Praise for

TERI WILSON

"*Unleashing Mr. Darcy* is a wonderful modern-day fairy tale
that especially appeals to dog lovers. Readers unfamiliar with dog shows
will find the premise interesting without being overwhelming.
The interactions between the main characters are delightful
and the secondary characters add greatly to the reader's enjoyment."
—*RT Book Reviews,* Top Pick, 4½ stars

"Wilson wisely avoids repeating Austen's plot
or attempting to emulate her sharp satire, but she manages to
get in more than a few bits of homage.... Devoted Austen fans
will find much to enjoy in this fun contemporary rendition."
—*Publishers Weekly*

"Dog lovers and readers who love Austen pastiches
will savor this latest showing of the famous couple."
—*Booklist*

"*Unleashing Mr. Darcy* is a delightful story full of charm, wit and heart.
I didn't want to see it end.... A truly romantic tale."
—*USA TODAY* bestselling author RaeAnne Thayne

Also available from Teri Wilson and Harlequin HQN

Unleashing Mr. Darcy

And be sure to look for Teri's third modern classic, *Unschooling the Professor,* a retelling of *My Fair Lady,* coming in January 2015 from Harlequin HQN!

TERI WILSON

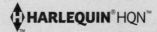

Recycling programs
for this product may
not exist in your area.

ISBN-13: 978-0-373-77875-1

UNMASKING JULIET

Printed in U.S.A.

HARLEQUIN®
™ www.Harlequin.com

Dear Reader,

Thank you for reading *Unmasking Juliet,* the second in my series of retellings of classic romances for Harlequin HQN. Of all the stories I could have chosen for inspiration, why *Romeo and Juliet?* I really wanted the chance to give these star-crossed lovers the happy ending they deserve. I'm a romantic at heart, so of course I've always longed for a different conclusion to Shakespeare's tale of ill-fated love.

Would you like to hear a secret? In college, I made all A's and B's, with just two exceptions. The first was a C in calculus. I'm actually quite proud of that C. Hello, it was *calculus.* I'm still not even sure what the word *calculus* means, other than it is some sort of torturous math. The other exception was also a C, but this one was in Shakespeare. *Gasp!* Please don't tell my editor.

I adore Shakespeare. I always have. It was my very last semester in college, and I think I was simply burned out. Alas, now I've had the chance to redeem myself. While working on this book, I've absolutely fallen in love with the Bard. More so than ever before. I could probably recite *Romeo and Juliet* backwards and forwards now. So there, Professor Clark.

It is my hope that you, too, will fall in love with this timeless story. Sure, I've given it some fun, new twists. There are two adorable dogs, wine and more chocolate than anyone could ever want. But the spirit of the original tale remains true, and for the Shakespeare aficionado, there are plenty of hidden treats. I had a wonderful time incorporating as much of the Bard's original language as possible in a modern story. It's like an Elizabethan Easter egg hunt!

If you enjoy *Unmasking Juliet,* be sure to look for the third book in this series, *Unschooling the Professor,* a retelling of *My Fair Lady,* early next year. And if you missed *Unleashing Mr. Darcy,* my debut book for HQN, it's still available. Take a peek at it, too.

Happy reading!

Teri Wilson

For the Bard, the Poet
With everlasting gratitude for his beauty and inspiration

"In winter with warm tears I'll melt the snow
And keep eternal spring-time on thy face."
—*Titus Andronicus; Act 3, Scene 1*

"Love is a smoke made
with the fume of sighs."

William Shakespeare
Romeo & Juliet, Act I, Scene 1

1

Thus with a kiss, she lived...

Midway through the Tenth Annual Mezzanotte Masquerade Ball, Juliet Arabella had the irrepressible urge to flee. The more she thought about what had transpired during the limo ride to the party, the more difficult it became to breathe. What was she even doing here? She didn't belong in this room, with these people.

Most of the guests who milled about the grand ballroom with their faces hidden behind Venetian-style masks would be flabbergasted to discover she was even in attendance. She'd thought she would feel secure at George's side, but she'd been woefully mistaken. She doubted she'd ever feel comfortable accompanying him anywhere again. And she hadn't forgotten for a moment about the diamond in her evening bag.

There was no way she was keeping it. No matter what George or her parents had to say about it. She was a twenty-eight-year-old woman. She could decide for herself whom she would marry. As much as she loved her family's chocolate boutique, loved bringing smiles to their customers with her special confections, loved the comforting predictability of knowing she could pour heavy cream over hot melted chocolate and end up with a perfect, glossy ganache, she couldn't sacrifice everything for it. Wouldn't. George was not the man for her. And after tonight, he never would be.

It was as easy as turning on the glittery heel of her stiletto and bolting for the door. George was deep in conversation with someone she didn't recognize, but she still didn't waste any time getting out of the ballroom before he could catch a glimpse of her escape. She held her breath and didn't release it until she'd pushed open one of the heavy oak doors that led to the outdoor terrace. To freedom, however temporary.

There was a chill in the night air, and a crisp breeze nipped at her bare shoulders. She remembered reading somewhere that the cold nights in Napa Valley were what made the area perfect for growing grapes. Her gaze drifted beyond the stone terrace, to the rows and rows of grapevines that followed the hillside in perfect symmetry. Their leaves fluttered in the wind above heavy clusters of red-and-purple fruit.

It was so serene, so quiet. Such a stark contrast to the dancing and busy hum of conversation inside. The pounding of Juliet's heart slowed. Her head began to clear, and she found she could breathe again. She took in a lungful of air, perfumed with the sweet scent of ripe grapes.

Behind her, the door to the ballroom opened, and a wave of music and laughter drifted out onto the terrace. She wasn't ready to go back. Not yet. And she certainly didn't want to get stuck making idle conversation with any of the other partygoers. So she tiptoed across the smooth tile floor and followed a wide stone staircase that spiraled downward, away from the house.

The steps fanned out and grew wider until they leveled out onto another smaller patio. Juliet got the distinct feeling she'd ventured somewhere she wasn't really supposed to be. The terrace had an intimate feeling to it, perhaps because it held nothing but two small chairs and a single café table, upon which rested two half-empty glasses of red wine.

She should leave. Whoever that wine belonged to would probably be coming back for it and would be less than happy to find her here. If they recognized her, they'd probably accuse her of spying. Or worse. Not that she'd blame them.

She turned around, fully intending to head back to the party, which now seemed like the lesser of two evils. But the sight of what lay beyond the terrace gave her pause. The sunflowers she'd only gotten a glimpse of when the limo pulled up to the vineyard were right there, close enough for her to touch. She took a tentative step forward, reached out and stroked a thick green stem with the tips of her fingers. It was soft to the touch, covered with a faint white fuzz that reminded her of the velvety smoothness of her dog Cocoa's ear. Up close, the flowers were even more spectacular than she'd imagined. The fat gold blooms loomed high above her head, and for an insane moment, Juliet had the urge to kick off her shoes and disappear among them.

Why not? George would never think to look for her here.

She slid her feet out of her stilettos and stepped off the tile floor onto the cool, damp earth. A chill coursed through her, but she didn't consider turning back. Not for a moment. She wrapped her arms around her waist and took another step. It was crazy, but wading barefoot through the dirt in a ball gown made her feel better somehow. The numbness that had come over her during the awful limo ride began to slip away. She felt alive again. Almost.

She pushed a leaf as big as the palm of her hand aside and stepped through the row of sunflowers. Her toes sank deeper in the soil, and she found herself among the intricate rows of grapevines. The vines were heavy with fruit. Thick bunches of grapes hung about waist high, such a deep purple that they appeared almost black in the twilight. And they smelled divine. She closed her eyes and took a deep, intoxicating breath.

"An escapee from the party, I take it?"

Juliet's eyes flew open. In that first, panicked moment she thought she was hallucinating. Could heartbreak actually make a person crazy? Because there was a masked man standing among the grapevines.

Then she remembered—it was a masquerade ball.

"Something like that." Her voice trembled slightly from the shock of being discovered. She took another deep breath, this time to steady herself. Why was she so nervous? She couldn't see his face, but he couldn't see hers, either. She blinked up at the stranger from behind her mask. "And you?"

He echoed her words. "Something like that."

Heavy lidded eyes gazed at her from beyond the silver satin of his mask. They were blue. Startlingly so. She lowered her gaze and took in his dinner jacket, his crisp white shirt unbuttoned at the neck. And his tie, seductively loosened, the exact same shade of blue as his eyes.

"Are you a regular at this annual shindig?" His voice carried a hint of disdain, as though he weren't any happier than she was to be in attendance.

Who is he?

"Not exactly. You?"

"God, no." The corner of his mouth lifted in a sardonic grin.

Juliet's mood lightened ever so slightly. The mystery man wasn't a Mezzanotte. He couldn't be. This masquerade ball had been an annual thing for a decade. "I suppose I look crazy, wandering around out here in the dark. I just had to get out of there."

"No explanation needed. As hiding places go, this is a rather nice one." His smile grew more genuine.

He had a nice mouth—full lips, perfectly balanced by a strong, chiseled jaw lined with just a hint of stubble. Not that Juliet was particularly prone to evaluating such things. But with the mask covering the rest of his face, it was hard not to notice.

Maybe it was the moonlight. Maybe it was the sense of mystery evoked by their Venetian masks. Or maybe she was simply at loose ends after all that had transpired, but this secret conversation had an oddly intimate quality. She wondered if he felt it, too.

"For the record, you don't look the least bit crazy." Yes, he did feel it. She could tell.

She wiggled her bare toes and glanced down at her dress. The rhinestones scattered among the folds of deep blue tulle glittered in the starlight. "I don't?"

His gaze swept her up and down. "Far from it. In fact, you look quite lovely."

Butterfly wings fluttered in her belly. Why did a compliment from this total stranger carry so much weight? "Thank you."

"You're quite welcome." Behind his mask, he gave her a devilish wink. Then he plucked a grape from the closest vine and popped it in his mouth.

Nervous laughter bubbled up her throat. "Did you really just do that?"

"What?" He shrugged.

He had a muscular build. Juliet could see that much, even

through the tuxedo jacket. "Steal a grape and eat it, right off the vine?"

"Surely they won't miss just one." He plucked another grape from the cluster. "Care for a taste? You don't know what you're missing."

His voice was low, rich and emphatically masculine. Had he purposely added that note of innuendo, or was she simply hearing things?

And why did she get the feeling that he was right, and that up until now she'd been completely clueless as to how much she'd been missing for a long, long time?

"I dare you." He took a step closer, holding the grape between his index finger and his thumb. In his eyes, Juliet saw an unmistakable challenge.

Before she could stop herself, she closed her eyes, tipped her face toward him and slowly opened her mouth.

What am I doing? This isn't me, flirting with a complete and total stranger, at the Mezzanottes' party, of all places.

But that's exactly what she was doing. And it felt good.

"Here, taste." His thumb brushed across her bottom lip in a feather-light touch.

Then the grape dropped into her mouth. She bit down, and an explosion of flavor burst on her tongue. Sweet, tangy and forbidden. It was the best thing she'd ever tasted. At the moment, even better than chocolate. She felt the last vestiges of her numbness slip away. In its place was a kaleidoscope of sensation—the taste of sun-ripened fruit, the sound of her full tulle skirt rustling in the night wind, the perfume of sunflower blossoms and the feel of the cold, damp earth between her toes.

"Well?" he asked, his voice barely a murmur in the darkness. He must have come closer. She could sense his warmth on her face, across her bare shoulders. She leaned into it and felt as though she were soaking in the heat of the sun after an unbearably long winter. "Delicious doesn't even begin to describe it."

She opened her eyes.

He stood a whisper away. His proximity sent a ripple of awareness dancing across her skin. She bit her lip and took in the sudden seriousness of his expression, the distinct look in his eyes she was surprised she could even recognize.

Desire.

It positively smoldered in his blue eyes. George had never come close to looking at her like that. No one had. Not with this kind of intensity. To think she'd spent her entire life on this earth without a man ever looking at her like he wanted to devour her was almost inconceivable. And sad. Maybe she needed to start spending less time in the kitchen making chocolate and more time with people. Specifically, people without the last name Arabella.

Now, however, was not the proper moment to reexamine her priorities. He was right there, his predatory gaze sliding over her, as though he was aware of her on some unparalleled level.

How could this be happening? She was a mess. A barefoot, lost mess. And he was a total stranger.

She swallowed. He might be a stranger, but right now he was looking at her as though he knew exactly who she was. And that look made her...

Breathless.

This was it. This was what had been missing for so long. Maybe she'd even been running from it. Was it possible that her passion for her work had become tangled up with her sense of duty to her family's chocolate boutique to the exclusion of everything else? Had she really come that close to losing herself?

He took a step nearer. He didn't make a move to touch her, but somehow Juliet knew exactly what his hands would feel like on her waist, her shoulders, sliding through her hair. *Exquisite*.

The way she saw it, she had two choices—she could either go back to the party and be the dutiful Arabella daughter, or she could stay right here and, even if only for a moment, finally know what it felt like to be wanted by someone with no ulterior motive, who didn't even know her last name. Someone who just wanted her.

Her heart thundered beneath the sparkling bodice of her ball gown. And suddenly, walking away was no longer an option.

Before she could change her mind, she lifted her hand, wrapped her fingers firmly around his tie and yanked. Then she kissed him. Hard. With the confidence of a woman who acted this way all the time.

It was a beautiful thing, that kiss. The thrill of it sparked a memory from long ago of the very first time a boy's lips had touched hers.

His hands found her face, tipped it back so his lips came down on hers instead of the other way around. He kissed her with purpose, as though he was dying of thirst and she was a pool of glistening water. And she found she was no longer capable of coherent thought. Everything slipped away—the limo ride, the party, even that elusive memory of her first kiss.

There at the Mezzanotte Masquerade Ball, Juliet Arabella was swept off her feet by a man whose name she didn't even know, carried away on a wild grape-scented river of kisses, sweeter and more decadent than any chocolate she'd ever tasted.

2

Two hours earlier…

"A plague on the house of Mezzanotte!"

Juliet's father uttered those archaic words while her mother pushed her into the limousine bound for the heart of Napa Valley. The uniformed chauffeur somehow managed to keep a straight face as he held the car door open, and Juliet's father continued his rant, his face turning a more vibrant shade of crimson with each expletive. He shook his fists and cursed the heavens for allowing a family as corrupt as the Mezzanottes to walk the earth. He might have even spit when he said their name, as though they were living in the Old Country. Or a *Godfather* film. The idea would have been utterly ridiculous, except that it was true.

Sort of.

Not that the Mezzanottes or Juliet's own family, the Arabellas, were Mafia. As far as she knew, none of her ancestors had ever been involved with any kind of crime syndicate.

Although at times, their family business was arguably more contentious.

Running a chocolate shop wasn't all sugar and bonbons. It was a business, like any other. And if the fact that everyone who collected a paycheck shared the same last name didn't complicate matters enough, the only other gourmet *chocolaterie* in town was located right across the street.

Napa's foodie scene was intensely competitive under normal circumstances, but there was nothing normal about the rivalry between the Arabellas and the Mezzanottes. Tonight Juliet was scheduled to attend the annual Mezzanotte Chocolates Masquerade Ball, and dealing with the Mezzanottes was never normal. Or pleasant. Or anywhere near the civil end of the spectrum.

The Mezzanottes had been crafting artisan chocolates in Napa Valley as long as the Arabellas had. At one time the two families had even worked alongside one another, Juliet's grandmother pouring dark couverture chocolate into delicate bonbon molds while her best friend, Donnatella Mezzanotte, ran the business end of things. But that was years ago. The relationship had long since soured into a bitter rivalry.

Emphasis on *bitter.*

Now Mezzanotte Chocolates could be found in grocery stores around the state. And their shop still stood right across the street from Arabella Chocolate Boutique.

"I don't like this. I don't like it one bit." Juliet's father aimed a glare at George as he helped Juliet into the car.

Her head began to throb as she slid into the buttery interior of the limousine and waited while George exchanged quiet words with her parents. George had always been a calming influence on her father. She wanted to think this was because he was her boyfriend, but in all likelihood it had more to do with the fact that he was also Arabella Chocolate Boutique's biggest champion.

George Alcott III was the heir apparent to the single most lucrative gourmet food distributor in Northern California. The Arabella Chocolate Boutique had been doing well enough for a small family-run business, but once Royal Gourmet Distributors came into the picture, things turned golden. Now, thanks to George, Arabella Chocolates could be found on the menus of some of Napa's finest restaurants. For the first time in decades, the Arabellas finally had the upper hand on the Mezzanottes.

"Everything will be fine. I won't let her out of my sight," George murmured, his voice syrupy smooth.

Juliet's father let out a noise somewhere between a growl and a sigh.

Then her mother weighed in. "We agreed on this, remember? Joe Mezzanotte is making a big announcement tonight about the future of Mezzanotte Chocolates. George was invited. Let him take Juliet. She'll find out firsthand what exactly is going on over there. You know what they say—keep your friends close and your enemies closer." Her mother's hatred had always been more shrewd in nature than her father's, though no less intense.

There were a few more urgent whispers, but Juliet tried to tune them out. Truth be told, she was a little nervous about this whole ordeal. It was one thing to come face-to-face with the Mezzanottes on the street or at the occasional food festival or dessert fair. But it was quite another to walk into their masquerade ball as though her name appeared somewhere on the guest list.

At least her face would be covered. She ran her fingertips over the edge of her rhinestone-encrusted, Venetian-style mask. She'd intentionally chosen the most feathered, bejeweled one she could find. *All the better to hide behind.*

At last George climbed in, his cell phone already glued to his ear, and sat down opposite her. The car began what seemed like an excruciatingly slow crawl toward the Manocchio Winery, the site of the fancy masked ball. At least the party was being held at a neutral location. She'd sooner die than walk into the Mezzanottes' family home.

"How are the Cabernet Sauvignon truffles coming along?" George asked when he finally ended his call.

He removed a dark bottle of champagne from the limo's built-in bar. The movement struck Juliet as profoundly odd. As many times as Juliet had been in his limo, she couldn't remember drinking anything more exotic than Fiji water.

"Great. I think I've finally perfected the recipe." She smiled.

You couldn't swing a stick in Napa Valley without hitting a piece of chocolate that had been infused with wine. The proliferation of such treats was precisely why Juliet had avoided them like the plague in her own chocolates. She much preferred the challenge of creating something new and unexpected. But the restaurants George worked with wanted Cabernet truffles, so Cabernet truffles they would have.

"Then maybe we should toast in honor of your latest creation." George offered her a champagne flute.

"Of course. To Cabernet Sauvignon truffles." Juliet wasn't altogether sure she wanted to drink to that, but she lifted her glass, anyway.

"To Cabernet Sauvignon truffles." George tapped his flute against hers.

Bubbles danced on Juliet's tongue. The champagne was perfect—light, delicate, fizzy. She shouldn't have been surprised. George had a definite taste for the finer things in

life. But she'd never glimpsed a bottle of Dom Pérignon in
the limo bar before.

During the course of the year they'd been dating, she
could count on one hand the number of times she'd seen him
drink. His restraint was noteworthy, a rarity among those living in the wine country. Now here he was—popping open
a bottle of Dom on the way to a formal event at a vineyard
where, no doubt, the wine would be flowing.

Those Mezzanottes drink like fish.

The voice of her mother. Again.

Juliet drained her glass.

"More?" George refilled her flute without waiting for an
answer.

While he poured, she let her gaze fall on the impeccable cut of his tuxedo jacket, the black sliver of a bow tie at
his neck and the tasteful silver cuff links at his wrists. He
looked perfect. Like royalty, which was fitting since he was
the reigning prince of Napa Valley's gourmet scene.

She glanced back down at her champagne and, for the
first time, noticed the Royal Gourmet Distributors company logo on the glass. Why a food company—gourmet or
otherwise—needed engraved champagne glasses was a mystery she couldn't fathom. Of course, the limousine itself didn't
exactly scream practicality, either. The one time she'd asked
George about it, he'd shrugged it off and said something
about image being everything. Royal Gourmet wasn't just
any food distributor. George's business catered to the most
exclusive eateries in Northern California. His clients owned
the sort of places where people waited months to get res-
ervations. Restaurants like La Toque, Ad Hoc and the biggest jewel in Royal Gourmet's crown, The French Laundry.

"I've been looking forward to tonight for quite some

time." He cleared his throat and straightened his already-straight tie.

"You have?" He'd been looking forward to a party thrown by the Mezzanottes? They were about to be plunged into the *den of vipers* as her father liked to call them. What was there to look forward to besides an awkward evening of forced merriment?

"Yes. Here we are, all dressed up. Alone." He took her hand in his. "You look beautiful, by the way."

Juliet looked down at her dress—midnight-blue, sprinkled with tiny rhinestones on a ruched bodice that led to miles of frothy tulle. She'd found it in her favorite vintage shop in Yountville, just around the corner from Arabella Chocolate Boutique, and was struck by the whimsy of it, even though part of her wondered if George would find it too quirky. Apparently, he didn't.

"Thank you. You look rather handsome yourself." She smiled demurely behind her champagne flute.

They didn't normally talk like this. Had George ever told her she looked beautiful? She didn't think so. He'd said as much about her chocolate creations on countless occasions. But that was to be expected. Her truffles and other confections were drool-worthy. And Royal Gourmet was responsible for getting those chocolates into Napa's finest restaurants, so it was completely normal for him to take an interest in her work to the extent that he did.

Sometimes, though, she wondered what it might feel like to be considered drool-worthy herself.

"I've been thinking…." George ran his thumb in a gentle circle over the back of Juliet's hand. It was another atypically tender move.

Finally.

She should have been thrilled. She'd begun to wonder if they were dating or if they were just business associates who hung out together on the occasional Saturday night. Not that George didn't treat her well. On the contrary, he was a perfect gentleman at all times. That in itself was part of the problem.

She'd seen more passion from him when he bit into a chocolate-dipped pretzel than he'd ever displayed on the handful of occasions when they'd come close to sleeping together.

She was keenly aware of the fact that it took a special man to put up with her unique profession. And in that department, she and George were a perfect match. He never complained when she was late for a date simply because she'd lost track of time and got caught up in the kitchen. Special holidays like New Year's Eve and Valentine's Day weren't times to be spent on romantic getaways, but days she worked her longest hours. The week of Easter, she'd made so many chocolate bunnies she'd begun to see them in her dreams. She'd drifted off once during a movie with her head on George's shoulder and awakened from a nightmare of an army of chocolate rabbits with bite marks on their ears coming after her.

George had soothed her back to sleep and given her a rundown of the movie's plot on the way home in the limo. He never made demands on her, even when they went weeks without seeing one another. The relationship might be lacking in the sparks department, but it was easy. And that went a long way, especially during February when she and her family couldn't make the candy fast enough to fill the heart-shaped boxes.

George understood. He was patient and undemanding. What more could she want?

Romance.

"Juliet? Did you hear me? I said there's something I want to ask you." George leaned forward and cupped her face in his hand.

He was looking at her exactly the way she'd wanted him to look at her for months now. At least she'd thought it was what she wanted. Now that it was finally happening, the moment seemed strangely out of place.

She saw George gazing tenderly into her eyes and her own reflection mirrored back in the dark brown of his irises, and it was like watching two complete strangers. A perfect couple, riding in the perfect limousine. She was struck with the abrupt realization that something was missing. As perfect as everything ought to be, it simply wasn't.

She swallowed. "You have something you wanted to ask me?"

Wordlessly, he reached into the inside pocket of his tuxedo jacket. Juliet's head began to swirl. Suddenly, everything made sense—the compliments, the champagne, the unexpected display of affection. All the romantic trappings were there. Why hadn't she seen the signs?

George was going to propose.

Panic welled up in her chest at the sight of the black velvet ring box in his hand. She wasn't ready for this. *They* weren't ready for this. What was he thinking, anyway? He was going to ask her to marry him on the way to the Mezzanotte Chocolates Masquerade Ball? She might be dressed in a fanciful cloud of tulle, but this was a business event. A business event she'd been dreading for weeks now. Why would he choose this wholly inappropriate moment to pop the question?

She grew lightheaded from the champagne. Her stomach

gurgled, and she wished she'd eaten more than a handful of chocolate-covered strawberries for lunch. She wondered if she might actually throw up all over the interior of the limo when he got to the actual proposal. Maybe she could blame car sickness.

"Juliet, we're good together." George's expression was a mask of calm assurance.

They *were* good together. They got along. They'd never had an argument. They'd never even raised their voices at one another.

They'd also never made love. A girl couldn't live forever on chocolate alone. George had never touched her in a way that made her weak in the knees. She'd never grown breathless at the thought of seeing him. Not once.

But was that really so bad? Did that kind of passion ever last, anyway?

Doubtful. Still, she couldn't imagine actually marrying the man. He was nice. He loved her family. He'd invested loads of time and energy into their business. Were those real reasons to spend the rest of her life with him?

She had to stop him before this went too far. "Yes. Yes, we are, but..."

Unfazed, he pressed on. "I think we'd be even better as husband and wife."

He toyed with the velvet box in his hand. The sight of it made Juliet a little nauseated.

He popped open the box, displaying an enormous glittering diamond solitaire on a background of stark black velvet. "Will you marry me?"

All she felt was the strange emptiness surrounding his question, and two thoughts crystallized in her mind with perfect clarity. First, she couldn't marry him. She just couldn't do it.

And, second, her parents were going to be absolutely livid once they found out she'd turned him down. What would it mean for the business? Would they lose the support of Royal Gourmet?

She couldn't think about that now. Things were already awkward enough. "George, I'm sorry."

His expression remained unchanged. "Sorry? I don't understand."

"I can't."

"You can't?" His brow furrowed as realization began to set in. "What do you mean?"

"I can't marry you. I'm fond of you. You know that, but I don't think this is the best idea for us."

God, this was difficult. The look of bewilderment in his eyes was almost too much to bear. If he'd uttered a single word about love, her resistance might have faltered.

He hadn't. There'd been Dom Pérignon. There'd been a diamond. But there'd been no mention of love.

"So your answer is no?"

She cleared her throat. "I'm afraid so."

He snapped the jewelry box closed and leaned back in his seat. The confusion in his eyes had morphed into something darker, more dangerous. At last, an inkling of passion. The irony of the situation was hard to ignore. "Not the *best idea?* I'm afraid your mother doesn't seem to agree."

His words fell heavily between them.

The inside of the limo began to swirl around Juliet. "You discussed this with my mother? Why would you do that?"

She wasn't some virgin ingenue to be sold off to the highest bidder. She was a grown woman, twenty-eight years old. Granted, her relationship with her parents might be a bit atypical due to the family business. Still, the idea of him asking her mother's opinion on the matter rubbed her entirely the wrong way.

He shrugged. "Why wouldn't I? Our marriage would affect your family's business as well as mine. I talked about it with both your parents. They were in complete agreement, by the way."

She imagined the three of them sitting around a conference table discussing her future. *Marriage? We concur. Children, negotiable. Love, optional.*

Turning him down was becoming less and less difficult with each passing second. "That hardly seems appropriate. Shouldn't something this personal be just between you and me?"

His laughter sounded condescending, and Juliet had the distinct feeling they were on the verge of their first argument. "That's impossible. Our marriage is about more than the two of us."

She wished he'd stop staying *our marriage*. There would be no marriage. The reasons why not were becoming even clearer.

George straightened his tie. "The foundation of our relationship is, and always has been…"

Love.

Juliet's heart gave a little twinge. There was still a tiny part of her that wanted to believe he'd asked her to marry him because he was in love with her, and that someday she could love him, too.

"Business," he finished, leaving no doubt in her mind exactly where she stood. "Imagine what joining Royal Gourmet with the Arabella Chocolate Boutique would accomplish. I urge you to reconsider."

She shook her head. A single tear slipped down her cheek, leaving a hot trail of humiliation in its wake.

George's gaze softened. He reached for her hand, pressed the tiny velvet box in her palm and wrapped her fingers closed around it. "Think about it. We'll be happy together. I promise we will."

Impossible. Not after this.

How could she be happy living side by side with a man who'd chosen her as though she were a Royal Gourmet acquisition? Worse, she didn't love him. And now she didn't see how she ever could.

The intercom crackled overhead, breaking the tense silence in the car, which, despite its stretch proportions, had begun to feel far too small.

"Sir, we've arrived," the driver announced.

"Thank you." George buttoned his tuxedo jacket and checked the time on his wristwatch.

His ring was still clutched in Juliet's fist, but when he looked up she felt as though she were invisible.

Had it always been this way? Had she really wasted the better part of a year wishing the two of them could have something that so obviously wasn't there?

She'd never felt so foolish in her life. Even the time she'd mixed up the sugar with the salt in her first batch of chocolate kiss cookies as a teenager paled in comparison.

She gazed wistfully out the window of the limousine. The Manocchio Winery stretched out before her in endless rows of green tangled vines and rich, red earth. A border of tall sunflowers surrounded the vineyard, the wide faces of the blooms lifted toward the sky. At the forefront of it all

stood a grand house, with a gabled roof that gave it a certain
Old-World charm. Its creamy white exterior glowed almost
amber in the light of the setting sun. If she hadn't known
better, she would have thought the limo had carried her all
the way to a Tuscan hillside.

At the entrance, a handful of people milled about—women
in elegant ball gowns, dashing men in perfectly cut tuxe-
dos. The guests looked especially stylish and otherworldly
in their Venetian masks.

Beautiful, she mused.

She wasn't sure what she'd expected. A group of thugs who
looked like extras from an episode of *The Sopranos?*

A plague on the house of Mezzanotte!

Plague or not, she couldn't wait to walk into that party.
She'd rather be anywhere right now, doing anything, talk-
ing to anyone other than George. Even someone named
Mezzanotte.

Leo Mezzanotte had been back in the United States for less
than two hours following a twelve-year absence and had a
case of jet lag the likes of which he'd never experienced.
Even his dog, Sugar, was feeling the aftereffects of the long
international flight. Her little white body was strewn across
his lap in a lifeless heap.

Leo envied her unconscious state with every fiber of his
being. His throat felt as though he'd just swallowed a mouthful of sand, and he had a killer headache. What he needed
most was a long hot shower and a bed. Instead, he was dressed
in a tuxedo, with a silver Lone Ranger-style mask strapped
to his face.

Now that he thought about it, perhaps the mask had something to do with the pounding in his head. He peeled it off

and tossed it on the tiny café table next to his glass of wine, an action that earned a disapproving glare from the man seated across from him. Sugar, on the other hand, didn't so much as flinch.

"What are you doing? We're at a masquerade ball." Leo's elderly uncle Joe pushed the mask back toward Leo with a shove of his shaky index finger. "Hence, the masks."

"The guests have barely begun to arrive. I'll put it back on before I get to the ballroom." God, the ballroom. There would be music. Dancing. People.

Was it too late to find someone he could pay to wear his mask and take his place? Just for the next few hours, while he took a nap?

Uncle Joe frowned. "Don't forget. This party is a tradition."

So much for cloning himself. Leo knew better than to mess with tradition. Uncle Joe was Italian through and through, as old school as they came. Tradition and family were everything. Leo already had a few ideas for shaking things up with regard to the family business, starting with the chocolate shop itself. Things he knew that might be met with resistance if Uncle Joe's reaction to his mention of *mendiants* was any indication.

"*Mendiants?* Why the hell would an Italian want to make something French?"

Leo would have to pick and choose his battles.

He'd wear the damned mask. He'd shake a few hands and schmooze with Uncle Joe's friends. But he wasn't about to give in on the *mendiants.* Or the chocolate hazelnut macarons. He hadn't spent three years at Le Cordon Bleu and another five as an apprentice at La Maison du Chocolat to come back to California and dip cherries in melted chocolate all day. Or worse, sit in an office overseeing the mass production of candy bars.

"This night is most important. Everyone who's anyone in the Napa food scene will be here. And I want them all to meet you, so they'll know the torch has been passed. You're the future of Mezzanotte Chocolates." Uncle Joe flicked an imaginary speck of lint off the knee of his tuxedo trousers.

Leo stared at his wine and wished it would somehow transform into a vodka martini. Or maybe just plain vodka. He reached for his glass of Cabernet and took a generous sip. It was excellent. Full-bodied. Fruity. He may have left his soul in Paris, but he was still enough of a Californian to know that French wines had nothing on Napa's finest. Of course, the first-rate Cab was a total waste at the moment. He could be drinking gasoline for all he cared.

You're the future of Mezzanotte Chocolates.

There was a time when those words would have meant the world to Leo. That time had passed.

"It's a shame your father didn't live long enough to see this moment. He would have been so proud." Uncle Joe smiled.

"Let's try and avoid the topic of my father, shall we?" Leo took another gulp of wine and rested his hand on the gentle rise and fall of Sugar's back.

"You're going to be working in the kitchen where he worked for over fifty years. You can't avoid his memory forever, now that you've finally come home."

Home.

Leo didn't feel as though he'd come home. He'd felt more at home in Paris. Specifically, in the modest, unfinished brick building in the third *arrondissement* where he'd planned to open his own *chocolaterie*.

He wouldn't be here, on the verge of a coma, if he'd just

sucked it up and gone through with the wedding. Rose had been ready and willing to pledge him her heart along with her supersize bank account. He would have had more than enough cash to open his own shop. In Paris.

But in the end, he just couldn't do it. He couldn't take advantage of a woman like that. He'd been known to bed a woman without being in love, but he drew the line at marrying one. Call him sentimental.

He'd sat Rose down after the invitations had been mailed out and told her she deserved better. Once he'd admitted he wasn't in love with her, and never had been, she agreed. She'd been the one to propose, and he never should have let things get so out of hand.

So this is what he got for having a sentimental streak? A future of moving about in his father's shadow?

He had no right to be dissatisfied with the turn of events. The worsening of Uncle Joe's arthritis was rather fortuitous. He needed help with Mezzanotte Chocolates, and Leo needed a soft place to land. It wasn't Paris, but it was home. More importantly, it was honest.

And honesty was key. He'd watched his father lie to his mother his entire childhood.

No, I didn't bet on the game.

I don't know where the money went. Honest.

In a way, marrying for money was its own form of gambling. And Leo couldn't bring himself to repeat the past.

"The Arabellas will be seething with jealousy when they hear about you." Uncle Joe's lip curled in a triumphant sneer. He'd always had a certain flair for the dramatic.

Leo lifted a brow. "The Arabellas?"

"You know the Arabellas. Our archenemies, those evil swine." There was that dramatic flair again.

"The name rings a bell." Leo hadn't heard the name Arabella in years. Not since he'd left for Europe at eighteen.

When he was a kid, he'd actually thought it was a curse word since it was usually uttered with revulsion. He could remember his parents talking—usually in raised voices—about their rivals, another Italian family-owned chocolate enterprise. He knew there was no love lost there. He'd just never known why. And he hadn't realized the rivalry was still in full force.

"It should sound familiar. And it should stoke the fires of hatred deep in your gut every time you hear it." Uncle Joe pounded his fist on the desk. The empty wineglass jumped a few inches.

"Consider my fires stoked," Leo said dryly.

"This is no laughing matter, Leo. As a member of this family, you are required to despise the Arabellas to the same extent as the rest of us. The Arabellas are traitors of the very worst sort."

"How so?"

"There was once a time when my mother, God rest her soul, was friends with an Arabella. The very best of friends. Way back before Mezzanotte Chocolates could be found in grocery stores, they owned the shop together."

"Our chocolate shop?" This was news. The competing shops were now right across the street from one another, but Leo had never known they were once the same store.

"You could say that. It stood where our store stands today, but at the time it was known as Bellanotte Chocolates."

Bellanotte. *Beautiful night.* It had a nice ring to it. "What happened?"

"That Arabella woman was a selfish snake. That's what happened." Uncle Joe wrinkled his nose.

"A selfish snake? In what way, exactly?"

"The shop was doing well. Very well. Like any smart businessperson, your grandmother saw an opportunity to expand it. She had visions of seeing Bellanotte Chocolates on grocery store shelves, right alongside names like Hershey and Mars."

Leo could take a wild guess who had ended up winning that argument. "That's where our chocolates are today, so I'm assuming Grandma got her way."

"You might say that. She grew weary of trying to convince that Arabella snake to see reason, so she went ahead and made a deal with an industrialist who could really put the chocolates on the map. Then she handed over the Bellanotte recipe."

"Without her partner's consent?" Hell, it was like a bad soap opera.

"She was doing them both a favor. As a Mezzanotte, you should know that. Really, Leo. Why must you vex me so?"

Sugar opened one eye and growled.

Leo gave her a scratch behind the ears, and she fell back into a dead sleep. "Whether it was in the best interest of the business or not, they were partners. Surely you could see how that might cause some hard feelings."

"Hard feelings?" Uncle Joe released a loud snort. "Your grandmother would have made that woman a millionaire. But before they saw a dime Sofia Arabella packed up her candy molds and opened up shop right across the street. Less than twenty feet away! The nerve. Then she proceeded to tell everyone in Napa what a sellout your grandmother was. She even claimed to put some weird voodoo hex on our entire family. It became a full-scale chocolate war." Uncle Joe's voice trailed off, and his expression grew pensive.

So, that was the big mystery. Five minutes with Uncle Joe,

and Leo knew more about his own family than his father had ever bothered to share with him. But that was nothing new. He could count on one hand the number of civil conversations they'd had before hd left the country. And after he'd moved to Europe there'd been no more conversations.

Until the night he called to tell Leo that his mother had died. Lymphoma. He'd never even known she was sick. *Thanks, Dad.*

Try as he might, Leo still couldn't drum up an ounce of hatred for the Arabellas. He actually couldn't care less about them. "Chocolate war? Really? Don't you think it's time for someone to fall on a caramel grenade and let bygones be bygones? All of this happened years ago."

"I could say the same about your feelings for your father," Uncle Joe said softly.

Leo cleared his throat. "Point taken."

He hadn't given a thought to forgiving his father. The man was dead and buried, as were Leo's feelings. So long as he was far away, he could forget about everything to do with home. Family. Mezzanotte Chocolates. Being surrounded by all of that now was one of the more unpleasant aspects of being back.

His uncle stood and attached a Phantom-of-the-Opera style mask to his face. "Enough talking. We're late. Let's head to the ballroom. You've got a great number of people to meet."

For someone who'd done his best to convince his nephew that he was on his last legs, Uncle Joe was remarkably strong-willed.

"In a minute. I need to clear my head. It was a long flight. Do you mind?" What time was it in Paris? Four in the morning.

"I suppose not. But don't keep everyone waiting. You're a big star. The toast of the town." Uncle Joe lingered at the foot of the stairs, his mouth turned down in a frown. His hand rose to the front of his tuxedo shirt, and he pulled at his collar. "I'm getting indigestion. It must be all this talk of those filthy swine, the Arabellas."

Then he spit on the tile floor of the terrace, as if the very name Arabella was so utterly revolting he couldn't bear the taste of the word in his mouth.

Alone at last, Leo dropped his weary head in his hands. Sugar craned her tiny neck and swiped the side of his face with her tongue. Her fluff ball of a tail beat against his thigh.

He was home, all right.

Home, sweet home.

3

At the first brush of the mysterious woman's lips on his, Leo was fully aware he should stop her. He really should. She was clearly acting on impulse. And even though she was a most effective seductress—more so than she realized, he suspected—he had the distinct impression this wasn't the sort of behavior she often engaged in.

Maybe that's why he found it so damned hot that he lost control of his senses. Still, somewhere in the periphery of his consciousness, he knew he should just gently unclench her hands from around his tie and remove his lips from hers.

That's what a gentleman would do.

But being passionately kissed by a beautiful masked woman in the golden light of a harvest moon had a way of making him forget he was a gentleman. He'd forgotten pretty much everything altogether, including his headache.

Jet lag...what jet lag?

She tasted exactly as a barefoot goddess standing in the middle of a vineyard should—warm, sweet, like a sun-kissed cluster of merlot grapes. A predatory thrill surged through him, the likes of which he'd never experienced. Not with Rose. Not with anyone.

He was in the middle of what was probably the sexiest experience of his life, and he didn't even know her name. He couldn't see much more than a hint of her face. Her mask glittered in the moonlight and left everything to his imagination, save for a pair of jade-green eyes and her full-lipped, most kissable mouth.

He groaned into that mouth. He couldn't help himself. She responded with a helpless whimper that just about drove him to his knees. His tie slipped through her fingertips as her hands found his back, sliding over his muscles in a path of brazen exploration. His own hands fisted in the wispy netting of her dress and pulled her closer until she was crushed fully against his chest.

God help him, he was on the verge of unzipping her fluffy ballerina gown right there among the canopies of grapevines. What was wrong with him? It wasn't like him to abandon every last shred of restraint. Although he should have known he was in trouble when he first spotted her standing there.

She'd painted such a pretty picture among the grapes, with her strapless midnight-blue gown exposing a perfect pair of feminine shoulders, waves of dark hair tumbling down her moonlit back. Her mask was decorated with an abundance of dazzling crystals that formed dramatic cat eyes. He wasn't sure if he was looking at an actual woman or a vision—a lifelong fantasy that until that moment he hadn't even known he had. He'd taken one look at her and wanted to sink his teeth into her creamy white shoulder. The image had flashed through his mind, as vivid as a fiery Tuscan sunset. Strange. He wasn't ordinarily the shoulder-biting type. Or the biting type at all.

Maybe the near-death experience of his bachelorhood had done something to him. Something potent. Something primal. Or maybe it was just her.

He'd wandered back out on the patio in search of a moment of peace before he had to drag himself to the ballroom and let his uncle parade him around like the prodigal son. Instead of clarity, he'd found a woman. It had been those bare feet that did him in. Barefoot. In a ball gown. In the dirt. The contrast had been so striking, he'd done a double take. And when he did, something about the sight of her pink-polished toes spoke of a heartbreaking vulnerability that reached straight to his core.

With his mouth still on hers, he tangled his fingers in her hair until he found the smooth satin bow that held her mask in place. He nibbled the corner of her lips and gave the end of the ribbon a gentle tug.

She stiffened in his arms.

He dipped his head and whispered against the slender column of her neck, "I want to see your face."

His lips found the curve right above her collarbone, and she melted into him once more.

"Please," he murmured, sounding far more desperate than he cared to.

She lifted her chin and fixed her gaze with his. Green eyes framed with lush black lashes peeked out at him from behind her bejeweled mask. Ever so slightly, she nodded.

Leo cradled her face in his hands, slipped his thumbs beneath the ribbons on either side of the mask and lifted it free. His breath caught in his throat as he waited for the first glimpse of her face. She bowed her head as he untangled the ribbons from her hair, and when she looked up his heart stopped.

"Lovely," he whispered.

It was perhaps the biggest understatement of his life. She was gorgeous, with large, luminous eyes, high cheekbones and pink, bow-shaped lips.

She shook her head. "I really shouldn't be here."

Leo couldn't think of a single place she belonged more.

"Don't go." There was that note of desperation in his voice again. What was happening to him?

"I'm afraid I must." She took a step backward and cast a panicked look toward the house.

Before Leo could say another word, she dashed past him, the skirt of her elegant gown swishing in the darkness. He reached for her and managed to catch her wrist right before she slipped away for good. "Wait. At least tell me your name."

She shook her head. "I can't."

He couldn't just let her leave. Not now, before he even knew who she was. "Please. After all, what's in a name?"

"I'm sorry," she whispered. Then she pulled away, and her wrist slid through his fingertips.

In his other hand, Leo still held her mask. Its crystals glittered in the night, like stars in the Napa Valley sky. He started after her to return it, but she'd already disappeared through the tall stalks of the sunflowers.

She was gone.

And the bewitching spell that had been spun among the grapevines was broken.

Temporary insanity.

To Juliet, it seemed the only explanation. She'd suffered some sort of breakdown. Why else would she have wandered around the Mezzanotte ball, throwing herself at the first random man who crossed her path?

It hadn't felt random, though. Quite the contrary. Their meeting had somehow felt predestined, orchestrated by the hands of fate.

Fate? Destiny?

Really?

Now she knew for a fact that she'd lost her mind. She didn't believe in such things. She believed in free will. Life was a product of the choices one made, day in and day out. She'd never been one to believe in *la forza del destino*—the force of destiny. That was superstition, like the *Malocchio,* the Evil Eye. Or her mother's bizarre belief that wearing red panties on New Year's Day would bring good luck. It was crazy.

Odd, she didn't feel crazy. She felt fantastic. Invigorated. Her skin tingled all over. If this was what a breakdown felt like, then sanity was highly overrated.

That kiss had been a work of art. An all-consuming masterpiece. She'd forgotten anything and everything the moment his lips had touched hers. Had her mystery man not removed her mask, who knew how far things would have gone?

The exposure of her face had served as a powerful reminder of exactly who she was. An Arabella.

She couldn't jeopardize everything she'd worked so hard for by ridiculing the family name and making a spectacle of herself at the Mezzanottes' party. Wouldn't any member of that family be delighted to find out what she'd been doing only a handful of minutes after the heir to the Royal Gourmet dynasty had proposed to her? Her secret would be exposed. George would no doubt put an end to his association with Arabella Chocolate Boutique, not that Juliet would blame him. They would be right back where they started—

struggling to make it with their tiny shop while Mezzanotte candy bars flew off grocery store shelves.

Of course, George might even decide to end their business arrangement based solely on her refusal to marry him. And that would be fine, too. Fiscally devastating, but fine nonetheless.

Her actions in the vineyard, however, were a flagrant slap in his face. The Mezzanottes would surely scream the news from the mountaintops. Her father would have a coronary. And her mother...

There was no telling what her mother would do. That was a horror that Juliet couldn't bring herself to consider.

Things had to change. She'd decided that much in the wake of George's proposal. But not like this. Any necessary changes to her life would be made on her own terms. She wasn't about to let the Mezzanottes dictate her future any more than her parents, or George.

She gathered the floaty layers of her tulle skirt in one hand, her discarded shoes in the other and ran up the stairs toward the ballroom like a Cinderella in reverse. Music swelled from the party as she slid her feet back in her stilettos. Enough lingering. She just needed to make haste, get back inside and pretend nothing had happened.

The party was in full swing upon her return. The center of the ballroom was overflowing with couples spinning in graceful circles across the dance floor. They almost outnumbered the row of chocolate fountains ringing the room atop gleaming silver stands. Seriously, she'd never seen so many chocolate fountains in her life. White, dark, milk. It was like a Hershey's version of Niagara Falls. Juliet nearly toppled one of them while she was craning her neck looking for George.

She found him in the far corner near the wine bar. He

was chatting with an older gentleman wearing a white half-mask like the one from Phantom of the Opera.

At the sight of George, the afterglow of her tryst in the vineyard lost some of its luster. She couldn't believe she had to go stand beside him for the rest of the night. It made her feel like the biggest imposter in the world.

Get a grip. You just need to make it through the next hour or two, and then everything will be better.

She took a deep breath, pasted a smile on her face and joined George and his companion. "Hello."

"You're back." George cast a cursory glance in her direction. As usual, he seemed to look right through her.

Juliet no longer cared. Her lips still felt swollen from stolen kisses, and she carried the memory of how the mystery man had looked at her right from the start. As if she mattered. She didn't think she'd ever forget it.

She cleared her throat. "Yes, sorry. I just needed to get some air."

"Juliet Arabella? What are you doing here?" The exposed side of the Phantom's face turned an angry red.

Juliet took a closer look at him. She would have recognized that one beady eye and thin-lipped mouth anywhere. No doubt there was a forked tongue in there, waiting to dart out.

Joe Mezzanotte.

Mask or no mask, she'd seen him skulking around across the street enough times to know exactly who was standing in front of her.

But how did he know who she was?

Her hand automatically flew to her face, making contact with bare skin. Her mask. Where was it?

Oh, no.

She'd left the vineyard in such a hurry that she'd forgotten it, which meant she was standing in the middle of the Mezzanotte ball completely exposed. Less than a foot away from Joe Mezzanotte.

"Um, yes. It's me. Surprise!" She smiled. If memory served, this marked the first time she'd ever smiled at someone with that particular surname.

Joe tore his mask off. The right side of his face was equally as red as the left. "May I ask what you're doing here?"

"Um, well…" She looked pointedly at George. *A little help?* Why had she ever let herself get talked into coming here?

George removed his mask. "Mr. Mezzanotte. It's me, George Alcott from Royal Gourmet. You were so gracious as to invite me to this evening's event, and Miss Arabella is my…"

"There you are, Uncle Joe." A familiar voice cut him off. A voice that sent a thrill up Juliet's spine. "I've been looking everywhere for you. Let's get this over with."

Oh, my God.

It was *him.* Her mystery man.

She would have recognized those blue bedroom eyes anywhere. And that mouth…the mouth that had been on her neck only moments before. He'd straightened himself up a bit—the top button of his shirt was now fastened, and his tie was arranged in a perfect knot at his throat. Although, upon further inspection, she could make out a series of indentions in the vibrant blue silk. A rush of heat filled her cheeks as she realized those indentions were from her own fingers, where she'd grabbed him by the tie and reeled him in for a kiss.

None of those visible clues mattered, really. She would have recognized him even if she'd had her eyes closed, simply by the way his very presence sent a wave of awareness crashing over her. She nearly swayed on her feet.

Make no mistake. It was most definitely him. And he was standing right there, talking to Joe Mezzanotte. *And calling him Uncle Joe!* "I see we've dispensed with the masks already. Good."

Then the world around Juliet seemed to move in slow motion as he reached for his mask and lifted it from his face. She might even have stopped breathing as she waited for her first full glimpse of his appearance.

It was well worth the wait.

God, he was handsome. No wonder she'd thrown herself at him. If George and that awful Joe Mezzanotte weren't present, she would do it all over again in a heartbeat.

Except why had he said *Uncle Joe?*

He raked a hand through his rich espresso-colored hair and looked up, his gaze meeting hers for the first time since he'd breezed into the ballroom. The breath left Juliet's lungs at the impact of that single glance. She experienced a moment of recognition so intense that her heart stopped beating as his expression changed from shock to extreme pleasure.

"You." He studied her, his gaze burning a searing path from her eyes to her lips to her throat.

Juliet forgot how to breathe. She couldn't have felt more exposed, more vulnerable if she'd shed her ball gown on the cool marble floor.

"I believe this belongs to you." He reached into the inside pocket of his dinner jacket, removed her mask and offered it to her.

She stared at it, unable to move a muscle.

"Leo? You two know each other?" Joe Mezzanotte's voice dripped with disgust.

"Yes," he said at the precise moment she blurted a hasty denial.

"No." She shook her head.

George touched her elbow. She could feel his irritation travel clear through his fingertips. "Which is it—yes or no?"

"Um…" Her heart thumped wildly in her chest. "No, of course not."

Her mystery man's eyes narrowed ever so slightly. "My mistake."

Joe crossed his arms. His head swiveled back and forth between the two of them. "Then what are you doing with her mask?"

A ribbon of dread snaked through Juliet as she wondered what he would say.

"I found it out on the terrace. It belongs to this lovely lady, obviously. She seems to be missing a mask." He held it toward her once again.

He'd saved her. *Interesting.* She reached for the mask, her hands shaking for reasons that now left her more confused than ever. "Thank you…Leo, is it?"

"Yes. Leonardo Mezzanotte, but please call me Leo. And you are?"

Leonardo *Mezzanotte?*

Bile rose up the back of Juliet's throat.

What have I done?

In her single moment of indiscretion over the course of a lifetime of being the good girl, she'd kissed a Mezzanotte?

Leonardo Mezzanotte. She struggled to absorb the name and its myriad of implications. Funny, he didn't look like the devil's offspring. Truthfully, he looked delicious. Every bit as delicious as he'd tasted only minutes before.

"Cat got your tongue, Miss Arabella?" Joe's beady eyes slid over her, dark with malice.

"*Arabella?*" Leo asked slowly.

Beside her, George cleared his throat. It startled Juliet out of her shell-shocked state so badly she jumped. "Permit me to do the honors. Mr. Mezzanotte, I'm George Alcott, of Royal Gourmet Distributors, and this is my fiancée, Juliet Arabella."

Leo's eyes flashed. "Fiancée? Congratulations must be in order."

Fiancée? *Fiancée?*

Juliet had been so rattled that she hadn't even processed George's presumptuous use of the word. Before she could issue any sort of denial, George nodded and smiled, the picture-perfect groom-to-be.

"Thank you." He released her elbow. Finally. He'd marked his territory with about as much subtlety as a Great Dane.

"Would the bride-to-be care to dance?" Leo extended a hand toward her.

She took a step backward, stepping on George's toe in the process. "Oh, I don't think…"

"I insist," he ground out.

He snagged her hand in his and dragged her toward the dance floor.

"Please, let go of me," she huffed as he pulled her into a dance hold. She hated to admit it, even to herself, but it felt right to be back in his arms. As if she belonged there, which was clearly not the case.

"Save it. We both know how much you like my hands on you." His gaze burned into her, deep, reminding her of things better forgotten.

She took a ragged breath. "That was before."

"Before what, exactly?" He lifted a seductive brow.

"Before I knew who you were."

He leaned in close, so close that his next words sent a ripple through her hair and a cascade of goose bumps over her skin. "Perhaps you should have checked my ID before you kissed me."

Juliet wanted to die right there on the spot. "Shh. Someone might hear you."

"Not my problem. You're the one who's spoken for. Tell me something, though. I'm curious—do you kiss your fiancé like that?" His palm in the center of her back slid lower, perilously closer to her bottom.

Her cheeks blazed with heat. "No."

He smiled the smile of a man most pleased with himself. "That's what I thought."

Could this get any more humiliating? "I meant no, as in no, he's *not* my fiancé."

He glanced over her shoulder, toward the spot where George and his uncle stood watching them, both looking equal parts mystified and annoyed. "Have you told him that? Because he seems confused."

She lifted her chin. "I made things very clear when I turned down his proposal earlier."

His confident smile wavered. "Earlier? Are we talking earlier *tonight?*"

"Why do you care?"

"I don't."

Yes, he did. She could see it in the tense set of his jaw and the angry vein that throbbed in his right temple.

"Just tell me one thing—did this proposal take place before or after you kissed me?"

That again. Was he ever going to let the kiss thing go? Doubtful. As far as kisses went, it was pretty memorable. "Stop saying that. Please. I beg of you."

"Why? You don't want anyone to know what happened between us earlier?"

She let out a most unladylike snort. "Of course I don't."

"I suppose this has something to do with the fact that I'm duty-bound to abhor the sight of you." He rolled his eyes.

"Yes, it has everything to do with it. Didn't you see how your uncle reacted when you asked me to dance? He looked like he wanted to kill me with his bare hands." And he probably would have if Leo hadn't dragged her away.

"What my uncle thinks of my romantic pursuits is of no concern to me whatsoever."

Had he lost his mind? "If you're a Mezzanotte, why have we never met before?"

"I've been away for a while. And now I'm being dragged into the family business." His droll expression left no doubt about his feelings on the matter. Juliet wasn't any happier about it than he was.

This could *not* be happening. "Away? Where exactly?"

"Paris."

"And what did you do there?" Why did she even care? *Shut your mouth, Juliet.*

"I studied at Le Cordon Bleu and then interned at La Maison du Chocolat. Is that an adequate summation of my résumé?"

Juliet's head moved in the subtlest of nods. "It'll do, I suppose."

Le Cordon Bleu? La Maison du Chocolat? Who was this guy, Willy Wonka?

Apparently, that's exactly who he was. Willy Wonka, albeit a mouthwateringly hot version of him.

"I suppose that means we'll be seeing more of each other. My uncle told me that the fires of hatred should burn deep in my gut at the mere mention of your name. I'll admit you've stirred a fire in me, but it doesn't feel anything like hatred." He took advantage of their dance hold by running the pad of his thumb up the curve of her neck.

Juliet grew dizzy. Whether it was from the swirl of their feet on the dance floor or his boldly flirtatious words, she wasn't sure. "You don't know what you're saying. This thing, this feud, is bigger than the both of us. Trust me."

"So, that's it? We're destined to despise one another simply because of our last names?" His arms tightened around her, holding her flush against him.

"I'm afraid so." Although when he put it that way, it didn't make much sense. She didn't believe in destiny. Did she?

It didn't matter. He was a Mezzanotte. She was an Arabella. If that weren't bad enough, he was the heir apparent to the entire Mezzanotte operation.

"What if I kissed you? Right here, right now. Do you suppose that would put an end to this whole ugly feud?" His voice was smooth and sweet as honey. It made her limbs go limp.

And for a nonsensical second, she actually considered his proposition.

She blinked in an effort to clear her head. He was the competition. And he was awfully arrogant. She hadn't noticed that before, in the vineyard. Then again, it was difficult to notice such things with his tongue halfway down her throat. "Don't you dare. Do it, and I'll slap your face."

His eyes flashed. "Would you now?"

She was bluffing, of course. If he so much as gave her a peck on the cheek, she'd probably melt into a puddle at his despicable Mezzanotte feet. "Try me."

"Relax. I won't force myself on you. I won't kiss you again

until you ask me to do so. And you will. Sooner or later." The corner of his mouth quirked up into a smirk.

"Don't flatter yourself."

He shook his head. "I'm right. You know it, and I know it."

She couldn't even meet his gaze. It was as if he could see right into her thoughts, wanton and inappropriate as they were. "For the time being, we'll have to agree to disagree."

He said nothing. He didn't have to. The smug look on his face spoke for itself.

She peered up at him. "You're going to tell your uncle what happened in the vineyard, aren't you?"

"I'm not sure I know what you're talking about, Miss Arabella." He placed special emphasis on her last name, drawing out each syllable. "Refresh my memory."

Juliet huffed out a sigh. "I kissed you."

"And you would prefer that to be our little secret?" There was that naughty smile again.

Boy, was she in trouble. Trouble of the worst sort. "Yes. Very much."

The music stopped. All around them, the other couples drifted apart and left the dance floor. An eerie quiet fell over the ballroom. It was then, and only then, that Juliet finally took her eyes off Leo. And when she did, she saw that every pair of eyes in the room was watching the two of them.

"Thank you for the dance," he said politely, just loud enough for people standing nearby to hear.

"You're welcome. It was nice meeting you." It *had* been nice. Not in the conventional sense, but definitely nice. She couldn't help but wonder what might have been, if he weren't a Mezzanotte but someone else. *Anyone* else.

He leaned close one last time and whispered in her ear,

his breath warm and sultry against her skin. "The pleasure was all mine. Not to worry, Juliet—I may be many things, including a Mezzanotte. But I'm not the kind of man to kiss and tell."

Then he walked away, toward his uncle, who'd been joined by Gina Mezzanotte and her husband. More of Leo's relatives. All three of them looked as though they wanted to rip him apart limb from limb.

It gave Juliet the creeps, until she turned around and saw a similar expression of disdain on George's face. How was she going to explain the dance? How could she explain any of this?

I'm not the kind of man to kiss and tell.

She wanted to believe him. She really did.

But a lifetime of loathing told her things weren't quite so simple.

4

"Hello? Anybody home?" From the moment Juliet walked through the front door of her parents' house with her big dog, Cocoa, trailing beside her, she knew something was dreadfully wrong.

Where was the usual chaos?

Sunday was the one day of the week that Arabella Chocolate Boutique was closed, and she was right on time for their big weekly family breakfast. Where was the smell of bacon? And hot coffee?

After the disastrous night she'd had at the Mezzanotte ball, she could use some coffee. Lots of it. Although she feared there wasn't enough caffeine in the world to help her process the fact that she'd kissed a Mezzanotte.

And she'd liked it. She'd liked it a lot.

What she didn't like was how often her thoughts had drifted to Leo in the twelve short hours since they'd met. He'd even made a rather hot appearance in her dreams. It was downright irritating.

She was certain he hadn't spent the night pining away for her. He'd probably forgotten about her altogether. And moved on to someone else. A man didn't learn how to kiss like that by embracing celibacy.

Her lips tingled.

Why was she thinking about kissing him again?

Because kissing Leo had been nothing short of divine.

She bit down on her bottom lip as a form of self-punishment. She had no business thinking about kissing Leonardo Mezzanotte. None at all. The first time had been an honest mistake. It could have happened to anyone.

Anyone who went around making out with anonymous strangers, which was a category that didn't include Juliet... until recently. But that was beside the point. Now she knew exactly who he was. She wouldn't be repeating that horrific mistake. Kissing him again would be suicide.

But what a way to go...

"Ugh." Disgusted at herself, she shook her head.

Cocoa reached up and licked her hand, which made her feel marginally better. She gave the dog an affectionate pat on the head. Puppy kisses would be the only type of kisses in her future, at least until she managed to get Leo out of her head.

"Mom? Dad?"

Where was everybody? Her stomach growled. She unclipped Cocoa's leash and headed toward the dining room with the scruffy dog on her heels.

"Oh, here you all are." Juliet's smile faded as she took in the empty table and the somber faces of her relatives.

The gang was all there—Mom, Dad, her brother, Nico, and even her cousin Alegra, who doubled as Juliet's closest friend. She was practically a sister, since she'd been orphaned when she was only twelve and Juliet's parents had taken her in as if she was a daughter rather than a niece.

Yep, the entire cast of characters was present, but there

wasn't a strip of bacon in sight. And everyone was stone-faced.

"What's going on? Is this a hunger strike? Or some kind of intervention?" Juliet snickered, but the laughter died in her throat when she realized no one else seemed to think it was a joke. "Wait. This *is* an intervention, isn't it?"

"Don't be silly. We all just want to sit down with you and have a rational, calm conversation." Her mother's voice was as serene as a yoga teacher's. Juliet had never before heard her mother sound that way.

It was eerie. Like the calm before a very intense, very bad storm.

Juliet gritted her teeth and waited for her mother to lose it. The wait would be brief, if past history was any indication.

"Have a seat." Her father motioned toward the chair at the head of the table. The turkey-carving chair. If memory served, neither she nor her brother had ever occupied that place at the table.

She sat down slowly, half expecting to be electrocuted when her bottom hit the seat. Clearly, some kind of major chastisement was in the works. She wished the yelling and screaming would start. Waiting for the fireworks was akin to torture.

Cocoa sighed and rested her massive head in Juliet's lap. At least someone was on her side. "I suppose this is about George."

Her father's fists clenched on top of the table. One of her mother's eyes twitched.

Yep, this was about George all right.

Had he already gone behind her back and told them that she'd refused his proposal? What was this—the Elizabethan Era? Did they think she didn't have any say in the matter?

"Do you have something to tell us regarding your evening with George last night?" her mother asked evenly. How long was she planning on keeping up this whole Stepford Wife act?

"Mom, you can stop pretending. George told me you and Dad knew about the proposal." Juliet's gaze shifted toward Nico and Alegra. There wasn't a trace of shock on either of their faces. If they hadn't been privy to George's plans before, they'd clearly been filled in this morning.

Alegra's expression turned almost sympathetic until Juliet's mother cleared her throat. Then any compassion in her eyes was replaced with stone-cold fear.

"So, where's the ring?" her mother said, a hint of annoyance finally creeping into her tone.

All eyes shot toward Juliet's unadorned ring finger.

She drummed her nails on the table in a defiant tempo. "There is no ring. Actually there was one, but I couldn't accept it. I don't want to marry him."

"So you turned him down. He's completely devastated. He was practically falling to pieces when he called here last night. You've made a mess of things, Juliet. A real mess." Her father's disappointment echoed off the surface of the bare table.

George had called her parents *last night?* Had he even waited for the limo to back out of the driveway of her condo before he'd dialed their number?

She found it impossible to believe George had been devastated. If anything, she'd hurt his pride. Certainly not his feelings. She was no longer sure he even *had* feelings. "Didn't you hear what I said? I don't want to marry him."

"Give me one good reason why not." Her mother raised an index finger. It trembled with what Juliet could only assume was rage.

Her mother's whole body could tremble, and it still

wouldn't change her mind. "I'll give you two. I don't love him, and he doesn't love me."

Her father snorted. "Nonsense."

"It's not nonsense. It's true. I'm not in love with him. And he doesn't love me, either. He told me so point-blank. He loves his business. He loves what it would mean for Royal Gourmet if we got married. He wants a merger, not a marriage."

She buried her fingers in Cocoa's wiry chocolate-colored coat for emotional support. She'd promised herself she wouldn't cry. Not over George. But confessing all this in front of her parents, Nico and Alegra made her feel humiliated all over again.

"Like I said—nonsense." Her father shrugged.

Had he not heard a single word she'd said? *"What?"*

"Love is certainly a reason to get married, but not the only one. There are plenty of others. Better ones, in fact. You and George work well together. He would provide you with a comfortable living, and he couldn't be more supportive of your work. Do you think they'd be dining on Arabella chocolates at The French Laundry if not for George? It's a perfect match. He's a good man."

A good man? That was highly debatable.

Would a good man have point-blank said that the reason he wanted to marry her was because it would be good for business?

Her mother's forced smile wavered ever so slightly. "I don't know what you're waiting for. You're not going to do better than George."

Ouch. "I will not marry a man I don't love. Period."

No one said a word for a long, excruciating moment. No

doubt they were shocked. Juliet had never gone against her parents' wishes. Not once in her entire twenty-eight years.

She sneaked a glance at Nico, who flashed her a quick wink. Her brother—the wild child. Who knew they'd ever be on the same side of an argument against their parents? That was something Juliet hadn't seen coming.

At last someone said something. Her mother, naturally. "Tell her, Dom. She needs to know."

Her father sighed.

"Tell me what, Dad?"

"We're ruined, that's what!" her mother screamed. Her cool exterior had finally cracked. It was almost a relief.

Cocoa's tail drooped between her legs. Juliet was feeling rather droopy herself at the moment. "Ruined, because I won't marry George? Isn't that a tad melodramatic?"

Her father rested his interlocked hands on the table. He might have appeared calm, especially in contrast to Juliet's mom, but upon closer inspection he had dark circles under his eyes that hadn't been there the day before. He looked tired. Tired and very worried. "We're no longer going to be represented by Royal Gourmet. They're dropping us effective immediately."

Juliet's heart sank. "All because I won't marry George?"

"That, and the way you carried on last night with Leonardo Mezzanotte." Her mother didn't yell this time, but her words dripped with venom. The whole effect was far more terrifying than a raised voice.

Cocoa released a sharp bark, and everyone around the table jumped.

They knew about Leo?

Beads of sweat broke out on Juliet's forehead.

"Did you think you could let a Mezzanotte touch you like that and we'd never find out? Ha!" This was followed by a stream of curse words in Italian. At least Juliet assumed they were curse words by the way her mother spat them out.

Her Italian was rusty these days. Not that now was the time to worry about her foreign language skills. What exactly did they know? Had her mother somehow found out about the kiss?

Oh, God. Please, no.

A wave of nausea hit her hard and fast. Leo had told his uncle, just as she knew he would. And now everyone knew what she'd done. How could she have thought for a moment that she could trust him?

"It's not what you think...." Juliet said. *But wasn't it exactly what they all thought?* "I didn't know his name."

Her mother rolled her eyes. "What are you talking about? You knew precisely who he was. The two of you had just been introduced, and for some reason you agreed to dance with the man. George was standing right there."

Oh. Relief coursed through Juliet. So this was about the dance, after all. Leo hadn't shared their secret.

This pleased her far more than it should have.

She let out a measured exhale. "We danced, Mom. It was nothing."

"It most certainly was not. George said he was all over you and that you appeared to enjoy every minute of it. He was humiliated." Her mother's furious gaze bored into hers.

Once again, Juliet found herself on the verge of tears. So George had been humiliated? As humiliated as she'd felt when he'd told her he wanted to marry her for business reasons? As humiliated as she'd been when he'd introduced her as his fiancée, even after she'd turned down his proposal?

As humiliated as she felt right now, watching her parents take his side?

"Let's just hope it's not too late to fix things." Her mother smiled a dangerously composed smile.

"Mom…" Nico started.

She stopped him with a pointed glare. "As I was saying, you will fix this, Juliet. You will call George today and apologize. Tell him you had too much wine last night, and you let your guard down. Tell him you've given it more thought and you realize you can't live without him. I don't care what you tell him, or how you do it. Just fix it."

Juliet's stomach tightened. She'd made her feelings clear. And still her parents wanted their only daughter to marry a man against her own wishes, simply to profit the family business.

She looked around the table. Her father appeared slightly less anxious now that her mother had issued her decree. Alegra stared down at the table, refusing to meet her gaze. Nico just yawned, as if he'd witnessed this sort of exchange all his life, which she supposed he had.

Juliet, eat your vegetables.

Juliet, put on a sweater. It's cold outside.

Juliet, marry George Alcott.

They all expected her to comply, and she really couldn't blame them. That's what the old Juliet would have done. But something was different about her now. What happened in the limousine had changed her, and what happened afterward in the vineyard had only strengthened her resolve. Even if Leo was a Mezzanotte.

She took a deep breath. "No."

Leo had been hoodwinked.

That much was obvious when he accompanied the rest of the Mezzanotte clan to the Manocchio Winery on Sunday morning to retrieve the dried-out chocolate fountains.

"He doesn't look sick. And he certainly doesn't act like it," Leo muttered to his sister, Gina, as he watched Uncle Joe heave one of the fountains on his shoulder and head out of the ballroom toward the parking lot, speaking into his Bluetooth all the while.

"He's not." Gina frowned and attempted to lift another of the fountains herself. It didn't budge.

"Here, let me." Leo picked it up. The thing had to weigh at least eighty pounds. "Then why did he tell me otherwise? He made his arthritis sound so bad that I half expected to find him crumpled up on the floor when I got back here."

"Please. You know why he said that. He wanted you home." Gina held the door open for him and followed him out of the ballroom.

They stepped out onto the terrace and into the morning mist. The sky swirled overhead in smoky shades of pink and lavender, and the vineyard rustled with the soft footfalls of day laborers tending the vines. Leo had been away so long he'd forgotten how the valley was usually bathed in a thick blanket of fog in the early morning hours. It gave the Manocchio Winery a mysterious, almost-romantic quality.

Not quite as romantic as it had been under the silver light of the moon, however. The memory of Juliet Arabella standing barefoot among the vines was hard to shake—those cool green cat eyes, those porcelain shoulders, those cute pink toes.

Those lips.

"He missed you. We all have. It's been years." Gina sighed, dragging Leo's attention back to the present.

Just what he needed. A guilt trip. He'd foolishly thought that, since his father was buried, he might avoid this part of coming home. "I missed you, too, sis."

"You could have called me, you know. I would have told you what Uncle Joe was up to." She squinted into the fog. The cargo van with Mezzanotte Chocolates emblazoned on its side was swallowed up in the mist.

"I called. Didn't I?" Leo adjusted his grip on the fountain.

He was half-tempted to let it fall. Didn't Uncle Joe know that once chocolate fountains had made their sticky sweet way into the mainstream, they had no place in a specialty *chocolaterie?* As a rule, Leo's plans for overhauling Mezzanotte Chocolates included avoiding anything the average person could buy at a warehouse discount store.

There were no warehouse discount stores in Paris.

Leo's jaw clenched. How was it possible to feel homesick for a place that wasn't truly your home?

"Once a month, maybe. You're family. You belong here, not Paris." Gina gave him the older sister glare he'd managed to forget about over the course of the past decade.

"Well, I'm here now."

Uncle Joe marched back toward him through the fog. He looked distinctly displeased.

"Leo, I'd like you to explain to me what you were thinking when you asked that gate-crasher to dance with you last night." He crossed his arms and planted himself directly in Leo's path.

Leo walked right around him, continuing on toward the van. He'd managed to avoid a dressing down over the whole Juliet Arabella thing thus far. Uncle Joe had been on his cell phone for the majority of the morning. Clearly whatever business he'd been taking care of was now settled.

"Don't ignore me, Leo. I'm still waiting for you to explain yourself." Uncle Joe scurried behind him.

Leo opened the door of the van and rid himself of the fountain. "It was a ball. Don't people typically dance at such parties?"

"But why *her*, of all people?" Gina scowled.

Leo shook his head. *Et tu, Gina?*

"There were easily seventy-five women there to choose from, and you picked *her*. She wasn't even invited. I should have called the police and had her removed at first sight. Maybe even arrested for trespassing." A smile made a brief appearance on Uncle Joe's face at the thought of Juliet Arabella in the slammer.

"It would never have worked. She came with one of your invited guests. She had every right to be there." Leo clicked the doors of the cargo van shut and began making his way back to the main building of the winery.

Gina and Uncle Joe were hot on his heels, of course. Every move he made was apparently now a family matter.

"A man can dream, can't he? An Arabella incarcerated— that's the stuff fantasies are made of." Uncle Joe's laugh boomed throughout the valley.

Leo cleared his throat. He'd had a few fantasies involving Juliet over the course of the past twelve hours, none of which involved her being behind bars. "What do you know about that George character she was with, anyway?"

He shouldn't care about the guy. He knew he shouldn't. He and Juliet had shared an encounter, nothing more. He had no claim on her. What's more, he didn't want any such claim. He'd been down that route before with Rose. He had no interest in revisiting that particular brand of disaster.

Yet the thought of someone else proposing marriage to Juliet on the very night he'd had his hands all over her...

It riled him. And he wasn't usually one to be riled.

Gina's response did little to alleviate Leo's irritation. "George Alcott? He's kind of a big deal. You should probably know who he is."

"Do enlighten me," he ground out.

Uncle Joe paused on the terrace. His face took on a sudden red hue, and his eyes bulged, like one of those French bulldogs that were all the rage in Paris. "For your information, dear nephew, the man's full name is George Alcott III."

Leo's annoyance grew threefold, in direct proportion to the Roman numerals after George's name.

And he was no doctor, but by all appearances, Uncle Joe suddenly looked as if he were on the verge of an aneurysm. "His family owns Royal Gourmet Distributors. They place specialty food items in local four- and five-star restaurants. For the past two years he's been putting chocolates from the Arabella Chocolate Boutique all over the area's finest eateries. They're mopping up the floor with us. It's no wonder Juliet Arabella is going to marry him."

So, for practical purposes Juliet's boyfriend held the purse strings to her business? That was a situation that sounded uncomfortably familiar.

Leo leaned against the stucco wall of the winery and crossed his arms. "She's not."

"Wait...what?" Gina blinked.

Uncle Joe's complexion paled a degree or two back toward normal. "Pardon?"

"She's not going to marry him. She turned him down."

Gina gasped in obvious delight.

Uncle Joe's eyes narrowed. "How do you know?"

Leo's shoulders lifted in a nonchalant shrug. "She told me."

His uncle lifted a sardonic brow. "I assume this confession occurred when you were busy fondling her on the dance floor last night?"

Fondling her?

He didn't know the half of it.

"For your information, that was dancing. If I'd been fondling her, you'd have known it. I would have put forth greater effort."

Uncle Joe wagged a finger at him. "That's not funny, Leo. Not funny in the slightest."

"It wasn't meant to be funny. I'm dead serious." There were few things Leo was ever serious about. The list pretty much consisted of chocolate and women. In that order.

"What's up? Are you all having a meeting out here?" Gina's husband, Marco, sauntered out of the building. He carried another godforsaken chocolate fountain in his arms.

Gina nodded toward Leo. "According to my brother, Juliet Arabella isn't really going to marry George Alcott."

The third. George Alcott III, Leo's subconscious screamed. Sometimes his subconscious could be a real bitch.

Marco's eyebrows rose to his hairline. "That's big news."

"Wait a minute. She could have lied," Gina said. "Just to throw us off track."

Yeah, right. When he'd dragged her onto the dance floor, she'd been way too rattled to make something up. "Trust me. She wasn't lying."

"There isn't something going on between the two of you, is there?" Gina looked wholly horrified at the prospect.

Uncle Joe answered on his behalf. "Of course there isn't. It's not possible. She's an Arabella, and Leo is a Mezzanotte."

As if it were a law. Or based on any sort of rational thinking.

Leo opened his mouth, but before he could say anything, his uncle raised a hand to silence him. "You can forget any ideas you have about wooing Juliet Arabella. Juliet wouldn't give you the time of day. She's well situated under her mother's thumb. Charming as you may be, you're a Mezzanotte. That makes you her mother's worst nightmare."

His description of Juliet didn't sit well with Leo. Not at all. "You're wrong about her."

"And what would you know of Juliet Arabella?" Uncle Joe scowled heartily.

I know what her lips feel like, sliding against mine.

I know what a whimper of desire sounds like, coming from her lush mouth.

"I know she's not marrying George Alcott III. That speaks volumes, don't you think?" Leo couldn't help but feel a certain affinity with her in that regard. The two of them had both had a chance to marry into fortunes, and they'd each turned it down. He wasn't quite sure whether that made them respectable or the same brand of crazy.

He pushed off the stucco wall and crossed the threshold into the ballroom. He'd had about enough of this conversation.

Uncle Joe called after him. "At any rate, I forbid you to see her again."

Forbid? Didn't he know the surest way to pique a man's interest in a woman was to declare her off-limits?

Not that he needed much piquing. He was plenty piqued

already after that hot encounter in the vineyard, regardless of her last name.

He turned back around and planted his hands on his hips. He couldn't help but notice that Gina and Marco had made themselves scarce all of a sudden. "Since when do you give me orders?"

"Since last night. You're a vital part of the family business now. It's time to start acting like it."

Be careful what you wish for. "You want me to start acting like a 'vital part' of Mezzanotte Chocolates? Fine. We'll start with the store."

Uncle Joe's mouth fell into a flat line. "There's nothing wrong with the store."

"Look, you can stop pretending. I know what's going on."

"I'm sure I don't know what you're talking about, Leo." Uncle Joe flexed and unflexed his fingers, no doubt in an attempt to show off his imaginary arthritis.

"You're not sick. Admit it." Leo crossed his arms and waited.

"I'm seventy years old," Uncle Joe said.

"There's nothing wrong with you," Leo countered.

Uncle Joe let out a sigh of resignation. "You don't understand. The Arabellas are driving me to my grave. For years, they've been struggling away in their tiny little shop while our chocolates have been the crème de la crème of Napa Valley. And then George Alcott III came along. I refuse to die until we're back on top."

Leo released a long, frustrated exhale. This was California, not Le Cordon Bleu. He'd thought his days of cutthroat competition were behind him. "First of all, no one wants you to die. And second, if being the best in the valley is what you're really worried about, then you need to let me do my job."

"I'm not sure you understand how important this is. Otherwise, you wouldn't be dancing cheek to cheek with the enemy."

Again with the dancing. He could have stripped naked and waltzed around the ballroom solo, and it would have been less controversial that what he'd actually been guilty of. "Being the best has absolutely nothing to do with who I choose to dance with."

Or sleep with.

Although bedding Juliet Arabella was beginning to look less and less like a possibility. He was somewhat stunned that the earth hadn't toppled right off its axis when they'd kissed.

"What is it you want, Leo? To marry the girl?" Uncle Joe looked nauseous.

"Don't be ridiculous." Hell, no. Hadn't he just narrowly escaped the noose? Marriage was the last thing on his mind. Didn't he have enough people trying to tell him what to do already? "I'm talking about creative control. I want free rein over the chocolate shop. I will create whatever I like, whenever I like. For the store, the catered events and all our food festival appearances. And, yes, that includes *mendiants* and other distinctly French items. Do we have a deal, or should I catch the next plane back to Paris?"

His words hung between them in the damp air of the valley. No doubt Uncle Joe thought he was bluffing.

He wasn't. He might not have enough capital to start his own store in France, but he could always go back to La Maison.

"Free rein, hmm?"

"Have a little faith. I know what I'm doing. Isn't that why I'm standing here?" Leo gestured to the valley, the grapes, the gently swirling fog. The Mezzanotte shop might not be technically visible from where they stood, but it was a part of Napa as much as a good merlot.

"Okay, we have a deal." Uncle Joe extended his hand.

Leo took it and tried to shake the feeling that he'd just made a deal with the devil instead of his own flesh and blood.

"Ha!" Uncle Joe raised a fist in victory. "We're going to crush the Arabellas. Decimate them."

Just as Leo began to release his fingers from his uncle's grip, Uncle Joe squeezed his hand even harder. He leaned close, and his eyes grew dark. Deadly. "And you, my dear nephew, will be the weapon that puts an end to them once and for all."

5

Oh, how the mighty had fallen.

Aside from the annual Napa Valley Chocolate Fair, Juliet hadn't participated in a food festival, wine event or any other type of fun-filled outdoor gathering since Royal Gourmet Distributors had joined forces with Arabella Chocolate Boutique. In fact, George had preferred them not to participate in such events, calling them *pedestrian* and saying that peddling their goods at such affairs weakened the exclusivity of their brand.

Their *brand*.

She should have known what a pretentious ass he was the first time she'd heard him use that word. They weren't the Kardashians, they were chocolatiers. And now that Royal Gourmet had so unceremoniously dropped them, they were no longer above offering their chocolates to the masses of hipsters who flocked to the wine country in search of the latest and greatest food trend. In fact, participating in such events was a crucial part of Juliet's new strategy for making sure Arabella Chocolate Boutique stayed on the map. Truth be told, it was pretty much the entirety of her strategy.

She'd tried contacting a few of the restaurants that only days ago had been proud to feature Arabella creations on their menus. Every one of those calls had gone unreturned. She couldn't bring herself to call on The French Laundry. Being ignored by a chef like Thomas Keller would have been an omen too menacing to even contemplate. So she'd moved on to Plan B—create a demand for their products that was so great, the chefs would eventually come crawling back to her. And in order to do so, they needed to venture beyond the boutique and out into the world.

Since the Napa Valley Chocolate Fair was still two weeks away, first up was the Nuovo Winery's famed annual hot air balloon festival. Fortunately for Juliet, it fell on the Saturday immediately following the Mezzanotte Masquerade Ball.

*Un*fortunately, her mother's fury over her refusal to marry George hadn't waned over the course of the past five days. If anything, she was even angrier. So angry that she'd ordered Juliet to handle the balloon festival entirely on her own. She'd outright forbidden every member of the family to lift a finger.

The snub was no doubt intended to be a penance, but Juliet couldn't help but feel somewhat relieved. She had no desire to spend any more time with her parents right now than absolutely necessary. And if that meant staying holed up in the chocolate shop by herself until past midnight on the eve of the balloon fest, then so be it.

Except she wasn't quite alone. Cocoa's heavy bulk rested on Juliet's feet as she sat putting the finishing touches on her chocolate-dipped strawberries. Not just any berries— locally grown, organic berries. And not just any chocolate— she'd used a beautiful mixture of dark Belgian chocolate, and topped it off with a heavy dusting of luminescent, edible gold glitter. The berries couldn't have looked more beautiful if Midas had brushed them with the tips of his magic fingers.

A quiet knock on the shop door startled Cocoa into wakefulness. She lifted her shaggy head and let out a single deep bark. Juliet thought she saw a puff of glitter fly out of Cocoa's mouth, but she might have been hallucinating. It had been a long week.

She hurried to the door, Cocoa's toenails clicking behind her on the tile floor. Then she peered into the darkness as she opened the front door just wide enough for Alegra to dart inside. "No one saw you, right?"

"This is crazy. I can't believe I'm sneaking into this place." Alegra pushed back the hood of her sweatshirt, revealing her close-cropped platinum blond hair and signature giant hoop earrings. Even in a hoodie, Alegra was easy to spot. "I spend over forty hours a week busting my butt here. You'd think I'd be welcome any time of day or night."

Juliet closed the door and clicked the dead bolt in place. "It's not you. It's me."

"That's what they all say." Alegra grinned.

"Seriously, I don't want to get you in any trouble. I'm supposed to be in solitary confinement. You didn't see anyone outside, did you?"

Alegra shed her sweatshirt and pulled a frilly, ruffled apron over her head. "No one but your secret boyfriend."

Juliet's cheeks grew hot. Alegra and Nico had taken to teasing her unmercifully about dancing with the enemy. Of course, neither of them would think it was quite so hilarious if they knew her association with Leo hadn't been limited to the dance floor. "Leonardo Mezzanotte is *not* my boyfriend, secret or otherwise."

Cocoa let loose with another bark.

Alegra frowned at the dog. "Is Cocoa barking glitter?"

"Maybe, but look at the strawberries."

Alegra gasped at the sight of the gilded berries shimmering under the light of the crystal chandelier that hung overhead. "Oh, my God, they're gorgeous."

"Gorgeous enough to compete with whatever the Mezzanottes will bring?"

Woof.

"Cocoa, shh." Juliet ran her hand over the dog's head.

"Since when do you worry about your beautiful chocolates being outshone by anything the Mezzanottes do?"

Woof.

Juliet wagged a finger at Cocoa.

Alegra shrugged and went to work gently placing the strawberries in clear plastic boxes. "I mean, the Mezzanottes are drugstore candy bars and we're refined elegance."

Woof.

If only things were so simple. "I don't know. I have a feeling that's about to change. Did you know he studied at the superior level at Le Cordon Bleu in Paris?"

"Who? Your clandestine lover?"

"Yes." Juliet's hands trembled. What happened in the vineyard had become so ingrained in her memory that it had become a part of her, every bit as physical as it was emotional. Even now, standing in the Arabella Chocolate Boutique, she swore she could feel the silky smoothness of his tie slipping through her fingers, feel his breath, hot and sultry against her skin. "I mean, no. Leonardo Mezzanotte is not, and never will be, my lover."

Woof.

The scissors fell from her hands and landed on the counter with a clatter. God help her if she ever actually slept with him. She'd probably lose all ability to function. Good thing that would never happen. Because it wouldn't. Ever.

Alegra picked up the scissors and handed them back to her. "Take it easy, there. I was only kidding. I know you'd never do something like that. Your mom might be a piece of work, God help us all, but family is family. We stick together. Always. Besides, you're way too smart to ever get involved with one of them. They're nothing but liars and crooks. Look what happened to Grandma when she made the mistake of trusting a Mezzanotte."

Woof.

"Cocoa, hush!" they both shrieked in unison. Then they looked at each other and laughed.

Alegra cleared her throat, and suddenly she had a rather uncharacteristically pensive look on her face. "Juliet, there's something about Leo you should probably know. It's something your mom heard, but I thought it would be better coming from me."

"No, there's nothing I need to know." She shook her head. "I told you. Leonardo Mezzanotte is none of my concern. Zero. None. At all."

Alegra lifted a dubious brow. And that tiny, seemingly inconsequential gesture spoke volumes.

Thou doth protest too much.

Damn it. Juliet twisted the dishrag in her hands into a knot. "Fine. Spill. What is it?"

"He was engaged to be married."

"So? Lots of people have failed engagements." Juliet shrugged.

It was true. No big deal.

Then why are you wringing out that dishrag so tightly that your knuckles are white?

She threw it on the counter. "Look, I know he's a Mezzanotte and therefore on equal moral footing as the Antichrist. But this is silly. We danced. He was once engaged. I see no connection between the two."

"That dance you two shared—" Alegra picked up the abandoned dish towel and folded it into a neat square "—was on what would have been his wedding night."

Juliet blinked. A couple times. "Wait. What?"

Alegra nodded. "Yep. The invitations had gone out and everything. Just a couple weeks ago he called it off. Out of nowhere. Poof. That poor girl. Can you imagine?"

No. No, she couldn't. Nor did she want to.

Her stomach did a little flip. She'd kissed the man. And danced with him. On his almost-wedding night.

Common sense told her she was reacting over nothing. There'd been a diamond engagement ring in her evening bag at the very moment she'd grabbed Leo by the tie and reeled him in for a kiss. Who was she to judge?

Yet for some reason, she couldn't get the image of him dancing with a woman in a fluffy white wedding gown out of her head. Nothing—not one thing—about her encounter with Leonardo Mezzanotte made sense. Common, or otherwise.

"Be careful. That's all I'm trying to say. I don't want you to get hurt." Alegra cast her a cautious glance.

"I don't need to be careful. I told you. Leo Mezzanotte is nothing to me, other than a competitor. The only thing I'm worried about right now is what he's making for the festival tomorrow." She told herself what she was saying was true.

"Enough talk of what's going on across the street. We've still got loads to do if we're going to be ready by tomorrow morning." Alegra clamped the lid closed on the last box of glittery strawberries.

"I couldn't agree more," Juliet said, more than ready to abandon talk of Leonardo Mezzanotte, his degree from Le Cordon Bleu and his erstwhile fiancée.

She had over two hundred sea salt and maple bacon hearts ready and waiting to come out their silicone molds. And she couldn't very well show up at Nuovo tomorrow without a few wine-inspired offerings. This was Napa Valley, after all. She'd already prepared dozens upon dozens of truffles—both milk chocolate champagne and dark chocolate Cabernet Sauvignon varieties—but they still needed to be rolled in confectioners' sugar and cocoa powder. In short, she and Alegra still had plenty to keep them busy.

They worked silently, side by side, with Cocoa snoring at their feet, until sometime around one in the morning. Finally, when every last truffle, chocolate heart and strawberry had been packed up in insulated containers, it looked as if the bulk of the work was done.

"Why don't you head on home? I can finish cleaning up this mess by myself." Juliet grabbed a spray bottle of eco-cleanser and aimed it at the countertop.

"Are you sure?" Yawning, Alegra picked up a sponge. "Because I can stay."

Juliet plucked the sponge out of her hand. "Go home. You're dead on your feet."

Alegra slipped her apron over her head. "Okay, but I'll see you bright and early tomorrow morning. You're picking me up at five, right?"

Five. Less than four hours away. Why, oh, why, were the hours just after sunrise the most stable for hot air ballooning? It hardly seemed fair. "I'll be there."

Juliet gave Alegra a quick hug and locked the door behind her. Cocoa whined and paced at the doorway, no doubt wondering if they'd ever get to go home, too.

Juliet gave the dog a comforting scratch under her chin. "Be patient, girlie. We're just about done here."

She wiped everything down as quickly as she could, starting with the countertop and finishing with the stainless steel sink. By the time she reached for Cocoa's leash and flipped off the overhead light, her eyelids were growing heavy. She was weary to the bone.

Cocoa took full advantage of Juliet's exhaustion by taking off into the darkness as soon as they stepped outside. The leash slipped right through Juliet's fingers, and the big dog darted into the street.

"Cocoa!" she screamed, her heart leaping straight to her throat. "No!"

Great. This was the last thing she needed.

At least it was far too late at night to worry about Cocoa being hit by a car. This area of town was typically deserted after midnight. Still, she didn't know what she'd do if Cocoa got lost. And it really wasn't like her to run off.

Juliet ran after her and soon found the impetus for the dog's hasty getaway—a tiny white ball of fluff masquerading as another dog. The miniscule thing was quivering on her back, belly-up in the grass on the opposite side of the road while Cocoa sniffed her from head to tail.

"Cocoa, what have you got there, a new little friend?"

Cocoa's tail beat against the ground in a happy tempo.

Juliet bent to pick up the end of the leash and to check the little white poodle for identification tags. As soon as she squatted down, a familiar masculine voice pierced the darkness.

"Her name is Sugar."

Juliet flew upright. "Leo. What are you doing here?"

"I could ask you the same thing." He nodded to the quaint shop less than five feet away, with its delicate white gingerbread trim and scrolling, decorative window script.

Mezzanotte Chocolates.

Oh, God. For all practical purposes, she was standing in the Mezzanottes' front yard.

"I'm sorry. It's my dog...she ran across the street, and I just followed her. I wasn't thinking." Panic coiled in Juliet's belly. At least she assumed it was panic, even though it felt oddly like anticipation. Maybe even some sort of longing.

Clearly she was sleep deprived.

Leo's mouth curved into a wicked smile. "By all means, don't apologize."

Juliet took a giant step backward and almost tumbled over Cocoa and her petite companion.

"Careful, there." Leo reached for her, and before she could register what was happening, he'd managed to scoop her up in his arms and deposit her back on her feet in perilously close proximity to himself.

The words *sweep me off my feet* swirled in Juliet's consciousness. She blinked. Hard. "Thank you. Well, I should get going before someone sees..."

Her gaze darted toward the warm cozy light coming from the windows of Mezzanotte Chocolates.

"No one's here. Just me. Your secret is safe." He lifted an amused brow. "Again."

She cleared her throat. Why did this keep happening? She'd managed to avoid Mezzanotte territory her whole life up until the past week. Accidentally, of course.

There are no accidents. Only fate.

Isn't that what her mother was always saying? She wondered what her mom would think about the hands of fate leading her daughter to the door of Mezzanotte Chocolates.

On the other hand, maybe she didn't want to know what her mother would think about anything having to do with Leo.

"I've been meaning to thank you, actually," she said.

"For?" His voice was like melted caramel. Warm. Rich. Smooth.

"For keeping your promise and not saying anything to your family about the circumstances surrounding our meeting. I owe you a debt of gratitude." A salty ocean breeze drifted through the valley, lifting Juliet's hair and sending it flying in all directions.

"'The circumstances surrounding our meeting?' That sounds awfully clinical. Forgive me, but I don't remember it quite that way." He reached for an errant strand of her hair and tucked it behind her ear.

A shiver coursed through her. Juliet would have loved to blame it on the gentle wind, but she would have just been fooling herself. "Fine. Thank you for not mentioning the kiss."

He tilted his head, his blue eyes searching, probing. "Don't you mean the kisses? I'm certain there were more than one."

Like she'd kept count. He'd pretty much kissed away her ability to reason, much less undertake anything involving math. "You know what I mean."

"Yes, I believe I do." His gaze fell squarely on her mouth.

She needed to get out of here. Immediately. Before she did something monumentally stupid.

She took a deep breath and squared her shoulders. "Like I said, I should go. I have an early day tomorrow."

She gestured to the dogs. Cocoa had lowered herself to a

commando crawl position and was thus now on even ground with the poodle. The little dog was pawing at the big one with dainty swipes of her paws. "You said her name was Sugar? Do you know who she belongs to?"

His muscular shoulders rose and fell. "Sure, I do. She's mine."

Juliet snorted with laughter. "You're telling me that this is your dog?"

"Yes."

Why wasn't he laughing? Surely this was a joke. "You've got to be kidding."

He furrowed his brow. "What's wrong with my dog?"

"Look at her." Juliet waved a hand at the petite poodle and saw something twinkle in the moonlight. Was that a rhinestone collar? Oh, this was just too good to be true. "She's miniscule. And a little on the feminine side. And you're... well, you're..."

Now she was in trouble. How was she supposed to complete that thought without mentioning his obvious masculinity? His commanding presence? His big, strong hands? The lean, hard muscles she knew lay buried beneath his shirt?

He crossed his arms and narrowed his gaze at her. Even in the semidarkness, the mischief in his blue eyes was clearly visible. "I think the words you're looking for are *virile* and *manly*."

Bingo.

She swallowed and looked away. "Those work, I suppose."

"Come inside." He nodded toward the chocolate shop.

Surely she'd heard him wrong. "What?"

"You heard me. Come inside."

He'd thrown out the invitation so casually, as if it were

no big deal. As if crossing that threshold wouldn't be tanta-mount to treason.

He was delusional. She'd never in her life come close to setting foot in the Mezzanottes' store. To her knowledge, no Arabella ever had.

"No. Absolutely not." She turned to go, picking up Co-coa's leash and giving it a gentle tug.

"Suit yourself," he called after her. "I was experimenting with a new menu item and thought you might like to try it. But if you're not interested..."

Juliet's footsteps slowed.

A new menu item?

All week she'd been dying to know what he'd been up to over here. She found it impossible to believe the Mezzanottes would waste the kind of specialty training Leo had under-gone in Paris. They were far too shrewd to make a mistake like that. Hadn't history proven as much?

His grandmother had stolen her grandmother's recipe right out from under her nose. And the decades since had been filled with backstabbing rumors, innuendos and acts of sabo-tage. When she was a little girl, she'd seen Leo's father sneak into their store and drop a live rat from his pocket. The health department had shown up in less than ten minutes. So she knew good and well the Mezzanottes had something up their sleeve. They always did. Why would now be any different?

She could stay for a minute. Five, tops. Just to check things out. It could be an investigation of sorts.

"How about it?" The timbre of Leo's voice dropped a notch, and she couldn't help but remember the way he'd sounded when he'd gently lifted her mask from her face at the masquerade ball.

Lovely, he'd said, gazing down at her, his tone riding a fine line between tenderness and heat.

Sometimes when she closed her eyes she could hear that word, exactly as he'd said it that night.

Exactly as he sounded right now.

She turned to face him. The memory of a black velvet night spent kissing among the grapes of the Manocchio Vineyard danced between them, a sultry, irresistible rumba. Juliet could feel its slow, beckoning rhythm, beating in time with her heart.

Who was she kidding? Leo's chocolates weren't the only things she wanted to investigate.

That would have been his wedding night.

"I don't think so." She sounded breathless, maybe because she *was* breathless. Again.

Damn it.

She'd held on to a slender thread of hope that their first meeting had been a fluke. She'd even prayed for it to be so. It didn't seem possible that the one man who could make her feel this way was the only one who was so strictly off-limits.

It was no fluke. That much was certain.

"You disappoint me, Juliet. As you said, you do owe me a debt of gratitude. The least you can do is act as my taste tester on this one occasion." He tilted his head, and his gaze traveled from her eyes to her lips, down to the base of her throat, where her pulse had begun to pound wildly out of control.

She couldn't think of anything more dangerous than spending another second alone with Leonardo Mezzanotte.

On the other hand, what harm could one little bite of chocolate do?

Loads.

There were no words for the kind of harm that could

come from an Arabella crossing the threshold of Mezza-notte Chocolates. Swimming with sharks would no doubt be a safer activity.

She opened her mouth, fully intent on saying no, but what came out sounded an awful lot like, "Okay, just this once."

Probably because that's precisely what she said.

6

Leo couldn't help but notice Juliet looked a little shell-shocked as she stood in the entryway of the shop, her enormous dog leaning against her legs.

"I can't believe it. I'm standing inside Mezzanotte Chocolates." She shook her head, sending waves of hair the exact color of a perfect Belgian praline tumbling over her shoulders, down her back.

Her dog—he thought she'd called it Cocoa—released a single, ear–splitting bark.

Sugar flinched. Leo doubted she even recognized the sound. Nothing remotely that loud or deep had ever come from her tiny mouth.

Juliet spun in a slow circle, her eyes wide, taking in her surroundings. "It's really quite charming."

"I know the Mezzanottes are your sworn enemy." *Woof.* "But surely this isn't the first time you've been here."

She laughed. "Oh, I assure you, it is. When I was a little girl, I thought I would burst into flames if I ever walked through the door of Mezzanotte Chocolates."

Woof.

Leo narrowed his gaze at Cocoa. "Is it my imagination, or does your dog bark every time she hears my last name?"

Juliet's cheeks flushed a stirring shade of pink. "Maybe."

Leo refused to believe it. There were already more than enough opinions about this heated flirtation he and Juliet had going on without adding her dog's to the mix.

He looked at Cocoa again. She'd slumped to her belly, and was resting calmly with her head on her shaggy, outstretched legs at Juliet's feet.

The only way to know for certain was to put his theory to the test. "Mezzanotte."

Cocoa's head popped up. *Woof.*

Leo slid his gaze to Juliet. Her flush intensified.

"Arabella," he said, doing his best to ignore the musical way the word rolled off his tongue.

Cocoa simply yawned.

"Butter."

Nothing. No reaction at all.

"Cream."

Still more silence.

"Mezzanotte."

Woof.

Leo shook his head. "Well, I'll be damned."

"Sorry." Juliet bit her plump bottom lip, which was enough to make Leo forget about the crazy dog.

Almost.

"Did you teach her to do that?" He nodded toward Cocoa.

"Don't be silly. Of course not. It's just something she picked up. I don't know why you're so surprised." She rolled her gorgeous green eyes.

"You don't know why I'm surprised that your dog hates

me?" He frowned at Cocoa. "And she's rather vocal about it, too."

"She doesn't hate you. She's just accustomed to your name being said in the heat of the moment, that's all. It's kind of brilliant, actually. She picked it up all on her own. You should be impressed."

"Oh, it's made an impression." Animals loved him. He'd rescued Sugar off the streets of Paris. Her coat had been so matted and filthy, he'd been surprised to discover she was white once he'd cleaned her up.

Maybe it was time for Sugar and Cocoa to have a chat.

"I tried to tell you the feud was serious. You wouldn't listen." Juliet rested her hand on Cocoa's head. The dog's tail thumped against the hardwood floor.

Leo would be willing to bet the dog had no idea where she was. And he wasn't about to tell her. "Trust me. I've since been properly schooled in the seriousness of the matter."

"You, too?" Juliet smiled, but there was subtle sadness about her that unsettled him.

He'd heard about Royal Gourmet dropping the Arabellas like a stone. The news had been delivered courtesy of his uncle Joe, of course, who'd been beside himself with glee. No doubt the hostility between their families only exacerbated the situation.

She felt responsible. He could see that much in her eyes. And it gave him the very sudden, very real urge to wring George Alcott III's pretentious neck.

"I'm sorry if our dance played any part in what happened with Royal Gourmet." Even if it hadn't, he was still sorry. From the looks of things, the turn of events had taken its toll.

She snorted. "Sure you are."

"I mean it." He gave her a half grin. "Although I can't

say I'm sorry you're not marrying that idiot." As one who had so recently escaped a similar fate, he could empathize.

Her eyes went melancholy again for a beat. "Why are you being so nice to me?"

He shrugged. "I like you."

It was inconvenient to say the least, but it was the truth. His relief at her single status wasn't fueled solely by empathy. He liked her. That didn't mean he wanted to marry her. Marriage and all it entailed was as far off his radar as Paris. But he could simply like a woman, couldn't he?

"You can't like me." Her voice went softer. Quieter. "And I can't like you."

"The hell I can't. The feud has nothing to do with me. I don't believe in it."

She rolled her eyes. "What do you mean you don't believe in it? It's a thing. It exists, whether you believe in it or not."

"Plenty of people believe in Santa and the Easter Bunny, but that doesn't make them real." He moved closer to her, keeping one eye on her dog. Just in case.

She looked him up and down. "Believe whatever you want. Or don't. But I do."

"Yet here you stand, inside the lion's den." He had her there, and they both knew it.

She glanced around at the shelves stocked with boxes of rum-flavored chocolate cigars and rich chocolate dessert wines, then at the cases filled with hand-rolled truffles, chocolate dipped orange peels and what he'd been working on for the better part of the evening—Pavé Glacé, melt-in-your-mouth blocks of hazelnut, saffron, dark chocolate and butter, covered in cocoa powder and meant to resemble cobblestones.

He got the distinct feeling she was on the verge of turning

on her heel and walking right out the door. And for some reason, it had become very important to him that she stay.

"I didn't invite you here so we could talk about our families." Without waiting for a response, he wound his fingers through hers and led her by the hand toward the kitchen.

She followed willingly, so that was something. He hadn't been altogether sure she would. The dogs trotted behind them—Cocoa first, followed by Sugar, who scrambled to keep up.

"Sit." He nodded toward the butcher-block countertop next to the stove.

Both dogs plopped into sit positions.

When Juliet hesitated, he put his hands on her waist and lifted her up and onto the counter. She gasped and clutched at his shoulders for balance. But even after she was situated, she held on to him, the fabric of his shirt gathering in her fingertips. He had a flashback of his favorite tie being crushed by those same hands, and a wave of arousal rocked through him, as it always did when his thoughts drifted back to the night. Which they did with alarming frequency.

His palms slid to her hips, pausing for just a moment to appreciate the wholly feminine shape of her.

How long had it been since he'd touched her? Less than a week? Hard to believe. The hunger gnawing at his insides gave him the sense it had been ages.

She removed her hands from his shoulders, finally, and resituated them primly in her lap. With more than a little reluctance, Leo released his hold on her. She cleared her throat and blinked impassively, her expression a carefully arranged mask of detachment.

Leo had to give her credit—she was putting up quite a front, feigning indifference like that. But he could see the faint trembling in her lush bottom lip, as well as the subtle darkening of her irises. And there'd been no mistaking the way her breath had grown quicker when he'd lifted her off the ground and deposited her on his countertop.

Feud or no feud, she still reacted to him on a purely physical level. He got to her. And, hell, was it ever a turn-on. Obviously, she'd rather pretend otherwise. Fine. Two could play at that game.

Leo gave her a cool look, turned his back on her and strode to the refrigerator. He whistled as he pulled out cartons of cream and whole milk and carried them back to the stove. Eyeballing it, he poured a dollop of cream into the waiting saucepan. Unlike a lot of chefs, he was usually a fan of measuring cups. But Juliet was watching him like a hawk, clearly intent on memorizing his every move. He might be attracted to her on an unparalleled level, but he wasn't an idiot. As much as he liked the idea of feeding her *le chocolat chaud*, this wasn't a cooking lesson.

He turned the burner on low and slid his gaze back in her direction. "Nightingale or lark?"

"Pardon?" Her eyes met his once again.

Leo tossed a generous handful of bittersweet chocolate chunks—the finest quality he had on hand—into the cream mixture. Good *chocolat chaud* was all about the quality of the chocolate. "Nightingale or lark? Are you a night person or a morning person? Given the late hour, I'm guessing nightingale. I'm still fighting off jet lag. What's your excuse?"

"I typically don't work through the night. This week I happen to have an unusually heavy workload." She glared at him as if he had something to do with the fact that she'd been up half the night making chocolate.

And that's when Leo saw it—a glittery sparkle that caught

the light when she turned her head. She moved again, and he saw another shiny twinkle just above her cheekbone. And yet another by the corner of her mouth.

"You have glitter on your face." His gaze dropped to the open square-cut collar of her dark blue blouse, where her slender collarbones glimmered like stardust. "And elsewhere."

"No, I don't." Her face flooded with color.

She did the flushing thing a lot, he'd noticed. He wondered if it had anything to do with him or if she was always this bashful. He rather liked the idea of the former.

He released the whisk from his hand, stepped closer to Juliet and brushed the pad of his index finger along the side of her neck, letting it glide toward the soft dip between her glittery clavicles. A gentle gasp escaped her lips as her skin broke into shimmery goose bumps.

Leo smiled and held his finger up for inspection. Just a simple swipe, and he suddenly looked as if he'd spent his day scrapbooking. "I rest my case."

She crossed her arms. "I know what you're thinking."

"And what might that be?"

"That I moonlight as an exotic dancer." Her lips curved into a smile that could only be described as naughty. "You'd love that, wouldn't you?"

Guilty as charged. He could think of worse things, although he would have preferred that particular activity to take place somewhere private. Like his bedroom.

He backed away a fraction and tried to rid his mind of the image it was currently fixated on. "Of course not. I'm sure there's a perfectly reasonable explanation why you're covered in glitter in the middle of the night." He shrugged. "Maybe you're the tooth fairy."

She laughed. Loud and carefree. "I thought you didn't believe in things like the tooth fairy. Or Santa."

"Touché." He grinned.

And just as he was thinking they'd finally gotten somewhere, to a place where neither of them was thinking about
the feud, chocolate or their respective families, Juliet said,
"Hey, there, Willy Wonka. Aren't you forgetting something?" She nodded toward the stove, where his *chocolat chaud*
was within a millisecond from bubbling over.

Merde.

He switched the gas burner to the off position. Then,
while Juliet smirked at him and petted her giant, Mezzanotte-
hating dog with the tips of her toes, he attacked the concoc-
tion with the whisk and gave it a sniff. It smelled heavenly.
Like Paris.

Thank God.

He'd never burned something as simple as hot chocolate
in his life, and he wasn't about to start now.

He added a dash of brown sugar before pouring a generous portion into a demitasse cup and then handed it to her.
"Here you go."

She stared into the cup as he slid onto the counter beside
her. "What is it?"

"*Le chocolat chaud.* Parisian hot chocolate."

She eyeballed it again. He wished she'd just taste it already.
"What makes it Parisian?"

"Secret ingredient." He took the cup from her hands and
brought it to her mouth. "Sip. Now."

She did.

Leo could tell the precise moment the chocolate hit her
tongue. Her beautiful green eyes grew wide, then drifted

closed. Her head fell back, giving him a full view of her glittery throat, of her slightly parted lips.

"Oh, wow." Her voice was nothing more than a husky moan.

Oh, wow, indeed.

That sound was enough to get a rise out of any man. Even a Mezzanotte. Perhaps *especially* a Mezzanotte.

"Thoughts?" he asked, wondering if she remembered that he'd told her he wouldn't kiss her again until she asked him to. Because he was just about ready to forget that hastily uttered promise.

Her dark lashes fluttered open. "I think if you start serving this, my family will be out of business in a matter of days. What in God's name did you put in it?"

"Bittersweet chocolate. A little milk, a little cream and sugar." That was it. For the most part...

"And?" She lifted a wary eyebrow. He was holding out on her, and she knew it.

"And a secret ingredient." He slid closer, until the length of Juliet's thigh rested against his.

Leo shot a glance at her dog, just in case that old adage about its bark being worse than its bite didn't apply. Cocoa was curled on the floor, with Sugar nestled between her giant paws. They both peered up at him and wagged their respective tails. Clearly, Cocoa still had no idea who he was.

"You're really not going to tell me?" Juliet took another dainty sip of the chocolate, then licked her upper lip.

Leo had to stop himself from blurting it out right there and then—*fleur de sel.* His secret ingredient was a very special sea salt harvested from the salt marshes of South Brittany and packaged by Le Guérandais. He had no intention of sharing that information with her. Or anyone, for that matter.

But sitting there, watching her lick her pillowy lips while the heavy scent of good chocolate swirled around them, the words almost fell off his tongue.

He reminded himself who they were and where they were sitting. It might be fun to toy with Juliet, but there were limits as to how far this flirtation could go. And those limits stopped short of sharing recipes. Obviously. "As everyone is so intent on reminding me, you're an Arabella. And I'm a Mezzanotte. If the shoe were on the other foot, would you tell me?"

Her gaze flitted to the demitasse cup and back at him. A century's worth of secrets, betrayals and strife ricocheted between them. "Yes, of course."

"Liar." He cupped her cheek in his hand.

There was the barest moment of hesitation in her eyes before she leaned into his touch. "What if I kissed you? Would that make a difference?"

A kiss in exchange for a simple ingredient? It almost seemed like a bargain.

She didn't wait for an answer but laid her graceful hand on his chest and reached up to brush her lips against his with the barest of touches. It was an innocent kiss. In a way, cautious. But the instant their lips met, Leo was consumed.

There was still no way he was telling her about the *fleur de sel.*

He smiled against her lips. "The secret ingredient is…"

She inhaled, and the warmth of her body, the softness of her breasts, pressed into him. Her heart pounded against his. *Stay strong.* "Unicorn tears."

She laughed, but made no move to back away. "That hot chocolate is so yummy, I almost believe you."

His hands moved from the countertop to her waist and

paused there a second before sliding to the small of her back. She made the tiniest mewing sound, almost like a kitten. Or maybe Leo only imagined it. He was aware of little else but the way the air between them pulsed—with desire now, more than secrets—and the feel of her silky skin sliding against his palms. Somehow his hands had slipped right beneath her wispy thin blouse, but she hadn't made a move to back away.

She was warm. So warm. Almost hot to the touch. And every bit as delectable as a soufflé fresh from the oven.

He splayed his fingers and pulled her against him. Her heartbeat careened nearly out of control, and Leo went abruptly hard as granite.

"Who says I'm lying?" he whispered, his lips a breath away from the curve of her ear. A shiver coursed through her. Leo felt it all the way to his core.

Her arms wrapped around his neck in a slow, sultry movement. "Unicorns aren't any more real than the tooth fairy."

"Or the feud?" His hands slid up to her rib cage, his thumbs scarcely skimming the lacy edge of her bra.

On some barely conscious level, he was aware this might not be the best idea. But he couldn't stop himself from touching her. And if he didn't taste her again—really taste her, right now—he was going to lose what was left of his mind.

"What feud?" she murmured.

It was music to his ears.

Then her mouth sought his, and this time there was nothing chaste, nothing careful about her kiss. It was like the vineyard all over again.

Only this time, she tasted like the salty shores of Brittany, the Eiffel Tower, the Place des Vosges under a starry sky. Every place that Leo loved most in the world. And as his tongue slid against hers, he experienced some kind of fundamental shift inside. For the first time since he'd left Paris, he felt as though he'd come home.

Which made no sense at all.

But he wasn't about to stop and analyze what was happening. In fact, stopping wasn't anywhere on his radar. The urgent need to take her had rendered him incapable of rational thought. The fact that he was seriously considering making love to Juliet Arabella on the kitchen countertop of Mezzanotte Chocolates seemed wholly reasonable. The best idea in the world. At that moment, he probably would have bedded her right in the front window display. In broad daylight.

Until he thought he heard ducks splashing in a pond. Somehow, between one desperate kiss and the next, the sound managed to reach his ears.

Juliet didn't seem to notice. She arched toward him and tangled her fingers in his hair. Her mouth opened in the softest of sighs and a fresh, needy wave of lust surged through Leo. So he told himself he was only hearing things. He slid his hands under her bottom and lifted her up clear off the counter. Then he shifted until that soft, supple body of hers was in his lap, pressed fully against him as he rocked into her so she could feel his arousal.

But when the splashing sound grew louder and was suddenly accompanied by the thumping of metal against metal, Leo could no longer ignore it. Still, it took a superhuman effort to remove his mouth from Juliet's. She whimpered in protest, a breathy sound that nearly killed him, as he reluctantly opened his eyes and peered over her shoulder toward the source of the invasive racket.

And there he saw Juliet's enormous dog standing on her

massive hind legs, paws planted on the edge of the stove, pink tongue flying as she guzzled down every last drop of his *chocolat chaud* straight from the saucepan.

7

Juliet had gone positively boneless. Her limbs felt languid and heavy, every bit as liquid as that extraordinary hot chocolate Leo had made for her. And whatever his secret ingredient might be—she was fairly certain it wasn't unicorn tears—it must have contained some kind of potent aphrodisiac. Because, oh, God, she was straddling Leo right there on the kitchen counter of Mezzanotte Chocolates, kissing him as if he were her last meal.

Somewhere in the back of her mind, she knew this was a mistake of the very worst sort. This wasn't like the vineyard, when she'd had no idea who she'd been canoodling with. This time, she knew precisely who he was.

Leo Mezzanotte, whose grandmother had betrayed her own grandmother's trust and stolen the family chocolate recipe right out from under her. Leo Mezzanotte, whose father had once gotten into a fistfight with her dad in the middle of the street. Leo Mezzanotte, with his fancy degree from Le Cordon Bleu and his chocolates that looked like works of art, whose sudden reappearance was sure to guarantee her a place in the unemployment line.

Leo Mezzanotte, whose talented fingers were currently unbuttoning her blouse.

Could she have possibly chosen a worse partner for a sexual reawakening? What had gotten into her? She didn't do this. She didn't sit on men's laps on kitchen counters. She didn't make the kind of breathy noises that were coming from her lips. And she most definitely didn't have sex in the Mezzanottes' chocolate shop.

Not that she'd done that last one.

Yet.

But when Leo pressed himself against her, letting her know how much he wanted this, wanted *her,* she knew it was only a matter of time. And right here, right now, she was perfectly fine with that.

Wasn't this precisely the kind of passion she'd wanted all along?

And then Leo's mouth abruptly left hers. Juliet felt as though he'd taken the air right out of her lungs. Every cell in her body mourned the loss of that mouth.

"Um, what...?" How pathetic. She couldn't even form a simple question.

"Oh, no. No, no, no, no, no." Leo scrambled out from underneath her, causing her backside to land on the countertop with a humiliating thud. "This can't be happening."

Seriously?

Her feet slid to the floor. Her knees had gone wobbly, so she kept a firm grip on the counter even though she would have loved nothing more than to turn tail and run.

Either that, or wring Leo Mezzanotte's neck.

It might have been a while since she'd done this sort of thing, but she was fairly certain it was bad form to kiss a woman within an inch of her life and then dump her on her ass. Literally.

"You know, if you've changed your mind about this, you could have just said so," she spat. What was his problem? Did he have a sudden yearning for his mysterious ex-fiancée or something?

His back was to her. Not that she was actually looking at him. She was too mortified to look anywhere but the floor.

"What? Of course I haven't changed my mind. But, Juliet, we need to get Cocoa to the vet."

That got her attention. Even faster than being tossed off his lap. Her head snapped upward. "The vet?"

Leo turned around. His hair was mussed, his blue eyes dark and serious, and there was a rather captivating knot in his jaw. "She got into the chocolate while we were…otherwise occupied."

"What? No." Juliet shook her head, not wanting to believe what she was hearing. Chocolate was toxic to dogs. Everyone knew that, especially chocolatiers.

He held up an empty saucepan as evidence. Not a trace of *chocolat chaud* remained. Cocoa had licked it clean, not that Juliet could blame her. It was *that* delicious.

She looked at her dog, standing beside Leo with her big tail swinging like a pendulum. Every shaggy hair on Cocoa's normally cream-colored muzzle was covered in rich dark cocoa.

"I can't believe this." Juliet was fanatic about keeping Cocoa away from chocolate. She had to be, seeing as it was an occupational hazard.

And the dog was trained. Hadn't Juliet taken her to eight weeks of doggy obedience school at that big pet store in Sonoma Valley? She was perfectly behaved, other than the unusual Mezzanotte-induced barking habit. But that was more of a personality quirk than problem behavior. Right?

Counter-surfing had never been an issue before, which meant that the lure of Leo's special hot chocolate was irresistible even to dogs. Wasn't that great news? Super. Just super.

She was on the verge of tears all of a sudden. "How did this happen?"

The corner of Leo's mouth curved into a smirk, and his gaze dropped to her opened blouse. How it had happened wasn't exactly a mystery.

She looked down at her bra, on full display. Red lace, with tiny satin bows on the straps. It had actually been a gift from her mother, who'd taken the whole Italian belief in wearing red underwear for New Year's a bit too far and gone for the whole matching set. It looked awfully brazen in the fluorescent light of the kitchen, as if she'd planned this entire encounter.

Damn her cultural heritage.

She wrapped her blouse around her torso, and a hot tear slid down her cheek.

Leo closed the small gap between them and wiped it away with the pad of his thumb. "Hey, don't worry. We're going to get her to the vet. Everything's fine."

She nodded, but she didn't see how it could be true. Things were far from fine. The first time she'd kissed him, she'd managed to lose the support of Royal Gourmet for Arabella Chocolate Boutique. But apparently that wasn't bad enough, because she'd gone and kissed him again.

And now her dog was poisoned.

This was all her fault.

"Come on, let's go." Leo grabbed her hand and led her to the back door of the shop, flipping off lights as he went.

The two dogs trotted alongside, as though they were all headed to the dog park for a rousing game of Frisbee. It was all happening so fast. Juliet didn't have time to think long enough to devise any sort of sensible plan. Before she even realized what she was doing, they were all buckled into Leo's car. A sporty little number. Very racy. Very Leo.

Oh, God, what was she doing in his car? She couldn't be seen out in public with him.

She reached for the door handle, even as he was pulling out of the parking lot. "Leo, just take me across the street. I can deal with this on my own."

He shot her an irritated glance. "I'll do no such thing."

"Leo, please." She glanced over her shoulder. Arabella Chocolate Boutique, with her car parked in its drive, was rapidly disappearing into the darkness.

"Juliet, your dog just consumed about ten ounces of bittersweet chocolate. Seventy percent grade. And I had a little something to do with it. What kind of man would I be if I just dropped you off at your car?"

Well. What was she supposed to say to that? *You're a Mezzanotte. I can only assume you're evil incarnate.*

"I think it's probably a good thing that she's so big. That much chocolate would probably kill a tiny dog." Leo nodded toward Sugar burrowing quietly in his lap.

The little poodle looked even tinier snuggled against him like that. "How on earth did you wind up with a toy poodle? I'm sensing there's a story there."

His mouth tilted in a half smile. "Well, since you asked nicely this time, I'll tell you. I rescued her. She was a stray, nothing but skin and bones and terrified of people. I started leaving a bowl of milk out for her by the back door of La

Maison, and after a few weeks she finally let me pet her. She's come a long way."

That explained it. But he'd left out a crucial piece of information. "And the girly rhinestone collar?"

His expression darkened. "That was my fiancée's doing. *Ex*-fiancée."

A hot spike of...something...hit Juliet right in the solar plexus. She was horrified to realize it felt an awful lot like jealousy.

"So you were engaged?" she asked, trying her best to sound disinterested. And in all likelihood, failing miserably.

"Yes."

That was it. Just yes. Apparently he wanted to discuss his ex as much as she wanted to talk about George Alcott III. It was no surprise when he abruptly changed the subject. "What kind of dog is Cocoa, anyway? Some kind of wire-haired pointer?"

It was a common mistake. Juliet shook her head. "She's a Spinone Italiano."

He took his eyes off the road for a moment to glance at her. "That's quite a mouthful."

"It's an Italian breed. I first saw one when I was about thirteen, and I was instantly besotted." She'd seen the dog at a wine fair. All these years later, she couldn't remember which one. The Napa Wine & Arts Festival, maybe? The memory of that sweet dog had stuck, and as soon as she'd moved into her condo she'd adopted Cocoa. "They're such sweet-natured dogs, and I suppose it didn't hurt that their name reminded me of spumoni. I've always called them ice-cream dogs."

"Spumoni, huh?"

"You know—the Italian ice cream with three layers and

bits of cherry inside?" Her favorite dessert. Besides choco-late, naturally.

"I'm familiar." Of course he was. He'd gone to Le Cor-don Bleu. He could probably whip up a batch of spumoni in his sleep. "So, an Italian dog for an Italian girl."

Her thoughts went at once to her red bra. Ugh. "I guess you could say that."

He grinned. "My mother would have loved you. She was Italian through and through."

Right. Cara Mezzanotte was probably spinning in her grave this very instant. "Leo, please. I think you and I both know your mother would have hated me with a passion."

His grin faded, and the knot in his jaw made a sudden reappearance. Mmm. Quite appealing, in an angry sort of way. Every bit as sexy as she remembered. "I suppose you're right about that."

They rode in silence for the remainder of the trip to the emergency vet clinic in Sonoma, unless the sound of Cocoa retching in the backseat counted as conversation. Oddly enough, the prospect of an eighty-pound dog vomiting all over his leather seats didn't appear to faze Leo in the slight-est. He looked cool as a cucumber over there in the driver's seat, with his charmingly rumpled dark hair and his lean, muscular arms stretched toward the steering wheel.

How did a pastry chef end up with arms like that? It wasn't natural.

Not that anything about the current state of affairs was natural. She shouldn't be here with him. She shouldn't ever have set foot in Mezzanotte Chocolates. And she most defi-nitely shouldn't have kissed him.

Cocoa gagged again. Juliet turned and rested a comforting hand on her dog's broad back. She would have given anything to turn back time, to have another chance to just walk away when Leo had invited her inside his shop.

She'd known good and well what she was doing. An investigation? Ha! She'd wanted to see what would happen when they were alone together again, to see if it was possible to recapture the magic of the vineyard.

She certainly had her answer.

"There might be dog vomit all over your backseat," she said in a quiet voice. Eerily quiet. How could she sound so calm when everything was such a mess? "I'm sorry."

"Don't worry. We're here." He reached over and gave her hand a quick squeeze before maneuvering the car as close as possible to the front door of the emergency pet clinic.

He was being awfully nice about all this. Far nicer than George would have been under similar circumstances. It was sweet.

And very confusing.

She hopped out of the car and coaxed Cocoa from the backseat. The poor thing looked terribly droopy as she climbed down. She peered up at Juliet with her big brown eyes, wagged her tail in slow motion, and Juliet's heart melted.

And sure enough, there was an ungodly mess all over the back of Leo's car. Somewhere in the afterlife, Juliet's grandmother was probably doing victorious cartwheels.

"Thanks for your help. I can get this from here." She'd allowed him to drive her to the vet. He was free to go. Preferably before someone—anyone—saw them together.

Leo ignored her. But a telltale twitch in that knot in his jaw told her he'd most definitely heard what she'd said.

He scooped Cocoa up in his arms and murmured in the

dog's chocolate-covered ear as he headed for the door. "Poor girl. Not feeling so good now, are you?"

Juliet sighed.

Again with the niceness. He looked downright heroic, cradling her dog like that. Just like the type of guy who would save a pitiful stray off the streets of Paris. A lump lodged in Juliet's throat as she followed him inside.

They explained to the receptionist what had happened, and a vet tech in blue scrubs came for Cocoa at once. She thought the vet tech seemed surprised to see the two of them together. And was the receptionist looking at them funny?

Get a grip on yourself.

She was already a dog poisoner. And now she was becoming paranoid. Leo had only been in town for a week, after all. She didn't even want to contemplate what she'd do next.

"So she got into some chocolate?" the vet tech asked, his gaze swiveling back and forth between the two of them.

"Yes, close to ten ounces." Leo nodded solemnly. "Baking chocolate."

The man in the scrubs winced. "Ouch. That's the worst kind for a dog to ingest. You did the right thing bringing her in right away. We can administer some activated charcoal and get all the chocolate out of her system before it's absorbed."

Juliet nodded mutely. Activated charcoal. That sounded horrid.

"She should be okay. With any luck, the two of you can take her home in twenty-four hours or so."

"Oh, we're not…" Juliet glanced at Leo. He gave her a steamy look. She tried not to notice how his biceps were bulging under the dead weight of Cocoa's limp form. "I mean, we're just…"

Archenemies.

The vet tech lifted Cocoa from Leo's arms and headed toward the back of the clinic muttering something that sounded an awful lot like *whatever*.

Paranoia. Definitely.

"Okay, then." Juliet released a nervous breath. Maybe she should just stop talking altogether.

"I should probably get the car cleaned up and check on Sugar." Leo waved toward the door.

Of course he wanted to leave. Why wouldn't he? Cocoa was in good hands now, and Juliet was ready to see him go. More than ready.

Wasn't she?

"Sure, you go on home. Thank you again for everything. I'll give my cousin a call to come pick me up later." Why was it suddenly so difficult to say goodbye? She should be feeling nothing but relieved.

He jammed his hands on his hips. He didn't look so nice anymore. In fact, he looked angry. "I wasn't planning on leaving you here alone. I was planning on going out to the parking lot for a minute and coming right back, but since you seem so determined to get rid of me, maybe I should rethink my plans."

She lifted her chin and reminded herself that the last thing she needed to worry about right now was Leo Mezzanotte's ego. "Maybe you should."

"Fine," he spat.

Good. This was for the best. She shouldn't spend another second in his presence. The more time they spent together, the worse things got. As much as she hated to admit it, her mother was right.

Oh, dear God, did she just agree with her mother? Things were even worse than she'd thought.

But it was true—Arabellas and Mezzanottes weren't destined to be together. Her grandmother had known that fifty years ago when Leo's grandmother had stabbed her in the back. Her father knew it. Her mother, brother and cousin all knew it. Even the Mezzanottes knew it.

The crazy thing was that Juliet knew it, too. But when she was around Leo, she had difficulty thinking straight. Or keeping her clothes on, apparently. So the prudent thing to do was to keep her distance. No more Leo Mezzanotte.

Starting right now.

Leo didn't particularly want to stay with Juliet at the vet's office. He really didn't. The heat they'd managed to generate in the kitchen had cooled considerably, and in the aftermath, he'd begun to seriously question what he was doing. He'd very nearly married another woman. Recently. What on earth was he doing with Juliet? He should be avoiding anything remotely resembling a romantic entanglement like the plague. He needed time to get his bearings. Time to get his head on straight.

Time. Lots and lots of time.

And even if he'd had all the time in the world, the last woman he should be attempting to bed was Juliet. The ridiculous Mezzanotte-Arabella feud aside, she was still his competition. She'd made no secret of the fact that she wanted his *chocolat chaud* recipe. And if his uncle got wind of the fact that he was gallivanting around with an Arabella in the middle of the night, Leo would never hear the end of it.

It wasn't as though he was the nurturing type, anyway. Rose could have testified to that. He might have had it in him to rescue a stray dog, but that was completely different. Dogs didn't harbor any expectations. They were simple creatures. Women, on the other hand, were not. And Juliet was an Arabella, which meant she was as far from simple as she could get.

But abandoning her didn't feel right. And the fact that Juliet fully expected him to do just that infuriated him.

The nagging headache he'd had all day blossomed into full-blown jackhammering behind his eyes. All his life, Leo had seemed to disappoint people at every turn. Most recently, Rose. But she was just the latest person who'd expected more from him than he'd been willing or able to give. His father had wanted him—*ordered* him, basically—to stay in Napa and help run the family business.

Leo had seen the handwriting on the wall. He'd seen himself working, holding down the fort at the store, making excuses for his father when he disappeared to pursue his extracurricular interests. Since he'd been a kid, his dad had used him as an alibi in one way or another. At least once a month, his dad had taken him to the track under the guise of spending a day with him at the park. To say his father hadn't taken the decision well would be an understatement.

And then there'd been his mother, whom Leo had let down in the cruelest way possible. He liked to think he would have done the right thing and come home before the lymphoma claimed her...if his father had bothered to tell him she was sick. Until he'd been called home from France for the funeral, he hadn't had a clue.

And now Juliet Arabella seemed to think that by virtue of his last name, he was some kind of monster. A monster she had no trouble seducing, he noted with a heavy dose of irony. But a monster nonetheless.

He should have been relieved. For once, he was dealing with someone who expected nothing from him. Yet the more Juliet acted as though she was waiting for him to up and leave, the more determined he became to stay.

Until she finally got her way, and he stormed out.

He pushed his way through the doors of the animal clinic, trying mightily to ignore her reflection in the polished panes of glass. She looked so pitiful standing there all alone, with her arms wrapped around herself and her hastily buttoned blouse all askew.

Pitiful, yet undeniably cute.

He did his best to push that image of her out of his head as he cleaned what seemed like a gallon of dog puke from his backseat. All the way back to Napa from Sonoma Valley, he tried to forget the way those sad eyes of hers pulled at him, even as she'd ordered him to leave. But when he guided his car down the only street he'd ever heard of that boasted not one but two gourmet chocolate boutiques right across the road from one another—a sight he'd never even come across in Paris—she was still at the forefront his mind. Along with the things they'd said to one another.

Since you seem so determined to get rid of me, maybe I should rethink my plans.

He cringed. It sounded like something a lovesick kid would say.

Then he remembered Juliet's response. *Maybe you should.*

He jerked the steering wheel into a U-turn. He'd never been good at taking orders from his father. Taking them from Juliet Arabella was flat-out unacceptable. She could get as angry as she pleased, but like it or not, he was going back to that vet clinic to wait with her while her dog vomited up a pound of chocolate.

Only a handful of cars remained in the parking lot when he got there. Even fewer than when he'd left a half hour ago.

He pulled into a spot close to the entrance, snapped Sugar's leash to her collar and strolled back inside. His dog trotted at his feet, her tags jangling in the silence of the smooth tile entrance of the animal hospital.

He nodded at the receptionist and rounded the corner toward the waiting area, fully expecting to find a lonely Juliet slumped in one of the orange vinyl chairs that seemed standard issue for waiting rooms the world over. Despite the drama surrounding their goodbye, he didn't quite believe she'd be unhappy to see him. Who truly wanted to be alone at a time like this?

He couldn't have been more wrong. Juliet didn't look the least bit pleased, and she was decidedly *not* alone.

She was still right where he'd left her. Only now a young woman sat beside her, holding her hand exactly the way Leo had envisioned himself comforting her when he'd hightailed it out of Napa and back to the vet clinic.

"Leo." Every drop of color drained from Juliet's face. She looked as if she might faint. Or strangle him. One of the two, definitely. "What are you doing here?"

His gaze darted from Juliet to her companion—she looked to be in her midtwenties with ultra-short blond hair, sizeable gold hoop earrings and an even more sizable scowl. Leo would have bet every penny he'd ever earned, plus his ex-fiancée's sizeable bank account, that her last name was Arabella.

He half expected her to bark at him. Instead, she let out a shuddery, horrified gasp. "Leo? As in *Leonardo Mezzanotte?*"

Leo could have sworn he heard Cocoa's deep-throated *woof* from somewhere deep in the bowels of the animal hospital.

"Yes. And you are?" He answered as politely as he could

manage, considering he would have been more comfortable addressing a firing squad.

"This is my cousin, Alegra. She just arrived." Juliet swallowed. Leo traced the movement up and down the slender, graceful column of her throat. He tried not to think about the fact that not long ago, his lips had been on that throat. "Alegra, this is Leo Mezzanotte. I have no idea what he's doing here."

Leo narrowed his gaze at her. "Don't you?"

For a split second, he actually thought about faking some sort of emergency with Sugar in order to explain his presence. Then he realized how ludicrous that would have been. He was a grown man, not some love-struck teenager sneaking around after curfew. Besides, Sugar was too busy bouncing around at the end of her leash to fake any kind of viable illness.

"Um." Juliet blinked.

Alegra shot daggers at him with her eyes.

He backed up, out of spitting distance. "I'm here for the same reason I was here earlier. I was worried about you and your dog."

"Earlier?" A look of horror flashed across Alegra's face as she turned to face Juliet. "He was here earlier? With you?"

Leo half expected her to deny it. So he was rather surprised when she nodded, although she still didn't quite look him in the eye.

"Yes," she said. The calmness in her voice was completely at odds with the way her knuckles were turning white from gripping the armrests of her chair.

Alegra glared at Leo again. He simply shrugged. He'd wandered deep enough into this bucketful of crazy without opening his mouth and making things worse.

Sugar let out a yip and launched herself onto Juliet's lap as if the two of them were long-lost friends.

Alegra shook her head and stared at his dog as though *Mezzanotte* was an unfortunate medical condition rather than a surname. Some kind of sickness, like rabies. Clearly she presumed Sugar was a carrier. "I'm confused. What exactly is going on here?"

"Absolutely nothing. Nothing at all." Juliet met his gaze full-on. Finally.

Something about the indifference, feigned or otherwise, in her cool green eyes made Leo's temples throb with fresh intensity. "Cocoa got into some chocolate. I happened to be…" He shot a purposeful glance at Juliet's still-askew blouse. Her cheeks flamed as red as that bra of hers. All that lace. Those tiny bows. He'd probably dream about that bra for weeks. "Nearby."

Alegra threw her hands in the air. "Neither one of you is making a lick of sense. Cocoa knows better than to get into chocolate."

Leo couldn't help the almost-smile that crept to his lips. "It must have been some really great chocolate. Extra tempting."

Juliet snorted. Loudly.

Oblivious, Alegra resumed her interrogation. "And what exactly were you doing nearby? In the middle of the night?"

First his uncle Joe, now Juliet's cousin. Never before had so many people been this interested in what he did in his free time.

He crossed his arms. "Is that really any of your business?"

"Not helping," Juliet muttered. Sugar craned her tiny white neck and gave Juliet's cheek a dainty lick.

Judging by the look on Juliet's face, Sugar was the only

Mezzanotte that would be getting within kissing distance for the foreseeable future.

Then again, they'd been down that road before. And they'd ended up lip locked for a second time. Leo still fully intended to finish what they kept starting, which made him either the most desperate man on the planet or the craziest. Because no sex was worth this kind of trouble.

Except maybe the sex he wasn't having with Juliet Arabella.

Alegra's steely gaze bored into him. If she could read his mind, he'd be a dead man. "Oh, my God. I totally know what's going on."

Well, that made one of them. For the life of him, Leo couldn't remember why he'd been so dead set on coming back here. His behavior was beginning to exceed that which he could blame on jet lag or good old-fashioned lust.

"You!" Alegra flew out of her chair and jammed her index finger at Leo's chest.

Ouch.

And he'd thought his own family was nuts. This cousin of Juliet's made Uncle Joe seem mellow. Leo would have gladly traded places with poor Cocoa right about now.

"I'm onto you, Leonardo Mezzanotte." She poked him again. "You tried to murder my cousin's dog, you dog poisoner."

8

What a mess.

Juliet thought the night had taken its turn for the worse when Cocoa had ingested a saucepan full of bittersweet chocolate. But apparently, the fun had just been getting started.

The Nuovo Winery's Annual Hot Air Balloon Festival was scheduled to begin in two short hours. She should be in bed right now. *Alone.* But somehow she was standing in the emergency vet clinic watching her cousin accuse Leo of premeditated dog murder.

Or would that be attempted dogslaughter?

His innocence notwithstanding, his piercing blue eyes went instantly lethal. "*Dog poisoner?* Right. Because that's the sort of guy I am. I get off on hurting innocent animals."

His voice ricocheted off the polished floor and sterile tile walls of the waiting room. Thankfully, no one else was there to witness this train wreck. Just their dysfunctional little trio.

"Well, you *are* a Mezzanotte. I wouldn't put it past you." Alegra pulled her cell phone from the pocket of her hoodie. "I'm calling the police."

Juliet snatched the phone from Alegra's hands. "No one is calling the police."

Juliet hadn't seen much in her life outside the four walls of Arabella Chocolate Boutique. But of all the things she'd managed to bear witness to, the sight of Leo Mezzanotte cradling her dog in his arms and carrying Cocoa inside the animal hospital was something of a standout.

Alegra couldn't have been more off the mark. Not about this.

"Leo hasn't done anything wrong," she said quietly.

Leo responded with only a soulful look.

Alegra jammed her hands on her hips and looked him up and down. "How can you know for sure? He's—"

"A Mezzanotte." Leo rolled his eyes. "That's some powerful evidence. I'm sure it will hold up in court. Shall I refuse my name? Change it to something like Smith or Jones? Would that put an end to any of this nonsense?"

Things were far, *far* from being that easy to fix. A rose by any other name was still a rose. "Enough. Leo, you're not changing your name. And, Alegra, you're not calling the police. Cocoa drank some hot chocolate that Leo made for me. It was an accident, pure and simple. He didn't hurt her. Quite the opposite, in fact. He was actually pretty fantastic."

She stopped talking, as she'd begun to tear up. Over a Mezzanotte. She would never hear the end of this. And if her parents ever found out, she would probably be banished from the family, or suffer some other equally antiquated consequence.

"Cocoa consumed Mezzanotte chocolate? No wonder she's vomiting. Please tell me you didn't drink any of it. Why in the world was Leo making you a midnight snack, anyway?" Alegra's confused gaze darted between them once, twice, three times before finally landing on Leo. "Leo has gold glitter on his face. And his neck. And his hands. Why is Leo covered in glitter?"

Juliet glanced at him. Sure enough, he was as sparkly as a unicorn. A super hot, angry-looking unicorn. With perfect lips and spectacular, muscular shoulders.

"The strawberries for the balloon festival." Alegra's voice danced somewhere between astonishment and disgust. "Oh, my God. *Oh, my God.* I was only joking when I said you two were secret lovers. It's true, though, isn't it? You're actually sleeping together, aren't you?"

"Secret lovers. That has a rather romantic ring to it." Leo lifted a sardonic brow. "For the life of me, I can't see why you'd consider that worse news than if I'd actually poisoned the dog."

Juliet would have given anything right then for a swirling abyss to open at her feet and swallow her whole. "Leo and I are not sleeping together, Alegra. Absolutely not." She couldn't seem to shake her head hard enough.

So what if it was somewhat of a technicality? She wasn't lying. They hadn't crossed that line. Maybe they'd danced around the line a bit, dipped a toe close to the edge, but they hadn't crossed it.

And they weren't going to.

She glanced at Leo. He smoldered back at her. Who knew it was possible for someone with glitter on his forehead to smolder like that?

Juliet cursed her knees for growing weak. "We're friends. Sort of."

Friends who couldn't keep their hands off each other after dark, but pretended they didn't know each other in the light of day. That was normal, right?

"Now that we've got that cleared up, I think I'll be going." He lifted Sugar off the floor and nestled her in the crook of his elbow. The sight of him with that dog made Juliet go all mushy inside.

She looked away.

"Don't leave on my account, Sparkle." Alegra released a less-than-subtle snort.

"Sparkle?" A vein throbbed in Leo's right temple. "Really?"

Alegra shrugged. "Would you prefer I call you Butthead?"

He let out a little laugh. How he could laugh at a time like this was a mystery Juliet couldn't quite comprehend. "Good night, ladies. Or should I say good morning? I suppose we'll all see each other in just a matter of hours."

"Yes, we will." Juliet nodded. At the same time, she sent up a silent prayer that Leo would go home and wash off all that glitter before the balloon festival.

"You can bet on it. We're going to kick your pathetic drugstore chocolates to the curb." Alegra gave him a smug smile.

She wasn't going to look half that smug once she got the barest whiff of Leo's *chocolat chaud*.

Juliet's heart sank. With all the drama surrounding the night's events, she'd forgotten about that decadent hot chocolate. She had a sick dog on her hands and a cousin who'd learned her deepest, darkest secret, but she still didn't have a clue about Leo's secret ingredient.

Unicorn tears. Right.

"Kick my chocolate to the curb? We'll see about that, won't we?" He grinned. Nothing but a tiny, wicked quirk of his lips. "Good night, Juliet."

"Good night, Leo." The words nearly stuck in her throat for some ridiculous reason. Why did this keep happening?

Never in her life had she experienced so much difficulty saying goodbye to a person who she was more than happy to see go.

Then he walked toward her, took her fingertips in his and kissed the back of her hand. It was the softest, gentlest touch of his lips, but it very nearly took her breath away. She was barely conscious of Alegra gaping, slack-jawed, at the two of them.

And as Juliet watched Leo walk out those doors again, she was filled with an inexplicably sweet sorrow. In spite of their respective last names and all the secrets floating between them, she wondered what it might be like to stay with him as the sun came up, bathing the valley in soft hues of pink and gold. To keep whispering *good night,* again and again, until night became tomorrow.

The strawberries were sweating.

All that time, all that effort, all that godforsaken glitter, and now Juliet was watching her precious strawberries turn to mush.

"I don't get it. Why is this happening?" Alegra dabbed at the berries with a paper towel in painstakingly measured movements. She reminded Juliet of a nurse gently wiping perspiration from a doctor's brow during surgery.

Clearly Juliet had spent too much time around medical personnel in recent hours. She'd left the animal hospital only an hour before arriving at the majestic grounds of Nuovo Winery for the hot air balloon festival. And she would be headed right back to the vet clinic once it was over. The vet had wanted to keep an eye on Cocoa for the remainder of the day. With any luck, Juliet could bring her home by nightfall. She longed for the comfy warmth of her bed and Cocoa's big shaggy head in her lap.

Huge, colorful balloons hovered above the lush green grounds of the vineyard, waiting for takeoff. But Juliet couldn't seem to appreciate the beauty of it all. Not with her strawberries suffering like they were. "It's the change in temperature. Strawberries are ninety percent water, and all this cool, damp air is drawing out their moisture. It's freezing out here."

She should have known this would happen. Any decent chocolatier knew better than to store chocolate below sixty-five degrees, and to never, ever keep it in the fridge. This was one of the major tenets of chocolate known as Belgian Wisdom. But it had been so long since Juliet had prepared anything for an outdoor fair of any kind, not to mention untold years since she'd been up and about at five, that she'd forgotten just how frigid Napa Valley could be this early in the morning.

Weather had been the least of her concerns. She'd been consumed with one thing and one thing only—making sure the chocolates she brought to the balloon festival outshone whatever the Mezzanottes sold. And now here she was, with row upon row of sweaty strawberries on her hands while dozens of hot air balloon enthusiasts lined up at the Mezzanotte Chocolates booth for Leo's *chocolat chaud.*

"People are going back to Leo for seconds and thirds." Alegra shook her head. Beyond her rose Nuovo Winery's famed *castello,* its central building, which had been constructed to look like an Old World Italian castle, complete with turrets and arrow slits. "What's he putting in that stuff? Crack?"

Crack. That would explain a lot. "You should taste it. Then you'd understand."

"No way. Mezzanotte chocolate has never passed my lips. And it never will," Alegra announced with a heavy dose of indignation. Guilt wound its way through the sleepy fog in Juliet's head.

Alegra kept on talking. "Hey, maybe we can start a rumor that Leo's hot chocolate put someone in the hospital last night. There's an element of truth to it, so he probably couldn't sue us or anything."

"Let's just forget last night ever happened, okay?" She didn't want to talk about it. Or think about it. Or even remember it. Maybe the doctors could somehow empty her head the way they'd emptied Cocoa's stomach.

"I have to admit, hot chocolate was a great idea. I mean, it sounds so simple. But really...genius." Alegra's teeth chattered slightly as she gazed longingly at the elegant white tent where Leo was filling a cup from a fancy silver server. There wasn't a drugstore candy bar in sight over there. It was strictly white-glove service. And the pristine tent was the perfect canvas to showcase the vibrant balloons floating in the background. "Don't ever tell your mom I said that."

"I think we can agree that as far as secrets go, you pretty much have me over a barrel." She was indebted to Alegra now for life. She shuddered to think how her cousin might use this to her advantage once Cocoa was all better. For the moment, Alegra just seemed to feel sorry for her.

As sorry as someone who couldn't stop smirking could feel, anyway. Once the shock had worn off, Alegra's horror over the discovery of Juliet and Leo's secret had quickly changed to intense amusement with just a lingering dash of revulsion.

She managed to stop smirking long enough to sell four

dark chocolate Cabernet Sauvignon truffles to a pair of tourists with fanny packs strapped to their waists. At least the wine-inspired truffles were moving. And they'd nearly sold out of the sea salt maple bacon chocolate hearts. Deep down, Juliet still harbored the tiniest bit of hope that her chocolate bacon hearts would win the coveted Best of Balloon Fest Award, an honor bestowed on the finest culinary or beverage item featured at the festival. This being the wine country, the prize was typically awarded to one of the many local wines on offer. Once an olive oil made from locally grown olives had taken the prize, though. So winning wouldn't be completely without precedent.

She had a good feeling about the maple bacon hearts. Bacon was very trendy at the moment. Who didn't love bacon? Besides vegetarians and, well, pigs.

Speaking of pigs...

"Is that George, the self-proclaimed prince of everything, over there talking to your lover?" Alegra had apparently forgone any attempt at subtlety and was staring blatantly at the Mezzanotte tent.

Juliet gave her a sharp nudge in the ribs. "Stop looking at them. Please. Just pretend they don't exist, George in particular. And for the last time, I'm not sleeping with Leo."

"Yes, you mentioned that. In fact, you've said it so many times that I don't believe it for a minute. If you haven't slept with him yet, it's only because your dog's suicide attempt threw a kink in things." Alegra's gaze darted again to the Mezzanotte tent. "I have to admit, though, I almost understand. He's hot. Like, crazy hot. Why didn't anyone tell me how gorgeous he is? He probably heats up that hot chocolate just by winking at it."

"He actually does it the old-fashioned way and uses a saucepan." Not that the winking wouldn't work.

He looked awfully good in those chef's whites he was wearing. Oh-so-proper and quite French, with Le Cordon Bleu stitched discreetly in blue embroidery in the region of his left pectoral muscle. Juliet had first caught sight of him as she'd been hauling her chocolates from the van to her setup, and her knees had gone nearly as soft as her strawberries. She'd always had a major addiction to the Food Network. And she might have developed a certain appreciation for men in culinary uniforms, but neither Jamie Oliver nor Alain Allegretti could hold a candle to Leo Mezzanotte in a crisply ironed chef coat.

"Wait. How do you know that?" Alegra said, frowning.

Juliet was probably frowning, too. Just what was George doing over there in the Mezzanotte tent? And why was he grinning his smarmy grin and shaking hands with Leo? "How do I know what?"

"How do you know that Leo makes his hot chocolate in a saucepan?" Alegra smiled at a few customers. They smiled back, looked closely at the strawberries and fled.

Juliet sighed. "I watched him make it."

"He made it right there in front of you?"

"Pretty much, yes." Juliet was barely aware she was even talking. She'd begun to have a very uneasy feeling about whatever was going on over there between George and Leo.

When Royal Gourmet had dropped the Arabellas, the one mitigating factor was the knowledge that George and his company would never join forces with the Mezzanottes. Not only had George said as much on numerous occasions, but he seemed to have developed a nasty sore spot where Leo was concerned after seeing Juliet dance with him the night of that woefully disappointing marriage proposal.

George had his pride. He had pride in spades. Juliet would have bet money he would never even consider a working relationship with the Mezzanottes. Not while Leo still went by that last name.

But there they were, shaking hands, giving Juliet a glimpse of Leo's beautiful forearm where it emerged from the immaculate white sleeve of his chef coat.

She released a long, breathy sigh. So, now she was enchanted by the sight of a man's forearm? Surely this was a new low.

"Would you pay attention? I'm trying to have a conversation with you." Alegra planted herself directly in Juliet's line of vision. "Geez, and you were getting after me for staring."

"I'm sorry. Really. It won't happen again. No more Leo Mezzanotte."

No more Leo Mezzanotte.

Maybe if she repeated it to herself enough times, it would sink in. What was she doing even thinking about him, anyway? Wasn't her poor dog still lying in the hospital, sleeping off the effects of a stomach full of chocolate and charcoal?

She was a horrible person. Animal Planet could do an entire television special about how horrible she was.

"If you saw Leo make his *chocolat chaud,* doesn't that mean you know what he put in it?" Alegra blinked in hopeful expectation.

"Mostly. He used whole milk, cream, vanilla, brown sugar and bittersweet chocolate. Ten ounces, seventy percent grade." She was fairly sure he hadn't meant for her to know the specifics of the chocolate. But once Cocoa had eaten it all, any secrecy in that regard went out the window. "With a little playing around I might be able to figure out the rest."

"I suggest you start playing. The sooner the better." Alegra glared at George. Or maybe Leo. It was hard to tell because the two of them were still standing there chatting as if they were old friends. And now Leo's creepy uncle Joe sidled up next to them, making the intimate little gathering even more worrisome.

Juliet's stomach churned. "That could take a while. He said he used some sort of secret ingredient that makes it Parisian. I've never been to Paris. The closest I've come is the Eiffel Tower in Vegas."

And that had been for a food convention with George. They'd been there a grand total of twenty-three hours. God, she needed a vacation. She'd had more than one chance in the past few years to go to Rome, but she'd never gone, choosing instead to put the family business ahead of everything. As usual.

Those days were over. And now the family business was wilting all around her, much like her strawberries.

"That's what Google is for. I'll help you. I'll even go over there and buy some so I can taste it." Alegra tapped away on her cell phone, no doubt commencing an internet search for secret French ingredients.

"Do you think it really matters?"

"Of course it matters. You know why Leo is talking to George, right? If no one else can make that *chocolat chaud,* every restaurant in Napa will want it. And it's Royal Gourmet's job to make sure they get it. I'll bet Parisian hot chocolate will be on the menu at The French Laundry by tomorrow night."

The French Laundry. As recently as last week, it had been

the most beautifully plumed feather in Juliet's cap. Oh, how times had changed. "It will never happen. George despises Leo."

"Does his hatred for Leo outweigh his love of money?" Alegra directed a meaningful look at the Royal Gourmet limo parked at a pretentious angle across two spaces in the crowded parking lot.

Oh, God, she was right. That limousine and the ridiculous engraved champagne flutes in its rolling bar weren't going to pay for themselves.

Maybe she was worrying too much. After all, she'd been on quite a roll with the whole paranoia thing lately. Yes, the *chocolat chaud* was astonishingly delicious. And Parisian. But that didn't necessarily mean it would be a good fit for The French Laundry. Not everything they served was French. Their menu changed daily, and the chef prided himself on serving things that were new and exciting. Leo's *chocolat chaud* was certainly special, but it was still simple hot chocolate. And it wasn't as if it had won any awards or anything.

But even as she tried her mightiest to convince herself that the Arabellas had nothing to worry about, Juliet spied Alfred Richardson, the head of Nuovo Winery, walking through the crowd, making his way toward the Mezzanottes' elegant white tent. And in his hands he carried a gleaming silver loving cup, with lavish filigree handles and a shiny ornamental hot air balloon balancing on its lid.

The Best of Balloon Fest trophy.

The trophy was huge.

Leo's first thought upon accepting it was that it must have weighed nearly as much as Juliet's dog. As enormous as it was, it was nowhere near as big as the smile on Uncle Joe's face.

"Excellent work, Leo." He beamed. "Simply excellent."

"Good job, bro." Marco slapped Leo on the back. "Best of Balloon Fest. That's quite an accomplishment. You know they usually award that prize to one of the Napa wines, right? And you just walked away with it by cooking up some hot chocolate. Gina is going to be ecstatic when she hears the news."

Gina had been the Mezzanotte to draw the short straw earlier that morning. She was holding down the fort at the chocolate shop while Leo, his uncle and his brother-in-law manned the tent at the balloon festival. Leo had completely overhauled the plans for the tent, of course. If it had been up to Uncle Joe, the three of them would probably be surrounded by chocolate fountains right about now.

Leo nodded and accepted their praise, trying his damnedest to ignore the pounding in his head. If he hadn't been operating on a mere two hours of sleep, he would have been concerned. He'd never had this much trouble battling jet lag before. But he supposed his headache and general feeling of lethargy had more to do with the fact that he'd been up nearly all night with Juliet and her chocolate-guzzling dog than a twelve-hour flight he'd endured a full week ago.

Either way, he would have gladly sold his soul for an Advil. Or three.

To be fair, it didn't look as though selling his soul would be on the agenda anytime soon. At least according to one George Alcott III, who'd assured Leo that he could capitalize on the balloon fest victory and get *chocolat chaud* into some of the best restaurants in Napa. The numbers he'd batted around had been impressive enough to make the idea of doing business with Juliet's ex somewhat palatable. And now

he and Uncle Joe had their heads together at the other end
of the Mezzanotte tent.

Leo had been annoyed when George had first shown up.
Not jealous, of course. Just annoyed. Annoyed at the thought
of him kissing Juliet. Touching her. Tasting her. Slipping the
silky red straps of that bra off the smooth skin of her shoulders...

And doing all the other things that had been occupying
an alarmingly large portion of Leo's waking thoughts.

The chocolate rum cigar in his hand snapped in two.

Perhaps he was still slightly annoyed.

"Dude. A little tense?" Marco raised his eyebrows.

"I'm fine. Just a headache." Leo popped half the broken cigar in his mouth. It melted on his tongue in a pool of
sweet milk chocolate goodness, leaving behind the perfect
amount of warmth from the rum. He always used the real
thing instead of rum extract. There was just no substitute
for the genuine article.

"Relax. Take five. Maybe go for that balloon ride you
won." Marco took over the task of unloading the last of the
cigars. They were going nearly as quickly as the *chocolat chaud*.

Leo frowned and massaged his temples. "Balloon ride?"

"It's part of the prize." Marco nodded toward a green-and-
purple hot air balloon decorated with the Nuovo Winery
logo tethered in place at the entrance to the festival. "But
don't get any ideas. I was only kidding. If you disappeared
for an hour right now, Uncle Joe would have a fit. You're
the big star. I'm sure he wants to parade you around in front
of the press."

Oh, joy.

Leo bent to pick up the half of the chocolate cigar that
had landed in the grass and frowned at a colorful square of

thick paper that blew past his foot. He grabbed it before it tumbled away.

"What is this?" he snapped, flashing it in front of Marco's face.

Marco squinted at it. "Looks like a lottery ticket. Correction—a losing lottery ticket. So trash, basically."

Leo ripped it down the middle, then tore the remaining pieces in half for good measure. "What's it doing in our booth?"

Marco shrugged. "I don't know. I guess someone dropped it. What is wrong with you? For someone who's had such a successful day, you seem miserable."

"I'm fine." He wasn't fine. He suspected George Alcott's presence was exacerbating his headache. And finding the lottery ticket wasn't helping matters. He knew he was being irrational. Like Marco said, it was trash. There were people everywhere. Anyone could have dropped it. Just because it had found its way into the Mezzanotte booth didn't mean one of his family members had put it there. Odds were, they hadn't.

Still. He didn't like it. It brought back too many memories. Memories of his dad. Memories he'd just as soon forget, like the time Santa had left a roll of lottery tickets in his stocking instead of the comic books he'd so desperately wanted.

Who puts lottery tickets in a nine-year-old's Christmas stocking? His dad. That's who.

"For God's sake, what is she doing here?" Marco's gaze fixed on something over Leo's shoulder. He suddenly looked every bit as sick as Leo felt.

Leo turned to see Alegra Arabella marching toward the Mezzanotte tent. He thought surely she was on her way somewhere else—*anywhere* else—but, no. She walked right up to him. Just the sight of her made the throbbing in his head increase tenfold.

She smiled sweetly at him. Too sweetly. "Hey there, Sparkle."

Make that elevenfold.

Leo nodded. "Alegra."

Marco simply stood there, apparently stunned into speechlessness by the fact that a Mezzanotte and an Arabella would have anything to say to one another.

Or maybe it was the Sparkle thing. Yeah, probably that.

"To what do I owe the honor?" Leo asked, glancing over her shoulder to check and see if she'd brought along law enforcement. Not a badge in sight. This encounter was already an improvement over their previous one.

She huffed out a sigh. "Since no one will shut up about your fancy-pants hot chocolate, I thought I should check it out."

Marco managed to find his voice. "No. Absolutely not."

"I wasn't talking to you. I was talking to him." Alegra pointed at Leo.

With her middle finger.

Marco flipped her off right back, using both hands. Which officially made this the most ludicrous conversation Leo had been a part of since he'd been accused of attempted dog murder.

Leo shook his head. "How about we all try to act like grown-ups?"

Alegra slapped a five dollar bill on the table. "Look, I'm a paying customer. Give me the *chocolat chaud*. Now."

"We don't want your dirty Arabella money." Marco pushed the bill back toward her.

Leo ignored his brother-in-law and poured her a helping from the last of the silver servers. "Here you go. On the house."

Marco looked at him as if he'd sprouted two heads, which might have explained the headache. "What are you doing? You know she's only trying to figure out the recipe."

"She won't." Leo shrugged.

"Don't be too sure about that." Alegra peered into her *chocolat chaud*. She wouldn't find any answers there. Leo had heard of reading tea leaves, and even reading Turkish coffee. But never hot chocolate.

Marco's eyes narrowed. "How do you know she won't?"

A little faith would have been nice. "Because it's a secret. She can't."

Alegra snorted. "Secret ingredient? Like what? A packet of instant cocoa?"

"Yes. The kind with mini-marshmallows," Leo said, with the utmost sincerity.

"Whatever." She pocketed her five dollar bill.

Good. Leo wasn't about to take money from her. Not because it was dirty Arabella money, but because he'd noticed a distinct lack of customers at the Arabella booth over the course of the morning. He'd almost felt bad for them. Almost.

Juliet is not your girlfriend. She's not your fiancée. She's not your wife. Thank God. *Her business is no concern of yours.*

"Congratulations and all that, Sparkle. Enjoy it while it lasts, because it won't for long." Alegra managed to aim one last sneer in Marco's direction before sauntering off.

The silence that hung in the air after she'd left lasted just long enough for Leo to think that maybe Marco was going to let the whole thing go.

That was a pipe dream of the highest order.

"Do you want to tell me why Alegra Arabella is calling you Sparkle?"

"Not really. No."

Some things were just better left unsaid.

9

Leo should have known that Marco wouldn't take no for an answer.

His brother-in-law glowered at Alegra's retreating form and then directly at Leo. "Something's going on, and you'd better tell me what it is. Because there are a few potential scenarios going through my head, none of them good."

At some point, Leo was going to have to go toe-to-toe with him about what was family business and what wasn't. Leo's love life fell squarely into the latter category.

The look on Marco's face was an unspoken ultimatum. If Leo didn't explain himself soon, Marco was going to run to Gina and tattle on him. Then Gina would no doubt go straight to Uncle Joe, and the whole family would be breathing down his neck.

Leo had the distinct feeling he might be waking up to a horse head in his bed in the very near future.

He had no choice. He had to talk to Marco about Juliet... Soon.

Marco was a Mezzanotte by way of marriage, not blood. So the way Leo saw it, he was the only one of the lot who might be reasonable about the situation. Emphasis on *might*. After last night, Leo had pretty much given up hope that anyone on either side of this vendetta possessed an ounce of sense. At least where the Mezzanotte-Arabella dispute was concerned.

Two households, both alike in their overwhelming lack of dignity.

He shook his head and considered his brother-in-law. "Meet me for a beer tonight, and I'll tell you everything." Well, almost everything. He was a gentleman, after all. "In the meantime, cover for me."

Leo unfastened the top two buttons of his white coat and began making his way out of the Mezzanotte tent. He'd had about enough of being a Mezzanotte for the day.

"Cover for you?" Marco repeated, incredulous. "What is this? *Starsky and Hutch?*"

"You said I needed a break. I'm taking one." Leo gave him a single, firm nod. "Right now."

Marco released a weary exhale. "When will you be back? And in the meantime, what am I supposed to tell Uncle Joe about where you've gone?"

"A while. And as for Uncle Joe, I'm sure you'll think of something." He only knew he had to get out of there. A little space would do a world of good.

And if he could somehow arrange for Juliet Arabella to share that space with him, all the better. They were two consenting adults. They could fool around. It didn't mean they were a couple. It didn't have to mean anything.

Unless they wanted it to.

"See you later for that beer." He tossed a wave at an exasperated-looking Marco—clearly, Leo would be paying for every last drop of alcohol consumed tonight. He broke into a jog in order to catch up with Alegra.

She was sipping her *chocolat chaud* when he edged up beside her. For once she had a pleasant expression on her face. Actually, it bordered on one of ecstasy.

"I see you're enjoying my fancy-pants hot chocolate," he said with a grin.

She gave a start. *Chocolat chaud* spilled over the edge of her cup and dribbled down her hand.

Cue her customary scowl.

For some reason, it made Leo smile this time. "Caught you, didn't I?"

She rolled her eyes. "What do you want, Sparkle?"

"A moment with your cousin." Or an hour or two, give or take.

She snorted. "Good luck with that."

"I don't need luck. I've got you."

She stopped in her tracks and jammed her free hand on her hip. "First of all, *any* Mezzanotte who has a thing for an Arabella needs luck. Loads of it. And second, why don't you take the arrogance down a notch? It's not attractive."

He crossed his arms. "Neither is snorting."

"Insulting me isn't going to get you any brownie points, you know." She heaved out a sigh and ducked behind a large tent, out of view of the general public.

Leo followed her.

This wasn't going nearly as well as he'd expected. He'd assumed he could reason with Alegra, which in retrospect seemed like a really stupid assumption. "Look, I know she doesn't want me walking right up to her at a place like this. Perhaps you can help me arrange something. I'd really appreciate it."

She didn't say anything at first, but merely swept her steely gaze up, down and back up again. Was it his imagination, or did her expression soften ever so slightly? "And why on earth would I help a Mezzanotte get cozy with an Arabella?"

A question. Not a yes, not a no, but a question.

Some of the tension in Leo's head eased. Finally, he was getting somewhere. "Because this Mezzanotte wants to take a particular Arabella on a ride in a hot air balloon. Nothing evil, nothing sinister. Just a hot air balloon. And maybe some champagne."

"Oh." A rare smile made its way to her lips. "That actually sounds nice."

Leo told himself it didn't mean anything that as soon as he'd heard about his balloon ride prize, he'd imagined sharing it with Juliet. A quiet ride in the clouds, high above the complications and reality of their respective lives in Napa Valley, did sound nice. Better than nice, actually. It sounded like heaven.

That didn't mean he was a traitor. Or on the verge of proposing marriage. He wasn't doing anything wrong. It was a ride in a hot air balloon. A perfectly harmless activity.

A rather intimate one. And romantic. Definitely romantic.

Maybe it does mean something, he told himself.

Then he told himself to shut the hell up.

"So, you'll help me?"

"Sure." She nodded. "I'll help you, Sparkle."

Relief—somewhat worrisome in its intensity—coursed through him. "Great."

Her smile broadened. "But it will cost you."

Of course it would. How could he have thought, even for a moment, that she would be anywhere close to cooperative? "Name your price."

She dropped her gaze to her cup of hot chocolate. "The

secret ingredient. Tell me what it is, and I'll help you arrange a meeting with Juliet."

No way in hell.

His jaw tensed. "Not going to happen."

He turned to walk away, not that he actually intended to give up so easily. But as much as he liked the idea of some quiet time with Juliet, he wasn't forking over his *chocolat chaud* recipe, and Juliet's cousin needed to get that through her thick Arabella head.

"Okay, fine. Come back. There might be something else I'd consider." She looked around to make sure they were still alone and not being watched.

He raised his brows and waited.

"An iPad," she said, sweeter than orange blossom honey.

An iPad? Those things didn't come cheap.

But before she could change her mind, he heard himself agreeing. "Done."

He was down a round of beers for Marco and an iPad for Alegra Arabella. All because he wanted to spend an hour floating above Napa Valley with Juliet. Maybe it really was time to get his head examined.

She nodded, clearly pleased with herself. "Okay, then. I can arrange a clandestine rendezvous."

Clandestine rendezvous. He was beginning to feel as if he was in a Jason Bourne movie. A smile tugged at his lips. "You really go for the spy lingo, don't you?"

"I call it as I see it." She shrugged, and her giant hoop earrings grazed her shoulders. "Like I said, I can arrange a meeting, but I doubt she'll get in the balloon. She doesn't want anything to do with you anymore."

That was humbling news. If there was any truth to it, which he suspected there was.

At least some. They might have unfinished business in
the intimacy department that he suspected kept her awake
at night the way it did him, but he wasn't the most convenient man she could have chosen. And then there was the
unfortunate poisoning of her dog. "Is that so?"

"*No more Leo Mezzanotte*. Her words, not mine. It's kind of
her new mantra." Her eyes were wholly unapologetic. iPad or
no iPad, Alegra wasn't about to spare his feelings. Or his ego.

It was a crime how little the latest in tablet technology
could buy nowadays. "We'll see about that. I can be a pretty
persuasive guy when I set my mind to it."

"I can imagine." She flushed, not unlike her cousin, then
cleared her throat. "And one more thing. If you happen to
get her up there, *no* strawberries. Champagne oftentimes
comes with strawberries, but I don't want her laying eyes on
a single berry. Got it? I need you to promise that."

It was an odd request, but one that Leo could bear. "I
promise."

She seemed to consider things for a moment, then nodded. "Give me ten minutes."

Ten minutes. That seemed optimistic, but Leo wasn't about
to argue with her. "Will do. Meet me by the entrance to
the festival."

She groaned. "Could you pick a more public area, genius?"

He'd be willing to throw in an iTunes gift card if she'd
abandon the sarcasm. Talking to her was exhausting on every
possible level. "That's where the balloon is. It's the green-
and-purple one with the Nuovo logo on the parachute."

"Fine." She sauntered past him, in the direction of the
Arabella booth. "See you in ten, Sparkle."

Leo sighed as he jerked loose the remainder of the buttons

of his chef coat. Sooner or later, he and Alegra were going to have a chat about that nickname.

But first, he had a date with Juliet Arabella.

If he could convince her to go for a ride.

"I have something to tell you," Alegra announced when she returned from the Mezzanottes' tent, a half-empty cup of *chocolat chaud* in her hand.

Juliet motioned toward the hot chocolate. "Please, let it be that you've already figured out what's in there."

She didn't see how it was possible, but a girl could dream, right?

"What?" Alegra glanced at the cup in her hand, frowned, and looked back up. "Oh. No, I haven't a clue. But you were right. It's the best thing I've ever tasted." She tilted her head back and swallowed what was left of the *chocolat chaud*.

Juliet dropped her head in her hands. "Well, that was helpful."

Alegra gave her a playful hip bump. "Cheer up. I told you I have news."

"Spill. If this news is anything remotely cheerful, I'm all ears." She straightened up and pasted on a smile. Ever since Cocoa had done her best to eat her body weight in chocolate, things had gone from bad to worse.

Technically, the downward spiral had begun the night she'd made the fatal mistake of kissing Leo in the vineyard. She really didn't want to believe that a simple kiss could have anything to do with all the bad luck that seemed to be coming her way. That was just crazy. The world didn't work like that. But the more time she spent with Leo, the more things around her seemed to fall apart. It was as though they were defying the stars or something…and that was probably the single most absurd thought she'd ever had.

She was losing it. The only thing she was absolutely clear about was that she'd never needed good news quite this badly before. "Well?"

"I've arranged a secret meeting for you and Leo." Alegra glanced at her bulky lime-green wristwatch. "We need to head over to the rendezvous spot in about eight minutes."

Juliet stared blankly. Surely she was hearing things. "I'm sorry. Is this some kind of joke? Because it's not remotely funny."

Alegra shook her head. "It's no joke. He wants to see you. Pretty badly, from what I can tell."

"And you agreed to help make that happen?" This made no sense at all. Not to mention that it was a flagrant violation of the *No more Leo Mezzanotte* policy. "I don't understand. Just last night you tried to get Leo arrested. And weren't you the one who said I was way too smart to get involved with a Mezzanotte?"

"That's when I thought you were thinking with your head and not your feminine bits," she said dryly.

Juliet opened her mouth to protest and promptly closed it. What could she say? Her feminine bits had been doing a lot of thinking lately. Far more than her brain. That was for sure.

"There were more sparks flying between the two of you last night than I ever saw in the entire year you and George were together. The way I see it, you could probably use a good ravishing. And Leo certainly seems willing and able." She glanced at her watch again. "You have six minutes to decide. Not to influence your decision or anything, but he seems to genuinely like you."

Juliet raised a dubious eyebrow. As appealing as being ravished by Leo-of-the-gorgeous-forearms sounded, something about this dramatic turnaround in Alegra's attitude wasn't making sense. "And how did you manage to glean that from a single cup of *chocolat chaud?*"

Alegra shrugged. "The hot chocolate had nothing to do with it."

She was being evasive, which was definitely not normal for Alegra. Juliet glared at her. "What did, exactly?"

"He might have promised to buy me an iPad if I could deliver you—" she checked her watch yet again, then looped her arm through Juliet's "—right about now. Let's go."

"An *iPad?* Are you kidding me?" Juliet snatched her arm free.

So Leonardo Mezzanotte thought she could be bought with an iPad? Wasn't that charming?

"Relax. He can afford it. You should see how much business they're doing over there. He's making money hand over fist. An iPad is just a tiny drop in the Mezzanotte bucket. I should have held out for something bigger. Like a flat screen." She gave Juliet's arm another tug. "Are you coming or not?"

"I can't believe him." Juliet shook her head. She tried to keep herself from thinking the obvious—Leo was a Mezzanotte. Of course he'd think he could steamroll over people just to get his way.

But her thoughts went there, anyway.

Isn't that what his grandmother had done when she'd shared the Bellanotte chocolate recipe against her own grandmother's wishes? And isn't that what every other Mezzanotte had been doing since?

"And I can't believe you." Juliet frowned at her cousin. "Since when do you sell me out like that?"

"Chill out, would you? I'd have done it for free. Like I

said, after witnessing the yawn-fest that was you and George, it's kind of exciting to see you in such a state over someone. But Leo is a Mezzanotte, so I couldn't very well pass up the opportunity to mess with him a little. I'm sure you understand." Alegra batted her lashes innocently. "I'd like to take this opportunity to remind you that there's an iPad on the line, though. And I could sure use one. Nearly as badly as you could use a roll in the sack with Leo."

A roll in the sack.

To Juliet's horror, those aforementioned feminine bits of hers gave a rebellious clench. Ugh.

"Where is he?" she asked through gritted teeth.

"Near the entrance to the winery. By the big Nuovo hot air balloon." It was one of the few still tethered to the ground. The sky above them was dotted with balloons, their parachutes as colorful as a handful of jelly beans.

Juliet untied her apron, yanked it over her head and tossed it next to the untouched chocolate strawberries.

"So, you're going?" Alegra asked hopefully.

Good grief. Wasn't she having enough trouble avoiding Leo without her own cousin trying to push them together? "Yes, I'm going. And I don't require an escort."

"Great. Don't worry about me. I can hold down the fort as long as you like." Juliet could practically see visions of iPads dancing in her head.

"Trust me. This won't take long." How long could it possibly take to tell him she had no intention of rendezvousing with him? This had to stop. He could rendezvous all he wanted with his shiny, new, gigantic trophy. They could go dancing and drink *chocolat chaud* together until the wee hours, for all Juliet cared.

"You say that now...." Alegra gave her a knowing smile.

"I'll be back in less than five minutes. If not, I want you to come find me and drag me back to this booth. Kicking and screaming, if necessary." She had to get a handle on this situation.

"Yeah, I'll get right on that," Alegra said with a wry grin.

Juliet let out a huff and stomped through the cool green grass toward the Nuovo balloon. With each step, she vowed she was putting an end to things once and for all. She had plenty to worry about right now, like explaining to her mother how she'd managed to make the rookie mistake of screwing up chocolate-covered strawberries, and figuring out how to get her chocolates back into restaurants without the help of Royal Gourmet. Not to mention the monumental task of identifying the secret ingredient in the *chocolat chaud*.

Spending time sneaking around with a Mezzanotte was nowhere on her priority list.

But when she arrived at the Nuovo balloon, the Mezzanotte waiting for her looked awfully list-worthy. He'd shed his chef coat and was dressed casually in faded jeans and a chambray button-down with the sleeves rolled up, exposing those delicious-looking arms. She had the sudden nonsensical urge to rest her cheek against that impressive chest of his and take a whiff. She'd be willing to bet he smelled like ripe grapes and damp Napa air.

And chocolate. Obviously.

"Juliet." A smile creased his face, and her heart fluttered wildly in her chest.

It couldn't be normal, this intense physical reaction she experienced every time she was in his presence. In all the time she'd yearned to feel this way, she'd never imagined how frightening it would be. Feelings this powerful, this violent could only lead to violent ends.

"Leo." She squared her shoulders. "I heard you wanted to see me. Pretty badly, according to my cousin. Or should I refer to her as your minion now?"

"Minion?" Blue eyes gazed coolly back at her. "That's a bit extreme, don't you think? Alegra and I have come to an understanding that makes it possible to tolerate one another. That's a far cry from her becoming one of my flying monkeys."

"Do you have many of those? Flying monkeys?" She glanced at the balloons floating overhead, bobbing among the cottony clouds. Not a monkey in sight.

"No. I'm really more of an independent villain. I prefer to do my own dirty work." The spark in his gaze turned sultry.

I'll bet.

She took a step backward. "You can't do this. You just can't. My affection isn't for sale. Not to a Mezzanotte, not to *anyone*. I'm sure you wouldn't understand, but it's not a pleasant feeling to be controlled by someone with a fat checkbook." Someone like George Alcott.

She inhaled a ragged breath.

He appeared to study her for a long moment, his jaw growing more firmly clenched the longer he looked at her. "To be clear, I wasn't attempting to buy your affection. I was trying to have a conversation with Alegra without the threat of imprisonment looming over my head. I didn't think it was out of line to compensate her for acting as a go-between. Believe me, I plan on making her earn her keep. More importantly, just what makes you think I don't understand what it feels like to be with a person who mistakes money for affection?"

Mistakes money for affection. She hadn't thought about it quite that way before, but the phrase was perfect.

And intriguing. What did Leo Mezzanotte know about such things?

Quite a bit, apparently. "You're not the only one with an ex, Juliet."

His fiancée. Of course. "My mistake."

"You and I have more in common than you might imagine." His blue gaze bored into her.

She didn't want to ask. She really didn't. If she did, he would just get the wrong idea. If she did, he'd think that it mattered to her that he'd been so recently engaged. He'd think she was jealous. And she wasn't.

Except that the tiniest part of her sort of was.

"Tell me," she said, unable to resist the idea of knowing the story behind the wedding that wasn't.

"Tell you what, exactly?" His eyes narrowed.

"About your engagement."

He glanced at the ground and then back up to meet her gaze. "There's nothing to tell. I was engaged. I realized I was about to make an enormous mistake, so I ended it."

"Why would it have been a mistake?" And why, oh, why, did she care so much about his romantic past?

"I didn't love her."

Harsh. "Then why did you ask her to marry you?"

"I didn't. She asked me. I should have said no, but I didn't. I got caught up in the idea of what we could build together. A business, not a life. I may have ended things late, but at least I ended them." He crossed his arms. "Is your curiosity satisfied now?"

Juliet swallowed. "I suppose so."

"Good." He nodded, and something in his eyes softened.

He'd been honest with her about his engagement. Painfully so. Juliet wasn't sure what she'd expected, but not that.

It was too much. She closed her eyes for the briefest of moments so she could strengthen her resolve. But instead she saw Leo returning her mask and pretending not to know her at the Mezzanotte Ball, saw him carrying Cocoa inside the animal hospital, saw him kissing her hand as he told her goodnight. In that moment, she saw everything but his last name.

Don't be stupid.

She opened her eyes. "Look, Leo. I don't know what you want, but..."

"All I want is to take you on an actual date. Wouldn't you agree that it's about time?" He walked toward the Nuovo balloon that loomed above them and rested his hand on the edge of its wicker basket. "It's not a marriage proposal. It's a date. I'm not any more interested in marriage than you are."

Juliet managed to tear her gaze away from him long enough to give the balloon operator a weak smile and take a peek inside the gondola. She'd never been this close to a hot air balloon before. The basket was roomier than she'd imagined. It had a nice cushioned bench along one side, and in the center sat a sleek silver ice bucket filled with ice, two red plastic cups and a familiar-looking cobalt-blue bottle that could only be Nuovo Napa Cuvee X. Her favorite.

A hot air balloon and sparkling wine in plastic cups? As dates went, it sounded awfully cozy. But surely he didn't think she was going to get into that thing with him. "A date? Now? In the middle of the balloon festival?"

"No time like the present." He reached out to cradle her face in his hand, his thumb grazing her cheek, then the underside of her bottom lip.

Somewhere deep inside, she trembled. A tremble almost painful in its intensity.

Violent ends, she reminded herself. He'd just won the Best of Balloon Fest trophy. Not twenty minutes ago, she'd seen him shaking hands with George. If she climbed inside that balloon, something awful would probably happen. She'd fall overboard.

Or just fall...for Leo, which would be far worse than hurling toward earth from high among the clouds.

"I..." *Can't. Won't.*

Leo offered her his hand. "Let's do this, Juliet. A real date. I promise I won't bite." He paused, his gaze roaming from her face to her neck to her shoulder. His lips curved into a devilish smile. "Unless you ask me to."

She bit her lip—hard—to prevent a *yes* from flying out.

"Juliet, is that you?"

Leo's eyes widened at the sound of someone else calling her name, and every one of the impressive muscles in his body appeared to tense. He glanced over her shoulder and back at her. "Ah, do we have a problem?"

"Juliet?"

There it was again.

Juliet couldn't move. Couldn't turn around. Couldn't seem to breathe.

She was suddenly hyperaware of every sight, every sound, every sensation around her—the dim glow of fireflies spinning graceful pirouettes over the grapevines, a baby crying far off in the distance, the whoosh of the propane-fueled burners of the hot air balloons as they lifted off the ground, the look of real alarm on Leo's face. But she couldn't seem to make herself react to any of it. She wasn't sure she'd ever had a classic deer-in-the-headlights moment before, but she was undoubtedly having one now.

"Juliet, do we have a problem here?" Leo whispered again. Then he rested a hand on her shoulder.

The weight and warmth of his touch stirred her back to life.

"We most definitely have a problem. A big one." She heard the hysteria in her own voice, and her panic ratcheted up a notch. "My mother is here."

10

Fight or flight?

It was the timeless struggle—the instinct that separated zebras from lions, antelope from tigers, field mice from hawks.

And Juliet from her mother.

Juliet didn't turn around, nor did she wait to see if her mother had actually seen her. She acted without thinking, planting her hands on the edge of the balloon's wicker basket and vaulting up and over.

She landed inside the gondola in a graceless heap, her head making contact with the ice bucket.

Ouch.

"Are you hurt?" With his feet still planted on solid ground, Leo frowned down at her over the edge of the basket.

"I'm fine." Her pride had taken a serious hit, but she supposed that went without saying. God, this was humiliating. She was hiding from her mother like a five-year-old.

She should stand up. What was there to be afraid of? Hadn't she decided she was going to run her own life from now on? Make her own decisions?

And that had been going so incredibly well so far, hadn't it?

Things could be worse. You could be engaged to marry George.

The hot air balloon operator cleared his throat, dragging Juliet back to the degrading present. She didn't even want to contemplate what he must be thinking.

The corners of Leo's mouth crept upward. If he laughed, she might lose it. "I would have been more than happy to give you a hand, you know. You didn't have to throw yourself into the basket."

She sat up, straightening her clothes and hair. She might be cowering at the bottom of a hot air balloon gondola, but she could at least look presentable. "Are you getting in here with me or not?"

"I wouldn't dream of missing our first date." He leaped over the side of the basket with the grace and ease of an Olympic hurdler. Naturally.

"For the record, this isn't a date." He could call it whatever he wanted, but to Juliet it was more of a desperate escape plan.

"Keep telling yourself that, babe." He winked at her, leaned against the side of the gondola and crossed his feet at the ankles. Having him loom over her like that did nothing to lessen her humiliation.

"Is she still out there?" Juliet asked.

Leo took a glance around and shrugged. "I don't know. I've never met your mother. Should I be on the lookout for horns and a forked tail?"

He wasn't that far off the mark. "You'd probably know her if you saw her. She'd be the one coming after you, hell-bent on tearing you limb from limb. She knows exactly who you are, and if she just saw us together, the result would not be pretty."

Leo eyed the padded bench but crouched down on the

bottom of the gondola to sit beside her instead. The sweetness of the gesture wasn't lost on her. "How bad can she be?"

Bad enough to expect her only daughter to marry someone she didn't love. "Alegra is terrified of her, if that tells
you anything."

Leo's brow furrowed. "The same Alegra who tried to get
me incarcerated and accused me of trying to murder your
dog?"

She nodded.

"I suppose that does put things in perspective." He grimaced. "My uncle Joe has a pretty nasty streak himself. But
you know what?"

"What?" she asked.

"I don't want to talk about either of our families. Not
now. Not here. Date or no date, this balloon is a feud-free
zone. Agreed?" He arched an eyebrow and waited for her
to respond.

It sounded nice.

It also sounded like a pipe dream. But she could use an
hour or two without thinking about the feud. It seemed as
though lately she'd thought of little else.

She glanced over at Leo. Why did she get the feeling that
there was more between them than there should have been?
More than just physical attraction, as if that wouldn't have
been forbidden enough.

Feud-free zone. The words dangled meaningfully between
them, and Juliet realized she'd held her breath without intending to. It seemed Leo had, too.

She took a slow, measured inhale. "Agreed."

"All right, then." He smiled at her, not his usual mischie-
vous grin, but a genuine smile. Then he gave the balloon
operator a thumbs-up. Presumably the signal for takeoff.

The gondola shifted a bit as the ground crew untethered the balloon. Then the burner released a blast of hot air, ruffling Juliet's hair and warming her cheeks. She closed her eyes and lifted her face toward the heat, letting it wash over her. The chill that had settled in her bones sometime around dawn slowly lifted.

The burner grew quiet, and she opened her eyes.

Leo was watching her intently, with a look on his face that she couldn't quite read. "Shall we stand up now and enjoy the view?"

"Sure." She nodded.

Leo rose to his feet, offered her his hand for support and pulled her up off the floor of the basket.

What was she doing here with her hand in Leo Mezzanotte's, floating above Napa Valley as if she didn't have a care in the world? Today had been an unmitigated disaster.

As a single episode, it would have been bad enough. But this was only the beginning. Next weekend was the Napa Valley Chocolate Fair, an event that Arabella Chocolate Boutique had dominated for the past decade. Juliet's entry had taken the top prize year after year.

Somehow she doubted things would be so easy this time. And the one man who could steal the prize out from under her was standing right beside her. She tore her gaze from him and focused instead on the view. The lush green landscape of the Nuovo Winery spread below them in perfect, symmetrical rows of grapevines and pristine white tents. From above, the tents all looked alike. If Juliet hadn't known exactly where the Arabella and Mezzanotte booths were situated, she wouldn't have been able to tell them apart.

"It's peaceful up here, isn't it?" Leo handed her one of the red plastic cups, filled nearly to the brim with the Nuovo Cuvée.

"Yes. Very." Despite the gentle silence of the blue sky, and the way the balloon drifted so slowly among the clouds that she felt as though they weren't moving at all, but rather suspended in time and place, Juliet felt anything but serene.

On the contrary, she was worried. Worried to the brink of panic.

She took a taste, thinking about how different this was from the last time she'd sipped champagne. The limousine… George…it all seemed so far away now. And so vastly different from the current circumstances. How was it that someone she'd dated for so long hadn't really known her at all, and Leo, of all people, seemed to have a sense of exactly who she was? Maybe there was something else between them besides a special brand of heated chemistry. Maybe there was more.

Stop it.

How many other men were there in the world? Millions. Any one of them would be a better choice.

"Juliet," he whispered against her hair as he wrapped his arms around her from behind and planted his hands on the edge of the wicker basket, effectively locking her in place. "Do you have any idea how difficult it was not to march over to your booth this morning and kiss you senseless?"

She kept her gaze fixed on the horizon and did her best to ignore the way those words, and his nearness, sent an illicit tingle coursing through her. "I don't kiss on the first nondate."

Thank God for the presence of the balloon operator. Otherwise, she wouldn't have a chance of sticking to such a policy. Given past history and all.

A soft laugh escaped him. "Very well, then. No kissing.

Although I could accuse you of sending mixed messages, considering the way you're dressed."

She glanced down at the sweater and jeans she'd tossed on after leaving the animal hospital. The sweater was cashmere and the jeans were her favorite pair, perfectly worn and soft. But nothing about either article of clothing screamed *kiss me.* "What's wrong with the way I'm dressed?"

"Absolutely nothing." He dipped his head and let his lips barely graze the sensitive skin of her neck.

She held her breath and willed herself not to react.

"It's just that every time I've seen you, you've been wearing the Mezzanotte color," he murmured. "It's beginning to bring out a rather predatory feeling in me."

"The Mezzanotte color?" She laughed. "You're a family, not a sports team. What in the world are you talking about?"

He ran his fingertips up and down her arm. "Surely an Italian girl like you knows what Mezzanotte means."

She had to think about it for a second. All her life, the name had been synonymous with the very worst sort of evil. She'd never actually thought about the literal translation.

Mezzanotte.

Midnight.

Visions of a moonlit vineyard danced in Juliet's head. She squeezed her eyes shut. "It means midnight, doesn't it?"

"Yes." He ran a fingertip up and down the deep blue cashmere of her sleeve.

Midnight-blue. It had always been her favorite color. Her subconscious clearly had a twisted sense of humor. "I suppose I'll have to rethink my wardrobe."

"Don't stop wearing it on my account. It suits you." He gathered a pinch of cashmere in his fingers.

Juliet swallowed. "It does?"

"Very much," he all but growled.

The balloon operator cleared his throat. Thank goodness. Juliet had forgotten he was even there. She'd forgotten pretty much everything except Leo.

And how very much she needed his lips on hers.

Except that wasn't what she needed at all, was it? *Wanted,* perhaps, but definitely not needed.

What she really *needed* was to get her head out of the clouds. It was one thing to feel a physical connection to Leo. After what had transpired in the vineyard...and beyond... she couldn't exactly deny that there was something between them. Heat. Passion. Desire. But it was another thing entirely to entertain the notion that she might be developing real feelings for him.

Nothing so drastic as love. Obviously. Not even close. But definitely a feeling that went beyond mere tolerance, which in itself would have been scandalous with regard to a Mezzanotte. Ever since she'd watched him carry Cocoa into the vet clinic like some kind of animal-loving superhero, she couldn't deny that there was an inkling of something more than heat simmering beneath the surface.

She shook her head. It was impossible. Downright unthinkable.

Then why was she thinking about it?

She swallowed a gulp of champagne and took in the panoramic view of the valley's rolling green hills, the rich, clay-colored earth and the soft light of the rising sun, bathing the grand estates of the vineyards below in a warm, dreamy glow. Around them, other brightly colored balloons drifted on the wind, as graceful and weightless as feathers. It was breathtaking. All of it. The view, the champagne.

The company.

How exactly was she supposed to get her head out of the clouds when she could practically reach out and touch them?

Think about something else. Anything else.

She took another swig and blurted the least romantic thing that popped into her head. "George."

Leo's arms stiffened around her. "No. I'm Leo. Leo Mezzanotte. Surely you haven't forgotten. We just had an entire conversation about my last name."

"I know perfectly well who you are." As if she could forget that particular detail.

She spun around to face him. Maybe if she turned her back on the romantic view, she could get through the remainder of the balloon ride without growing weak in the knees.

Then again, maybe not. Leo's eyes flashed and grew darker, dangerous, until they were a fitting shade of midnight-blue. The mention of George had clearly stirred something proprietary in him, just as it had at the Mezzanotte Ball.

Knees definitely weakening.

Juliet crossed her arms in an effort to hold herself together. "Earlier today I saw you talking to George. What was that about?"

Leo's eyes softened. "Juliet…"

He didn't need to say another word. So it was true. The French Laundry would be serving Leo's *chocolat chaud* while Arabella Chocolate Boutique faded further into oblivion.

"I see," she said, swallowing what little was left of her pride.

"It's nothing personal. It's business." The wistfulness in his tone seemed to scrape Juliet raw, from the inside out.

Everything about him—the concern in his gaze, the care with which he chose his words—told her that he had a good idea of how much trouble her business was in, and he felt badly about it. He probably even felt sorry for her.

The look on his face was the wake-up call she so desperately needed. As much as she'd been through in recent weeks, being on the receiving end of pity from a Mezzanotte was a new low.

"Everything about this is personal. It was personal between our grandmothers, and it's personal between the rest of our family." She drained her cup. The sparkling wine fizzed on her tongue, and her head spun a little, but with each sip she was forgetting how heroic she'd found Leo before he pitied her. "Why wouldn't it be personal between you and me?"

"So, you'd have me refuse the generous offer from your former fiancé?" His eyes narrowed. The knot in his jaw throbbed to life. And he looked a little less intent on kissing her.

Good.

"Of course not. I'm simply saying we can't separate ourselves from our businesses. That's precisely why this balloon ride, romantic as it is, is not a date."

He smiled again. A cocky, satisfied grin this time. "So, you find it romantic. I knew it."

"You're impossible." She grabbed his arm, lifted it over her head and slipped out from his grasp. "And you're going down next weekend at the Napa Valley Chocolate Fair. I'm going to murder you. Consider yourself warned."

He reached for the bottle of Nuovo, refilled her cup and poured one for himself. Then he winked at her as he clicked their cups together in a toast. "I look forward to it."

"Let me get this straight." Marco frowned into his beer and shook his head. After a long, painful pause, he finally looked up at Leo. "You and Juliet Arabella."

Leo nodded reluctantly. He wasn't exactly thrilled to be having this conversation. Not one to beat around the bush, however, he'd taken the direct approach as soon as they'd found a table at what had to be the noisiest sports bar in Sonoma Valley, and served up the truth, along with Marco's bottle of Fat Tire. Not that Leo had a full grasp of the truth himself.

There's something going on between Juliet and me. That had been the extent of his announcement.

Vague much? He tipped back his bottle of beer and took a long, cold swallow. He might have been more forthcoming with his brother-in-law if he'd had half a clue about what he was doing with Juliet. He still wasn't sure if they'd actually gone on a date or not.

"You and Juliet," Marco repeated, as if saying it enough times would make it more believable.

"Yes. That's the big secret. The cat is officially out of the bag." Behind Leo, a bowling ball thundered down the lane and crashed into a cluster of pins. His head thundered along with it. Between the bowling, the shuffleboard and the half-dozen big screen TVs, this place was killing him. "But this is between you and me only. I have enough of a headache as it is without Uncle Joe getting wind of this."

Marco's brow furrowed. "Wait. Isn't Juliet engaged to George Alcott?"

Why was he constantly having to answer that question? And why did the thought of George and Juliet together never fail to make Leo's blood boil?

"No," he said through clenched teeth.

"I know. I'm just messing with you, bro." Marco laughed. "I've been wondering why you seem to hate that guy so much. Now I know—you're jealous."

The night was getting better and better. "Shut the hell up, would you? I'm not jealous. I just wish you'd get your facts straight."

Marco pinned him with a look. "Gladly. Although you've pretty much blindsided me. What exactly *are* the facts?"

Leo had no idea. But he knew she wasn't marrying George Alcott. That was the one fact he was perfectly clear on.

He managed not to sigh. "It's complicated."

Marco's bottle of beer paused midway to his mouth. "Complicated? That sounds like more than just a one-time thing. Are you two a couple now?"

Leo's memory snagged on their balloon ride. She'd stuck to her guns. There'd been no kiss. There'd been a threat or two, but definitely no kiss.

I'm going to murder you.

For some sick reason, he'd enjoyed that as much as a kiss. Almost as much, anyway. She wanted to murder him, and he had no interest in being someone's soul mate. "No. Definitely not."

Marco shrugged. "Then you need to put a stop to it. Whatever *it* is. Sooner rather than later."

Leo's grip tightened around his beer bottle. "Not going to happen."

Marco groaned. He looked about as thrilled as Alegra Arabella had when she'd been dialing the cops. "Have you lost your mind? This thing has disaster written all over it. Gina will have a fit when she hears about it."

Leo glared at his brother-in-law across the table. "No, she won't. Because you're not going to tell her."

"I don't have much of a choice. I can't keep something like this from her. That's how marriage works." Marco shook his head. "You'd know that if you'd gone through with the wedding."

So now they were going to discuss his failed engagement, too? Great. He was beginning to appreciate how much easier life had been in Paris, when he didn't have to worry about his family meddling in every aspect of his life.

But if life in Paris had been so grand, what was he doing back in the States?

"Rose has nothing to do with this."

"You sure about that, bro? I mean, the timing screams rebound. And if that's what this is, couldn't you pick someone else? *Anyone* else? Except her cousin. That Alegra Arabella is downright scary."

Leo signaled the waitress for another round. Clearly, this was a multi-beer discussion. "This isn't a rebound thing."

He'd never loved Rose. He wasn't even sure he liked her much. He wasn't proud that he'd let things get so out of hand, but it was what it was. He knew better now. He wasn't made for marriage.

Besides, things were different. He was home. And in the short span of a week, things at Mezzanotte Chocolates were better than they'd been in years. He was a success here. As opposed to Paris, where he'd been just another French-trained chocolatier.

"This thing with Juliet is…" He had trouble choosing an adjective. So many applied. *Intense. Unexpected. Maddening.* "Different."

How could he explain what had come over him when he'd first seen her standing barefoot in the vineyard that night? When he'd lifted the mask from her face and gotten his first full glimpse of her emerald eyes and her pillowy, blush-colored lips? Something had shifted inside him at that moment. Whatever it was had felt every bit as real as the moist, fertile ground beneath his feet, the grape-scented night breeze swirling around them and the starlight twinkling overhead. He'd had the surreal feeling that their meeting had been orchestrated by a higher power. Like fate, or destiny. Or some other nebulous force Leo had never before believed in.

Which made him sound crazy.

So he kept his mouth shut about all that.

"Look, when I met Juliet, I didn't know who she was. All I know is that I felt like I'd never seen true beauty until that night. I realize that doesn't make sense, especially now that I know she's an Arabella. It's inconvenient, to say the least. But you can't tell Gina. Not yet. I need more time." He still sounded borderline nuts. Just how much alcohol had he consumed over the course of the day?

Marco exhaled a long, weary sigh. "I can't believe I'm even considering lying for you about this. More time to do what? Get her out of your system?"

That actually sounded reasonable. Juliet had made it more than clear she had no interest in a real relationship with him. And Leo certainly wasn't looking for love. But he wasn't ready to let her go, either. What he really wanted was to be rid of the overwhelming need she'd created in him and clear his head of these ridiculous notions of fate and destiny. "Yes. Exactly."

"How much time are we talking about?" Marco drummed his fingers on the table.

"I don't know." He would have thought he'd have been more than happy to move on once he'd discovered what a mess he'd wandered into. He should have run for the hills when Alegra got involved, or when Juliet's first instinct at getting caught with him was to hide in the bottom of a hot air balloon gondola. But apparently he was a glutton for punishment. Besides, she'd looked kinda cute huddled at his feet like that.

"You've got a week. I won't say a word until we get through the Napa Valley Chocolate Fair. Gina will be too preoccupied worrying about it to even notice anything else. But after that, all bets are off."

Marco set his empty beer down and headed toward one of the shuffleboard tables. He glanced over his shoulder. "Are you coming, or what?"

Apparently, his time frame was nonnegotiable. Fine. Leo was actually somewhat surprised. He'd expected Marco to be on the phone with Gina ratting him out before they'd finished the first round.

Leo swallowed what was left of his beer and rose from his chair.

A week. Seven days to come up with a winning entry for the Napa Valley Chocolate Fair.

Seven days to seduce Juliet Arabella without interference from his family, all while she was plotting to take him down in the chocolate war.

Seven days to come to his senses.

It wasn't much time, but he'd take what he could get.

11

After dusk had fallen, after all the white food tents had been dismantled, and after Juliet surmised that every last drop of Leo's award-winning *chocolat chaud* had been consumed, the rolling hills surrounding the Nuovo Winery were still dotted with illuminated hot air balloons. They shone like a string of oversize Christmas lights in the darkness.

Closing the balloon festival with a Night Glow was a long-held tradition. The balloons were inflated as if they were going to ascend, but instead were held in place by the ground crews. Their burners ignited every so often to keep the balloons full of hot air. The result was a spectacular display visible from one end of Napa Valley to the other.

Juliet was grateful for the light show as she drove from the winery to the animal hospital. She couldn't remember the last time she'd been so sleep deprived. A few hundred oversize lightbulbs bobbing on the hillside might have been the only things keeping her from falling asleep at the wheel. All she wanted to do after she picked up her sick dog was relax on the sofa with Cocoa's head in her lap while they watched *Cupcake Wars*.

She'd pretty much had the day from hell. Yesterday hadn't exactly been a cakewalk, but today was no improvement. She wasn't sure which had been worse—the epic strawberry disaster or Leo being crowned king of hot chocolate. And then there'd been her mother's surprise visit. Thankfully, by the time Juliet had floated back down to earth in the hot air balloon, her mom was already long gone, no doubt making Nico's life miserable behind the counter of Arabella Chocolate Boutique.

Juliet had felt guilty when she'd realized that while she'd been sipping champagne and doing her best to somehow *not* end up in Leo's arms again, Alegra had taken the brunt of the strawberry fallout. Well, she'd felt guilty for a little while. Until she realized that if Alegra was truly scarred from the experience, she could always cry into her shiny new iPad.

The animal hospital was more hectic than it had been the night before. A line of worried-looking people, some cradling kittens or puppies, snaked around the waiting area. Juliet took her place in line behind a man holding a coughing dog. At least she thought it was a dog. It was completely hairless. As smooth as a baby's bottom.

Juliet wiggled her nose. Was it her imagination, or did the animal smell like baby lotion?

"Miss Arabella?" The vet tech who'd helped Cocoa the night before motioned to her from the hallway.

Oh, no. What now? Had Cocoa taken a turn for the worse, or was she suffering from withdrawal from Leo's award-winning *chocolat chaud* like everyone else in Napa Valley?

Juliet left her place in line behind the naked dog and approached the vet tech. "Yes? Is something wrong?"

He shook his head. "No. Cocoa is doing as well as can be expected. She's lost a fair amount of weight, but that's normal. She's tired and ready to go home. You'll need to limit her activity for a week or so, which shouldn't be much of a problem since she's feeling a little lethargic. You'll also need to keep her on a special bland diet. Boiled chicken and white rice are best. I can also give you a few cans of special prescription food."

Juliet nodded. "I understand."

She'd be cooking for her dog now, while she still dined on her usual Lean Cuisines and grilled cheese sandwiches. But that was perfectly fine. She would have made Cocoa a heaping portion of Julia Child's famed Beef Bourguignon if necessary, so long as her dog was okay.

"No. More. Chocolate." The vet tech wagged a finger at her.

"Of course not. It was an accident—one that I promise we won't be repeating." Because she wasn't getting within a foot of Leo or his *chocolat chaud* ever again.

It was time to get her head in the game. And that meant she had two big priorities. First, she needed to figure out Leo's secret ingredient so she could duplicate his hot chocolate recipe. And second, but no less important, she had to create something special for the chocolate fair. Special enough to make Leo Mezzanotte look like an amateur.

"Good. I'm glad to hear it." The vet tech jerked his head in the direction of the exam rooms and kennel area. "I'll go get Cocoa. Give me five minutes to wake her and put together a case of that prescription canned food for you."

"Great. I need a minute or two to pay the bill, anyway." She hated to even think about how much all of this would cost. It wasn't as if she was rolling in money. And now without Royal Gourmet backing Arabella Chocolate Boutique, she had a feeling there was a significant pay cut in her future.

The vet tech shrugged. "The bill has already been taken care of. That's why I pulled you out of the line."

He turned to go.

Um. *What?*

"Wait a minute." She grabbed his arm before he disappeared into the recesses of the vet hospital. "What do you mean it's been taken care of?"

"You have a zero balance." He formed a perfect O with his index finger and thumb, and he spoke with exaggerated slowness, as if trying to explain something to a toddler. "That means you don't owe us any money."

She *so* did not need sarcasm right now. Not after the day she'd had. "I know what it means. I want to know who paid my bill."

"Does it matter?"

Yes, it mattered. It mattered very much. "I simply want to be able to thank the person, whoever he—or she—is."

There was no doubt in her mind it was a *he*. A very specific *he* who liked to go around buying people iPads and, apparently, paying exorbitant veterinary bills.

"I'm not sure I'm authorized to give you that information." The vet tech glanced longingly toward the kennel area, then fretfully at Juliet's fingers, where they still clutched the blue fabric of his scrubs.

She let go, before he decided she was a crazy person. Although from the look in his eyes, she was too late. "It was him, wasn't it? The guy who carried my dog inside last night?"

"The one who you insisted you weren't with?" He raised his eyebrows.

She swallowed.

He nodded. "Yeah, it was him. Sounds like a real jerk. Good thing you guys aren't together."

Juliet's cheeks blazed with heat. "We are *definitely* not together."

"Yeah, I got that." He rolled his eyes.

"You don't understand. It's complicated." Why was she explaining herself to a total stranger? Didn't she have enough problems with people who she actually knew voicing their opinions about things?

"I'm sure it is. Here's a news flash for you—no one cares." He jerked a thumb toward the exam rooms. "Is it okay if I go get your sick dog now?"

She blinked. If her face got any hotter, she might burst into flames. "Yes. Please."

She took a deep breath and didn't allow herself to exhale until he'd gone. Embarrassment butterflied in her chest. What had gotten into her? She'd brought this on herself. Why didn't she just keep her mouth shut and pick up her dog, like a normal person? And why had she invited Cocoa's vet tech, of all people, to weigh in on her personal life?

Because everything about Leonardo Mezzanotte made her crazy. That's why.

She wanted to scream. Or cry. When would this day ever end? Her vision blurred, and the vet tech's words bounced around in her head.

No one cares.

If only that were true.

Leo left the sports bar and drove straight to Mezzanotte Chocolates under the pretense of getting a head start on planning his creation for the chocolate fair. Aside from his near-constant headache, he finally seemed to be getting over his jet lag. But he'd always done his best work alone, and quiet hours at the family chocolate shop were few and far between.

Who was he really kidding, though? He wasn't fooling anyone, least of all himself. He was actually hoping to spot Juliet—preferably alone, although he could deal with Alegra if the situation required—across the street at Arabella Chocolate Boutique.

She wasn't there. The windows were dark, the parking lot empty. She was probably at home with Cocoa, running her graceful fingers through the sweet dog's fur. He'd seen to it that the bill at the emergency animal hospital had been paid. Knowing all too well what Juliet's reaction would be if he tried to pay the balance with her knowledge, he'd stopped by the clinic on the way to his scheduled drinks with Marco. She'd had a rough week. It was the least he could do to help, seeing as he'd played a rather big part in the tumultuous situation.

But enough of Juliet Arabella.

He'd been victorious today, but next week all anyone would care about was the Napa Valley Chocolate Fair. And as Uncle Joe had told him countless times, Juliet was the reigning champion. The *undefeated* reigning champ. Leo would wager his degree from Le Cordon Bleu that there wouldn't be a single soggy strawberry in sight next Saturday.

He flipped on the lights in the kitchen of Mezzanotte Chocolates and slipped his arms into his chef coat. So long as he was here, he may as well get some actual work done. He didn't want to think about what it would mean if he left and went home simply because Juliet wasn't around. He might have had one too many beers tonight, and he might be suffering from a serious case of unrequited lust, but he wasn't quite ready to confess that he'd become that pathetic.

He opened the refrigerator and pulled out a dozen eggs. Then he thought for a minute and reached inside for a dozen more. He'd planned on making macarons. Genuine Parisian macarons, like the ones that sold for four euros apiece at Ladurée on the Champs-élysées. Dark chocolate, filled with a creamy orange blossom ganache. White-on-white chocolate, dusted with sea salt and rosemary, the perfect, unexpected blend of sweet and savory. A bittersweet chocolate-coffee blend, filled with sweet cream and topped with espresso powder. And Leo's personal favorite—rich, decadent cocoa with a key lime filling so tart that it bordered on bitter but, when combined with the delicate cocoa cakes that made up the outside pieces of the macarons, was the epitome of French culinary perfection.

He wasn't sure when he'd begun to have doubts, only that they'd taken root somewhere around the time Juliet had thrown down the gauntlet.

You're going down next weekend at the Napa Valley Chocolate Fair. I'm going to murder you. Consider yourself warned.

It was sexy as hell.

It had also made him more determined than ever to win.

Leo separated the eggs and whipped the whites with a dash of salt until they were foamy. Then he flipped the speed on the standing mixer to high for exactly fifty-six seconds before folding in the almonds and sugar with a well-rehearsed twirl of his spatula. He piped the batter into disks with a pastry bag and tried not to obsess over them while they sat at room temperature, waiting for soft skins to form over the outer layer.

They were beautiful. Even less than halfway through the process, they were still magnificent. Elegant and refined in their simplicity.

But did elegant and refined win trophies? He needed to somehow transform them into an eye-catching attraction. Something spectacular that even non-foodies who'd never before laid eyes on a macaron could appreciate. Something along the lines of the extravagant window displays of Ladurée.

That's it.

He let out a laugh as he slid the macarons into the oven, leaving the oven door slightly ajar. He would take the macarons and make a showpiece out of them. The windows of the Paris tea shops were always fitted with towering macaron towers or colorful, sculpted macaron trees. He would do something along those lines. It would be tricky—doubly tricky as simply making the perfect chocolate macaron, since he'd also be constructing what amounted to a food sculpture—but if it worked, it would sure as hell be memorable.

And it *would* work. Because it had to.

An hour later, satisfied with his plan, he locked up the shop. His test batch had turned out to be acceptable. A crack here and there. Perhaps the *pied,* the notoriously temperamental ruffle at the base of the cookies, could have been a bit more voluminous. But the flavors had been dead-on. Once he invested in a portable dehumidifier for the store, he'd be golden.

Even though it was so far into the wee hours that the dramatic lights of the Night Glow had begun to grow dim and there was still no sign of Juliet across the street, Leo felt downright triumphant as he drove home. He could win this thing. And if the powers that be at The French Laundry were at all excited about his *chocolat chaud,* they would turn back-

Unmasking Juliet

173

flips over a prize-winning tower made up of four varieties of Parisian chocolate macarons.

The thought of his arrangement with George Alcott and The French Laundry brought with it a stab of guilt to his consciousness as he pulled into his driveway.

It's not personal. It's business.

Juliet sure didn't seem to agree.

He slammed his car door shut more forcefully than necessary. If the shoe had been on the other foot, she would have done the same thing. He'd done nothing wrong. She'd get over it. She couldn't very well hold it against him forever.

His foot bumped against something bulky and solid on the porch as he slid his key into the front door. He bent to pick the mysterious object up, but couldn't tell what it was in the dark. Once inside, he switched on the lights and saw it was an envelope. Even though it was held closed with a rubber band, the thick manila paper of the envelope strained at the seams.

His teeth ground together as he pulled off the rubber band. Surely this wasn't what he thought it was.

Oh, but it was.

An avalanche of dollar bills fell to floor. All ones. Leo didn't count them. He didn't have to. He knew precisely how many there were—1,232 of them. The sum total of Cocoa Arabella's veterinary bill.

Leo's headache returned with unparalleled vengeance.

She'd get over it. She couldn't very well hold it against him forever.

And yet he suddenly found himself with 1,232 new reasons to believe she could.

For the second Sunday in a row, the thought of the weekly Arabella family breakfast filled Juliet with a sense of dread.

But she showed up right on time, just like the dutiful daughter she'd always been. Up until a week ago, at least.

"Here goes nothing," she muttered to Cocoa as she opened the front door of her childhood home and walked inside.

The scent of bacon and freshly brewed coffee immediately invaded her senses. So there was actual food being prepared this time? That was certainly an improvement over last week. At least if she was going to be confronted with an intervention again, there would be snacks. And caffeine. She still wasn't fully caught up on her sleep. Although in the grand scheme of things, sleep deprivation was the least of her problems.

The family was all there—Alegra, Nico, Dad. And of course, Mom, who stood at the stove wearing a pink ruffled Arabella Chocolate Boutique apron. It looked as if she was stirring eggs, which was somewhat of a relief. Juliet had half expected to be force-fed the leftover strawberries for breakfast.

"Hey there, sis," Nico said around the slice of bacon hanging from his mouth as he poured himself a cup of coffee. The last cup, apparently. He held the coffeepot upside down until the last drop landed in his mug.

"Morning." Juliet wasted no time heading for the pantry for a new filter and the bag of Lavazza Classico blend her mother always kept on hand.

"Juliet, I have something for you." Her mother turned to face her. "*Dio mio!* What happened to Cocoa?"

Everyone stopped what they were doing to stare at the dog. Cocoa, who loved any occasion in which she was the center of attention, wagged her tail. It beat against Juliet's legs.

"She looks like a bag of bones." Juliet's mother jammed her hands on her hips. "Have you stopped feeding her?"

Juliet rested a protective hand on Cocoa's shaggy head. "Oh, she's eating. She's eating plenty. In fact, she got into some chocolate and had to have her stomach evacuated."

"Evacuated?" Nico frowned around his bacon. "What exactly does that mean?"

"Trust me. You don't want to know. But the end result was that they got all the chocolate out of her system." The fact that it had been Mezzanotte chocolate was a detail Juliet didn't feel the need to share.

She glanced at Alegra, but Alegra's eyes were glued on her new iPad. Juliet wondered when Leo had managed to find time to purchase the thing, much less deliver it to Alegra. He sure managed to get around.

Well, if he was busy throwing his money all over Napa Valley, that was fine. The less time that man spent in the kitchen, the better.

"Since when does Cocoa get into the chocolate?" Her mother frowned and gave the omelet on the stove a flip.

Alegra glanced up. Finally. But she managed to keep her mouth shut.

"Believe me, I was as surprised as you are. She's doing okay, though. Aren't you, girl?" Juliet ran her fingers through Cocoa's fur and prayed no one noticed the nervous tremor in her hands.

Juliet's mother snatched the slice of bacon hanging from Nico's mouth. He yelled in protest. "Hey!"

Their mother swatted him with her spatula. "Nico, don't be selfish. Share that bacon with Cocoa. The poor dog is at death's door."

She tossed the bacon at Cocoa, who threw her newly slimmed-down frame in the air and lunged at it, proving that bacon apparently was a cure for lethargy. Juliet would have to remember that in case she lost to Leo at the choc-olate fair and needed something to pull herself out of the deep depression she was sure to succumb to in the event of another crushing defeat.

She snagged the bacon out of reach in the nick of time and tossed it in her own mouth instead. *Mmm. Crunchy.* "She's not at death's door. She's just lost a little weight. But she can't eat bacon, or anything else we're having. The vet put her on a special diet for a few days."

Her mother rolled her eyes. "Nonsense. Dom, get the bag of meatballs out of the freezer."

Her father obeyed.

Juliet didn't bother trying to tell him otherwise. Her mother had spoken. Juliet would simply have to somehow intercept those meatballs. Besides, so long as everyone was focused on Cocoa's scrawny state instead of the disaster at the balloon festival, she could breathe somewhat easy.

Her relief was predictably short-lived.

"I stopped by the Nuovo Winery yesterday, Juliet, but you weren't at the booth." Her mother picked up a knife to slice some bell peppers that were spread out on the cutting board. At least that's what Juliet hoped it was for. "I thought I spot-ted you when I first arrived, but I must have been mistaken. Alegra said you were networking."

Networking. So that's what the kids were calling it nowa-days? "Yes. I had a nice chat with one of the other vendors."

Technically, it wasn't a lie. Leo was a vendor. And they had chatted.

"I'm sorry I missed you, Mom." Now that *was* a lie. "And I'm sorry about the strawberries. The sea salt maple bacon hearts were a hit, though."

An awkward silence fell over the kitchen. Juliet's brother,

father and even Alegra seemed to look everywhere but at Juliet. She cleared her throat. "And I'm already working on plans for the chocolate fair this weekend."

Her mother stopped slicing the peppers and set the knife down on the cutting board. Then she wiped her hands on her apron with excruciating slowness. Every move she made caused Juliet's heart to beat with increased anxiety. She couldn't ever remember wishing her mother would say something, anything, but she wished that very much right now. The waiting was almost unbearable.

Finally, her mother finished wiping her hands. She smoothed down the front of her apron, looked straight at Juliet and then walked right out of the kitchen.

Juliet exchanged glances with Alegra, then Nico and her dad. Alegra and Nico, obviously as much in the dark as she was, simply shrugged.

Her father held up a hand and nodded. "Be patient. Your mother has something up her sleeve. I'm sure she'll be right back."

That's what I'm afraid of.

Where had she gone? In search of Juliet's pink slip?

Apparently not. She returned to the kitchen with a book resting delicately in the palms of her hands. It was an old book with a worn leather cover that was peeling back at the edges. The spine was cracked in numerous places, making it look as though it might fall apart if someone opened it.

Juliet tilted her head, and a feeling of vague recognition washed over her. The book looked familiar. She could almost remember seeing it long ago, when most of the books she'd read had titles like *Goodnight Moon* and *Where the Wild Things Are.*

She glanced at Nico out of the corner of her eye. He shrugged. Clueless as usual.

"Do you know what this is?" her mother asked, still holding the book as though it were a treasure on par with the Gutenberg Bible.

Juliet shook her head. "Not really. No. It does look sort of familiar, though."

"This is your grandmother's recipe book." Her mother's eyes misted over.

Juliet might have remembered seeing that book, but she'd never once seen her mother cry. Ever. Her own throat grew instantly tight. "Grandma's recipes. Wow."

"Yes, and I want you to have them." Her mother offered the book to her.

Juliet stared down at it, almost afraid to lay a finger on it. "I don't understand. Why?"

It wasn't as though the recipes were top secret. Not anymore. The Mezzanottes had sold those very recipes years ago. What was she supposed to do with them now?

"Just take the book." Her mother thrust it toward her again.

Juliet took it from her hands as gingerly as possible, certain it would crumble the moment she touched it.

"Promise me you'll read it." Her mother crossed her arms. "Now."

"Now? As in right this minute?" She still hadn't had a drop of coffee, much less breakfast.

"Yes. You can read while you eat. This is important, Juliet. There's more to this than a few lists of ingredients and baking instructions. You'll see." Her mother tapped the cover of the book with her pointer finger. It was a subtle gesture, yet somehow still eerily ominous.

Juliet gripped the book more tightly. "Okay, I will."

Of course she would. She'd expected to be chastised again, and instead she'd been asked to read her grandmother's recipe book. She would have done so without prompting. In her hands was the foundation for everything she'd ever held dear. These recipes were what had started it all. Even though they'd been stolen, their secrets mass-produced and packaged in cheap paper and foil and sold to the public for less than a cup of Starbucks coffee, they still represented her family's history. In a way, they were like an inheritance.

But why now?

"All right. It's settled, then." Juliet's mother cast a fleeting look at her father. And that one glance spoke volumes.

He nodded ever so slightly in return.

Juliet watched their exchange with mounting curiosity. She'd spent a lot of time with her parents over the years. And they still worked together, side by side, nearly every day. Juliet had witnessed similar silent communications before.

Her mother's eyelashes fluttered, and for a cryptic, fleeting moment, her lips curved into a satisfied smile. If Juliet had blinked, she would have missed it—the unmistakable look of triumph on her mother's face. It had been quick and oh-so-subtle, but very much there.

Her father began to whistle and went about setting the table for breakfast.

No doubt about it. They were up to something.

And whatever it was had everything to do with the book in Juliet's hands.

She flipped open the book's cover, and the spine creaked. Juliet suppressed a shiver and told herself she was being ridiculously overdramatic. It was a recipe book, for goodness' sake. She'd probably only get a glimpse of her grandmother's attempts at creating the perfect chocolate candy.

She got far more than she bargained for as her eyes skimmed the yellowed pages. The book wasn't simply a collection of family recipes. The dates and notations scribbled in the margins chronicled her grandmother's struggles, both culinary and nonculinary alike. Those faint, penciled-in notes recorded every detail of her friendship with Donnatella Mezzanotte, along with the crushing loss of that friendship and the pain of Donnatella's betrayal.

Page one: *May 10, 1938, Donnatella and I opened the shop today. Our dream has finally come true!*

Then later, scribbled next to a recipe for a rich Mexican chocolate sheet cake that Juliet remembered learning how to make on her tenth birthday: *August 1, 1939, Donnatella has been so quiet of late. Baking her favorite chocolate cake as a surprise.*

August 15, 1939, above step-by-step instructions for orange ginger white chocolate disks, *Worried about my dear friend.*

A few pages later, beside the step-by-step instructions for dark cappuccino chocolate candy, now a Mezzanotte Chocolates bestseller: *September 10, 1939, Donnatella thinks we should sell our recipes to a candy bar company. Thinking of giving away everything we've worked so hard for hurts my heart.*

And on and on it went, until the final page: *I don't know which pain cuts deeper—the loss of these recipes I've been working on for years, or my closest friend. She was like una sorella to me.*

Una sorella.

A sister.

There was no recipe on that page, or any of the blank sheets of paper that followed.

Juliet closed the book and rested her hand on the worn leather cover. She knew it was silly, but she could have sworn she could feel the beat of her grandmother's heart pulsing beneath her fingertips. Those pages held the real secrets Juliet's mother had wanted her to uncover. No doubt her mother thought reading of her grandmother's pain at the hands of a Mezzanotte would serve as a warning to Juliet, would make her think twice about trusting anyone with that last name, no matter how genuine he seemed.

12

Sugar scrambled out of Leo's lap and let out a high-pitched whine as the car slowed to a stop in front of the address Leo had procured from Alegra.

He took the whining as a good sign. Maybe Sugar somehow sensed Cocoa's presence, meaning he'd truly found out where Juliet lived. Alegra didn't seem to hate him with quite as much passion as she had at first, but her feelings for him still appeared to vacillate between intense dislike and mere tolerance. He half suspected she'd given him a fake address.

But as he grabbed the canvas grocery bag from the passenger seat and approached the front door, he caught a whiff of bittersweet chocolate, and he knew Alegra had told the truth.

After four fruitless days and nights, he'd given up trying to catch Juliet alone at Arabella Chocolate Boutique. From what he could tell, she was always surrounded by a bevy of Arabellas during the day. Arabellas who would sooner see his head on a platter than let him walk through the front door of their store. And as soon as the purple shadows of twilight descended on the valley, Juliet made herself scarce.

He sometimes wondered if she was intentionally avoiding him. His ego wanted to believe that was nonsense, that she'd simply been just as busy as he had preparing for the chocolate festival.

His macarons were done, finished just this morning. Since they were best eaten one to two days after baking, they were currently biding their time in the walk-in cooler at Mezzanotte Chocolates. Tomorrow he would get started crafting the tower, but in the meantime he had an entire evening ahead of him. An evening he planned on spending with Juliet.

Waiting to see her again had been excruciating. With the macarons to distract him, he'd somehow managed. But now that he had a moment to breathe, he simply couldn't take the loss of her any longer. It was a loss that made no sense to him, but a loss nonetheless.

He had to see her straightaway. Before he went mad.

He knocked three times, glanced down at Sugar spinning small circles on the welcome mat and smiled. If Juliet was tempted to slam the door in his face, Sugar's antics just might buy him a minute or two to convince her to let him in.

The door swung open more quickly than he expected. He jerked his head up and took in a surprised, somewhat disheveled Juliet. Clearly, he'd caught her in the middle of a cooking frenzy. Her hair was piled haphazardly on top of her head, and she had a smudge of what looked like cocoa powder on her cheek.

Adorable.

His gaze traveled lower. The sight of her long bare legs stretching out from beneath the hem of a saucy red apron went beyond adorable, venturing into more tempting territory. He had the sudden, intoxicating thought of how great those lithe legs would feel wrapped around his waist as he moved inside her, pushing in deep.

A spark of electricity shot straight to his groin.

He almost dropped the groceries. "Juliet."

"Leo." Predictably, she sounded less than happy to find him at her door. "What are you doing here? This isn't a good time. I'm in the middle of a…" Her luminous green eyes flitted somewhere over her shoulder. Toward the kitchen, Leo presumed. "Project of sorts."

"I know all about your 'project.'" The *chocolat chaud*. If Alegra hadn't told him that Juliet had been holed up for days trying to duplicate his recipe, he would have been able to guess what she'd been up to simply from the aroma emanating from within her home.

From the smell of things, she was getting close. Closer than he'd anticipated.

"I doubt that." She crossed her arms. Her tank top shifted, giving him a brief glimpse of a wisp-thin, lacy bra strap. Red again.

Another jolt of electricity zinged through him. If she didn't let him in, he'd have a long, lonely night ahead of him.

"You think I can't recognize the scent of my own recipe?" He narrowed his gaze at her. Even Sugar's tiny nose appeared to quiver in recognition.

"*Your* recipe." She grinned. At last. "So I'm that close, huh? I knew it."

"Why don't you let me in? I can give it a taste and let you know exactly how close you are." He gave her door a slight nudge with his foot.

She rolled her eyes. The front door didn't budge. "Right. You're here to help me duplicate your *chocolat chaud*. Do you really expect me to believe that?"

He gestured to the bag in his arms. "See for yourself."

She rose up on her tiptoes, lowered her lashes and peered inside. Then she went very still for a prolonged moment until she looked back up and fixed her gaze with his. "Chocolate. Vanilla. Cinnamon. What is this, Leo?"

"Supplies. I told you—I'm here to assist with your project." He took advantage of her surprise and maneuvered past her. Sugar scrambled to her feet and romped across the threshold alongside him.

With its soft, violet-colored walls and abundance of drippy candles, her condo was warm, feminine and inviting. Three black-and-white photos of cobblestone streets, sidewalk cafés and arched doorways hung on the wall opposite the entryway. Italy. Rome, in particular, if Leo wasn't mistaken.

He waited for a twinge of homesickness for Europe to wash over him. But it never came. Strange.

Just as he was thinking how nice it would be to stretch out on her overstuffed sofa—preferably with Juliet beneath him, or at the very least, beside him—a massive, shaggy head poked up over the back of that sofa. Cocoa looked a fair bit better than the last time Leo had seen her, he noted. When she leaped off the couch to greet Sugar, he could see that she'd lost weight, but other than that, she looked none the worse for the wear.

Juliet bent to give Sugar a pat on the head, giving Leo a magnificent glimpse of her creamy, generous cleavage. In an effort to remain at least partially a gentleman, he averted his eyes. After a beat or two, the temptation proved too great, and he looked his fill. Until Juliet glanced up and caught him.

She abruptly straightened, her cheeks glowing pink in that way that always made his chest tighten. "The kitchen is this direction."

He followed her to a room with a terra-cotta tile floor and a rustic butcher block in the center. It was larger than he'd expected. More pictures of Italy were tacked up on the red vintage refrigerator, and every square inch of counter space was covered with open boxes and cartons. Whipping cream, milk, sweet cream butter, just about every variety of sugar Leo had ever seen, and bar upon bar of bittersweet chocolate.

An ancient-looking book was spread open on the center island. Its pages were brittle and as brown as a farm fresh egg. To Leo it looked like the type of thing that would hold secret magic spells, but he spied the words *caramel silk* and *roasted hazelnuts* and figured it must be a collection of recipes. Someone had written dates and notes in the margin in script that had faded over time until it was nearly invisible.

An oven timer went off, drawing Leo's attention to the red gas stove. Three burners were going at once, each topped with a simmering saucepan of warm chocolate. Juliet killed the heat to one of the burners and gave the contents of its corresponding pan a quick stir with a practiced flip of her slender wrist. Everything about the action suggested she'd been doing this for quite a while. If Leo had to guess, he would have estimated countless times over the past forty-eight hours alone.

He set the bag on the center island, next to the antique cookbook, and let out a low whistle. "This is quite the production. No wonder I haven't seen you around your shop. You've been busy."

"Yes. Well. When I commit to something, I give it my all." She gave her stirring spoon an innocent lick.

Leo's pulse kicked up a notch. He ground his teeth together, averted his gaze and focused instead on the interlocking pattern of the butcher block island. Sugar maple. He'd bet money on it. "Clearly."

He wondered if this staggering level of commitment applied to her relationships, as well. He suspected it did, given her devotion to her family. Did George Alcott III have any clue what a lucky man he'd once been? Doubtful, or his ring would have ended up on Juliet's finger.

Leo frowned. Since when did he consider anyone within striking distance of having a ring on their finger lucky?

Juliet reached into the canvas bag and began unpacking the ingredients he'd picked up on his way over, lining them up one by one. When she got to the vanilla paste, she turned the bottle over in her hand and inspected the label. "This is the good stuff from Madagascar. Nice. And I have to say, food was the last thing I expected to find in that bag."

"I like to think outside the box and carry actual groceries in my grocery bags. I'd hate to be predictable." He winked.

"Oh, you're anything but predictable," she said dryly.

He raised an eyebrow at her tone. "And what did you expect me to be carrying in that bag?"

"Honestly? Money. Lots of it. At least, oh, I don't know…1,232 dollars. Thereabouts." Her elegant shoulder lifted in a nonchalant shrug.

A jackhammering began in Leo's jaw and traveled up to his temple.

So they were going to talk about the vet bill? Marvelous.

It had taken every ounce of self-control he possessed, and then some, not to return her money. To march right into Arabella Chocolate Boutique and fling it at her feet. But as furious as he'd been to find all those dollars on his doorstep, he knew she'd be doubly furious if he tried to force her to take them back.

Her eyes blazed with indignation. Or was it hurt? "I have my pride, Leo."

And he didn't? "I felt responsible."

She waved a hand at Cocoa in the living room. The big dog was lolling on her back, letting Sugar bat at her face with one of her dainty paws. "Why would you? It was my dog."

"Yes, but it was my chocolate." Leo gave her a playful tap on the tip of her upturned nose. As strongly as he felt about wanting to pay for Cocoa's veterinary care, he was willing to let the matter drop. For now. They already had enough working against this attraction without adding 1,232 dollars to the mix.

"I think we're going to have to agree to disagree." She leaned toward him, bathing him in the intoxicating fragrance of chocolate and Chantilly cream, then appeared to realize what she was doing and righted herself.

What a pity.

It's okay, he wanted to say. *Lean in. Lean all the way in.*

He had to stop himself from reaching for her, from pulling her soft, lithe body against his so she could remember how perfectly they fit together. Like they were made for one another, last names be damned.

He'd already shown up uninvited. He certainly wasn't going to force himself on her. What he wanted most of all was for her to lose control again, to show him how much she wanted him. He wished she would stop thinking so much and just live in the moment with him, grab him by the shirt and kiss him so hard that she bruised his mouth. Hell, until he bled.

But he feared those days were over.

He moved closer to her, barely a heartbeat away. But he made no move to touch her. An ache throbbed to life deep in his center. The unfulfilled longing that had come over him that first night in the vineyard had blossomed into something he could no longer control. He was right there on the cusp of begging, of falling to his knees and pleading with her.

Must you leave me so unsatisfied?

"I didn't come here to argue with you, *bella.*" His words scraped against the inside of his throat, leaving him feeling raw and altogether too vulnerable.

She blew out a soft, shaky breath, as if she was trying to hold anything and everything she might be feeling inside. Out of his reach. But her eyes gave her away. They glittered, dark, lovely and full of unspoken desire.

Perhaps those days weren't over, after all.

"Leo." She swallowed, and for the briefest of moments those delicious lips of hers parted, rendering him spellbound. "Exactly why did you come here?"

Bella.

The endearment just about did Juliet in.

It meant *beautiful,* and it sounded infinitely more romantic in Italian than in English. Or maybe it was just the way Leo had said it. With complete and total abandon, rather as if he hadn't planned on saying it at all, and his use of it had surprised him every bit as much as it did her.

"Leo." She paused for a steadying inhale, as if anything could calm the beating of her heart at the moment. "Exactly why did you come here?"

"I already told you—to help with your project." He winked at her. That wink zinged straight to the center of her chest with laser-guided precision.

He was here to help her re-create his *chocolat chaud.* What a load of crap.

He smiled at her, grabbed a spoon from the countertop and dipped it in one of the saucepans. He appeared to be entirely comfortable in her kitchen. *Too* comfortable. And by all appearances, he was completely relaxed. If he was lying to her, he certainly wasn't nervous or anxious about it.

Then again, neither were psychopaths when they lied. Or serial killers, for that matter.

She dropped her gaze. It was easier to think without his dreamy blue eyes and perfect bone structure invading her senses.

Fate must have been smiling down on her at that moment, because her eyes landed on the one thing capable of dragging her back to reality.

Her grandmother's recipe book.

She had to hand it to her mother. Giving her the book had been deviously brilliant. God, why did her mother have to be such an evil genius? And what exactly had she seen at the balloon festival?

Juliet squared her shoulders and looked back up at Leo. He was busy tasting the batch of *chocolat chaud* that Juliet considered her best effort thus far. Still, it was missing that special something. Would she ever put her finger on it?

"This one's the closest." Leo nodded and rinsed the tasting spoon in the sink. Leonardo Mezzanotte…in her kitchen. Who would have ever predicted such an occurrence? "But you probably already knew that."

Okay, so he was being honest. For now.

She crossed her arms. "As a matter of fact, I did."

He leaned against the kitchen counter, crossing his feet at the ankles. Why did this room feel so small with him in it?

Juliet's head spun. She attributed it to the brandy she'd generously poured into one of the batches of hot chocolate.

It couldn't be because she was falling under Leo's spell again. "You know, if you truly want to help me as you claim, you could save me a lot of time and effort and simply give me your recipe."

"Ah, but what would be the fun in that?" His grin was nothing short of wicked.

"Fun?" She motioned toward the mess everywhere. Her kitchen had never been such a disaster. "You think this is fun?"

"Cooking is always fun," said Mr. Cordon Bleu himself. "Don't you think so?"

Not when she was cooking for her very life. "Under ordinary circumstances, yes. Nothing about this situation is ordinary."

"Again, what would be the fun in ordinary? I find ordinary quite boring." The grin slipped from his lips suddenly. "You're not wearing midnight-blue. I have to admit that's somewhat of a disappointment."

She glanced down at her white tank top and jean shorts, mostly obscured by her pink Arabella shop apron. "No, I'm not." Then she tossed his words back at him. "I'd hate to be predictable."

He laughed. "Touché, my sweet. Touché."

My sweet. Juliet's knees went as soft as gooey caramel.

"Why don't you dump out the chocolate on the stove, and we can start a fresh batch? If you're indeed serious about this venture." Anything to get him to stop talking, to stop saying nice things that she wasn't sure she could believe in, even though she wanted to. Very badly.

"Oh, I'm serious," he said, rolling up his shirtsleeves.

She handed him one of the pans and did her best not to stare at his forearms. "So you said."

He poured the rejected hot chocolate down the drain. "What's next? Are we starting all over?"

"Yes, I think so. I was going to keep tinkering with the batch that was the closest because I'd used up nearly all my supply of whipping cream, but since we have more now, we can start fresh."

We. She shook her head. This whole charade was absurd.

"See? I'm already helping." He picked up one of the cartons of cream he'd brought with him and handed it to her. She reached for it, but he held on for an extra beat, engaging her in a playful tug of war.

"How bad do you want it?" he asked, the tips of his fingers fluttering against hers.

So, so badly.

She rolled her eyes. "Is this your idea of working?"

"Maybe." He shrugged, released his hold on the carton and winked at her again. "But you're starting to have fun now, aren't you?"

She opened her mouth to issue a swift denial but realized she'd be lying. She was having fun. Damn it. "A little."

He plunged his hands in the sink full of soapy water. "Good. That means I've already made myself useful."

"Would you care to make yourself even more useful and tell me what we should add to the new batch?" She eyed the rest of the items he'd supplied, certain that the secret ingredient was nowhere among them. He was way too smart for that.

He rinsed the first of the clean saucepans under the cool, clean water and set it on the butcher block to dry. "Admit it—you'd derive much more satisfaction from figuring it out for yourself."

She gave his words some thought. "That's probably true."

He reached a soapy hand toward her, cupped her face and

wiped away the smudge of cocoa on her cheek that she'd completely forgotten was there. "Well, far be it for me to deny you such pleasure."

His skin was hot against hers. Juliet had to remind herself that they were still talking about chocolate.

Chocolate...chocolate...

A word, a taste lingered on the edges of her consciousness, but she couldn't quite grasp it. Something earthy and familiar that could possibly be the perfect counterpart to so much rich chocolaty goodness. Then it hit her, like a bolt from out of the blue.

Why hadn't she thought of it before?

"Sea salt," she blurted.

Leo froze for a second, then slowly removed his hand from her face. "Sea salt?"

She nodded. "Yes. Sea salt. It's the only thing I haven't tried."

His flirty demeanor seemed to harden, as did the all-too-familiar knot in his jaw. No sooner did Juliet notice the change than it appeared to pass.

He gave her a lazy, sultry smile, slipped an arm around her waist and pulled her close before she could even think about resisting. "Let's give it a go, then. Shall we?"

Her response was nothing but a sigh of contentment at the feel of his arms around her again. The spoon in her hand went clattering to the kitchen floor. Leo's lips dropped to her neck, and she inhaled a slow, quivering breath while he gave her a good and thorough nuzzling.

But even when Juliet began to feel as if she could no longer draw a pure lungful of air without shuddering, as she all but disappeared into a swirling fog of desire, she could feel the pounding of Leo's heart. It crashed against hers like the rumble of distant thunder warning of a coming storm.

And she knew she was onto something.

13

Leo stared into the demitasse cup Juliet pushed toward him once her latest batch of *chocolat chaud* was ready, more nervous than he cared to admit.

Relax. It's ordinary sea salt. Not the *sea salt.*

"Go ahead. Try it. I'm anxious to hear what you think." She nodded at the untouched cup, the look on her face bordering on triumphant.

She had every right to look that way. She was close, all right. Too close for any degree of comfort.

He sipped at the chocolate, a silver bullet of pain piercing his temple the moment the rich liquid hit his tongue. He made every effort to temper the anxiety out of his voice. "Not bad."

"I know, right? Tell the truth—I'm getting there, aren't I?" She smiled, and her joy sank into him, warm and silky.

"As a matter of fact, you are." What was the harm in admitting it?

She couldn't possibly know about the *fleur de sel*. Juliet's kitchen was a safe five thousand miles from Brittany. And as far as Leo knew, she'd never even set foot in France.

"I knew it. It's still not quite right, but close. So close."
She untied her apron and slipped it over her head, sending
those delicious waves of praline-colored hair tumbling out
of their clip, over her shoulders and down her back.

Leo was beginning to care less and less about the *chocolat
chaud*. His fingers itched to touch her again, his lips ached
to kiss her—full on her mouth this time.

He set down his cup. "Tossing your apron? You're not
giving up, are you?"

"In your dreams." She laughed, and the sound of it dashed
through him, settling in his gut in a tight knot of longing.
"But it's late, and I believe in quitting while I'm ahead. Tomorrow is another day."

"Tomorrow?" He raised his brows. "So you're going to be
back at it as early as that? Surely you haven't forgotten there's
only one day left before the chocolate fair."

"Of course I haven't. My entry is ready. What about
yours?" She crossed her arms. Those breasts, that tiny tank
top...

He blinked. Hard. Chocolate fair? What chocolate fair?
"All finished."

"I don't suppose you want to tell me what it is?" She gave
him a coy look.

He wasn't that stupid with lust. Not yet, anyway. "You
first."

"As grateful as I am for your help tonight, no." She shook
her head and brushed past him on her way to the sink.

This was his cue to leave. He should go get his dog and
head home. Of course, he had no idea where Sugar was at
the moment. The last time he'd seen her, she'd been curled
against Cocoa's side, exhausted after hours of tearing in cir-

cles around Juliet's living room. Not to mention the fact that he didn't want to go home.

Leaving was the last thing he wanted. What he wanted most was the woman standing just a few feet away from him—the one woman he shouldn't want, a woman who might not even want him in return.

After an evening in the kitchen, the sweet scents of heavy cream and vanilla clung to every inch of her, leaving Leo with the irrepressible fantasy that she smelled like she'd been dipped in chocolate, purely for his pleasure. Intellectually, he knew this made no sense. But since when had any of his feelings made sense where Juliet was concerned?

He ordered his feet to move, to walk out of Juliet's kitchen and to continue walking right out her front door.

They didn't so much as budge. A certain other body part, however, seemed to have no problem making its presence known.

To hell with leaving. He wasn't going anywhere unless Juliet kicked him out, lock, stock and barrel.

He moved behind her, quietly, softly, running his fingertips up and down the graceful length of her arms. A part of him expected her to stiffen at his touch or try to slip away from him. Every cell in his body sang a hymn of joy when instead she leaned back against him. Her hands went still in the soapy water, and her head fell back on his shoulder.

"Tonight was fun," she murmured, her eyelashes drifting closed.

The purr in her voice, coupled with the softness of her bottom pressed against him, was simply too much. His hands dropped to her waist, slid forward and splayed against her belly. He pulled her even closer, his arousal pressing into her until he thought he'd go mad with wanting.

"Tonight doesn't have to be over," he whispered into the delectable curve of her neck.

"I'm afraid it does." She moved ever so slightly, her backside sliding languidly against him.

He groaned through clenched teeth. "I should advise you not to tempt a desperate man."

She turned to face him, leaving less than a fraction of an inch between their bodies. The sudden distance felt like miles. For several long moments, the water dripping from her wet hands onto the tile floor was the only sound that pierced the quiet. "It's not that I don't want this every bit as much as you do. In fact, I'm sure I want it more."

Leo wholeheartedly doubted that. He was hard to the point of pain. He couldn't remember ever being this aroused in his life, except maybe the last time he'd kissed her. And the time before that.

He rested his forehead against hers and tried to slow his heavy breathing. "I'm tired of fighting this. Aren't you?"

"You have no idea." He could hear the struggle in her voice, see it play out in the bottomless green of her eyes.

He cupped her face and dragged the pad of his thumb against the swell of her lower lip. "Ask me to kiss you. I've been waiting for you to ask me since the night we met. I want to hear you say it."

"Leo." His name was a plea on her lips, but instead of looking in his eyes, her gaze landed somewhere behind him.

He turned his head and took in the butcher block island, the clutter of bowls and measuring spoons on it, and the leather-bound book he'd spotted earlier.

He looked back at Juliet. "Do you care to tell me what's in that book?"

"It's my grandmother's recipe book. More than that, really. It's a journal of sorts." She reached for it and held it toward him.

He wasn't altogether certain he wanted to touch it. Something about it gave him the sense that lifting the cover would be akin to opening Pandora's box. "What does your grandmother's journal have to do with me? With us?"

"Nothing." The crack of the book's spine as she opened it was like a bullet leaving its chamber. "And everything."

He looked down, his eyes snagging on the word *Mezzanotte*. Between recipes that were undeniably familiar, he read of the affection between his grandmother and Juliet's, of their optimistic plans for their business venture. And as he turned the fragile pages, he read of his grandmother's odd behavior and Elenore Arabella's fears that she was pulling away.

He could see where this was going, and it was nowhere he cared to visit. He slammed the book closed. He'd seen enough.

He handed it back to her. "So?"

"That's it? That's your reaction?" She lifted an accusatory brow. "So?"

"That book has nothing to do with me." He gave her a gentle tap, right below the exquisite dip that rested between her collar bones. "Or you, for that matter."

He could feel her heart beating beneath his touch, wild and fast, like a caged bird. And he wanted nothing more than to set her free.

"You make things sound so simple." She set the book back down on the butcher block, but her gaze lingered on it. Just for a moment. No longer than it took for Leo to breathe in and out. But he still would have liked to bury the thing in the deepest pit he could find.

"Things *are* simple. I want to make love to you, and I

don't give a damn what anyone else has to say about it." His
words vibrated between them, leaving them both breathless.

He bent toward her, and she rose on her tiptoes to meet
him, sending a thrill surging through Leo's veins. Her lips,
flushed pink with desire, parted. But instead of taking those
lips with his, he pressed a tender kiss to her forehead. "Your
beautiful head is full of quarrels. I assure you mine is not,
bella. Neither is my heart."

He lifted her chin and forced her to meet his gaze. "We're
not our grandparents. You're Juliet. And I'm Leo. It's just the
two of us here. No one else."

She reached up and wound her arms around his neck, tan-
gling damp fingers in his hair. "Kiss me, Leo."

A smile welled up from the deepest part of his soul. "I
thought you'd never ask."

He kissed her as softly, as slowly as he could at first, lest
he lose control and take her right there on the butcher block
island. But she began to make that little kittenish noise he
loved so much, the tiniest sigh, just short of a whimper, and
before he knew it, he was angling his head over hers, his
tongue plunging in deep.

Her hands dropped to his chest, and she clutched at his
shirt, pulling him closer, closer, until he could feel the crash
of her heart, thudding against his. So fast, so hard, he couldn't
help but wonder if he'd frightened her.

"Juliet." He pulled back. Just a bit, but it was enough to
spot a telltale tremor in her hands. "You're trembling. I'm
not going to let anything hurt you. Not even me."

"It's not that." She shook her head. Her cheeks glowed
pinker than ever, her lips already bee-stung from his kisses.
"It's been a while. I'm guess I'm a little nervous."

"Don't be nervous." He cradled her hands in his and lifted

each one to his lips and covered it with a tender, reverent kiss. "How long, exactly?"

She leveled her gaze at him. "Years." *Years?* He willed his face not to register his shock. That boyfriend of hers, George, was an even bigger idiot than Leo had originally thought. Didn't he know a priceless treasure when he saw one?

Years. How was that even possible? She'd nearly been engaged to the man. He couldn't even fathom it, but it explained a few things. Namely, that haunting vulnerability she'd seemed to possess when he'd come across her in the vineyard that night. She'd been equal parts fragile beauty and seductive goddess, a rare, intriguing combination that he'd never fully understood.

Until now.

He would fix this. He would worship her body like it had never been worshipped before. Every neglected inch of it. He would do everything within his power to show her just how desirable she was. They had all night. He would fix this, and he would savor every second he spent doing so.

"I'll be gentle, baby." Being anything approaching gentle would take every ounce of self-control he could muster, seeing as he wanted to devour her. But he would manage. Somehow.

She took a step backward, away from him, and he felt that small loss of her down to his core.

"I want you, Leo." Her damp fingertips ran along the hem of her tank top, and she peeled it up and over her head. Next she unbuttoned her shorts and stepped out of them, so she was standing before him wearing nothing but some tiny wisps of red lace and an expression filled with raw hunger and need.

He'd dreamed of undressing her since the moment he first saw her and had wanted to unzip her out of that fluffy bal-

lerina dress. But watching her bare herself for him was infinitely sweeter.

Her green eyes glittered like emeralds as she watched him
take in the sight of her. She was without a doubt the most
beautiful thing Leo had ever laid eyes on. Creamy porcelain skin, graceful long limbs and soft womanly curves that
somehow begged for exploration.

He looked his fill. *The things I plan on doing to that body.*
Then he lifted his gaze back to hers. "Do you have any idea
how gorgeous you are?"

A quiet, satisfied smile was her answer.

"You said you'd be gentle?" Her voice was somewhere
between a whisper and a purr as she took his hands and
placed them over the swell of her breasts. So supple. So soft.
The room could have burned down around them, and Leo
wouldn't have been able to take his hands off her. "Don't.
Oh, please don't."

Juliet had waited for this entirely too long.

She didn't want careful. She didn't want gentle. She didn't
want any kind of restraint on Leo's part.

She only wanted him.

And he seemed all too happy to oblige. He lifted her clear
off the ground and set her on the edge of the kitchen island.
Her measuring spoons and metal mixing bowls went teeter-
ing toward the floor, but before they'd even crashed onto
the terra-cotta tile, Leo had peeled back the lace cups of her
bra, and his mouth was on her breast.

Oh, yes, this was undeniably what she'd been waiting for.
Since before she'd ever heard the name Leonardo Mezzanotte, she'd been waiting for this moment. And this man.

She'd never experienced this kind of passion before. It was

like a wildfire moving through her body, and she would have been powerless to stop it, even if she wanted to. Which she most definitely did not.

"Leo," she begged. "Please."

He kissed his way up her neck, and as he dispensed with her bra altogether he leaned down and whispered in her ear, his breath hot against her skin. "Baby, we're just getting started."

Dainty red straps slipped from her shoulders and fell to the floor. Somewhere in the tiny part of her brain that was still capable of coherent thought, she was aware of the fact that, save for her panties, she was naked. In the middle of her kitchen. And somehow Leo was still fully clothed.

His hands and mouth were everywhere. And every place he touched tingled until she didn't think she could stand the wait another minute. She needed to see him, all of him. She needed to feel his smooth, bare skin sliding against hers.

She tugged at his shirt, but her movements were anything but effective. Her limbs felt languid, as though warm honey flowed through her veins, and the fabric slipped right through her fingers. She groaned in protest.

"What is it, baby?" he asked, his voice every bit as rough and wild as she felt. "Is this what you want?" He slipped his fingers beneath the lacy edge of her panties.

Oh, yes. Yes. Exactly that.

She arched toward him, her spine taut as a violin string. He played her to perfection until every part of her hummed with pleasure, and she thought she might break into a million pieces.

"Leo," she whispered.

He kissed her on the mouth. Once, twice. Mercifully soft,

feathery kisses. Then he bit down gently on her lower lip, while his fingers still teased and tormented her.

She gasped and opened her eyes to find him watching her with sleepy blue eyes that held a most satisfied smile. "Yes?"

She made a weak effort to push him away. "Take off your clothes. Now."

He let out a laugh, then winced as he took his hands off her, as if it caused him physical pain. Juliet was almost sorry she'd made the demand. She ran her toe up and down the hard muscle of his thigh while she waited, as he unbuttoned his top button, ripped open the next few and finally yanked his shirt over his head.

Then she got her first glimpse of his exposed chest, and she was no longer sorry. He was finely muscled in a way his glorious forearms had only hinted at, with the kind of washboard abs she would have never expected to find on a man who made his living making chocolate.

"My turn," she said, reaching for him, letting her fingertips dance across the firm planes of his chest, down his flat stomach, to where a fine line of hair disappeared beneath the waistband of his jeans.

He leaned closer, giving her what she wanted, the chance to explore him the way he'd explored her. He groaned as she wrapped her arms around him, pressed her breasts against his skin and ran her fingers over the broad muscles of his back.

"Your turn?" he murmured, burying his hands and face in her hair.

"My turn to tell you how beautiful you are." She dropped a slow, purposeful openmouthed kiss to his shoulder. His skin was salty and sweet, like the finest candy she'd ever tasted. "Mmm. How is it that you taste like sea salt and caramel?"

"I've got chocolate in my blood, same as you." He tipped

her face toward his and kissed her again, his lips ravenous and seeking, quickly losing patience.

She could have gladly drowned in those kisses. They were sweeter than oxygen.

She dropped her hands, somehow steady at last, to Leo's fly, and he released another low, sultry groan. She managed to get him unbuttoned, but before she could get any farther, he gathered her in his arms and lifted her off the butcher block and into the safe nest of his arms.

"I think it's time we moved this to the bedroom. Don't you?" he said, enveloping her in his embrace.

So, this was really happening. After tonight, there'd be no turning back.

"Yes." She nodded and buried her head against his shoulder, sinking into him, feeling as light as a puff of cotton in his arms.

He took a few steps, then stopped. "Maybe you should tell me where it is."

The smile in his voice made her laugh. "It's the open door on the left at the end of the hall."

Once he'd stepped gingerly past the sleeping dogs, his footsteps quickened. When they reached her bedroom, he kicked the door closed behind them and tenderly laid her down on the bed.

There was a final breathless moment of stillness as he stood over her, devouring her with his gaze. She felt his eyes on her, the sensation every bit as real as if he'd touched her with those magic fingers, and chills broke out over her exposed skin. He leaned down to kiss her, his tongue gently parting her lips as he traced her goose bumps with a whisper touch of his fingertips over her breasts, down her belly, all the way to the silky edge of her panties. She sighed into his mouth as his touch grew more urgent, and she felt the scrape of lace and fingernails traveling down the length of her legs.

Completely bare before him, she rose up on her knees and helped him out of his jeans. His hands cupped her breasts, his breath coming faster and harder as he watched her undress him. Then he was instantly beside her on the bed, touching her, kissing her, anywhere and everywhere.

"I want you, Leo. Please," she whimpered, convinced she wouldn't last another minute without him inside her.

He lowered himself over her, and something fierce and electrifying pulsed between them.

Violent ends.

She told herself she couldn't get hurt. She was going into this with her eyes wide open. She knew exactly who Leo was. Tonight he was here, in her bed, but the day after tomorrow they'd be competing against one another in the Napa Valley Chocolate Fair. One of them would win, and the other would lose.

The future was written in the stars, and there was nothing either of them could do to change it. But she didn't want to think about the future right now.

For tonight she wasn't an Arabella. She was his. And she would give herself to him in every possible way.

His body covered hers completely. The weight of all those firm, lean muscles on top of her was nothing short of exquisite. A thrill of anticipation shot through her, and she moved her hands over his hips, around to his backside and pulled him even closer. They groaned in unison as his erection pressed hot and wanting against her center.

"Juliet, baby." He gazed down at her, his blue eyes darkened to midnight, and tenderly brushed the hair from her face. "Just you and me, remember. No one else."

"No one else," she whispered in return, reaching for him to guide him home.

Then he was entering her, pushing deep, swallowing her cries of pleasure with a scorching kiss.

He was everything. Everything she'd always wanted, and everything she'd never before had. It had been a very long time since she'd had this kind of attention from a man, but not once had it ever been anywhere close to this intense, this completely overwhelming. How could she have so foolishly thought she'd known what she was doing? She'd had no idea.

No more resisting. No more waiting. It was only the two of them, just like he'd said.

Her and Leo.

At last.

She opened her eyes to watch him move over her, inside her, wanting to remember everything about this night— how perfect he looked in the silver rays of moonlight from her open window, how fully and completely he filled her, so much so that it made her want to weep with relief...and the fire, the unstoppable fire moving through her until she thought it would consume her, body and soul.

And despite all her plans to guard her heart, to keep it safe, she felt it crack wide open in blissful surrender.

14

Juliet woke to the sounds of happy barking and someone bustling around in the kitchen. She sat up, reaching for Leo, but he wasn't there. The sheets were still warm, and she could make out the shape of his jeans pooled on the floor in the darkness, so he obviously wasn't trying to sneak off.

Not that she'd expected him to. Over the course of the past few hours, he'd made it more than clear that there was no place he'd rather be than in her bed. She couldn't stop the smile that sprang to her lips as she remembered the things he'd said, the things they'd done.

She was happy. Happier than she'd been in as long as she could remember.

Too happy.

She closed her eyes and fell back on the pillow, craving sleep. She wasn't ready for wakefulness, nor for the coming light of day when she'd have to think about the line they'd just crossed.

Curiosity got the better of her after only a few sleepless seconds. She climbed out of bed, threw on a T-shirt that just happened to be a certain dark shade of blue and headed for the kitchen to see what he was up to.

She found him tearing chicken into tiny pieces and hand-feeding it to a rapt Cocoa while Sugar scrambled to catch any crumbs that escaped the big dog's mouth. There was a small pot on the stove with a cloud of steam hanging over it. He'd been cooking, apparently. His hair was charmingly disheveled, and he hadn't bothered to throw on a stitch of clothing.

Yet here he was, cooking chicken for her recuperating dog.

She paused in the dim light of the living room, taking it all in. A candle that they hadn't bothered to blow out on the way to the bedroom flickered its last breath. The cool breeze blowing off the bay threatened to snuff it out completely and left her gauzy curtains fluttering like butterfly wings.

An unexpected lump formed in Juliet's throat. She swallowed it down. "Hey there."

Leo looked up, his hand pausing midair until Cocoa voiced her impatience, and he tossed her another bite. He smiled. "Hey there, yourself. Did I wake you? I'm sorry."

"Don't be. I wouldn't have wanted to miss this." Cocoa didn't even swivel her head at the sound of Juliet's voice. That was a first. Good grief, even her dog was falling for him. Which meant that now there were two of them destined for heartbreak. "It's not every day that a French-trained chef cooks for my dog in the middle of the night. Naked, I might add."

The dogs sniffed the air for a few seconds, then stretched out on the floor when Leo failed to produce another chicken breast from thin air.

He lifted a brow. "Do you have a problem with the naked part?"

She tried her best to maintain eye contact with him and failed. Miserably. "Absolutely not."

"Good." He rinsed his hands in the sink, giving her a rather spectacular view of his ass. "Hungry? I could whip something up for the humans in attendance."

The lump in her throat doubled in size. "Oddly enough, no. But, thanks. What are you doing up?"

"I couldn't sleep." Was it her imagination, or did his gaze dart to her grandmother's recipe book?

It sat on the kitchen island, dead in the middle of the room, as if it was the center of the universe and she and Leo were helplessly destined to spin circles around it.

She looked back up at Leo. "Everything okay?"

"Everything is more than okay." He stepped closer and tucked a wayward lock of hair behind her ear. "Everything is perfect. I just thought I'd clean things up a bit. We left a rather good-size mess."

She remembered the bowls clattering to the floor, the avalanche of falling measuring spoons, the buttons flying off Leo's shirt. And everything that had happened afterward.

Quite a mess indeed.

"Thank you for straightening up," she said.

"You're most welcome." He ran a hand through his hair, somehow making it look both more and less tousled.

Yum.

"Tell me something. All the photos of Italy…" He nodded toward the refrigerator. "Have you ever been?"

"No, I haven't. I've always wanted to go, though."

"You would love it. It suits you." It was the same thing he'd said about her favorite color. "I can see you there, drinking wine on the Spanish Steps, wandering through cobblestone streets with the Mediterranean breeze blowing through your hair."

It was crazy how much she liked the idea of him thinking of her in a radically different way than anyone had before. Not as an Arabella, but as her own person. Juliet. "So you've been?"

He nodded. "A few times. For the *Roma Festa del Cioccolato*. You've heard of it, right?"

The Rome Chocolate Festival. Of course she'd heard of it. She watched it on the Food Network every year. She'd even qualified to compete in it every year for the past five years. The winner of the Napa Valley Chocolate Fair automatically qualified for entry in the festival in Rome.

"Yes. Were you a competitor?" She couldn't remember seeing him on television, and she was fairly sure he would have made an impression. "It's always been a dream of mine to compete there."

George had never seen the point. He'd steadfastly refused to loosen Royal Gourmet's purse strings so that she could go, reasoning that competing in Rome would have little impact on her commercial success in Napa. But his opinion no longer mattered, did it?

"No, I was just there to watch. La Maison du Chocolat only sends their best of the best to actually participate."

And Leo wasn't their best of the best? She found that somewhat difficult to believe.

"Tell me more about Rome," she said wistfully, running her fingertips along one of her black-and-white refrigerator snapshots—a panoramic view of the Eternal City's many rooftops with the dome of St. Peter's Basilica rising from the background.

Leo settled in behind her, winding his arms around her

and pressing a tender kiss to her cheek. At the feel of all that warm bare skin wrapped around her, her body hummed with awareness. "You can hear the sound of church bells and street music wherever you go. The food is fantastic, the tomatoes so ripe and fresh you can eat them out of the palm of your hand as if they were apples. And there isn't a building in sight less than three hundred years old."

It sounded wonderful. And a world away from Napa Valley. "I've heard there's a building there called the Wedding Cake. Is that true?"

"Absolutely. Although that's just a nickname. The actual name is the Altare della Patria. It's a monument in the center of one of the busiest piazzas in the city. The Tomb of the Unknown Soldier is there. The building itself is really something. And it does, in fact, look like a wedding cake."

"And the Spanish Steps? Have you seen them, too?" She pointed at the photo of the famed stairway at the Piazza de Spagna with its wide staircase spilling over with violet-colored azaleas and happy-looking people.

"Mmm-hmm," he said absently, gathering her hair and moving it aside so he could kiss her neck. She could feel him growing hard again behind her as his lips slid over the rapid beat of her pulse. "You know, they say Rome is full of secrets. Perhaps you and I should go there since we seem to be living the secret life."

Rome was full of secrets. At the moment, so was Napa Valley. So was this very room.

She turned in his arms and swallowed, lest her heart leap right out of her throat. "Leo, what happens after tonight?"

He shook his head, equally as mystified as she felt, then tightened his hold on her, drawing her close. "I don't know, baby."

What else could he say? He wanted to win the chocolate fair every bit as much as she did. And it wasn't as if she was going to give up on the *chocolat chaud*. The French Laundry was hers, and she wanted it back. There was also the pesky detail that he was pretty much the spawn of the devil.

I don't know, baby.

He'd never lied to her before, and he wasn't lying now. But she couldn't help wishing he would. Just this once.

"Come back to bed?" she whispered into his shoulder, wanting him again, and wishing with all her might that she didn't.

Maybe things weren't as bad as they seemed. Maybe they could keep whatever this was going while they still tried to destroy one another out there in the real word.

Right. That sounds plausible.

She looked up and found him gazing down at her with a smile on his lips.

Eyes, look your last. Arms, take your last embrace.

"I have a better idea, but I'm afraid you're overdressed." He dropped his hands to her hips, pausing for a leisurely caress of her backside. Then he lifted her shirt up and over her head, his fingertips skimming along her rib cage, her breasts, leaving her sighing once again with desire.

"That sound. Never stop making that sound," he murmured against her parted lips.

Then he wove his fingers through hers and led her to the sofa where he pulled her onto his lap, and they made love again in the glow of the flickering candlelight.

Gentle, soft and sweet this time.

Just as he'd promised.

Leo was late.

He'd headed straight from Juliet's bed to the little Italian coffee shop where Uncle Joe had mandated that all members of the Mezzanotte clan meet for breakfast before Mezzanotte Chocolates opened its doors, mindful of the fact that his tardiness wouldn't go unnoticed.

Too bad. They were lucky he was showing up at all. He still marveled at the fact that he'd had the willpower to bid Juliet goodbye when she'd been warm, naked and tangled in bedsheets, her green eyes all sleepy and sultry. If that didn't prove his family devotion, nothing would.

He deserved a medal. Not the scowl that Uncle Joe greeted him with when he finally arrived. As usual, his phone was glued to his ear. Who on earth his uncle spoke with on an hourly basis was a mystery. Leo didn't particularly care at the moment, as it gave him a split-second of calm before the storm.

"Leo." Uncle Joe switched off his cell phone and frowned at his wristwatch. "You're eighteen minutes late."

Eighteen. Not bad. He should have stayed for another kiss or two.

"It looks that way, doesn't it?" He wasn't about to apologize. That was exactly the kind of precedent he didn't need to set. "Good morning, all."

It was indeed a good morning. Despite the toxic combination of his sleep deprivation and the ungodly hour, he could still appreciate the beauty of a spectacular Napa Valley sunrise. The pink sky had barely begun to turn molten, and the leaves of the surrounding grapevines shimmered like gold dust.

He pulled out a chair and sat down at the outdoor café table where the three other Mezzanottes had set up camp. Sugar leaped into his lap and craned her little neck toward Gina's cup of espresso.

Gina moved it out of harm's way and narrowed her gaze at Leo. "You're a mess. What happened to your shirt?"

Leo glanced at his shirt, untucked, wrinkled and missing a good portion its buttons. He shrugged. "I threw on the first thing I could find."

The fact that he'd found it on the floor of Juliet's kitchen wasn't a detail he cared to share.

But Marco had already managed to figure it out. He pinned Leo with a knowing look. "Did you?"

Attitude from his brother-in-law. Just what he needed.

Leo responded with a glare and a firm nod of his head. "Yes."

They weren't doing this. Not now. A good twenty-four hours remained on the ludicrous deadline Marco had given him. Leo presently had no intention of abiding by that deadline, but Marco didn't know that yet. They could deal with that later.

Things had changed.

Leo was still trying to wrap his mind around what had happened between him and Juliet the night before. Because whatever it was had been more than just sex. Much more.

When he'd felt Juliet shatter around him for the first time and he himself had all but come apart, something fundamental had shifted inside him. Given the circumstances, it was less than convenient.

He supposed he should have seen it coming. If his interest in Juliet had been casual, or merely carnal, he would have been able to walk away the instant things had gotten complicated. Like any sane person.

But he hadn't walked away. The crazier things had gotten, the more he'd dug in his heels. Now he was even helping her re-create his *chocolat chaud*. Things had moved beyond complicated. The moment he'd carried her to bed, they'd charged headfirst into forbidden territory. They needed a whole new word for the situation they were in.

Just minutes ago, she'd been burrowed against his side, her graceful long legs still tangled with his and one of her hands resting lightly on his chest as she slept. He'd had to stop himself from picking up her hand and kissing each one of those fingertips until she stirred back to life so he could take her again. And again.

He shifted in his chair. Sugar stood, turned a few circles and settled back in his lap. "Now, what's this meeting all about? I'm assuming we didn't gather here to discuss my choice of attire."

Uncle Joe looked at him, incredulous. "The chocolate fair, of course. It's tomorrow."

"I'm aware of that." Leo nodded, trying his best to concentrate on the conversation instead of the elegant curve of Juliet's bare shoulders, the sensation of her hair slipping between his fingers. So soft. Everything about her was soft. And sweet. Sweeter than his godforsaken *chocolat chaud*.

"We need to be ready." Uncle Joe drummed his fingers on the table, dragging Leo's attention reluctantly back to the matter at hand. "Are we?"

"Yes. Stop worrying. The macarons are all perfect. And after we finish up here, I'm heading over to the shop to construct the towers." He'd sketched out a few ideas and settled on the one that made the most powerful statement. "I'm thinking of doing a cluster with one large tower in the middle, flanked by a smaller one on either side. Striking, yet simple and elegant at the same time."

"It's of the utmost importance that we win, Leo." Uncle

Joe's hands were shaking. Maybe he needed to lay off the espresso.

"I don't intend to lose, if that's what you're implying." Leo signaled for a server. This time of day, Uncle Joe's intensity was easier to take with a heaping dose of caffeine.

"I want you to promise me that we're going to win." His uncle polished off what was left in his cup. "There's a lot at stake here. More than you know."

Leo grimaced at the irony of the statement. He knew plenty. Uncle Joe was the one in the dark. Leo had done something that was an arguably worse offense than sleeping with Juliet.

It had happened in the middle of the night when he'd gotten up to clean the kitchen and he'd found Elenore Arabella's journal facedown in a pile of sugar on the kitchen floor.

He'd dusted it off and flipped through a few pages, if anything just to prove he wasn't intimidated by it. He'd meant what he said to Juliet—the contents of her grandmother's journal had nothing to do with either of them.

But as he'd read page after page of chocolate recipes framed by faded, pencil-scrawled words of heartbreak, he'd found himself caught up in the story. And even though he'd been fully aware that he was reading only one side of the age-old feud, he'd actually begun to feel a pang of sympathy for Elenore Arabella.

She'd been devastated when his grandmother had sold her recipes behind her back. And stunned, even though there'd been so many hints along the way. Stolen tears, outbursts of temper. There had to be an explanation.

I don't know which pain cuts deeper—the loss of these recipes I've been working on for years, or my closest friend. She was like una sorella *to me.*

The following page had been eerily blank. Nothing.

He'd stared at that blank sheet for a long, quiet moment, and for the first time, the seriousness of the feud between the Arabellas and the Mezzanottes had become real to him. They were stuck right there on that blank page. All of them. His uncle Joe, Gina, Marco, Juliet's parents, her brother, Alegra.

And as much as he'd hated to admit it, even he and Juliet.

He'd inhaled a steadying breath and told himself not to seriously consider the idea that had begun tumbling through his head. It wasn't possible to rewrite history. And yet his fingers had itched for a pen.

"Can I help you?" The server approached the table, and Sugar wiggled with excitement in Leo's lap.

"Yes, we'll have another round of *antoccinos,* please. And one for him, as well," Uncle Joe said, pointing at Leo.

The server nodded. "Great. They'll be right out."

"Excuse me." Leo smiled at her. "I'm sorry. I'd rather have a café au lait, please."

"Nonsense. You're not French. You're Italian." Uncle Joe shook his head.

Not this again. "I'd prefer café au lait."

His uncle waved a hand at him. "Don't be difficult. Get the *antoccino.* We're all having it. It's their specialty."

The server lingered in the periphery, looking distinctly uncomfortable.

Leo gave her an apologetic glance. "A café au lait, please."

"You've never had the *antoccino* here. How do you know you wouldn't like it better?" Uncle Joe pressed on. Good God, did the man have any idea how to mind his own business?

Leo opened his mouth to respond, but before he could say a word, Marco jumped into the fray.

"Yeah, Leo. Why must you stick with the café au lait when there are other *more appropriate* coffees out there? Coffees more suited to your particular background." He lifted a sardonic brow.

"He has a point." Uncle Joe nodded.

Leo ignored his uncle, his sights now set firmly on his brother-in-law. "I don't need to taste the other coffees to know that I prefer the café au lait."

An edge crept into Marco's voice. "That's rather short-sighted, don't you think? You can't possibly know what you're missing."

Leo's fists involuntarily clenched, and Sugar quivered with worry in his lap. "Why taste the *antoccino* when I know what I want? Café au lait is creamy and decadent. Absolutely sublime."

Gina blinked and stared down into her empty cup. "Now you're making me want one."

"You don't. Trust me," Marco ground out.

Leo met his gaze full-on. "She may not, but I most definitely do. I want the café au lait. I crave the café au lait. And I'm going to have the café au lait."

"So you're just going to keep drinking café au lait until the day you die, even though it's bad for you? Even though it's much like drinking poison?" Marco gave his eyes an exaggerated roll.

The server cleared her throat. "Actually, there's nothing terribly unhealthy about café au lait. Although if you're watching your cholesterol, we can make it with skim milk, or even soy, instead of whole."

"My cholesterol is fine," Leo said through gritted teeth. "And I never said I was making a permanent commitment to the café au lait. That's not at all what I meant. But my coffee is my business and no one else's."

Marco leaned across the table, his nostrils flaring. "Not necessarily. Not when a single sip of café au lait could destroy all of us."

Gina gave her husband a swat. "Marco, what in the world has gotten into you? Just let Leo order his coffee so we can get on with things. I really don't think a silly cup of coffee is going to destroy anyone."

"I wouldn't be too sure about that." Marco sat back in his chair and crossed his arms.

"So...um." The server's gaze swiveled back and forth between Leo and Marco. Poor girl. Leo would make sure she got a good tip. "What will it be?"

He wasn't backing down. "Café au lait, please. And another round of *antoccinos* for everyone else."

"Yes, sir. Coming right up." The server fled before anyone could object.

In the wake of her absence, Uncle Joe was the first to speak. "I'm not entirely sure what just transpired, but can we please move on and get back to business? Even I no longer care what Leo drinks."

Leo sat back in his chair, a smug smile playing on his lips. But his expression was solely for Marco's benefit. He might have won the tiny, inconsequential coffee battle, but he had a long, long way to go before he claimed victory in the chocolate war.

15

The Napa Valley Chocolate Fair rotated every year from one winery to the next, this time landing on the grounds of the Calantha Vineyard in the heart of Sonoma. Family-owned, it was one of the smaller wineries in the area but had always been one of Juliet's favorites.

Originally from San Francisco, the family behind Calantha had made their fortune in the city's booming flower district before venturing into the business of winemaking. They'd brought their floral expertise, as well as an abundance of blossoms, with them to the rolling hills of the valley. The winery was bordered on all sides by a dazzling display of flowers— Lily of the Nile, bougainvillea, camellias and roses of every color imaginable, lined row upon row like crayons in a box.

A grand archway of Blue Moon wisteria marked the entrance to the grounds. Strung between the posts of the pergola was a banner announcing the event, along with directions to proceed to the winery's barrel room for the judging of the entries.

Juliet's mother slowed to a stop. "The barrel room? Really?

TERI WILSON

Why would they hold the festival in the barrel room when they have such lovely grounds?"

Juliet didn't know, and after the disastrous outdoor adventure the weekend before, she didn't much care. Especially since the Arabella crew had shown up in full force. Her mother, father, Alegra and even Nico had accompanied her, leaving the shop in the hands of a part-time girl they typically only relied on under desperate circumstances.

Okay, so maybe this was one of those circumstances. Juliet was expected to redeem herself today. Not only herself but the entire family business. And now she had to do it in front of an audience of Arabellas while competing against the man she was sleeping with.

Slept with. Past tense.

Maybe.

She hadn't actually seen or spoken to Leo since he'd left her condo yesterday morning, but then again, she hadn't really expected to. Today was game day, after all. She shouldn't even be thinking about Leo in that sense right now. And she wasn't.

Right.

She cleared her throat, forcing persistent memories of the movement of sinewy muscles, strong shoulders and lean, perfect hips from the forefront of her mind. "I'm sure we'll be fine in the barrel room. Actually, now that I think about it, that atmosphere suits my entry."

"Oh, you're right." Alegra grinned and tightened her grip on the box in her hands.

Alegra, Juliet and Nico held one small box each. And that was it, the sum total of things they'd brought. She'd opted for simple this year. It was a gamble, but she was pretty certain it was one that would pay off, especially now that she knew her entry would be displayed in the winery's barrel room.

"I don't know. I still wish you would have gone with something more, oh, I don't know...spectacular." Juliet's mother gnawed nervously on her bottom lip.

"Trust me. I've got this." Juliet forced a smile, hoping she sounded at least a bit more self-assured than she felt.

"I certainly hope so," her mother muttered, doubt clouding every syllable.

Gee. Thanks for the vote of confidence, Mom.

They followed a curved pathway spilling over with camellias in alternating patterns of soft pink and creamy ivory, leading behind the glass-walled atrium that served as the tasting room, toward the barrel room at the back of the property. In the midst of the lush surroundings, the huge rectangular building with a simple metal roof looked rather out of place. Almost like a barn.

Then they stepped inside.

"Oh, wow. This is gorgeous." Alegra slowed to a stop, pausing to take in the atmosphere. "Look at all the candles."

Juliet was looking. How could she not? The entire barrel room had been transformed into a dreamy, candlelit wonderland. An oversize banquet-style table covered in an elegant ivory cloth stretched from one end of the room to the other. Tall candelabra dripping with strands of shimmering crystals and crowned with white hydrangeas separated the table into sections for the various competitors. The ceiling was draped with broad satin ribbons, waving slightly in the cool Napa breeze. The wine barrels had been moved against the walls, stacked floor to ceiling on their sides, each one balancing a white pillar candle on its rim. Brightly lit torches stood in each corner of the room, casting romantic shadows over the banquet table.

And at the center of everything stood Leo, dressed in his

impeccable chef's whites, his beautiful face awash in the soft glow of candlelight. He sent her a stealthy wink, so quickly that she almost thought she'd imagined it, until the corner of his mouth lifted in a subtle telltale smile.

Juliet's feet stuck to the floor.

She'd told herself she could do this. She could stand face-to-face with Leo, compete against him surrounded by their warring families and act as if nothing had happened between them. But she hadn't banked on the candlelight. And all the billowy satin. And the heady fragrance of hydrangea blossoms, fine wine and oak barrels assaulting her on every side.

And she'd completely forgotten he would be dressed like God's gift to the Food Network. Honestly. Did he have to look so…scrumptious?

"Juliet, what are you doing just standing there?" Her mother waved an angry hand at her, beckoning her to the competitors' table.

Mom seemed wound even more tightly than usual today. Goody.

Juliet took a deep breath and forced her feet to move in the proper direction. Which apparently was straight toward Leo, since it appeared that the space reserved for the Arabella Chocolate Boutique was situated right next to Mezzanotte Chocolates. Of all the luck.

"Where do you want me to put these?" Nico nodded toward the box of wineglasses in his arms.

"Just set them right here on the table." Juliet aimed her gaze at the empty spot in front of her. Then at Nico. Then at the red rim of a wine barrel.

Anywhere but at Leo or the display he was busy assembling.

Macarons. He'd made macarons, those woefully delicate,

temperamental confections that no one would dare try to make for a competition in the damp, humid climate of Napa Valley. And of course, they looked nothing short of perfect.

Not only that, but he'd arranged them in three huge cones. The one in the center was very tall, even taller than the fancy candelabra that towered over everyone. Two smaller cones were lined up alongside in perfect symmetry. The overall effect was gorgeous, like the shapely geometric beauty of the pyramids in Giza, Egypt.

A quick jolt of doubt coursed through her. Or was it desire? She glanced at Leo. His mouth curled at the edges. She could feel him watching her even though he appeared to be focused entirely on his fancy-schmancy macarons.

Juliet closed her eyes for a moment and concentrated on keeping her breathing even. It wasn't just the macarons, even though they were undeniably impressive. It was him.

Why was having him here, having him near, so terribly hard?

She opened her eyes.

Alegra was watching her with concern. She slid her gaze toward Leo, then back at Juliet. Her eyes widened just enough for Juliet to know she'd figured out that something significant had happened in recent hours.

"Are you okay?" she asked under her breath.

"I'm great." Juliet gave her a tight smile. "Don't I look great?"

"Of course you do." Alegra nodded, her expression filled with a tad too much sincerity. "You look positively ravished. Oops. I mean *ravishing*. Slip of the tongue."

The air stuck in Juliet's throat, and she coughed. Several times.

"Everything all right, Miss Arabella?" Leo asked, feigning

detachment. His blue eyes danced with devilish amusement. Surely she wasn't the only one who could see it.

"Don't talk to her," Juliet's mother barked. "My daughter is none of your concern."

Leo's jaw hardened, and he grew instantly still. Eerily so. Like a lion freezing in place in the final moments before pouncing on its prey and going for the jugular. Her mother being the prey in question.

Juliet couldn't decide if it was the most awkward moment she'd ever experienced, or the sexiest.

"Mom, he was only being polite," she said, stunned that she managed to sound anywhere close to normal when she actually felt like jumping out of her skin.

If the elephant in the room had been any bigger, it would have swallowed them all whole.

Her father pressed a calming hand to her mother's shoulder. "Now isn't the time, dear. Let Juliet prepare for the competition."

Her mom aimed one last death glare at Leo. He stared back, his gaze unwavering, until she finally backed down. That was a first.

"I suppose you're right. Do you need any help, Juliet?" she asked, crossing her arms, her elbow hovering approximately half an inch away from Leo's.

This was just too surreal. "Mom, I'm fine. Take a seat. Please. I've got this. Remember?"

Leo's shoulders shook the tiniest bit.

Was he laughing in the face of her confidence? She hoped so. She really did. She much preferred the idea of being angry to this…this…restlessness she felt being around him. It was altogether unsettling.

"Okay, then. We'll go find our seats. Dom, come on." Juliet's mom scowled one last time at Leo and headed toward the spectator area with Dad trailing on her heels like an obedient puppy. Nico and Alegra filed in line behind them, casting their own glares in Leo's direction as they went. Although Alegra may have sneaked a smile at him. Just a little one.

And of course, when her family reached the rows of white chairs marked for spectators, they all just happened to choose seats immediately behind Joe Mezzanotte, Leo's sister, Gina, and her husband, Marco. Joe and Gina swiveled in their seats, no doubt to make faces at the row of Arabellas behind them. Or something equally mature. Marco remained facing straight ahead, his gaze fixed steadfastly on Juliet. He looked as though he'd just plucked a rotten grape off the vine and eaten it.

What's his problem?

Let the drama begin.

Leo was running out of things to do at the competitors' table. He'd already moved each of the smaller macaron trees an inch to the left, then an inch to the right and then back again. It was ludicrous. He felt like a seventh grade kid standing beside his schoolgirl crush setting up a project at the science fair.

He couldn't look at her. Not again. Not so soon. Her mother had already just about clawed his eyes out because he'd spoken to her. And Marco was watching him and Juliet like a hawk. Gina, in turn, was watching Marco in a similar manner. Probably because he was acting like such a nutcase. Leo was beginning to wonder if his brother-in-law was morphing into a younger version of his uncle Joe. And wouldn't that be a horrid turn of events? One of him in the family was quite enough.

If he and Juliet could get through this chocolate fair without everything blowing up in their faces, it would be a miracle.

He sneaked a glance at her before he could stop himself. From the looks of things, she'd just about finished getting her entry set up. It consisted of six wineglasses—two white, two red, plus two champagne flutes. They were lined up in an evenly spaced row, as if being presented as a tasting group, better known as a *wine flight* in Napa Valley. Each glass was filled to overflowing with its own particular flavor of truffle. He was guessing the pale orange confections piled in the first champagne flute were some sort of peach Bellini-white chocolate combination. Other than that, he couldn't begin to guess what she'd dreamed up.

She'd gotten lucky with regard to the surroundings. A chocolate wine flight would have been nice outside on the grounds with the vineyard and the tasting room in view. Here in the barrel room, it was genius. Clever, creative and perfectly suited to the occasion.

She could win.

He wasn't sure whether to be impressed or threatened. He settled on a somewhat schizophrenic blend of the two. Would he be impressed if she won? Of course. Would he be happy about losing? Absolutely not.

Although the outcome was hardly a foregone conclusion either way. The majority of the judge's scores would come from the tasting round. He had the utmost confidence in his macarons, and he hadn't a clue what Juliet's chocolates tasted like. But he'd tasted her attempts at *chocolat chaud*. She knew her stuff.

From the looks of things, Juliet's chocolate wine flight and his macarons were the only serious contenders. The other dozen or so entries looked amateurish compared to the painstaking details of Juliet's truffles. She'd decorated each one with white or dark chocolate decorative swirls, bows and crisscross patterns. For the life of him, he couldn't figure out when she'd had time to do all that while at the same time cranking out gallons of experimental hot chocolate.

He nudged his center macaron tree forward less than a centimeter. Then he did the same with the two smaller trees.

Finally, he blew out a strained breath. He'd had about enough of this nonsense.

He turned toward Juliet and closed the small space between them. What would her mother, Uncle Joe or Marco possibly do if he and Juliet had a simple, innocent conversation? Leap out of their chairs, teeth bared, claws extended, ready to rip the two of them apart?

Possibly.

So he studiously avoided looking anywhere but at Juliet as he stood at her side. She, on the other hand, acted as though she was wholly unaware of his presence, busying herself with doing nothing. Polishing a glass. Twirling the slender stem of a champagne flute between her fingertips.

How he itched to feel those fingertips dance across his skin again. Desire welled up inside. He all but burned with it.

She did, too. He could see her pulse booming at the base of her throat, the flush of color in her softly parted lips. She burned just as brightly as he did. As brightly as the torches overhead.

"Good morning," he said as softly as he could.

Her hands trembled. A truffle went rolling from one of her wineglasses.

He picked it up and returned it to her, pausing to caress the palm of her hand with an understated swipe of his thumb.

She shied away. Oh, how he hated that. It was all he could do not to grab her slender wrist and reel her back in.

"What are you doing?" she asked through lightly clenched teeth.

"I'm talking to you. Surely there's no law against that." He concentrated very hard to keep his expression neutral. "Would it really be out of the ordinary for us to exchange pleasantries?"

She looked at him. Finally. "You know it would."

"Don't pay any attention to them." He gave a slight nod in the direction of their families. "I'm not."

It was almost the truth.

"That's not going to work, Leo. It's not just you and me this time. It's everyone. My whole family is here. And yours." Her gaze flitted to the barrel room's big double doors, and she stiffened. "And apparently, so is your new business associate."

"What?" He took his eyes off her long enough to see George Alcott III saunter in and shake hands with Uncle Joe.

He took the seat beside Uncle Joe as if the two of them were long-lost friends. Then he removed a large manila envelope from his slim leather briefcase and offered it to Uncle Joe.

The contract between Mezzanotte Chocolates and Royal Gourmet Distributors. Leo didn't need x-ray vision to know that's what was inside. His gut tightened. He'd known he couldn't put this moment off forever, but he hadn't anticipated having to deal with it here in the middle of the chocolate fair.

"Look, about that proposed business arrangement…" he began.

"Yes?" The expression on Juliet's face was half wary, half hopeful.

"I…"

Before he could utter another syllable, someone rapped on a wineglass with a piece of cutlery and the room grew quiet.

"Ladies and gentlemen! Welcome to the Twenty-Sixth Annual Napa Valley Chocolate Fair." The announcer waved a sweeping arm toward the banquet table. "Today's contestants are competing for the title of Napa Valley Chocolate Fair Grand Champion, and they represent the very best culinary talent that the bay area and accompanying wine country have to offer."

Leo took another look around at the other competitors. All appeared to be professional chefs. But unlike him and Juliet, none were specialty artisan chocolatiers. Mezzanotte Chocolates and Arabella Chocolate Boutique were the only such shops in the area. This competition was theirs to lose.

Well, one of theirs.

The announcer continued. "I'd like the esteemed judges to step forward, please."

Even after the judges were introduced, Leo still had no idea who they were. To say he was having trouble focusing was an understatement. The envelope in George's lap and the accompanying battle he was sure to have with Uncle Joe over its contents…Marco and the daggers he was staring at Juliet… all those angry Arabella faces watching his every move. He was being bombarded on all sides. A simmering discomfort started low at the back of his head as the judges moved from one competitor to the next, examining the entries.

When they reached him, he explained the flavors of each macaron and presented them with a tasting plate.

"Very nice." One of the judges—Leo really should have paid attention to who these people were—smiled and nodded.

The other two looked equally pleased, so he figured he was in excellent standing. Next up was Juliet.

Leo stood back, crossed his arms and pasted on an expression of unwavering confidence, all the while straining to hear her describe her creations.

"Good morning, Ms. Baker, Mr. Collins and Mr. Weatherton," she said, her voice smooth and professional.

Leo suppressed a smile of approval. Addressing the judges by name. Nice move.

"In keeping with the spirit of the wine country, today I offer you a chocolate wine flight, showcasing two each of red, white and sparkling wine varieties."

The judges looked as though they were hanging on her every word. Leo couldn't really blame them.

She picked up one of the red wine balloon glasses. "Here we have a heart-shaped pinot noir truffle with a sweet cream cocoa center that's been injected with a shot of raspberry cordial."

Red wine and cordial. That was a lot of liquor in one little nibble. Leo wished he could toss back an entire handful. It might make dealing with their families a bit more palatable.

The judges all took a bite. Then one by one, each of them polished off their remaining pieces of chocolate. This was atypical. Leo hadn't noticed them eating entire samples on any of their other stops. Not even his.

"The second red wine inspired offering on our flight is a chocolate red wine cupcake truffle, with a merlot cake batter center covered in a milk chocolate shell that's been rolled in cupcake crumbs. And for our first white wine chocolate, we have a classic white wine spritzer truffle with a delicate center of white chocolate ganache blended with pinot grigio and lemon-flavored Italian soda." She briefly allowed her gaze to wander in his direction.

Italian soda. He grinned and thought of all the photos of Rome in her condo.

"Next is a sweet Riesling gingerbread truffle, which is dark chocolate on the outside with an inside of spicy gingerbread milk chocolate ganache and a dash of sweet Riesling infused throughout."

Leo had to stop his eyebrows from creeping up his forehead. These flavor combinations were quite inspired. Red wine, chocolate and cake batter? Sweet Riesling with gingerbread? He wasn't sure he would have thought of either of those.

She finished by introducing her champagne duo, which she christened the Bellini—a peach puree truffle blended with a ganache of white chocolate and extra-dry Prosecco— and the Rossini—a decadent sounding confection of crushed strawberries with the seeds removed, blended with heavy cream, milk chocolate and a sparkling pink rosé.

"Very creative, Miss Arabella," the more portly of the two male judges said. Mr. Weatherton. Or was it Mr. Collins?

Damn. He'd never suffered from this kind of lack of concentration before. Whoever the man was, he'd eaten a full meal's worth of Juliet's truffles, as had the other judges.

"Thank you." Juliet smiled, and it seemed as if her entire being released a relieved exhale.

She was nervous. She really shouldn't have been.

The judges moved on to the next entrant, and she folded her hands in front of her just beneath the edge of the banquet table.

Thanks to the close quarters, Leo only had to shift a fraction to his left to be within reaching distance of her. Slowly, discreetly, he uncrossed his arms and dropped his hands to his sides. Then he reached under the table and took one of her hands in his.

He gave it a gentle squeeze and whispered under his breath, "Nice job. Good luck."

The secret smile that came to her lips was enough to cause a surge of victory to swell within him. For a fleeting moment, he felt as though he'd won a most precious prize.

No matter the outcome.

16

The warmth of Leo's hand calmed Juliet, creating a perfect moment of surreptitious stillness amid the pressure of the chocolate fair. The penetrating gazes of her family members and the scoffs of the Mezzanottes seemed to fade into the background. She wondered at the power of his touch to change everything in an instant. Then she wondered what it said about her that she seemed unable to let go of his hand.

"Thank you, ladies and gentlemen, for attending the Twenty-Sixth Annual Napa Valley Chocolate Fair. As you know, this event is part of the World Cup of Artisan Chocolate Competitions. As such, the winner qualifies for the prestigious *Roma Festa del Cioccolato,* to be held next month in Rome, Italy." The announcer paused while the audience applauded.

Juliet couldn't help but look at George sitting there in the front row alongside the Mezzanottes. George, who had failed to see the point of her traveling to Italy for the chocolate competition when she'd qualified last year and had refused to allow Royal Gourmet to foot the bill for her trip.

And she decided right then and there that she was going

this time. She'd pay for it all on her own if she had to. She'd put it on her credit cards if need be. She was going to Rome.

If she won.

"The contest this year was more competitive than ever before. We congratulate all the entrants on their imaginative use of chocolate and impressive culinary skills." The announcer accepted a sealed envelope from Mr. Weatherton, the head judge.

Juliet's stomach took a tumble. Leo squeezed her hand again, and she held on for dear life. Why did it feel as though they were in this together when they so clearly weren't?

The sound of the envelope's seal being broken echoed through the barrel room. Everyone's attention was focused on that small white square.

The announcer took a look inside, his face a perfect mask of calm. He cleared his throat.

Good grief, would he just get on with it?

"The contest results are rather surprising this year," he said. The quiet grew so tense that it was oppressive.

Juliet's senses became unnaturally heightened. Every inhale sounded like a tidal wave, her heartbeat a sonic boom. The perfume of the hydrangeas suddenly seemed too heady, too sweet. Her insides twisted into a tight knot. The room swirled around her in slow motion.

She let go of Leo's hand. The slide of his fingers slipping through hers seemed to last both a lifetime and an instant.

The contest results are rather surprising this year.

That meant she'd lost. What else could it mean? She'd won every year for the past five straight years. Winning again wouldn't be a surprise.

She'd lost.

Surprise!

Her eyes drifted closed. She couldn't bear to look at her family. It was over. They weren't going to bounce back from a defeat like this. She'd turned George down, gotten them dropped by Royal Gourmet, botched the balloon fest last weekend and lost the Napa Valley Chocolate Fair title.

Oh, and she'd managed to poison her dog and sleep with the enemy in the process.

How had her life spiraled so out of control?

This is what you wanted, remember? To be free of control.

She took a deep breath and opened her eyes.

The announcer was smiling as wide as a circus clown. "Ladies and gentleman, I'm afraid the contest isn't quite over. For the first time in the history of the Napa Valley Chocolate Fair, we have a tie."

She swayed on her feet. "What?"

"It's a tie?" Leo said beside her, his voice carrying a trace of bewilderment.

"The judges have awarded Juliet Arabella and Leonardo Mezzanotte identical scores."

Juliet's mother and Leo's uncle rose from their chairs at the exact same time, like a well-synchronized team. Scary.

"What?" Juliet's mom cried.

"A tie? That's absurd." Joe Mezzanotte's face was redder than Juliet had ever seen it before.

"Uncle Joe, sit down. Immediately. Or I will walk right out of here." Leo stood a little straighter, as if indicating he would indeed make good on his threat.

His uncle blanched and then lowered himself back into his chair.

"Mom," Juliet pleaded. "Please."

Likewise, her mother sat.

"Very well, then." The announcer paused, possibly to

make sure no one else was going to leap up and make a spectacle of themselves. Probably a good move, since there were still a half-dozen Arabellas and Mezzanottes who hadn't yet said their piece. And George. "In order to determine a winner, we will move on to another phase in the competition. Miss Arabella and Mr. Mezzanotte, please remain where you are. The other competitors are excused."

As the other chefs backed away from the banquet table and filed out, Leo leaned a fraction closer. The amused quirk in his lips caused pleasure to pool deep in her belly. "A tie. How's this for a turn of events?"

Staring into his startlingly blue eyes, she blew out a breath. *Focus.* "It's not a loss, so I'll take it."

"Still plan on taking me down in the next round?" His gaze dropped to her cleavage. Right on cue, she grew breathless.

Her body remembered him. Her skin, her pores, the little hairs on the back of her neck. And she leaned toward him, succumbing to his pull without even realizing it. "Absolutely."

He laughed under his breath and lifted his eyes back to her face. There was something different about the way he looked at her now, since the night they'd shared. A look filled with possession and secrets.

Juliet liked it. She liked it very much. Despite herself, she smiled back at him. Right there, with the whole room watching. "I don't know why you're laughing. I'm dead serious."

He brushed his hand against hers. Just the slightest touch. He had to stop touching her. She opened her mouth to tell him as much, but the words refused to come.

"I know," he whispered. "I'd be disappointed if you weren't."

A tie.

Leo hadn't seen that one coming. Not at all.

He'd thought he'd won. Juliet had thought he'd won, too, if the ashen hue she'd taken on when the announcer expressed his surprise at the results had been any indication. But he hadn't won. And Juliet was looking far less stricken now. Her color had come back. There was a rosy hue to her cheeks that made him think of things that weren't remotely connected to chocolate.

He dragged his eyes away from her. Time to regroup. Refocus. He still had every intention of winning. He needed to win. More so now than before. And apparently that was going to be a more complicated task than he'd originally thought.

A tie.

He looked at his macaron trees. All that time. All that effort. Now what?

"Henceforth, the competition will move to a tie-breaker phase." The crowd, which had begun to buzz in earnest after the announcement of the identical scores, settled down. No doubt everyone wanted to know what was involved in breaking the tie. Leo certainly did. In all his years in chocolate, he'd never witnessed this type of situation. "The tie will be broken and the winner determined with a taste challenge."

Beside him, Juliet grinned as if she'd just won the lottery.

In a way, she had. In a taste challenge the participants were given a finished creation and expected to duplicate it purely by instinct. The only tools at their disposal were the variety of ingredients presented and the judgment of their respective palates.

Which just so happened to be what Juliet had been doing for days on end with respect to his *chocolat chaud*.

He shook his head. Marvelous.

One of the judges took over the microphone. "Hello, everyone. My name Dan Weatherton, and I'm happy to present our two finalists with the tie-breaking taste challenge."

The other two judges wheeled a cart toward Leo and Juliet. It was piled high with every fruit, dairy product and variety of chocolate imaginable. And at the very front sat a platter of truffles. The mystery item, he presumed.

He glanced at Juliet. She looked at him, at the truffles and then back at him.

"You are *so* going down," she mouthed.

God, those lips.

A wave of arousal shot through him. Why he was in any way turned on by her dogged determination to bring him to his knees in defeat was a mystery he'd given up trying to figure out. Whatever the reason, he found it undeniably hot.

He averted his gaze and murmured, "Not if I can help it."

"The contestants will have five minutes to taste the challenge item and peruse the selection of ingredients." Weatherton eyeballed the two of them. "Then they'll move to the vineyard kitchen, where they will have a total of ninety minutes to duplicate the item that's been presented."

Ninety minutes.

That wasn't enough time to make a proper truffle even under normal circumstances. Truffles needed a good two hours in the refrigerator to cool. And that didn't even include the preparation time. He'd have to work at warp speed, then put them in the freezer and pray that they hardened to a respectable consistency.

And of course, that was after he figured out what the hell he was even making.

"Good luck, Leo!" his sister called out.

"He doesn't need luck. Leo will win. Mark my words," Uncle Joe said in a voice far louder than necessary.

Unsurprisingly, Juliet's mother felt prompted to join in the fray. "You may as well go home. Your nephew doesn't have a chance."

"Here we go." Juliet aimed her eyes at the floor, as if waiting for it to open up and swallow her whole.

They were like children. Worse than children. He'd seen better behaved two-year-olds.

"If the crowd will settle down, the five-minute time period will begin for the competitors to taste the challenge item." Weatherton aimed a pointed glare at the Mezzanotte-Arabella jeering section. "Ready, set, begin."

Leo and Juliet approached the cart and reached for the truffles at the same time, their fingertips colliding.

He took a step back. "Ladies first, Miss Arabella."

"Thank you, Mr. Mezzanotte," she said primly.

Juliet bit right into hers, but Leo took a few minutes to examine his first. He turned it this way and that, inspecting the outer shell for clues. A ribbon of white chocolate ran across the top, but the rest of the shell was obviously a dark chocolate blend. Exactly how dark remained to be seen.

He took a whiff. It had a far sweeter aroma than he expected, given the dark shell. He went ahead and took a bite.

It exploded on his tongue in an intense mixture of sweetness, creaminess and some sort of earthy flavor he couldn't immediately identify. He frowned and popped the rest in his mouth.

Beside him, Juliet was humming happily and already choosing a few of the offered ingredients. And she'd only eaten one of the truffles. Other than the obvious—white chocolate, dark chocolate and cream—Leo wasn't at all sure what to select. Some sort of fruit. Definitely. Berries, most likely.

His head began to throb, most of the pain concentrated in the area behind his left eye socket. Great. Just what he needed. Another headache.

He ate a second chocolate, then a third and tried not to take notice of which ingredients Juliet was gathering and piling into one of the small wire baskets they'd been given for such purpose. He didn't want his instincts to be in any way influenced by hers. But he couldn't help noticing that she still hadn't taken any of the fruits on offer.

Big mistake.

He definitely tasted berries. He grabbed a pint of straw-berries and added them to his basket. Then he had to squeeze his eyes shut for a moment because the pain behind his left eye had grown markedly more intense. Like someone was inside his head stabbing him with an ice pick.

"Are you okay, Leo?" Juliet's voice came to him, and he realized she must truly be concerned about him if she was calling him Leo in front of the whole world.

But it was just a little headache. Nothing to worry about.

He opened his eyes. Spots of bright light floated around Juliet's lovely face. "I'm fine, Miss Arabella. Just fine. And quite ready to beat the pants off of you."

Her cheeks colored—at his wording, he presumed. "We'll see about that, won't we?"

Before Juliet began to heat the heavy cream for her ganache, she dropped four tea bags in a small saucepan of water and placed it on the stove to boil. That sweet taste that had al-most tricked her into selecting berries as an ingredient was, in fact, fruit tea. She was sure of it.

She'd made fruit tea cupcakes once after seeing them on
Cupcake Wars, and the flavor had been nearly the same—
intensely rich and fruity, but absent any denseness that would
have resulted from using the actual fruit. And there was that
undefined hint of herbs from the tea, very slight but nonetheless present. Only the barest suggestion of a vineyard, or
perhaps a mossy forest floor.

Her plan was to let the tea bags steep in about a half cup
of water and then squeeze every drop of flavor from them
that she could manage. She hoped to end up with a good
syrupy mixture that she could whisk right into the ganache.

She fired up the burner and glanced over at Leo. He was
eating another truffle while staring at his collection of ingredients.

"Stumped?" she asked, pouring the cream into a separate
saucepan for her ganache.

He picked up a handful of strawberries and laid them out
on a cutting board. "Hardly."

"You sure?" She focused on his face, not trusting herself
to look at those woeful strawberries without giving away the
fact that she knew he was making a mistake.

"Quite sure." He winked at her, then aimed a slight frown
in the direction of the contest proctor who'd accompanied
them to the kitchen.

Juliet wasn't certain how she felt about the fact that they
had a chaperone. She'd been disappointed at first, thinking
that it would be fun to cook with Leo again. Just the two of
them. Upon reassessment, she realized it would have been a
dangerous proposition. She couldn't afford to get distracted
at this point. And Leo was nothing if not a distraction.

The cream arrived at its boiling point, and Juliet reached
for it while flipping the burner to the off position. She poured

the cream over a bowl full of broken bits of dark chocolate and immediately began to stir. As she was blending the ganache, her elbow grazed Leo's, and she felt a ribbon of longing wind its way down her arm.

Her hand tingled.

Distraction. Most definitely.

Leo poured warm cream over his chocolate, but instead of stirring it right away, he stuck it in the big, walk-in refrigerator. Interesting.

He looked at his watch, then approached the proctor. "Could I trouble you for some ibuprofen, or maybe an aspirin?"

"Certainly. I'll be right back."

And then they were alone.

"Aspirin? Are you feeling sick?" Juliet stared into her ganache as if it held the mysteries of the universe, willing herself to concentrate. She could not screw this up. No matter how good Leo looked in those chef's whites and no matter how her heart started beating harder and faster with each step that he took in her direction.

"Just a headache." He walked up behind her and slipped his arms around her, pressing his warmth into her back.

She closed her eyes, so she wouldn't have to look at those white sleeves, those forearms. But not being able to see only heightened her other senses. He smelled absolutely heavenly, like every kind of chocolate in the world. And with his arms surrounding her, she somehow felt both safe and in the gravest danger imaginable.

She took a shuddering inhale as he bent to rest his chin on her shoulder, wrapped one hand around her waist and the other around her stirring hand, moving the silicone spatula through the chocolate right along with her.

She really needed to put a stop to this.

"I thought you weren't feeling well. What are you doing?" she heard herself ask in a breathy whisper.

Way to go. You really told him, didn't you?

"Helping you." His breath hot on her neck almost made her crumple to the ground.

"Helping me or trying to sabotage me?" she asked, no longer stirring at all but letting the languid movements of his arm and wrist move her wherever they wanted. She hadn't realized that stirring chocolate could be so…well…stirring. But he moved with a confidence and finesse that was almost mesmerizing.

"You don't really think I would try to sabotage you, do you?" He kept guiding her arm in smooth, rhythmic circles, and it felt as if they were slow-dancing rather than cooking.

She sighed into him, letting her head fall to the side, welcoming his mouth when it dropped to her neck. The touch of his lips still shocked her eyes open, and she quite accidentally got a glimpse of her ganache.

Did it look runny? Surely not.

She peered into the bowl. "This isn't a joint project. I think you should get your hands off my chocolate."

"If you insist." He released the spatula.

Juliet watched it sink into the ganache, thinking that she should really pick it up. But Leo's hands slid to cup her bottom, and she decided to hold on to the counter because her knees were growing weaker by the millisecond.

"Leo." It was a good thing his name was short. She could barely form words.

"Yes?" His caress was slow, leisurely, as if he had all the time in the world.

When, in fact, the proctor could return any minute with

Leo's ibuprofen. And weren't they supposed to be making truffles? "Don't you think you should get started on your ganache?"

"I always leave it in the refrigerator for exactly five minutes before blending it with the cream. I've still got..." He removed one hand from her backside long enough to take a look at his watch. "An entire minute."

She could last another sixty seconds without completely falling to pieces and forgetting what she was doing. Right? "One minute. That's not very long."

"Long enough for this." He spun her around, pinning her between the counter and his wall of hard, lean muscles.

Then he pulled her against him and kissed her in a way that made her remember everything that she'd been trying so hard to forget over the course of the past few hours. Not that she'd been all too successful at forgetting.

He groaned into her mouth.

She remembered. Dear God, she remembered every forbidden detail.

"Time's up," he said, pulling back and grinning down at her with one hundred percent male satisfaction.

Leo was no dummy. He was well aware of the impact of that kiss. She was on the verge of forgetting all about the competition and begging him to take her right there on Calantha Vineyard's kitchen counter next to her runny ganache and the tea bags that still needed expressing.

"You're horrible." She swatted at his chest, right at the spot where Le Cordon Bleu was embroidered across his impressive pectoral muscle.

"Me? Horrible? You're equally as guilty. Just your presence is a distraction. And kissing you..." He aimed a smoldering look at her mouth. "Let's just say there's more peril in your kiss than twenty swords."

Well, then. She rather liked that.

"I'm getting back to my truffles now. I suggest you do the same," she said, reaching for her spatula and waving it between them, like one of those twenty swords he'd mentioned. A bit of chocolate flew off the end and landed on his white coat.

There. At least he looked a little less perfect now.

He removed the drop of ganache with the tip of his finger and licked it clean. "This isn't over. Not by a long shot."

She turned her back to him, reaching for her tea bags and grinning secretly to herself as she got back to work.

This isn't over.

She certainly hoped not.

17

By the time his truffles were finished, Leo was popping Advil like it was candy. He'd managed to ignore the throbbing in his head during his all-too-brief interlude with Juliet. But as the minutes ticked by and he worked frantically to produce something remotely resembling the challenge item, the pain worsened.

Juliet's truffles were already plated, and she was running over them with a last-minute swipe of her pastry bag, drizzling them with streaks of white chocolate. Leo had no idea what they tasted like, but on the outside they were certainly identical to the challenge truffles.

His didn't look half-bad, either. They could have been neater, but halfway through the allotted time period, his hands had begun to shake. Typically, he could pipe a line of chocolate drizzle finer and more delicate than spun sugar. Not so today. He wasn't sure if it was the Advil or the pain in his head, concentrated mostly on the left side of his face, that had given him the shakes. Either way, he could have done without the added handicap.

He took a bite of one of the sample truffles, chewed,

swallowed and then tasted one of his creations. His head-ache made it impossible to tell whether he was on the right track or not. The chocolate tasted like metal on his tongue. A wave of nausea hit him, no doubt due to the fact that he had nothing but chocolate and pills swimming around in his stomach. None of it mattered, anyway. It was far too late to change anything.

The proctor clapped his hands, and the noise resounded through Leo's head like a thunderstorm. "Are you two ready?"

"Yes." Juliet bounced on her toes.

Leo would have loved to gaze appreciatively at that bounce if only it hadn't made him the slightest bit dizzy to look at it.

"Ready," he said.

"All right, then. Shall we?" Their chaperone waved a hand toward the door.

As they headed back toward the barrel room, Leo won-dered how many of the spectators had bothered to stick around for the final results. He suspected a fair number of them were long gone by now. An hour and a half was a long time to wait just to watch the judges eat a couple of truffles and declare a winner.

He couldn't have been more wrong. If anything, the audi-ence had doubled in size. There were enough people packed in the barrel room to make him think the chocolate fair was in flagrant violation of the fire code.

A round of applause erupted as he and Juliet approached the banquet table with their plated chocolates. Leo closed his eyes in an effort to shut out all the noise and the light coming from the candelabras and torches, which seemed far brighter than they had before.

"Welcome back, Miss Arabella and Mr. Mezzanotte!" The

announcer's voice echoed off the wine barrels, hitting Leo
from all sides.

More clapping.

More shouting.

More pounding inside Leo's head.

He clenched his teeth. Couldn't everyone just pipe down
for a minute?

"Will the judges step forward, please?" The announcer approached the table and was joined by Ms. Baker, Mr. Collins
and Mr. Weatherton. "First, our esteemed judges will taste
the challenge item. Then they will sample each of our competitors' attempts to duplicate it. Once they've made their decision, I will provide you all with a detailed description of the
mystery truffle. And finally, our winner will be crowned."

Leo flinched at the mention of a crown. That had better
have been a metaphor, because he didn't relish the thought
of anyone or anything touching his head.

He watched as Weatherton and his cohorts tasted the sample truffle with looks of intense concentration. If Leo had
been psychic or capable of mind control, he would have
willed them to taste berries. Lots and lots of berries.

Juliet hadn't so much as waved a berry over her ganache.
Instead, she'd done something with tea. He'd thought she'd
made a fatal error until he got a whiff of her finished ganache as she'd scooped her truffles into small rounds using
a melon-baller. The smell of her chocolate definitely carried
fruity undertones. Concord grape, if he'd had to venture a
guess. But with his head about to split in two, he couldn't
be sure. The only thing he knew for certain was that one, or
possibly even both, of them had missed the mark.

He cast a fleeting look at Juliet. She looked back at him,
an almost-smile tipping her lips. He almost-smiled back.

Their family members still sat on the edges of their seats, also still in frighteningly close proximity to one another. It was a flat-out miracle that a fistfight hadn't broken out. What had they done for the ninety minutes when he and Juliet had been sequestered in the vineyard kitchen? He supposed he was better off not knowing.

He averted his gaze from the audience, Uncle Joe in particular. If there was one thing that was sure to exacerbate a headache, it was his uncle.

"And now the judges will test Miss Arabella's chocolates," the announcer boomed into his microphone.

So Juliet was first up? Leo wasn't sure whether that was good or bad news. At the moment, he didn't particularly care. He was more than ready to get this whole ordeal over with. It seemed as though the noise, the lights and, last but not least, the crazy feud, were all working together to render him incapacitated. His stomach churned. Bile made its way up his throat, and he felt as though he could no longer breathe.

What the hell kind of headache is this?

"Very good, Miss Arabella." Mr. Weatherton grinned and nodded.

"Yes. Exceptional job," Ms. Carter gushed.

Leo stared at his truffles, anxiety worming its way into the painful fog in his brain.

"Mr. Mezzanotte, the judges will now taste your offering."

Leo made his best attempt at a smile. It hurt to move any part of his face, especially anything left of his nose. "Welcome. And thank you for your consideration."

Weatherton bit into one of the truffles. He lifted an eyebrow, aimed a curious look at Leo and took another bite. "Nice work, Mr. Mezzanotte."

"Thank you, sir." Leo nodded, then thought it best to keep his head as still as possible.

"Very good." Ms. Carter was too close, and whatever perfume she was wearing seemed to lodge in Leo's throat.

His head began to swim. The room seemed to fade in and out, flickering like one of the many candles that surrounded him.

Keep it together. This will all be over in a few minutes.

"Thank you very much." He squinted as the three judges blurred into six, then back down to three.

Leo pushed his thumb against his left eye socket. Oddly enough, the pressure helped. A little.

He glanced at Juliet, standing less than two feet away. She gazed impassively at the audience with her hands folded in front of her. Everything about her posture was detached, but as her cool green eyes flitted ever so briefly in his direction, he could see something there. An engaged look that spoke of secrets and, if he wasn't mistaken, affection. It made him think that if he could lie down and rest his head in her lap, everything would be just fine.

He looked away. He told himself it was because he didn't want to bring hellfire and damnation raining down on her by daring to interact with her in public. But on some level he was aware of the fact that he shouldn't be thinking about resting his head in his competitor's lap when they were on the verge of hearing who had won the chocolate fair. He wasn't so incapacitated that he couldn't appreciate how ridiculous that sounded.

The judges didn't take long to come to a decision. After exchanging what appeared to be a few sentences and one or two head nods, they approached the announcer, and the deed was done.

Leo's head began to throb with renewed intensity. He could no longer blink without feeling like his skull was about to crack down the middle. He longed for someone to hit him between the eyes with a sledgehammer and put him out of his misery.

The announcer moved toward him and Juliet, drawing out the suspense by making sure not to focus on either one of them too long. "I'd like to thank everyone in attendance for sticking with us for the exciting conclusion to the Napa Valley Chocolate Fair. As I said earlier, this is a first for us. We've never had a competition result in a tie before. Let's have one last round of applause for both of our finalists."

Please. No more clapping.

Leo took a deep breath and held it until the noise stopped.

"Our finalists were asked to duplicate the flavor of a mystery chocolate, which I can now describe as a tea-infused black currant truffle."

Leo froze and waited for him to say something about berries. He didn't.

"And I'm thrilled to announce that our winner once again is Miss Juliet Arabella."

The world erupted in noise. And even though Leo could see the Arabellas jumping up and down and cheering and his own family yelling their objections to the ruling, the origins of the cacophony seemed to be coming from inside his head.

He turned to Juliet to congratulate her. She mirrored his movements, angling toward him at the same time. He reached for her hand, thinking that she looked so happy, so damned beautiful and full of life, much like she had when they'd first met in the moonlight. And as his fingertips barely grazed hers, her touch evoked the memory of what it had

TERI WILSON

been like to lift the bejeweled mask and gaze upon her face for the very first time.

Time slowed. All the noise around him quieted to a soft hum. Then his fingers fell away, unable to fully grasp her hand. She was right there, looking at him with those luminous eyes of hers. So close. Yet impossible to reach.

And everything faded to black.

One minute Leo was looking at Juliet as if they were the only two people in the room, and the next his hand was slipping right through hers. She searched his gaze for an explanation of why he suddenly no longer wanted to shake her hand, and that's when she knew something was wrong. Very, very wrong.

His eyes were dead, lifeless. Then they closed, and his body crumpled toward the ground.

"Leo!"

She reached for him, but it was too late. Instead of breaking his fall, she went right down with him. The two of them landed on the floor of the barrel room in a tangle of limbs. Juliet somehow ended up flat on her back with Leo's head facedown right between her breasts.

"Oh, my God. Leo, move." She nudged him in the shoulder, but he didn't move a muscle. "Leo, are you okay?"

"Oh, my. Mr. Mezzanotte?" The announcer didn't seem to know what to do. He just stood there with the judges gaping at Juliet and Leo sprawled on the floor.

"Someone, do something! That lecherous loser is accosting my daughter." Juliet's mother leaped from her chair and practically hurdled over the row of seats in front of her. It would have been amusing had it not been so abjectly mortifying.

"He's unconscious," Juliet said, tapping him again. He

stayed right where he was. If anything, the sheer weight of his motionless form caused his face to burrow farther into her cleavage. "See?"

She looked back up. Mom, Dad, Nico, Alegra, Joe Mezzanotte, Leo's sister, Gina, and Gina's husband, Marco, were standing in a circle over her, staring at Leo's head nestled in her breasts. Only a few feet behind them, the contest judges and announcer had moved in for a closer look. As far as fainting spells went, it couldn't have gotten any more awkward.

Then George chimed in, proving her wrong. "Unconscious? What happened?"

She didn't want to talk to him. Especially not with Leo on top of her, awake or otherwise. So she addressed her answer to everyone else assembled. "I think he fainted."

"In that position?" Marco blew out an incredulous huff. "Sure he did."

Gina jammed her hands on her hips. "What is wrong with you lately? My brother is flat on the ground, unconscious. Call 9-1-1. Do something."

Mr. Weatherton pulled a cell phone from the inside pocket of his jacket.

"I just called." George waved his iPhone in the air. "There's an ambulance on its way."

Joe Mezzanotte thanked him, while every member of the Arabella family pretended not to hear a word he'd said.

"I'm simply saying that's an awfully convenient position for him to land in." Marco crossed his arms and aimed a disbelieving glare at Juliet.

Then Leo stirred. Finally.

Juliet gave him a little shake. "Leo, are you okay?"

He groaned as if he was in pain. He lifted his head, just barely, and blinked at her with a faraway gaze. "Juliet?"

She nodded.

"Baby." He gave her a naughty smile and dropped his head again, moving his face back and forth over her breasts. Before she could stop him, he let out another, much less painful-sounding groan.

Marco threw his hands in the air. "I rest my case."

"Oh, my." The announcer averted his gaze.

One of the judges snickered, and Joe Mezzanotte turned such a dark shade of crimson that Juliet worried he might pass out, too.

Juliet scrambled to get out from under Leo. It was no use. He was pretty much dead weight. And there was the added problem that his hands had begun to close around her waist, holding her in place underneath him.

This was definitely not the ending to the chocolate fair that she'd envisioned. Well, perhaps it was. Only not with an audience. "Leo, you really need to get up. If you can. You're at the chocolate fair. You fainted."

"Get off of her." Juliet's mom picked up Leo's leg and tugged.

"Ouch," he mumbled, right into her chest.

Juliet did her best to act as if a semiconscious Mezzanotte talking to her breasts at point zero range was a perfectly ordinary occurrence and tried to wave her mother away. "Mom, stop. You're hurting him."

"Who cares?" Nico's voice had a distinct brotherly edge to it. "I'm on the verge of knocking him out all over again."

Leo lifted his head, squinted and frowned at her mother. He shook his leg, and she let go. His foot flopped to the ground with a thud. "No, it's not my leg. It's my head. Dear God, my head hurts."

Juliet propped herself up on her elbows so she could see

him better. "You had a headache earlier in the kitchen, remember? Do you think that's why you fainted?"

"I don't know, baby."

"Someone get him off of her. Right now." Her mother
had resorted to screaming, which was probably the last thing
Leo's head needed.

He groaned again. Louder this time.

"Why is he calling you *baby?*" Gina jammed her hands on
her hips, clearly more concerned about the intimate nature
of her brother's semantics than his health.

"He fainted. He's…disoriented. That's all." Juliet's face
grew hot. Her eyes darted toward Alegra.

A little help here?

"Of course," Alegra stammered. "He's confused. He has
a head injury."

"Well, he's about to have another one." Nico reached
down and grabbed Leo by the shoulders, hauling him off
of Juliet.

"Do not hurt him. If anyone is going to hurt him, it's
me." Gina swatted at Nico, until he released his hold on Leo.

Leo was upright finally. Sort of. He sat on the floor
slumped against a wine barrel. Gina reached down to whack
him in the head, and he pushed her hand away.

He kept his arms up like a boxer in a prize fight, just in
case she wasn't finished. "Enough with the hitting."

"Gina, stop hitting your brother." Leo's uncle Joe made a
feeble attempt at restraining her.

"Yeah, my head hurts enough as it is. Why are you so bent
out of shape? What the hell did I do?"

"Her!" Gina pointed a furious finger at Juliet.

Oh, no. Oh, no no no no no. Juliet wondered if anyone would notice if she crawled under the banquet table

and stayed there until the ambulance arrived. Given that every eye in the room was now glued on her, probably. She scrambled to her feet, figuring it would be easier to face this situation with dignity if she weren't sprawled on the floor. Besides, if she were standing, it would be easier to run away from Gina if the need arose. From the looks of things, fleeing was more a matter of when, not if.

"Gina." Leo still looked groggy, but he managed to inject a warning in his tone nonetheless.

"Oh, my God. I can't believe this." Gina shook her head and aimed a pointed glare at her husband. "She's the café au lait, isn't she?"

"The café au lait?" Juliet's dad echoed.

"The café au lait!" Joe Mezzanotte clutched at his chest.

Nico raised his brows and shrugged. "I could use a café au lait right about now. That sounds good."

Gina gaped at him. "That's disgusting. She's your sister."

"Why is everyone talking about café au lait? I don't get it." Alegra threw her arms up in the air.

Even Juliet had begun to lose track of the conversation. She didn't know any better than Alegra why everyone was talking about coffee. And she especially didn't know why they seemed to be comparing that coffee to her. But she had the distinct feeling that it wasn't good.

"Marco." Leo shook his head, winced, then squeezed his eyes shut. "Thanks a lot. I'll remember this next time you need me to keep a secret."

"Secret? What secret?" Juliet's mom had grown very pale in the past few minutes. She was as white as Joe Mezzanotte was red.

"Don't look at me. I didn't say anything, Sparkle," Alegra said. It was all Juliet could do to stop herself from clamping a hand over her mouth. "So don't even think about taking back my iPad."

"Sparkle?" Leo's uncle Joe and Gina said in unison.

"I didn't say a word either, bro. You're the one who let the cat out of the bag when you practically had sex with her right there on the floor." Marco smirked at Juliet.

His words pretty much cleared things up. Café au lait, iPads and sparkly nicknames aside, everyone in the room finally realized exactly what was going on.

Juliet braced herself for yelling, screaming and, especially in Gina's case, physical violence. Which only made the ensuing silence even harder to digest.

No one said a word. Not her mother, not her father, not Joe Mezzanotte. Not even Gina. By all appearances, each one of them seemed too shocked to utter a syllable. But words weren't necessary for Juliet to feel the tidal wave of disappointment, judgment and condemnation crashing down on her. Her father couldn't even meet her gaze. Someone sniffled, and to Juliet's horror, she realized it was her mother. She couldn't remember seeing her mother cry before. Ever.

George cleared his throat, walked to his chair and returned with a flat manila envelope. Silently, he tore it in two and tossed the pieces in Leo's lap.

"I'm sorry," Leo said, his voice rough with pain. "I'm so sorry."

He wasn't talking to George, however. He was looking right at Juliet.

Tears clouded her vision, and as she looked into his eyes, all she could remember was the way she'd felt that night when he'd held her face in his hands and whispered the impossible—and everything between them had changed.

You're Juliet. And I'm Leo. It's just the two of us here. No one else.

But that was no longer true, was it?

They were surrounded by people, all of whom wanted them apart. Even the ghosts of their pasts were conspiring against them. Juliet could feel the disapproving presence of their grandmothers looming over them as much as those whom she could reach out and touch. Maybe even more so.

The paramedics rushed in, and once again, chaos ruled the room. They bent over Leo, shining lights in his eyes and talking to him in loud voices. Everyone started talking, providing the EMTs with their own version of what had happened. In all the confusion, someone stepped on Juliet's foot. She wasn't even sure who it was. Her chest grew tight, and she had trouble catching her breath.

Just you and me, remember. No one else.

Without a doubt, she'd never stood in a more crowded room.

18

Two trips to an emergency room in less than two weeks. Leo wondered if it might be some kind of record.

Granted, the first time had been for Juliet's dog. But it still counted, especially once Leo found out that his diagnosis wasn't unlike Cocoa's.

"Mr. Mezzanotte." The ER doctor, who'd downed at least five cups of coffee since hooking Leo up to an IV and running every test at his disposal, frowned at the clipboard in his hand. "I think I've finally gotten down to the root of your problem."

"Exactly which problem would that be? I suddenly find myself with more than my fair share." He was only half joking.

As much as he disliked being poked and prodded for the entire afternoon and most of the night, Leo considered his curtained-off area of the emergency room a little slice of heaven. Uncle Joe, Gina and Marco had all insisted on accompanying him to the hospital, and as far as he knew, they were still camped out in the waiting room. Whenever he got out of here, he would have all three of them to contend with.

His crippling headache was sure to make a speedy return. He wondered if he could take his IV with him when he left.

He was fairly sure they were so upset to learn about his relationship with Juliet that they'd forgotten he'd also lost the competition at the chocolate fair. He furrowed his brow. *Relationship* wasn't quite the right word, was it? If what they had was a relationship, it had to be the most dysfunctional one on record. Especially now that the lid had so spectacularly blown off the whole thing. He had a feeling it would be a long, long time before he found himself back in Juliet's bed. If ever.

He suddenly felt sick again, and it had nothing to do with his headache.

The doctor glanced up from the clipboard. "I'm talking about your migraine, of course."

"Of course." Leo nodded, feeling faintly nauseous.

His headache had been labeled a migraine within minutes of his arrival, due mostly to the fact that it was concentrated on one side of his head, and the bright lights of the hospital made it exponentially worse.

"It's good news. You're not suffering from any major health problems." The doctor smiled and tucked the clipboard under his arm. "I'm afraid your fainting spell, which was brought on by the severe pain in your head, was simply a result of your chocolate allergy."

Leo blinked. Just what kind of hallucinogens had they put in his IV drip? "I'm sorry. I must have misheard you. I thought you said chocolate allergy."

"That's exactly what I said."

The metallic taste was returning to Leo's mouth. "But I'm not allergic to chocolate."

"I'm afraid you are. Quite allergic, in fact." The doctor pulled a pen from the pocket of his white coat, circled something on his clipboard and shoved it in Leo's direction.

Patient has tested positive for a level five chocolate allergy.

Leo stared at the printed words until he thought he might rip the clipboard out of the doctor's hands and throw it across the room.

"Level five." He swallowed. Instead of just metal, he now tasted pennies, nickels and dimes. "That doesn't sound so bad. On what scale? Ten? Fifty? One hundred?"

The doctor aimed a serious look at Leo. "Six."

"Six?" Whoever heard of a scale from one to six?

"Yes, six. Five is considered a very high-level allergen. Six would indicate an extremely high level."

Very high. Extremely high. What was the difference? Leo felt as if they were mincing words at this point. "There's been a mistake. I can't be allergic to chocolate. It's simply not possible."

"It's entirely possible. The tests don't lie, Mr. Mezzanotte." The doctor was beginning to look at him as if he were crazy, which could possibly be a side effect from the implication that he was allergic to his livelihood.

"But I'm a chocolatier. I work with chocolate all day, every day. I have for years." If he was really allergic to chocolate, wouldn't he be dead by now? He'd consumed enough over the course of his lifetime to kill a herd of allergic elephants.

"I'm afraid a person can develop an allergy to anything at any time. Just last night we had someone in here who went into anaphylactic shock after eating a slice of key lime pie. Turns out he was allergic to citrus. Forty-five years old and just started breaking out in hives last month. Came out of nowhere." The doctor shrugged.

Leo really didn't give a damn about the guy with the citrus allergy. Not now.

His doctor continued. "This has probably been sneaking up on you for a while. It's rare that your initial attack would be as severe as the one you experienced today. Have you been suffering from headaches lately?"

"No, I haven't. I mean, I've had some pain for the past few weeks, but that was just jet lag." *Dear God, please let it have been jet lag.*

"I doubt it was jet lag." Dr. Bad News raised a knowing brow.

The headaches had been bad, but not so excruciating that Leo couldn't live with them. Until today. Obviously, he couldn't go around losing consciousness on a daily basis. He would just have to deal with the situation. Consume less chocolate. He couldn't stop eating chocolate altogether, but he could cut back. "So, what happens now?"

"It's rather obvious, isn't it? You stop eating chocolate."

This doctor just wasn't getting it. Leo being allergic to chocolate was like him being allergic to sick people. "And if I don't?"

"Your symptoms get worse with each episode until you go into anaphylactic shock like Mr. Key Lime Pie. Then, if you don't get medical attention quickly enough, your throat closes up and you die."

Leo had trouble swallowing all of a sudden. He remembered standing in front of the judges at the chocolate fair and feeling as though he couldn't breathe as he presented his tasting plate.

"Any more questions?" the doctor asked as he stood with his hand on the privacy curtain. Clearly Leo's time with him was up.

"No. I think I've got it."

He sat on the hospital bed for a few more minutes waiting for the news to sink in. It started to feel a little more real
when a nurse in navy blue ER scrubs came and gave him
an epinephrine auto-injector that he was supposed to keep
with him in case of emergency.

She handed it to him. It looked sort of like a small flash-
light. "If you suffer a life-threatening allergic reaction, you
may experience swelling in your face. Your throat will begin
to close up, and you'll have trouble breathing."

Terrific. He willed himself not to swallow.

She showed him how to inject himself in the thigh with
the injector. Apparently, if he did it the wrong way, he could
give himself a heart attack. "In the event of any of those
symptoms, inject yourself with the EpiPen and get to the
nearest hospital immediately. A few gulps of liquid Benadryl
wouldn't hurt, either."

This was getting worse by the minute. What was he supposed to do? Carry around a flask filled with grape-flavored
children's allergy medication? "I understand. Thank you."

He shoved the EpiPen in the white paper bag she pro-
vided, and once he was unhooked from the IV, headed for
the waiting room. Still a little rattled, he didn't bother gird-
ing himself for an interrogation on the Juliet situation. So he
was relieved to find Marco watching television and waiting
for him alone in the row of orange plastic chairs.

"Hey." Leo slumped into the seat next to him. He still felt
a little off center, but at least it no longer seemed as if there
was an axe protruding from his head.

"Hello," Marco said, taking his eyes off the TV only
briefly. Leo was pretty sure *Dance Moms* was on the screen,

but he didn't have it in him at the moment to mock his brother-in-law. "Are you going to live?"

"Looks that way." Leo glanced down at his white coat, still streaked with chocolate from Juliet's spatula. He crossed his arms so he wouldn't have to see it. "Where is everyone? Home, I hope."

"Yep. Gina took Uncle Joe home. He said there were some important things he needed to take care of."

More important than his nephew being treated in the emergency room? Interesting. Leo didn't much mind, though. He simply counted his blessings that he wouldn't be forced to deal with the Juliet fallout right now. "Don't you wonder who he's on the phone with all the time? His cell seems permanently glued to his ear."

"Who knows?" Marco shrugged, and slid his gaze back to Leo. "Tonight he was in a panic over the whole Royal Foods contract, you know. I'm not sure I've ever seen him so upset."

The contract. Leo had forgotten all about it, since he no longer had any intention of signing it. Of course, no one else was privy to that information. Except possibly Juliet, but as far as he could tell, she was still in the dark.

"Can we not do this right now?" Leo jammed a hand through his hair. "I just want to get out of here."

"Sure." Marco stood and stretched his arms over his head. "What's up, though? Are you okay? Did the doctor find out why you passed out?"

"Yes, I am. And yes, he did." Leo rose to his feet and met Marco's gaze without elaborating.

"All right." Marco frowned for a minute and then dug his car keys out of his pocket.

They walked across the tile floor and out the automatic doors before he noticed the white paper bag in Leo's hand.

"What's in the bag?" he asked.

A needle full of drugs to keep everything I've worked for from kill-ing me. Leo gripped it more tightly in his fist. He felt physically incapable of saying the words.

He shrugged and kept his eyes focused fully forward. "You know. Ordinary hospital stuff."

Ordinary.

Right.

Juliet was being stalked.

By members of her own family.

If she'd been a teenager, she supposed she would have been grounded. But since she was a grown woman, her mother had to find another way to keep her under lock and key. And apparently her method of choice was making sure that Juliet was never alone. Every breath she took, every move she made, there was an Arabella right there beside her.

She wondered if they had a flow chart or something to keep track of who was on duty at any given time.

Nico had taken the first shift, driving Juliet home from the chocolate festival under the guise of helping her take the wineglasses and other leftover supplies to the shop on the way. But instead of just dropping her off afterward, he'd stuck around.

"I can't believe you let him touch you," he'd said at one point, staring at the road ahead of them with a twitch in his jaw.

Juliet had been too tired for a lecture. "Enough. Who are you? Mom?"

That had been sufficient to shut him up. Even though what she'd really wanted to say was, "Believe it. And someday I just might let him touch me again."

But she shuddered at the sort of surveillance such a statement might invite, so she'd kept her mouth shut. Besides, if
sleeping with Leo once had led to the kind of brouhaha that
had taken place at the chocolate festival, there was no telling what kind of chaos would rain down on them next time.

Nico had still been sprawled out on her sofa when she went
to bed that night. The next morning at the stroke of ten, right
when Nico finally dragged himself upright, Alegra rang the
doorbell. Naturally, she'd been carrying an overnight bag.

Such was Juliet's life at the moment.

Technically, she could have kicked them out. But she didn't
much feel like being alone, anyway. And Nico and Alegra
were far better than the alternative—her mother.

"How long are you all planning to keep this up?" she asked
Alegra as they climbed into her car and headed for Arabella
Chocolate Boutique on Monday morning.

Alegra slid on her sunglasses and cranked the engine. "I
have no idea what you're talking about."

Juliet rolled her eyes. "Please. Yes, you do."

Alegra shrugged. "Come on. It could be worse. First off,
you know I can be bought. Although at the moment, things
are so crazy that my price has gone up. Way, way up."

Juliet didn't even dignify that with a response.

"Besides, we had fun last night, didn't we?" Alegra turned
the car onto the main road that led to the store.

The street was lined with olive trees, their narrow leaves
covered with a thin layer of dusty white. Olive trees were
almost as common in Napa Valley as grapevines. They were
prettiest this time of year, when they bloomed tiny delicate
flowers that would one day become olives.

"Yes, last night was fun." There'd been a *Chopped* mara-
thon on the Food Network, and they'd fallen asleep dur-

ing the second-to-last episode. Juliet had dreamed of teams of men in white chef coats with indistinguishable faces and capable hands. "But that's beside the point. I want my life back."

"It's been two days. Less than two days, actually. Give it time. Everyone was thrown for a pretty major loop, you know." Alegra guided the car into the parking lot of Arabella Chocolate Boutique.

Juliet glanced across the street, and a ribbon of relief wound its way through her when she spotted Leo's sleek sports car. She hadn't heard a word about what had happened to him since the ambulance had carried him away from the chocolate festival.

She opened the car door a crack. "They're about to be thrown for another one."

"What exactly are you talking about?" Alegra's head spun around. "Oh, my God. You're not going to marry him, are you?"

"George? Of course not. I thought I'd made that clear. Besides, I'm pretty sure he no longer wants me as his wife." *Thank goodness.*

"I wasn't talking about George." Alegra lifted a brow.

Juliet's neck grew hot. "Leo? You can't be serious."

Marry Leo. The idea was so far-fetched she couldn't even imagine it.

Not that she wanted to imagine it. Or even think about it. Because of course, she didn't.

"Are *you* serious? That's the real question, isn't it?" Alegra's gaze darted across the street to Mezzanotte Chocolates.

Juliet wished she'd stop looking over there. "Hardly. I haven't even spoken to him since he passed out face-first in my cleavage."

"That was just the day before yesterday."

She squirmed in her seat. "I slept with him. That doesn't mean I'm going to marry him. Please."

"If you married him, that would mean you'd be related to Joe Mezzanotte." Alegra released an exaggerated shudder.

Related to Joe Mezzanotte. That was a sobering thought. She'd have to remember it if she was tempted to sleep with Leo again. Assuming she'd ever be free of her volunteer bodyguards. "I rest my case. I have no plans to marry Leo. Now or ever."

Never in her life had sleeping with someone blown up in her face in such a spectacular way. She climbed out of the car and slammed the door.

Alegra hustled to catch up with her. "Then what's this big bomb you plan to drop?"

"You'll see." She reached for the doorknob and strode inside.

Alegra could wait five minutes and find out with everyone else. Juliet had pretty much lost faith in anyone's ability to keep a secret around here.

"Juliet. Alegra. Good morning," her mother said crisply from behind the cash register.

Her father looked up, offered a weak smile and then went back to stamping white paper bags with the Arabella Chocolate Boutique logo. Nico just smirked. He'd been doing a lot of that lately.

Juliet stifled a sigh and marveled at the fact that her big win at the chocolate festival had seemingly been eclipsed by Leo's fainting spell and its subsequent mess. Okay, so she'd committed the unpardonable sin. But she'd managed to finally beat Leo. And from the looks of things, Mezzanotte

Chocolates was no longer affiliated with Royal Gourmet. That envelope-ripping episode had looked pretty damning.

Something that felt an awful lot like guilt nagged at her, which was profoundly absurd. Why should she feel bad about the whole Royal Gourmet mess? Hadn't she been slaving away for over a week now trying to duplicate the *chocolat chaud* recipe? She hadn't gone through all that trouble just for fun. Besides, the Mezzanottes were doing just fine over there across the street. They always had, and they always would, thanks to their mass-produced candy bars. She shouldn't feel the slightest bit guilty that her involvement with Leo had botched a possible arrangement between him and George, of all people.

And she didn't. Much.

"I have an announcement," she said, stowing her handbag beneath the counter.

"What is it?" Her mother paled. "I'm not sure I can take much more."

For a second, she thought about faking an affair with Joe Mezzanotte just to make a point. But it was too horrid a thought to even joke about. "I'm going to Rome."

Nico glanced up from the row of candied cordials he was arranging in the front display case. "Rome? As in Rome, Italy?"

Was there another Rome? "Yes."

"When?" Alegra looked equally confused.

So, everyone really had forgotten she'd won the chocolate festival. "In two weeks. For the *Roma Festa del Cioccolato*. I qualified because I won Saturday. Remember?"

Alegra slipped an apron over her head and tossed an extra one at Juliet. "But you qualified last year, too. And the year before that. You've never been before."

"Well, I'm going now." She squared her shoulders and prepared herself for a fight. Since she was already in a heap of trouble, she was sure there would be no shortage of opinions about her taking off for Italy.

"Right." Nico rolled his eyes.

"Honey, I'm not sure now is the best time for you to be competing in Rome. It sounds expensive." Her dad frowned at the cash register as if he could summon airfare simply by staring at the machine.

"Rome. Wow." Nothing about Alegra's expression indicated that she believed Juliet was actually going anywhere.

"Everyone, just wait a minute." A smile came to her mother's lips. Not a scary smile, but a genuine one, which made it all the more frightening. "I think Juliet going to Rome is a wonderful idea."

A protest was on the tip of Juliet's tongue, ready to fly right out, until she realized what her mother had said. She closed her mouth for a second, then opened it again. "You do?"

Nico peeled off his plastic gloves and threw them on the counter. "No way. You can't be serious. After what she's done?"

Her dad held up a hand in warning. "Nico."

It was as if she and her brother were in grade school all over again.

"I think it's a *wonderful* idea," her mom repeated, practically baring her teeth.

And then it dawned on Juliet exactly what was going on.

If she was a good six thousand miles away from Napa Valley, it would be hard to carry on an affair with Leo. She could roam around free of supervision and still not get into trouble. It seemed like an awfully extreme strategy, though.

Maybe she was reading too much into her mother's reaction. Maybe she really thought Juliet could compete in Rome and do well there.

"Perhaps you could even leave a few days early. You know, just to see a few sights before the contest begins." The weird smile on her mom's face grew even wider.

Okay, so maybe she really was trying to usher Juliet out of the country before she could see Leo again. That was fine. It still meant she was going to Rome.

"It's settled." Her mom nodded. "You'll go. We'll look into flights this afternoon. Maybe once the contest gets underway, the rest of us can fly out and join you. I'll need to look at the budget first, of course. But this is a huge event for Arabella Chocolate Boutique. If you do well there on the heels of winning the Napa Valley Chocolate Fair, it could mean big things for us."

Big things, as in getting back into Napa's finest restaurants. Now that George and Royal Gourmet were out of the equation, and she and Leo each had one win under their belts, it was anyone's game.

Win or lose, she was going to Rome. At last.

"You're going to Rome."

"Hmm?" Leo had only half heard whatever it was his uncle had said.

He'd barely crossed the threshold and was admittedly distracted. It was strange being in Mezzanotte Chocolates for the first time since learning the inconvenient truth about his new allergy. Everywhere he turned there was chocolate. Hell, he could smell it from the moment he'd opened his car door outside.

"I said, you're going to Rome. You leave in twelve days.

Get packing." Uncle Joe flipped the sign on the door from Closed to Open.

"Whatever for?" Leo crossed his arms.

He wasn't going to Rome. Boarding an international flight was the last thing he wanted to do. He'd had a grand total of one headache-free day since he'd climbed off the plane from Paris, and that day had been just yesterday. He hadn't even been able to enjoy it since he'd been grappling with how to handle his new reality.

Uncle Joe straightened his tie. The man was seventy years old, and he still wore a suit and tie to work every day. In a chocolate shop. "For the contest, of course. Why else?"

Why else indeed? The whole world revolved around chocolate.

Not anymore. "We need to have a talk."

"Yes, we certainly do. When were you going to tell me that you were sleeping with Juliet Arabella?" Leo's uncle slammed his fist down on the countertop. The chocolate straws next to the register jumped in their tall glass apothecary jar.

"Don't start in on that, Uncle Joe. There are more important things we need to discuss right now."

"What could possibly be more important? George Alcott has rescinded his offer of representation. No Royal Gourmet contract. No *chocolat chaud*. No French Laundry. All because out of all the women in the United States of America, you had to choose her."

"Forget about Royal Gourmet and George Alcott III. That man is an idiot." Leo could have told him that there would have been no contract regardless. But why stir that particular pot now? They had enough to sort out. "What makes you think I'm going to Rome for the *Roma Festa del Cioccolato?* I lost the other day. Remember?"

"A technicality." Uncle Joe shrugged, and his gaze dropped to the countertop.

"No. Not a technicality. I lost. Juliet won. Fair and square." It would have been nice to have won. He'd probably never compete again. Not now that he couldn't even eat his own recipes. And forget ever participating in another taste-test challenge.

But he hadn't won. Juliet had. No amount of pouting on Uncle Joe's part would change that.

Although Uncle Joe didn't exactly look like he was pouting. "You're in. Like I said, a technicality."

"What did you do?" Leo lowered himself onto one of the barstools across the counter from his uncle. He had a feeling he'd be better off sitting down for this conversation.

"I made a few calls. It didn't take long to convince the organizers that in the case of a tie in a qualifying event, both finalists should be eligible to compete in Rome. They were more than agreeable."

A few calls. Uncle Joe and that damned phone of his.

Leo lifted a brow. "Were they now?"

"Yes. Think about it from their point of view. They said if you and Juliet both made the trip to Rome, they could play up the rematch between the two of you. It could draw even more attention to the competition." Uncle Joe rolled his eyes. "Of course, that will never happen, but I didn't tell them that. I'm not about to shoot myself in the foot like that."

Something about this whole thing just wasn't right. "And why are you so sure it would never happen?"

Uncle Joe waved a dismissive hand. "Juliet Arabella isn't about to go to Rome. She could have already competed there five times over. She's going to stay right here and slave away under her mother's watchful eye like she always does."

Leo's hands balled into fists. "Uncle Joe…"

"Before you get all up in arms about it, think for a minute. Have you heard a word from her since you nearly died the other day?" Uncle Joe looked at him expectantly.

He hadn't heard from her. But that didn't necessarily mean anything. A lot had happened over the course of the weekend.

"I'd hardly say that I nearly died."

There was a grain of truth to it, though.

"You were unconscious on the floor. You'd think that the woman you're sleeping with would want to know if you'd lived or died. That's all I'm saying."

"Well, if *that's all*…" Leo rolled his eyes. He was sure there was no end to what his uncle wanted to say. "Can we not talk about Juliet? Please. Let's stick with the matter at hand. Why do you want me to go Rome so badly?"

"For the money, of course."

It was the last thing Leo had expected his uncle to say. "You mean the twenty-thousand-dollar prize money? The odds of winning aren't great. And it would cost an arm and a leg for airfare and accommodations. It would be a gamble."

Something in Uncle Joe's eyes flashed. "Any reason you're using that particular word?"

"No, I…" Leo paused. He remembered how tense Uncle Joe had been in the days leading up to the chocolate festival. All the phone calls. All the agitation. And he was suddenly hit with a sickening memory. His mother crying. His father begging for forgiveness. *I'm sorry. I'll never play cards again.* He searched his uncle's gaze and saw hints of that same look of regret he'd seen so often in his father's eyes growing up.

History was repeating itself. "Uncle Joe, did you gamble on the results of the chocolate fair yesterday?"

The lines in his uncle's face seemed to deepen. "Don't sound so self-righteous. It was a small bet, and you were sure to win. I was simply showing faith in my nephew."

Turn it around on someone else. Classic gambling addict behavior. Only his uncle wasn't a gambling addict. At least not to Leo's knowledge. "How small, exactly?"

Uncle Joe grew very quiet, and Leo realized that not only did they have a problem, but they had a big one. Really big.

He shook his head. "First, Dad, and now, you."

"This has nothing to do with your father," Uncle Joe said.

Was he actually delusional enough to believe that nonsense? "Our family has a problem, Uncle Joe. Face it."

Our family has a problem.

Our family.

No. Leo shook his head. *No, it couldn't be.*

He didn't want to believe it, but it was the only explanation. Clearly the family problem went much farther back than he realized.

He closed his eyes, and Elenore Arabella's faded pencil marks in her journal danced in his memory.

Donnatella has been so quiet of late…she thinks we should sell our recipes to a candy bar company. Thinking of giving away everything we've worked so hard for hurts my heart.

His grandmother hadn't been herself. She'd been quiet. Withdrawn. Desperate.

And then she'd betrayed her best friend.

For money.

Leo ground his teeth together and leveled his gaze at his uncle. "This is what's behind the feud, isn't it?"

"Don't be ridiculous, Leo. I made a few bets. Bets I should have won. The feud has been going on for years."

Leo pounded his fist on the counter. "I'm talking about our family history. You…Dad…who else? Was it my grandmother or my grandfather? I know it was one of them. Tell me."

Uncle Joe grew pensive and stared at Leo's fist for several long seconds before answering. "I'm not saying he had a problem, but your grandfather was known to make a bet or two in his day."

Leo let the news sink in while he blew out a strained breath. So this was it. The real reason behind the Arabella-Mezzanotte strife. "A bet large enough to put Bellanotte Chocolates in danger?"

"Maybe." Uncle Joe finally looked up. "But your grandmother still did that Arabella woman a favor. Mass producing those chocolates put them on the map."

Leo dropped his head in his hands, scrubbed them across his face. Uncle Joe could spin it however he wanted, but the fact was that the Mezzanotte gambling problem was at the root of the bad blood between his family and Juliet's.

And he'd thought he could come back home and pretend nothing that had happened in his childhood actually mattered.

"Leo, we need to talk about the matter at hand. Not things that happened fifty years ago," his uncle said quietly.

Leo supposed he was right. There would be time to deal with the feud situation. Later. Assuming the Mezzanottes still had a store to compete with the Arabellas. "This isn't the first time, is it? This is why you called me here from Paris. So I could help you get out of debt."

A tiny nod of Uncle Joe's head was his only admission.

Somehow the smallness of the gesture only underscored its magnitude.

Leo could have sworn he felt the scratch of a rope slip round his ankle and the weight of the anchor that was family responsibility dragging him off his bar stool.

It had been a long time since he'd worn that particular accessory. It didn't fit now any better than it had when he'd been eighteen. Or when he'd been a kid and his dad had made him promise to keep his secrets. "How bad is it? Just give me the bottom line."

Uncle Joe cleared his throat and took his time answering. The urge to wring his neck intensified with each passing second. "We're in danger of losing the shop. The proceeds from the candy bar side have been slipping for the past few years, and I've incurred other...expenses."

Expenses. As in gambling debts, no doubt.

"I took out a second mortgage," he continued. "There's a balloon note on the store due next month."

"Next month." Marvelous. "What exactly were you planning on doing if the Rome festival wouldn't let me compete?"

"Leo, don't be upset. Please. I had things perfectly under control. Of course I thought you'd win the chocolate fair. And we had the contract with Royal Gourmet all negotiated...."

The contract that George Alcott had ripped up and thrown in Leo's face.

"Do not try to turn this back on me," he said through gritted teeth.

He was tempted to walk out the door and never look back. He hadn't made this mess. Why should he be the one to clean it up? Just because his last name was Mezzanotte didn't mean he had to be the one to save the family business.

He could go home, grab Sugar and get on a plane back to Paris. And…

Then what?

La Maison du Chocolat would probably jump at the chance to rehire him now that he was allergic to chocolate, wouldn't they?

He was stuck. As much he wanted to resent it, this store, this business was all he had. At least for now.

He muttered a heartfelt expletive.

"So you'll go to Rome, then?" At least his uncle had the decency to ask this time.

Now that the secret was out, Leo's days of ignoring his uncle's attempts at ordering him around were over. "Yes, I'll go. On one condition."

"What condition might that be?" Uncle Joe pulled at his shirt collar. His tie went slightly askew.

It was funny how that one small detail could make him look older somehow. Vulnerable, which was a word Leo had never before associated with his uncle.

"If I win, the store is one hundred percent mine. Mine and mine alone. Got it?" If he was going to be the one to save it, then he'd be the one to make sure it stayed that way. Safe.

Of course, there was no guarantee he'd actually win. Especially now.

"All right." His uncle, in no position to argue, simply nodded.

"And this is the final contest. No more." He didn't need this kind of stress. For all practical purposes, he'd be competing with one arm tied behind his back.

Uncle Joe frowned.

"I mean it. No more. No more competing for me. No more gambling for you. If we get this straightened out, and you mess up again and the candy bar business goes down the drain, so be it. Is that understood?"

Another reluctant nod. "Any particular reason?"

"I've never been a fan of the mass production side of things. You know that." Leo had no interest in off-the-shelf chocolate. If that side of everything caved in, he could live with it.

He wondered if his willingness to sacrifice that part of the business had anything to do with the fact that it had been the root of the whole Mezzanotte-Arabella feud. Then he decided that maybe it wasn't best to examine his motivation right now. Rome…his chocolate allergy…Uncle Joe…

He felt as if he was juggling fire. And that was without even adding his feelings for Juliet Arabella into the mix. Feelings that he was in no way prepared to identify, yet were very much there.

Uncle Joe spoke up again. There was a tremor in his voice. Paired with the crooked tie, it gave Leo the sense that his uncle had aged ten years since he'd walked through the front door. "I meant the competing. Why no more contests? You're great at it."

Leo leveled his gaze at his uncle, fully intending to tell him the truth. He would worry. He would think the contest in Rome was hopeless. He would think Mezzanotte Chocolates would soon be a thing of the past.

He might be right.

Great at it.

I was *great at it. Now? Who knows?*

He swallowed. "I have my reasons."

Then he slid off the bar stool and pushed through the double doors leading to the kitchen. He wasn't quite sure why he'd spared his uncle the truth. God knows, the man deserved to worry.

But for the time being, Leo was worried enough for the both of them.

19

Juliet should have been delighted beyond reason. After only a handful of days of packing and frantic preparation for the *Roma Festa del Cioccolato,* she was in Rome.

Alone.

For the time being, at least. She'd been in the Eternal City for two days, most of which had been spent finalizing her plans for her entry in the contest's artisan division. Her first stop upon arriving at Aeroporto Fiumicino had been the Altare della Patria—the building more commonly known as the Wedding Cake.

She'd had her taxi driver take her there even before going to her hotel. With the windows of the little white car rolled down, they'd driven through the outskirts of the city where old met new and clothes dried on outdoor laundry lines strung across tightly packed, semi-modern-looking apartment balconies. The closer the car had crawled to the historic heart of Rome, the narrower the streets became. Pavement gave way to cobblestone, and when they'd passed through the gates of the Aurelian Wall, they left all traces of the modern world behind.

Everywhere she looked, Juliet saw the past. The cab driver had pointed out Circus Maximus, the Pantheon and Palatine Hill. He'd told her that Cleopatra had once ridden an elephant down the winding road that bordered the Roman Forum. Then they'd zipped right past the Colosseum, which of course, needed no introduction.

It was all breathtaking, and Juliet couldn't help feeling as if she'd stepped back in time. But remarkably, she also felt as if she belonged there. As if she'd been waiting her whole life to see these things, to breathe in the cool Mediterranean air and stand under the tall umbrella pine trees that resembled elegant parasols decorating the city sidewalks.

The car had carried her past churches, clay-colored buildings and piazza after piazza, until she'd spotted a glimpse of the purest white looming above the horizon.

She'd looked at so many pictures of the Altare della Patria in preparation for the trip that she'd recognized it at once. The Wedding Cake. But no photograph would have been preparation for the sight of the monument in its entirety as they cruised past the Piazza Venezia and curved around the busy circular intersection.

It was enormous, and its raised placement, carved into a portion of the Capitoline Hill, only made it look as though it loomed even larger.

"Here we are." The cab driver had waved a hand. "The Wedding Cake, just as you asked. Although we Romans call it *la macchina da scrivere.*"

He'd made a pecking gesture with his fingers until Juliet had realized he meant *typewriter.* She'd glanced back at the building. It had row upon row of wide stairs which she supposed could pass for typewriter keys. But she preferred the wedding cake nickname. It was far more romantic, for one thing. More importantly, it was the inspiration for her entry in the chocolate contest.

"You now sit in the very hub of Rome," the driver had said in heavily accented English. "This is the center of everything."

The center of everything.

Something about that phrase made her heart beat faster. And for some nonsensical reason, it also made her think of Leo.

She'd leaned toward the front seat and pressed three euro coins into the driver's hand. "Can you wait here for just a minute while I take a closer look? *Per favore?*"

"*Sì.*" He'd nodded.

"*Grazie.*" She'd grabbed her sketch pad and camera from her carry-on and climbed out of the taxi.

She'd already sketched out a plan for her entry. In great detail. But a few last-minute additions couldn't hurt. She wanted it to be accurate. As accurate as possible, anyway. There were limitations, of course, when working with food.

Basically, she planned on making the Wedding Cake into an actual, edible wedding cake. Over the course of her career, she'd made only a handful of wedding cakes. None of them had been nearly as decorative or made up of as many layers as the building standing before her. It was an ambitious plan. Overly ambitious, perhaps.

It was also perfect. Perfectly artistic. Perfectly impressive. And perfectly Roman. If she could somehow make it work, if she could make a cake that was recognizable as this famed Roman landmark and also tasted fantastic, she might actually pull off this whole *Roma Festa del Cioccolato* thing. She was here, after all. Not just to finally see Rome, but to compete. She may as well give it her all. If she did well, or possibly even placed on such a worldwide scale, it would be huge news back home in Napa. Those woeful strawberries and her close finish with Leo at the Napa Valley Chocolate Fair would be forgotten. Arabella Chocolate Boutique would once again reign supreme.

She'd finally made her way to her hotel that afternoon with a perfect picture of the Wedding Cake ingrained in her memory. The thing that had made the biggest impression on her hadn't been the colossal size of it or the elegance of its graceful columns or its many carved sculptures, but the stark whiteness of it. Her research had told her it was crafted of white marble from Botticino in Northern Italy, but book knowledge hadn't prepared her for the sight of a pure white spectacle sitting among the generally clay-colored back-drop of Rome. All the surrounding buildings were shades of muted brown, soft terra-cotta or creamy Tuscan beige. By contrast alone, the Wedding Cake was a standout.

Her white chocolate icing would have to be pristine. She'd need to give that particular challenge some serious fore-thought. Juliet had planned on using her grandmother's white chocolate frosting recipe and had even brought the fragile recipe book along with her from the States. But she was no longer sure it would work. Would it turn out white enough?

For two days, she thought of little else but the Wedding Cake. Her hotel was located a little over a mile away, on a quiet side street with a violinist who stood on the corner playing for change and a bountiful trellis of pink roses that climbed the walls. In the mornings she would drink deca-dent, creamy Italian cappuccino, then take a walk somewhere on her list of must-see places, like the Trevi Fountain or the lush, green Villa Borghese, an enormous park with sweep-ing views of Rome's crowded rooftops and its many domed churches. But she always ended up back at the Wedding Cake, staring at it, memorizing every angle of marble, the number of columns, the exact tilt of the wings on the goddess Victoria statues that topped the monument on either side.

On her final night alone in the city before her family descended, she forced herself to do something else. If anything, she was overprepared. And she still hadn't seen the place at the top of her list. The Spanish Steps.

She told herself she hadn't been intentionally avoiding that particular spot. A big, fat lie, of course.

She knew it was nonsensical, but ever since Leo had told her he could see her there—right there at that spot—and suggested they go together some day, an impossible fantasy had lodged in her heart. It was ridiculous. She hadn't even seen him since the chocolate fair. Just as she'd suspected, once their secret had been exposed, once it was no longer just the two of them alone in a room together, the reality of their impossible situation became all too clear.

She hadn't heard a word from him. Nor had she made any attempts to contact him. Cold turkey. That was the way to go. Why prolong the agony?

They'd been doomed from the start. But then again, she'd known that much all along.

Such forethought didn't make the yearning any less intense, though. Sometimes she found herself thinking about him at the oddest times. Case in point—this, her last night alone in Rome. He was invading her thoughts from all sides. She imagined him sitting across the tiny table at the café where she ate a dinner of homemade pasta dusted with pecorino cheese and cracked black pepper. She could have sworn she heard his voice drifting toward her on the salty Mediterranean breeze. She even thought she spotted him in

the crowd walking past the gelateria where she'd indulged
in a dessert of tiramisu gelato heavily sprinkled with cocoa
and powdered sugar.

She shook her head when she realized her feet had automatically started heading in the direction of the Wedding
Cake. She could draw a perfect picture of that building in
her sleep by now. She didn't need to go there again. She was
going to the Spanish Steps. Hadn't she been waiting nearly
all her life to walk up that grand outdoor staircase? She had
a photo of that exact spot tacked to her refrigerator, for crying out loud. Was she really going to skip seeing it in person
simply because she harbored some kind of fantastical notion
that she should be there with Leo?

No. That would be wholly irrational.

It didn't feel right going there alone. Which was precisely
why she needed to do it.

She turned around and headed in the direction of the Piazza di Spagna, home to the Spanish Steps. It also happened
to be one of the busiest piazzas in the city. The steps were a
huge draw, obviously. But the piazza was also situated along
one of Rome's most exclusive high-end shopping districts.
Shops with names like Gucci, Prada and Armani lined either
side of the street. The famed Hotel de Russie was just a block
away. And the home where romantic poet John Keats had
spent his last days in 1821 was located there, as well, tucked
into the right-hand corner of the steps.

As she approached the piazza, the buzz of happy conversation reached her ears and grew louder the closer she came.
Then, before she knew it, she'd rounded a corner, and the
grand staircase stretched before her. One hundred thirty-
five impossibly wide steps leading from the street level to
the Trinità dei Monti church at the top.

She paused for a moment in the middle of the street to appreciate the glory of the sight. While she'd been strolling with her gelato, the sun had fallen, leaving the sky a heavenly cerulean blue. The steps were awash in the pale golden glow of surrounding street lamps and overflowed with enormous pots of colorful azaleas. Crimsons, purples and hot, fiery pinks.

It was so *romantic,* she realized with a pang.

Around her, couples strolled hand in hand. Lovers sprawled on the steps, sharing bottles of wine and languid, sensual kisses. She was suddenly acutely aware of her aloneness. And in that quiet, vulnerable moment, Leo's words came floating back to her.

I can see you there, in Rome, drinking wine on the Spanish Steps, wandering through cobblestone streets with the Mediterranean breeze blowing through your hair.

Her throat grew tight. It had been a mistake to come here. She'd managed to keep thoughts of Leo at bay—mostly—but here they all came flooding back. And she realized just how very much she missed his touch, the warmth of his breath against her skin and, quite simply, *him.* She couldn't be here. Not without him.

This was the problem with wanting more. More life. More passion. More *everything.*

She'd been perfectly fine before she'd kissed Leo in the vineyard. Her career had been going well. Her family didn't blame her for ruining the chocolate shop. Her grandmother hadn't been rolling in her grave at the things she'd done.

She should have never played with fire. She would have been better off if she'd stayed inside the ballroom that night and never walked barefoot among the grapevines. Because now she knew exactly what it was she'd been missing for so long.

She stopped halfway up the world's most famous staircase to turn around abruptly.

And tumbled headfirst into another meandering tourist.

"Oh, I'm so sorry." She teetered on the edge of the narrow step, arms flailing, and the unknown victim of her hasty about-face grabbed her by the shoulders to keep her from falling.

"Careful there," he said, his hands solid and warm through the wispy fabric of her sundress.

At the sound of his melted caramel voice, her heart went still. She knew that voice. Intimately.

She breathed out a sigh. What was wrong with her? Was she really mooning over Leonardo Mezzanotte so much that now she was hearing things? She needed to get her head out of the clouds at once before she completely sabotaged her chances in the contest, or worse, broke both her legs falling down the Spanish Steps.

"So sorry," she mumbled, wanting nothing more than to escape to her hotel room and a bottle of Prosecco. She lifted her gaze to thank her rescuer for keeping her in one piece.

And everything went hazy, as if she were looking at the world through the emerald-green glass of a wine bottle.

She couldn't be seeing what she was seeing. *Who* she was seeing. It simply wasn't possible.

"Leo."

It took a moment for Leo to realize what was happening.

When he'd caught his first glimpse of the back of her head, that graceful curve of her neck, he'd thought it was her.

But he'd convinced himself he was imagining things. He

hadn't seen Juliet's name mentioned anywhere in conjunction with the *Roma Festa del Cioccolato*. Her name wasn't on the list of competitors he'd received with his registration materials. Of course, neither was his. His late entry meant he'd slipped in under the radar. Apparently unbeknownst to him, Juliet had been flying stealthily alongside him the whole time.

Still, that familiar glimpse of creamy white skin and up-swept hair had been enough to cause him to turn and follow. Only he'd thought he'd been following a ghost. An ethereal being conjured from the desire for her he still carried around like his love for good chocolate. Something he couldn't indulge, but at the same time refused to leave him.

"Juliet." He didn't know whether to release his hold on her at once or to follow his bone-deep instinct to pull her against him, wrap his arms around her and never let go.

Juliet. Here. In Rome.

She stared at him for a long moment until her gaze drifted to his fingertips, still resting on her shoulders. With no small amount of reluctance, he removed his hands from her.

She looked back up at him. "You're here."

It wasn't what he'd expected her to say. He'd anticipated questions. *What are you doing here? Why are you in Rome?* She seemed alternately surprised to see him and not shocked in the least. As if she'd fully expected to run into him on the Spanish Steps, a world away from the chocolate war in Napa Valley.

He nodded. "Yes, I am. For the..."

"Festa del Cioccolato," she finished, her voice going strangely hollow. "Interesting. I hadn't realized you'd qualified."

Damn you, Uncle Joe. "About that..."

"No explanation necessary. I can venture an educated

guess as to how that happened." The softness was slipping from her gaze. Once again, she was falling though his fingers.

"Would it make any difference if I told you that I didn't expect you to be here?" Should it? Even he didn't know the answer to that question.

"Well, surprise. Here I am." She laughed. But it was uncomfortable, nervous laughter. Not the kind of laughter he'd ever hoped to draw from Juliet's lips.

"Yes, here you are." In the spirit of supreme optimism, he reached for her hand.

She took a micro-step away from him, hovering once again on the edge of the stair where she stood. He almost wished she'd take another tumble, just so he could catch her when she fell.

He dropped his hand.

"Leo, what happened that day after the chocolate fair? The last time I saw you, you were being carried away on a stretcher."

"I'm none the worse for wear." It was a flippant answer, every bit deserving of the flicker of disappointment he saw in the subtle downturn of her mouth.

"Good to know." Church bells sounded from the Trinità dei Monti at the top of the steps. Her gaze lifted toward the bell tower. "It's getting late. I should probably get back to my hotel."

He could see she was on the verge of pulling a Cinderella and fleeing down the stairs.

Panic fluttered in Leo's chest.

This wasn't right. They were far from home in one of the most romantic cities in the world, and they were talking to one another like two damned strangers.

"Don't go," he said as she turned her back to him.

She gave him a final over-the-shoulder glance. That's when he saw it—the look of raw longing in her eyes that told him she still wanted him every bit as much as he wanted her. "Haven't we made a big enough mess of things already? We're competitors. More than competitors. We're enemies. We couldn't even tell one another we were coming here."

"I'm not your enemy, Juliet," he said quietly.

There were other things he could have said. Probably should have.

But how could he tell her that he was allergic to chocolate when they'd be facing off against one another in less than a day? His odds of winning were already slim at best. His family business was hanging by a thread.

His chest ached. He wanted to explain, to tell her everything. There was so much he wanted to say. And he would… once the *Roma Festa del Cioccolato* was over and done with.

She smiled at him. A bittersweet smile that all but ripped him in two. "Good luck tomorrow."

And then she was gone. Lost in the crowd of hundreds who gathered on the steps every night. Tourists. Friends. Lovers.

Lovers.

What the hell was he doing? She'd walked away from him, and he'd just stood there and let her.

Go after her, you idiot.

He took the stairs two at a time on his way down, hurdling over several bottles of wine and a few small children as he went. When he reached the piazza at the foot of the Spanish Steps, he searched for a glimpse of her breezy sundress but came up empty. Despite the late hour, the street was packed with people. Even the little round newsstand and the makeshift flower market down the block were still open.

Leo had no idea where she'd gone. She'd mentioned her
hotel, but of course, he didn't know where she was staying.
She could have already gotten into a cab for all he knew.
There was a taxi stand at the opposite end of the piazza from
the shopping district. He jogged toward it, narrowly avoiding a priest in full cassock juggling a cup of gelato.

He stopped at the first cab in line, bending to speak to the
driver through his open window. Hopefully the guy would
be forthcoming if he'd seen Juliet get into a car. *"Mi Scusi.
Ha fatto una bella donna che indossa un abito giallo entrare in una
di queste vetture?"*

"No, signore." The driver shook his head.

Leo breathed out a heavy sigh, resisting the urge to let
loose a string of Italian expletives. If Juliet had gotten into a
cab, there was always the slim chance another driver could
find out where she'd gone. Of course, things couldn't be so
simple. For once, it would have been nice to feel as if fate
wasn't working against him and Juliet. Just once.

"E andata cosi," the driver said.

She went that way.

Leo's head jerked up.

"E andata cosi," he repeated, pointing toward a quiet side
street behind the flower market. It was narrow enough to
be almost completely obscured by the flower stand's clay-
colored tent.

"Grazie." Leo dug a five-euro note out of his pocket and
gave it to the driver. *"Mille grazie."*

He ran down the side street, his feet echoing on the cold,
dark cobblestones. It was remarkable how quiet everything
seemed just a few short blocks from the chaos of the Piazza
di Spagna. Aside from a street musician playing a violin, its

case resting open on the ground at the player's feet, Leo didn't see another soul. Not anyone.

Not Juliet.

He stopped and looked at the buildings surrounding him. Most were nondescript with gated openings that he suspected led to enclosed private parking areas. Residences. But there was one modest-size building situated on the corner with roses climbing up its walls that had potential. The bottom floor was decorated with dark green awnings, and the upper floors were dotted with small balconies.

Of course, even if it was a hotel, even if it was *her* hotel, he didn't know what room Juliet was in and doubted very much that anyone would be willing to part with that information, no matter how many euros he tossed in their direction. He was contemplating other, more devious options when he heard something that slowed his footsteps.

A voice. *Her* voice.

"Oh, Leo."

He looked up and found her instantly. She stood on one of the second floor balconies enveloped in soft light, glorious in the night, looming over him like a winged messenger from heaven.

"Leo, if it weren't for your name, I'd give myself to you." Her voice was little more than a breathy whisper on the sultry Italian air, but he heard her loud and clear.

And at the sound of those magic words, his soul sang. "Juliet, I'm here."

"Leo?" She leaned over the balcony railing, squinting down at him in the darkness. "Is that you?"

"Yes. It's me." He planted his hands on his hips. Now that he'd found her, his patience was wearing thin. He wanted up there. Now.

"What are you doing here?" She sounded far more surprised to find him at her hotel than she had earlier on the Spanish Steps.

"I'll tell you exactly what I'm doing. I'm coming up there."

20

"I'm coming up there." Leo stood below with his hands jammed on his hips, staring up at Juliet. Even from two floors up, she could see the thunder in his gaze.

She peered down at him, butterflies swarming in her stomach. "What did you say?"

She'd heard perfectly well what he'd said. She just needed a minute to wrap her mind around the fact that he was here. In Rome. At her hotel. And he'd just announced that he was about to march up to her room.

How much of her wistful muttering had he heard from down there, exactly?

Her mind and body were at war. She knew good and well this wasn't a great idea. After the *Festa del Cioccolato,* maybe. But not now. Not here. She'd traveled over six thousand miles to compete in this contest. Not to mention the fact that her family was scheduled to descend on the place in less than eight hours.

Her body, on the other hand, was of a differing opinion. With one look, the smallest glance, she could practically feel his hands on her. The memory of their one night together was written into her flesh. Her heart beat hummingbird-fast, as though it wanted to leap over the edge of the balcony and throw itself at Leo's feet.

"You heard me. I'm coming up." His tone had a determined edge. Clearly he'd made up his mind.

He waited a beat, and when she didn't make a move to open her door, he marched straight toward the rose trellis that trailed up the side of the hotel.

Juliet leaned over the stone edge of the balcony. Surely he was bluffing. He wouldn't actually try to climb up there.

She rolled her eyes. "Leo, please."

He planted his foot on the bottom level of the lattice fencing attached to the wall, aimed a searing glance up at her and then gave the trellis a good shake. The roses trembled, and a lone pink petal drifted toward the ground as he pulled himself up about a foot off the ground.

"You're really planning on climbing all the way up here?" The building was five stories. Hardly a skyscraper. And her room was only on the second floor, but still.

He could get hurt. Could people die from falling two stories? She was pretty sure they could. Or at the very least be seriously injured.

"It looks that way, doesn't it?" He pushed past a cluster of rose blossoms and moved a bit closer.

The trellis seemed to be holding up, thank goodness. But he winced once or twice and muttered a string of expletives. He'd most likely encountered a few thorns. Well, that served him right. He was behaving like a crazy person.

She crossed her arms. "Leo, stop. This is insane."

She should go inside and forget he was even out here. Maybe then he'd shimmy back down the wall and go away.

But she couldn't seem to make her feet move. She stood rooted to the spot while he climbed his way farther up.

Her stomach tightened as the distance grew greater between Leo and the cobblestones below. She wanted to close her eyes, but they remained stubbornly open. He only suffered one little stumble. About halfway up, his foot slipped from the trellis. His body gave a little jerk. Roses shivered. But he managed not to fall to his death, so she released the breath she hadn't even realized she'd been holding.

Quicker than she would have imagined, he was level with her balcony. His lips curved into a cocky smirk. "Hello there, Juliet."

God, he wasn't even out of breath. If she'd attempted such a feat, she no doubt would have ended up with a nice collection of broken bones. Of course, he wasn't actually on the balcony yet. He was still hanging on to the trellis.

"What now, Spider-Man?" she asked dryly.

He swung his legs up and over the little cement wall that served as a railing, landing deftly on his feet. Impressive. She wondered how he'd managed to learn how to scale walls and hurdle barriers at the same time he'd been busy perfecting the art of making French macarons.

He glanced behind him at the railing. "Did you really think once I'd gotten up here I'd let a silly little wall keep me away? Stony limits can't hold me, Juliet."

Stony limits can't hold me.

It was a nice thought. Of course, there were plenty of other limits they had to worry about that were much stronger than stone. But at the moment, she was having trouble remembering what those limits were.

They stood face-to-face on the small balcony with the tangy scent of fresh lemons swirling in the air. It seemed as

if all of Rome smelled of lemons. There wasn't a star in the
sky. Somewhere in the distance church bells rang, and the
moon hung heavy and full over the grand dome of St. Peter's
Basilica. A harvest moon, gold and luminous, not unlike the
one that shone overhead the night they'd met in the vineyard.

The full moon. It must be to blame.

If the stars of fate could be blamed for keeping them apart,
it only seemed fair to credit the moon with bringing them
together.

She inhaled a steadying breath. Clearly the wine she'd
had with dinner had gone to her head. She wasn't thinking
straight. Fate, stars, the powers of a full moon…

None of it made sense. Then again, neither did running
into Leo on the Spanish Steps.

She had no idea what to say.

"Hi."

Hi? Really? The man had just scaled a wall to get to her
and all she could manage was a breathy *hi?* Pathetic.

He reached out and wound a lock of her hair around his
finger. "Hi there."

He continued to watch her with an intensity that she
felt down to her soul. It didn't help quell the romantic notions in her head. There was a wildness about that look in
his eyes, something primal and wholly unrestrained. A leaf
clung to his shoulder and a twig stuck in his hair, as if he'd
crawled through the jungle to get to her. Which, in a way,
he had. He had scratches on his hands and a small cut on his
left temple, no doubt from the thorny rose bushes. For some
crazy reason, that tiny glimpse of blood caused Juliet's heart
to thump violently in her chest.

He cast a glance over her shoulder toward the French doors
that led to her room. "Is your family here?"

She could lie. And then what? He'd pull a parachute out of thin air and glide back down to the ground? It wouldn't have surprised her in the slightest.

She swallowed. "Not yet."

"I see. So your family is no obstacle tonight." His grin broadened, equal parts wicked and triumphant. He released the lock of her hair, brushed his fingertips over her cheek and stepped even closer. His gaze was penetrating as it swept over her, and with each passing second she found it increasingly harder to breathe.

She'd never felt so utterly naked in her life. Not even when she'd undressed for him in her kitchen.

She reached to remove the twig from his hair, and he caught her wrist. "Come here."

She gasped as he pulled her hard against him, sliding his hands over her rib cage until they splayed against her back, holding her in place. She couldn't have moved anyhow. That look in his eyes that seemed to echo the need she felt deep in the pit of her stomach had paralyzed her. Her head grew fuzzy. The intoxicating fragrance of fresh roses clung to him, making her dizzy.

She blinked. They should discuss this like rational people instead of acting without thinking. The last time they'd done something like this, it had resulted in a spectacular mess. And here they were, a mere day away from facing off against one another again. Only this time, there was even more at stake.

She should be thinking about the chocolate contest. That's why she was here in Rome. But it was the last thing on her mind at the moment. Still, she managed to pay it lip service in case he was on a different page. "The competition…"

"Doesn't start for another sixteen hours," he growled, his hands sliding up her back and burying themselves in her hair.

Then his mouth came down on hers, hard, searching, demanding. Her lips throbbed from the force of his tender brutality, a bruise in the making.

When she'd implored him not to be gentle the last time, she'd thought he'd done as she asked. She was beginning to realize she'd been wrong. This was different from before. Darker. More dangerous. And even more intoxicating.

Violent ends.

She clutched at the lapels of his jacket, holding on for dear life as the kisses came too quick and too urgent to keep track of where one ended and the next began. But any attempt at anchoring herself was futile. She was falling into him again, just as she'd done since that very first night. Something about him drew her right in again and again, time after time. Like gravity. And now, as ever, she was incapable of resisting.

The words she didn't want to say slipped right out. She murmured against his lips, "God, I've missed you."

He took his mouth from hers and cradled her face in his hands, dragging the pad of his thumb along her throbbing bottom lip. "I know, baby, I know. Me, too."

He kept his gaze locked with hers as he dropped his hands to her waist, slid them over the curve of her hips and around to her bottom. His fingers dug into her soft flesh, and he rocked his hips, pressing the hard swell of his arousal into her belly to show her just how much he'd missed her.

She whimpered, and Leo's eyes went darker than ever.

"You know how I feel about that sound," he said, guiding her backward until she bumped up against the wall.

She gripped at the concrete with shaky hands while Leo braced his arms on either side of her head, hemming her in. She wanted to touch him, but she couldn't seem to make her limbs work. That familiar slow heat had ignited deep in her abdomen and seemed to be mirrored in the fire she saw in Leo's gaze. And as he leaned down and nipped gently at her neck, her most pressing thought was how very much she'd like to be burnt.

"You taste divine. I'd almost forgotten." Leo's tongue made a languorous trail from her neck to her shoulder. Hot openmouthed kisses, punctuated with the occasional bite. "Don't worry. I won't forget again."

His fingers made quick work of unbuttoning her dress. Before she could take in a lungful of fresh sea air, the garment fell to the floor. A gentle breeze fluttered over her exposed skin, intensifying each kiss, each nip of his teeth. Every cell in her body went on high alert.

"Leo," she breathed, sagging against the wall. If he didn't stop what he was doing, she'd never remain upright.

Leo. Lion. She'd been so preoccupied with his last name that she hadn't given much thought to his first. It suited him. He looked every bit a lion right then, all powerful grace. Even his eyes were lionlike as he let his gaze travel over her exposed shoulders and breasts. Like a wild cat stalking its prey.

"I want to touch you forever," he said with the utmost seriousness, sliding her bra off her shoulders until it too lay in a heap at their feet. His fingers hooked in the lacy edge of her panties and pulled, until she was completely naked on her hotel balcony.

Forever.

It was a dangerous word. And it made the heat flowing through her all the more scorching.

Juliet pretended she hadn't heard it. "Shouldn't we go inside?"

His hand slid up the back of her thigh, and he lifted her

leg until it was wrapped around his waist. "No. I want you right here. Right now."

A soft, shuddering moan pierced the quiet night, and Juliet realized it had come from her own lips. She wanted him so badly it was painful. Desire consumed her from the inside out. Each tiny nibble, each wet, hot lick of his tongue was agony. The cool, damp Roman air bit at each place where he kissed her, raising her skin into tiny, torturous goose bumps.

She reached for his fly, unbuttoned it and slid down the zipper, freeing him. He tensed when she took him in her hands. He was harder than she'd ever felt him. Solid, hot and ready. When she stroked him, he trembled and let out a long, agonizing groan that could surely be heard from cobblestoned streets below.

Then he took control, grabbing her wrists and pinning them above her head with one hand so she couldn't move. A tremulous shiver of desperate want coursed through her as he paused to look at her, his free hand holding her chin, his gaze wild and hungry.

"Leo," she breathed, wishing she could tell him how very much she wanted him no matter what the consequences. But she was unable to articulate more than his name.

He seemed to understand perfectly, though.

"I know, baby. I know," he said, his voice raw with desire.

He tightened his grip on her chin, tilting her face toward his. Then he kissed her as if his very life depended on it, and she arched toward him, utterly helpless. She couldn't move, and she had no choice but to simply kiss and give.

His free hand dropped to her breast, then her waist, then between her legs in a glorious trail of exploration that left her gasping for breath. Then he slipped his fingers inside her, and she thought she might die from longing. Her arms still pinned, she wrapped her leg more firmly around his waist, pulling him closer and closer still, until his body was crushing hers against the wall.

"Now, please," she begged, her eyes drifting closed, unable to wait another second to have him inside her.

"Open your eyes." he said. "I want you to look at me."

Her lashes fluttered open, and she found him staring down at her with those midnight eyes filled with an intoxicating combination of wonder, desire and something far more edgy that she couldn't quite identify.

Her breath caught in her throat during that final moment of anticipation as his erection pressed against her core. Her entire body went liquid. Music drifted to her ears, a mournful melody from the streets below. Strains of a violin floating on the errant night breeze. Leo's gaze never strayed, but remained fixed on hers, his face mere inches from hers.

And then she recognized it—that look in his eyes.

Possession.

"Mine," he groaned as he entered her, not with a push but rather an excruciatingly slow, aching grind.

It was too much—this overwhelming need to be taken, this pleasure, this fullness.

This man.

In that instant, he owned her. He knew it, and so did she. He was devouring her, and all she could do was give. She had no choice but to yield to desire, to the wild Italian night. To him.

And in the final moment before Juliet came apart, all she could do was whisper in return, "Yours."

21

Leo opened his eye a crack and then closed it again. If that was the morning light he saw peeking through Juliet's balcony window, he didn't want to know. Not yet.

He wanted another minute. Another hour. Another night. Sometimes he even thought he might want forever. Which was problematic, to say the least.

Whatever the future might hold, they'd at least had one perfect night. After their tryst on the balcony, he'd slowly and methodically helped Juliet back into her dress. Then they'd returned to the Spanish Steps with a bottle of red and two plastic cups from the hotel bathroom. It had been well past midnight, and they'd found the usually bustling piazza beautifully barren. Under a starless sky, they'd strolled hand in hand all the way to the top of the steps. There they'd sat and sipped wine while taking in the sweeping view of Rome under the inky blanket of night. They'd listened to the cry of seagulls, the peal of church bells from every direction, and they'd made out like teenagers.

It had been near dawn when they returned to her room—by way of the elevator this time—and Leo had wasted no time getting her out of that dress again. The things he'd done to her...the things she'd done to him...

The memory of it lingered in his waking consciousness, so that falling back asleep was impossible. He played with a lock of Juliet's hair, twisted it around his finger, and watched as she stirred to life.

"Mmm." She stretched against him, her body as supple and lithe as a cat's, until her eyelashes fluttered open. "Tell me it's not morning yet. Tell me that light I see coming in the window is starlight. A spectacular meteor shower setting the night on fire."

He was growing hard again. How was that even possible? He would have thought he'd reached the end of himself by now.

"It's not morning yet," he lied, shifting and snuggling against her backside. Two perfect spoons.

He'd tell her whatever it was she wanted to hear if it meant he could stay in this room, in this bed, just a little while longer.

He'd say the light coming through the window wasn't morning at all. He'd say it was the reflection of the low-hanging moon, shining just for them.

Juliet turned in his arms, and he kissed her, finding her lips warm from sleep. She sighed into his mouth, and for a lingering, drowsy moment, everything was exactly as it should have been.

"Oh, my God! It is morning." She sat halfway up in bed, the sheet dropping to expose her bare breasts.

Leo's lips strayed lower, moving down her neck, across her collar bone, to where his hands captured those beautiful breasts.

She melted into him for a moment, that purr he loved so

much escaping from her lips, and then she tensed. "Leo, you can't be here. It's getting lighter and lighter outside."

"More light," he murmured against her sweet-tasting skin. "More pain for us."

How long would they be destined to live in the dark?

"Seriously, do you have any idea what time it is? My family is scheduled to land at Fiumicino at nine o'clock."

He had no idea what time it was, as time seemed to have been suspended for a while now. But it couldn't be anywhere near nine o'clock already. Could it?

The click of a door being opened told him that, yes, actually, it could.

"Oh, geez. You've got to be kidding me." The always cheerful Alegra walked in the room and dropped her small suitcase on the ground with a thud, causing Juliet to bounce to the other side of the bed. Alegra expelled a loud sigh and shielded her eyes. "You guys are having sex, aren't you? I think my retinas have been permanently scarred."

Juliet's cheeks turned as pink as the climbing roses outside. "We're not having sex."

Alegra snorted. "At the moment, maybe."

Leo sighed and positioned himself in front of Juliet on the bed so she could have a modicum of privacy, which seemed a little irrelevant at this point. "Hello, Alegra."

"Hey there, Sparkle." Her gaze flitted to his naked torso for a second. "Nice biceps. I mean, I'm not sure why they're wrapped around my cousin. *In Rome*. But nice, nonetheless."

He wasn't at all sure how to respond to that sort of back-handed compliment, so he settled on a muttered, "Thanks."

Juliet dashed from the bed, pulled an oversize T-shirt from a drawer and slipped it over her head. Leo did his best not to fixate on the exposed length of lithe, sun-kissed legs stretching out from beneath the hem.

Juliet jammed her hands on her hips. She was flustered, clearly. The most gorgeous flustered woman Leo had ever laid eyes on. "Alegra, what are you doing here?"

"It's Tuesday morning. I'm supposed to be here, remember?" She aimed a pointed glance at Leo. "He, on the other hand, is not."

A muscle in Leo's jaw tightened.

Juliet's cheeks turned a brighter shade of crimson. "Alegra, now is not the time."

"Seriously. This is insane. What is he doing here?" Alegra crossed her arms and waited for an explanation.

Leo didn't care for her tone, but he was wary of getting into an altercation with Alegra while he was still undressed. He could see her throwing every stitch of his clothing over the balcony railing in a heartbeat.

"The same thing I'm doing here. He's here for the competition," Juliet said calmly.

Leo's jaw grew even tighter at the thought of standing in a kitchen with Juliet for two straight days, once again trying to trump one another. They'd spent an awful lot of time working in opposition lately. And they would continue doing so. Over and over. Again and again. It was their destiny.

Yet sometimes he couldn't help but wonder what might happen if they were on the same team. Not that being on the same side as Juliet was likely to happen anytime soon. Or ever.

"Are you serious? You two are going to be competing against one another in three hours?" Alegra groaned.

Three hours?

Leo frowned. Just how late had they slept? "Alegra, could you give your cousin and me a minute alone? Please?"

She snorted. "You don't have a minute, Sparkle. Juliet's mom is on her way up."

Perfect. Just perfect.

"What?" Juliet paled. In the span of a heartbeat, she grew whiter than death.

"Both of your parents are here. You knew they were on the same flight as I was. They just headed to their room on the first floor. Your dad is unpacking, and your mom wanted to come right up to see you. Honestly, what were you two thinking?" Alegra shook her head. "Never mind. I'd probably rather not know."

"Leo, you can't be here. You just can't." Juliet started tossing clothes at him in a fit of panic.

He ducked and narrowly avoided a shoe to the head.

"Don't worry, baby. She won't find me here." He pulled on his shirt. It would have been nice if Alegra had at least gone through the pretense of averting her gaze. Instead, she just stood there watching with an amused smirk on her face. But Leo supposed he had bigger problems at the moment.

"I'm worried. I'm *very* worried." Juliet was on the verge of tears, which was so not how Leo wanted the morning to end. "What are we going to do?"

He stood up, crammed his feet into his shoes and went to cup her face in his hands. God, she was so nervous she was trembling. "You're going to stay right here and have a nice visit with your mom, and I'm going to go out the same way I came in."

A glimmer of a smile came to her lips. "The balcony? Again? Really?"

"Yes, really."

There was a knock at the door. "Juliet!"

"I told you." Alegra lifted a self-righteous eyebrow. "Shall I answer that?"

"No," Leo and Juliet said in unison.

He looked into her eyes and tried desperately to ignore the knocking on the door. "Kiss me. One last time."

One *more* time. He'd meant one *more* time. Not last.

She threw her arms around his neck and, with her heart-beat pounding frantically against his, kissed the life out of him.

"Now? Are you kidding me?" Alegra began to pace circles around them.

The pounding on the door grew louder. "Juliet, Alegra, are you two in there?"

"Okay." Juliet pulled away from him, breaking their kiss. "Now, you really, really need to get out of here."

And then the window that had so cruelly let in daylight became his escape.

By the time Juliet finally gave Alegra the go-ahead to open the door, her mother had clearly begun to suspect something.

She sashayed right past both Alegra and Juliet and entered the room, her gaze darting to and fro. "What's going on in here?"

"Nothing," Alegra said a little too quickly.

Juliet willed herself not to cringe while her mother stared at the unmade bed, with pillows askew and tangled sheets hanging halfway to the floor.

"Why did it take you so long to come to the door?" She frowned at the messy bed for what felt like an eternity. "For heaven's sake, Juliet. Did you just wake up?"

Juliet faked a yawn. "Yes. I suppose I've got some lingering jet lag. I couldn't seem to make myself get out of bed this morning."

Alegra coughed. "Jet lag. I'm sure that's the culprit."

Juliet shot her cousin a warning glance and brushed past her to wrap her mother in a hug. Anything to divert attention away from the bed. "Mom, it's great to see you. How was your trip?"

Her mom hugged her back briefly. "Long, but fine. Your dad and Nico are downstairs. Shouldn't we be leaving soon for the competition? Goodness, you're not even showered."

She shook her head and tsk-tsked which, being typical Mom behavior, came as a great relief. Until she moved to the French doors that led to the balcony.

"What you need in here is some daylight. That will get you moving." She shoved the curtains aside and flung the doors open.

Alegra let out a little squeal and then clamped her hand over her mouth.

Juliet thought she might faint on the spot. She was sure Leo hadn't made it all the way down the trellis yet. There simply hadn't been time.

"Mom!" she shouted, loud enough to make Alegra jump again.

Her mother paused at the threshold of the balcony and turned around. Thank God.

She frowned. "Why are you yelling, dear? I'm right here in Italy, not back in Napa Valley."

"Um." What could she possibly say to get her off that balcony with its lovely view—Leo included—and back inside? "Um, I don't think I can go to the competition, after all."

That seemed to do the trick. Her mom did an immediate about-face. *"What?"*

Even Alegra was thrown for a loop. "Huh?"

"I don't feel well." Juliet sank down on the bed.

The sheets were still warm and smelled faintly of red wine and Leo. She battled the ridiculous urge to bury her face in the pillow where he'd rested his head.

"What do you mean you don't feel well?" Her mom's hand was on her forehead in an instant. "Your temperature is normal."

"It's my stomach. I feel queasy. I'm sure that's why I overslept." Juliet clutched her midsection. This kind of faux sickness had never worked when she was a kid and had wanted to stay home from school, but surely it would buy enough time for Leo to climb down the wall.

Alegra rolled her eyes and muttered, "Of course. Because nausea oftentimes goes hand in hand with jet lag."

Juliet's mom frowned. "Alegra, stop mumbling and go get Juliet a cool washcloth for her head. And a cup of chipped ice."

Alegra lifted a dubious brow. "For real?"

"Yes. And while you're at it, maybe a Coke. You should be able to get one from the bar downstairs. See if they have saltines, too."

Juliet mouthed *sorry* from behind her mom's back, but that didn't stop Alegra from breathing out a labored sigh.

She scowled. "I just got off a ten-hour flight, and now I get to be Juliet's servant when she's been doing nothing all day but rolling around in the sack...I mean lying around in bed. Awesome."

If Juliet hadn't been so fictionally ill, she would have strangled her cousin.

"Juliet, dear." Her mother sat down on the bed beside her while Alegra busied herself in the bathroom with the faucet and the requested washcloth. "Are you really feeling sick or, as I suspect, is this something else entirely?"

Her mother then proceeded to give her what Nico always called the *look of doom*. And Juliet suddenly did feel genuinely ill.

She swallowed. "Something else?"

Something like Leo Mezzanotte. Here. In Rome. In this very bed.

"Yes." Her mom gave a knowing, firm nod. "Nerves. This is a big contest. You're far from your comfort zone in Napa Valley, and you're worried about the competition. That's what this is really about, isn't it?"

Yes, it was. She was worried about her competition. Specifically, that her competition would get caught sneaking out of her bedroom. "There might be some truth to that."

"You can do this, dear. I know you can." Her mom smiled and, in a rare display of maternal affection, gave her shoulders a squeeze. Then she shocked the daylights out of Juliet by getting a little teary-eyed. It was almost enough to make Juliet feel bad about all the lying. But since telling the truth was not remotely an option, she could live with herself.

Her mom gave her a watery smile. "I'm so proud of you. We all are—me, your father, Nico and Alegra."

She probably could have left Alegra off that list. "Thanks, Mom."

"You've got nothing to worry about. This contest is going to go off without a hitch."

Alegra returned with a cold, dripping washcloth dangling from her fingertips, and flung it at Juliet. "Here you go, princess."

She managed to catch it before it hit her in the face. "Thank you."

Alegra crossed her arms, glanced at the balcony curtains rippling softly in the breeze and then back at Juliet and her mom. "What did I miss? Anything interesting happen while I was in the bathroom?"

"Juliet is nervous about the contest," her mother said, obviously satisfied that she'd gotten to the bottom of things.

"Oh, is that what she's nervous about?" The beginnings of a smirk danced on Alegra's lips.

Juliet buried her face in the cool washcloth. Admittedly, it felt good.

"I told her there's nothing to be anxious about. Things could be a lot more troubling. I mean, imagine if Leo Mezzanotte were here."

A very real wave of nausea washed over Juliet. She hadn't had much time to think about what Leo's entry in the contest meant. Was his family in Rome, as well? Probably. That meant they were in for a repeat of the drama of the chocolate fair back home.

Goody.

She removed the washcloth, opened her eyes and found Alegra grinning down at her. Her cousin flashed her a wink. "Yeah. Imagine."

The Roma Festa del Cioccolato was traditionally held at one of the many gourmet cooking schools in the Eternal City. This year, the venue was a seven-hundred-year-old Franciscan monastery that had been converted to a gourmet haven nestled near a quiet corner of Villa Borghese. The school's name—Il Cucchiaio di Legno—meant The Wooden Spoon, which Juliet found endlessly charming. And when she arrived for the preliminary round of the chocolate competition, she found the surroundings just as delightful as she'd imagined.

The building was square-shaped, with the center being an open courtyard shaded by a tall canopy of umbrella pines that stretched above bountiful herb and vegetable gardens, as well as a thriving cluster of Rome's ubiquitous lemon trees. A portico with tall arched walkways ran the entire length of the building, overlooking the gardens, ensuring that the lush courtyard could be seen from every room inside. The walls were buttery-yellow, and the floor was earthy tile. Juliet felt as though she'd stepped inside one of the postcards that she'd collected over the years.

She did her best to concentrate on these details and breathe in the essence of Old World Italy rather than think about the very narrow escape she and Leo had experienced just a few hours ago. If she thought too much about it, her hands began to shake. And that was the last thing she needed when she was trying to make a wedding cake.

As steeped in Old World charm as everything was, the commercial-size kitchen where the contestants each had an individually assigned workstation was sleek and modern, with every imaginable up-to-the-minute convenience. And surprise, surprise, Juliet's workspace was situated right next to Leo's.

He stood with his back to the countertop, leaning against it as if he didn't have a care in the world. And of course, he was wearing that impeccable white chef's coat again. Juliet's heart did a rebellious flip-flop at the sight of it.

She inhaled a deep breath. There were people milling around everywhere—fellow contestants, contest proctors, judges. People she preferred not to know that she'd spent the night in bed with one of her fellow competitors. It wasn't the most professional of circumstances.

But now was not the time for romance. Now was the time to kick some serious ass.

She gave Leo a polite nod as she approached her work area. "Mr. Mezzanotte."

He lifted a brow. "Miss Arabella."

Why did her name sound so different when he said it? Dangerous. Like poison.

She began checking the inventory of items at her workstation, doing her best to pretend Leo wasn't standing a mere two feet away.

Which was patently impossible. He was a force of nature.

"We've got to stop meeting like this," he murmured without looking at her.

"I couldn't agree more." She opened the plastic bins that contained her white chocolate sheet cakes.

Contest rules stated that competitors had eight hours to complete their entries for the artistic round of competition. These hours were to be spent mostly on construction. Certain cooking components, such as basic sheet cakes, simple chocolate or candied fruits, could be prepared in advance. Thank goodness. She would need every bit of those eight hours to carve her sheet cakes into shapes that resembled the Altare della Patria and get it decorated.

She glanced over at Leo. Compared to her crowded countertop, his workspace was barren. It held a single rectangular box that stood about a foot tall and a small leather sheath that held an assortment of odd-looking tools—tiny knives of various sizes, picks and armature wire. She wondered what on earth he was up to, but wasn't about to ask.

"Got everything you need over there?" she said, simply because she really couldn't help it. He had the fewest supplies of anyone in the room.

"Worried about me, Miss Arabella?" he asked, once again not looking at her, which for some odd reason made it all the more provocative.

"Of course not. I have my own entry to worry about." She double-checked to make sure her sketchbook and her grandmother's recipe book were among the items spread out in front of her.

"That's my girl," Leo whispered.

My girl.

She fully expected him to look away again, but he didn't. Their eyes met, and something intimate and unspoken settled between them. A memory.

A memory of the way he'd looked at her when he'd taken her in the sultry heat of that balcony. The way he'd claimed her.

Mine.

The way she'd given herself to him.

Yours.

Those weren't words uttered in the heat of the moment. They'd meant something. Still did. Those words echoed between them now. Here in the crowded kitchen.

Juliet could hear them whispering in her soul. She could see them shining in Leo's fierce blue eyes.

"Do you have any idea how badly I want to touch you right now?" His hands rested on the countertop in front of him, and, as he spoke, his fingertips inched closer.

"Leo." She bit her lip.

His gaze dropped instantly to her mouth. "Juliet."

"We can't do this here. You know that." She felt as if she was holding her breath, and she was so very desperate to exhale.

His fingers clenched on the edge of the counter, his knuckles turning white. "I know nothing of the sort. What's to stop me from taking you in my arms right here and now and kissing you within an inch of your life?"

It sounded very much like when he'd threatened to kiss her the night they'd met at the masquerade ball, for all the world to see. And she wondered suddenly what would have happened if she'd let him. Would they still be pretending they were mortal enemies when they were really anything but? Or would time and honesty have worked their magic, and allowed them to be free to love?

She blinked. Love? Was she in love with Leo? Surely not. "Oh, I don't know…the fact that we've both traveled all the way across the Atlantic Ocean to compete against one another in this contest?"

But even as she said the words, she realized the competitive fire that had burned in her since Leo had shown up back in Napa Valley had started to cool. She was tired. Tired of trying to beat him at every turn. Tired of pretending not to care for him. To herself and to everyone else.

"Try me." He moved toward her. Just a fraction.

Then a loud voice echoed off the ancient kitchen walls. Juliet jumped backward. Leo stilled.

"Competitors, *Benvenuti a Roma!*" The contest proctor stood in the center of the room, arms spread open wide in the universal gesture of welcome.

He scanned the room, his gaze finally landing on Leo and Juliet. "Let the *Roma Festa del Cioccolato* officially begin!"

22

Leo wondered if it was possible to absorb chocolate into his bloodstream through his skin. He hoped to hell not. If so, he was in deep trouble.

Chocolate was caked underneath his nails, in every possible crevice of his hands, in every tiny ridge and swirl of the pads of his fingers. If the kitchen in Rome had been a crime scene, he would have left his mark in an incriminating abundance of chocolate fingerprints.

He hadn't really thought about this inevitable result of his chosen project for the artistic round of the contest. He'd simply been searching for a way to avoid actually having to consume chocolate. He hadn't realized he would be taking a virtual bath in the stuff.

"That is really something." Juliet stared, wide-eyed, at his half-finished creation. It was only the first or second time she'd looked up from the pristine, white, oh-so-ambitious project she had going on beside him.

"Thank you," he said and nodded at the wedding cake within a wedding cake in front of her. The Altare della Patria. As an actual wedding cake. Brilliant. "So is your cake."

"Thanks." She looked almost bashful. That hidden smile and those pink cheeks, coupled with the smear of white chocolate frosting on her forehead and that creative mind she possessed, was enough to bring Leo to his knees with desire.

He'd had about enough. Even if he crossed the river and made a quick trip to the Vatican, and the Pope somehow managed to miraculously cure his chocolate allergy, he was done. No more competing. At least not against Juliet. He was ready to end this whole feud once and for all.

"I had no idea they taught sculpting at Le Cordon Bleu." She nodded at his project.

It was a replica of one of Italy's most well-known treasures—Michelangelo's David—carved from a solid block of chocolate. The head, face and shoulders were pretty much done, but he still had a good deal of work to do on the rest.

"They don't." Leo smiled. "I did a fair bit of sculpting at La Maison."

None as complicated as what he was attempting with the David statue. Not even close. At least he had some experience, though. With any luck, he'd make it through the first day of the contest and survive to compete on day two. If he could manage whatever the cooking challenge might be on the second day without consuming a morsel of chocolate, it would be a flat-out miracle. But he'd deal with that bridge when he came to it.

"Well, it looks great." Juliet pushed a wisp of hair from her eyes and ended up with another swipe of frosting on her face. Her cheek this time. Adorable.

He focused his attention back on his replica of David. "So long as his head doesn't topple off, I'm good."

Juliet eyed his sculpting mallet. "Don't put ideas in my head."

The naughty minx. "Watch yourself. That mallet could really do a number on a wedding cake. You know, if it were to fly out of my hand. Accidentally."

"Accidentally?" She narrowed her gaze. "You know what Freud said about accidents, right?"

"Refresh my memory."

"He said there are no accidents. My mother says the same thing. No accidents. Only fate. So watch your grip on that mallet, mister."

He slid it away from Juliet, just to be on the safe side. "Will do. Tell me, though. What do you suppose Freud would have had to say about the rest of our situation? I can venture a guess as to your mother's opinion, but what about our friend Freud?"

She flushed. "I'm not sure I'd want to know. The mind reels, doesn't it?"

"Indeed it does, Miss Arabella." He shot her a wink.

He didn't want to contemplate what Freud would say. He couldn't even make sense of it himself, and he was neck deep in it.

Juliet flipped her standing mixer to on, and the noise it created put an end to any further conversation. Just as well. He still had quite a great deal of work to do on chocolate David. Those six-pack abs weren't going to carve themselves.

Leo lost himself in the work. For that he was grateful. He couldn't very well go all day wondering if he would suddenly stop breathing, nor could he give into his urge to simply stand there and stare at Juliet. Watching her was fascinating. The slightest twist of her slender wrist as she iced her cake was enough to render him spellbound. He could see a world of radiance in that tiniest of movements.

And that cake. It was like nothing Leo had ever seen.

Nothing at Le Cordon Bleu or La Maison had come close to the intricacy she was busy weaving beside him. By the time it was finished, she'd crafted a replica of the Altare della Patria so exact that there was no doubt in Leo's mind who would win the first round of the competition.

"I should probably pack my knives and go," he said as they made their way to the courtyard where judging would commence.

Juliet laughed. "This isn't *Top Chef.* And only half us are going home, remember? The rest of us will still have another complete day of competition."

Leo was well aware. He couldn't have dreaded Day Two of the *Roma Festa del Cioccolato* more. Gladiators who'd headed to the Colosseum back in the day likely looked forward to their fate with greater enthusiasm. Today's competition was judged nearly exclusively on artistic merit, but tomorrow's round was all about taste. *If* he was still around tomorrow. He had no idea what to expect, as the rules varied from year to year. Sometimes the competitors were asked to create a recipe using a list of certain ingredients. In other years, there was one central ingredient that was required to be featured, but chefs could use whatever other ingredients they desired. And, yes, sometimes it was a blind taste challenge like the one from the Napa Valley Chocolate Fair.

He was banking on options one or two. Obviously. He didn't much care what he had to do, so long as it wasn't another taste challenge.

As they stepped from the confines of the building into the cool mist of the courtyard, Juliet's footsteps slowed. She peered up at him. "Good luck, Leo."

The self-control it took not to kiss her at that moment was staggering. "Thank you. Good luck to you, too."

He touched her hand with the slightest graze of his fingertips. For the barest of seconds, he felt it. The fire of connection. Every bit as real as it had been on the balcony the
night before.

Then she pulled away from him. And she was walking toward the silver wheeled cart that held her cake. The flash of
a camera went off. Leo blinked, and when the stars cleared
from his vision he saw Juliet's mother staring at him. Her
mouth was a perfect O of surprise. The camera in her hands
wobbled for a second, and he thought she might drop it right
on top of Juliet's cake.

Then, as quickly as she'd been thrown off guard, she re-
covered. Her face changed into its usual mask of cool indifference. Her lip curled in disgust ever so slightly before she
looked away.

The woman despised him. Maybe more so now than ever
before, since he'd turned up in Rome.

But he couldn't worry about such things now. The judges
were already milling about, moving from one entry to the
next. Leo took his place beside his sculpture, ready to answer
questions and discuss his entry. But none of the three judges
acknowledged him with more than a polite smile and nod.

This is not looking good.

He took a deep breath. The courtyard no longer smelled of
lemons as it had earlier. The overwhelming aroma of chocolate hung in the air. Leo took a bigger inhale. He still loved
that smell, probably always would.

"*Signore e signori.* Ladies and gentlemen. Welcome to the
first round judging of the *Roma Festa del Cioccolato*," the head
judge said in a booming voice that rose to the tops of the
umbrella pines looming overhead and threatened to topple
Leo's chocolate David off its pedestal.

Leo shot a glance at the audience, which seemed to be filled mostly with members of the media. But sure enough, he spotted Uncle Joe in the first row reserved for spectators. He looked drawn and worried, and just pale enough to take the edge off Leo's lingering anger. In fact, a flicker of genu‐ine worry passed through Leo until he realized that Uncle Joe had parked himself directly beside Juliet's mother. There they were—the Mezzanottes and the Arabellas, side by side, taking up the entire row.

Why they insisted on hating one another at such close range was a mystery Leo would never understand.

"The judges have evaluated the entries of the artistic round of competition. The competitors with the top five scores will move on to round two of competition tomorrow."

Leo took a look around. He was one of ten competitors. Half would move on, the other half would be finished.

"Those five, in no particular order, are Enzo St. Lucia, Arnaud Beaulieu, Carla Agostoni, Juliet Arabella and Leo‐nardo Mezzanotte."

Leo allowed himself to exhale. Of course his name would be called last. The seemingly unending millisecond between hearing Juliet's name and hearing his own had shaved at least a year off his life. He hadn't realized quite how much he wanted to win this thing until he'd thought he was out of it.

He grinned. He wasn't out of it. Not yet. And now his odds had increased from one in ten to one in five. He just might be able to pull off a win, after all.

The relief had barely begun to take form in Leo's mind, wasn't yet fully crystallized, when the judge spoke again. "Round Two of competition will commence tomorrow morning at nine o'clock. This year, the taste portion of the *Roma Festa del Cioccolato* will consist of a blind taste test.

Buona sera, signore e signori. And to our competitors, *in bocca al lupo!*"

In bocca al lupo.

Leo hadn't heard that saying in years. It was the traditional Italian way of imparting good luck and had always been a favorite saying of his father's. Literally translated, it meant *into the wolf's mouth*.

A blind taste test.

In bocca al lupo.

Leo's chest grew tight, and he suddenly found it difficult to breathe in a way that he knew had nothing to do with his chocolate allergy. Into the wolf's mouth, indeed.

Juliet focused every bit of her concentration on twirling her pasta around her fork. *Cacio e pepe,* a traditional Roman dish, perfectly simple and consisting of only three ingredients—homemade pasta, cracked black pepper and pecorino cheese. Growing up, she'd known it as Italian macaroni and cheese, and for as long as she could remember, she'd wanted to eat it in Italy.

Unfortunately, the experience wasn't quite as idyllic as she'd always imagined it since her mother was glaring at her from across the table.

"Juliet. What is Leo Mezzanotte doing here in Rome? Explain."

Juliet winced. As did her father, Alegra and Nico. On any given day, her mother could out-shrill the best of them. But right now, she'd ventured into nails-on-a-chalkboard territory.

"Now, dear, try to relax. We're having a nice family dinner in Italy. *Salute!*" Her father raised his glass of wine in a feeble attempt at a toast.

Paralyzed by her mother's death glare, no one else at the table moved a muscle.

"Juliet," she screeched. A flock of pigeons picking at crumbs on the cobblestones of the outdoor café where they were having dinner took flight and scattered.

For the first time in her life, Juliet longed to be a pigeon. "Leo is here competing in the chocolate contest. Just as I am. He's a chocolatier. Is it really so shocking?"

Nico's eyes widened. Alegra choked on her Chianti.

Juliet stabbed at her pasta again. Yes, she supposed she was being uncharacteristically bold. But since they'd left the cooking school, no one had said a word about her cake. Not a single word.

Did they have any idea how hard she'd worked on that cake? She'd thought of little else for weeks. She'd poured her heart and soul into that cake. It was more than just a pile of chocolate, sugar and flour. It was her heart wrapped up in creamy white frosting.

"He didn't win the Napa Valley Chocolate Fair. You did. He's not entitled to be here." Her mom threw her napkin on the table in disgust.

"Mom, everything is fine. I still made it to the final round, or hadn't you noticed?" She was a finalist in one of the most prestigious chocolate competitions in the world. It was more than she could have hoped for. And yet, nothing had changed.

"Of course I noticed." Her mother's face softened. For a millisecond. "But so did he. And he shouldn't even be competing."

"She beat him once. She can do it again," Nico said.

Her mother shook her head. "That's not the point."

Juliet's dad frowned. "It's not? Isn't it a competition? Isn't that why we're here? To win?"

Juliet dropped her fork. She couldn't eat another bite. She'd thought things would be different in Italy. Even when she'd first bumped into Leo on the Spanish Steps, for the most fleeting of moments, she'd thought they just might be so far away from Napa Valley that the feud wouldn't find them here.

She looked up at the swirling blue Italian sky. Same moon, same stars as back home.

Same problems.

"Actually, no. Winning is not why I came here," she said softly.

Juliet's mother narrowed her gaze. "Did you know Leonardo Mezzanotte was going to be here? Tell the truth."

"Does it really matter? In the grand scheme of life, does any of this really matter?" She didn't wait for an answer.

Ignoring the shocked expressions of her family members, she folded her napkin into a neat square and laid it beside her half-eaten meal. Then, for the first time her in her life, Juliet Arabella stood up and walked away from her family.

She couldn't sleep.

The peal of church bells drifting in through her open window told Juliet it was well past midnight, but she couldn't bring herself to close her eyes. Her body hummed with adrenaline. Whether she was nervous about the pending conclusion of the *Roma Festa del Cioccolato,* or simply still riding the high of finally refusing to take her mother's bait, she wasn't sure.

There had been knocks at her door. Her cell phone had rung. Several times. She'd ignored every single knock and call, choosing instead to take a nice bubble bath and order a split of Prosecco from room service. Then she'd watched *Roman Holiday* on television. In Italian.

Basically, she'd done the sort of things she'd always thought she would do in Italy. Well, what she could do in the wee hours of the morning. Without Leo.

Leo.

She couldn't stop thinking about him. Which was not good. Not good at all. She may have come to Rome because she needed to make a change, but she was certain he was here for one thing and one thing only—to win the chocolate competition. He'd been to Rome before. Numerous times. He'd been away from Napa Valley for years, seeing the world, doing things Juliet had only dreamed about. He wasn't here to fulfill some lifelong dream, unless that dream was winning the *Roma Festa del Cioccolato.*

The church bells rang again, and this time Juliet counted them. One, two, three, four, five. Five in the morning. Her alarm was set to go off in less than two hours. She had to get some sleep.

She reached into her bag for the book she'd started reading on the long flight over from California. But instead of her library book, she accidentally pulled out her grandmother's recipe book. She held it and ran her fingertips over the worn cover, wondering what her grandmother would think about things if she were here in Rome. Would she still be angry at Donnatella Mezzanotte, even after all these years? Or would she have forgiven by now? When she'd opened up shop across the street from her former best friend, her *sorella,* did she have any idea what she was starting? Years of name-calling. Years of hatred. Years of competition. It was still happening. And now Juliet and Leo were the ones squaring off against one another.

She opened the book and flipped through its pages, letting

her gaze wander over the familiar recipes. Mexican chocolate sheet cake. Orange ginger white chocolate disks. Dark cappuccino chocolate candy. *Chocolat chaud*.

She blinked.

Chocolat chaud?

She sat up straight in the bed, her eyes straining to focus in the semidarkness of her hotel room. Convinced she was seeing things, she flipped on the light on the bedside table.

She wasn't seeing things. There at the top of the page, in handwriting that wasn't her grandmother's, wasn't faded with age, were the words *Chocolat Chaud*. Only one person could have written it there.

Leo.

Juliet sat and stared at the page in disbelief. Her hands shook so hard, the book nearly slipped from her grasp.

The entire recipe was written out in careful script with exact measurements down to an eighth of a teaspoon. He'd even included the brand names for the ingredients. And right at the bottom of the list was the one thing that had managed to elude her for so long. The secret ingredient.

Fleur de sel, *packaged by Le Guerandais. A special sea salt harvested by hand from the South Brittany region of France.*

Sea salt, just as she'd suspected. Although she never would have gotten the specifics right.

A lump formed in her throat. The words began to swim before her eyes until she could barely make out the journal notation that Leo had written in the margin, just like the notes her grandmother had made. It included the date—from approximately three weeks ago—which Juliet instinctively recognized as the night they'd first made love back in Napa Valley. And beneath it, he'd written just one short sentence.

On this date, a Mezzanotte fell for an Arabella and tried to make things right.

She ran her fingertips over the words, wanting to touch them and make sure they were real, lest they disappear before her eyes. When had he done this? And how was it possible that she'd had this beautiful gesture in her hands all this time and never known?

She remembered waking late that night, finding Leo in the kitchen cooking for the dogs and his gaze snagging momentarily on the book. She'd thought he'd felt the presence of all those words standing between them, as she had. Words from so many years ago.

But she'd been wrong. He'd written a new ending to their story.

Before he'd passed out at the chocolate fair, before everyone knew their secret, before George Alcott had so ceremoniously ripped up the Mezzanotte-Royal Gourmet contract, Leo had given her his recipe. A sacrificial gift to make peace between their families.

So much had happened since that night.

If only she'd known.

23

Leo arrived at the cooking school the next morning for the competition, knowing full well that he was about to go down in flames. Big flames. Spectacular flames. Flames that could probably be seen all the way from Napa Valley.

As preoccupied as he was with the humiliation that loomed, and the fact that once he returned to Napa, he would have no job, no family business, no future to speak of, he couldn't help but notice that Juliet seemed uncharacteristically pensive.

She'd hardly said a word to him. Then again, they were back in the courtyard in full view of the press, the judges, the spectators. And their families.

The taste test challenge was to begin with the spectacle of each contestant tasting the challenge item. Leo wondered how he was going to pull that off in front of all the cameras, since he had no intention of actually eating any chocolate. He supposed he'd have to fake it somehow.

Right.

Okay, so he'd just have to cross that bridge when he

came to it. Surely he'd figure something out. One thing was certain—he would never, ever do this again.

He glanced at Juliet beside him and was surprised to find her watching him. Studying him, as if they were the only two people standing in the crowded courtyard. She was surrounded by the scent of lemons, cool basil and rosemary from the garden, chocolate. The perfume of Rome.

God, how he wanted her. Even here. Even now, standing on the precipice of doom.

"In bocca al lupo," he whispered.

She smiled in return, but still considered him with that hauntingly penetrating look. *"Crepi il lupo."*

Crepi il lupo. May the wolf die. Leo was about to lie down and die right alongside him.

Juliet turned to face the crowd again. She was close enough that he could reach out and touch her if he so chose. But what business would one competitor have reaching for another's hand or stroking the hair of one of his fellow chefs, right where the sunlight danced on her shoulders?

"This is it, Juliet. We'll never stand here again. Not like this," he murmured.

She glanced at him, and her emerald eyes grew wider. Softer. "What do you mean?"

He crossed his arms and looked away, once again carrying on with the ridiculous charade that they had nothing nice to say to one another. "I mean, I'm finished competing against you. I won't do it again. I don't even want to do it now."

His eyes flitted back to her, unable to stay trained elsewhere for long.

Her lips parted. A word, a question dangled on her tongue. *Why?* Leo could sense it as clearly as if it were visible, made up of color and form.

She closed her mouth, the word unspoken. Because she already knew the answer. "I don't want to compete against you anymore, either. But stopping isn't going to change anything."

He lifted a brow. "Won't it?"

She glanced toward the audience—no doubt dominated by a horde of feuding Arabellas and Mezzanottes—and then back at him. "My family won't all of a sudden like you simply because they won't see you at the next chocolate fair. They'll just hate you from afar."

Hate him from afar. Much as he'd been loving Juliet from afar.

He grew very still. *Loving* Juliet? Is that what he'd been doing?

He hadn't planned on falling in love. Didn't think he was capable of it. He'd been running from love his whole life, from the tumultuous love of his family to the business-arrangement-disguised-as-love that had been his engagement. He'd always considered love a heavy burden under which he'd just as soon not sink.

And here he was. In love with Juliet. His only love sprang from his only hate.

"You're right. I can't stop this on my own." One man fighting against history didn't stand a chance. "But if we try, maybe we can stop it together."

Juliet met his gaze. Full-on this time. No surreptitious glances, no fleeting looks. If she was worried about what her family would think, her expression gave no indication.

Electricity danced in the air between them. And its source seemed to be the sparkle in Juliet's eyes.

"Then let's start right now," she said, the slight tremor in her voice the only hint that something altogether different was happening.

Leo glanced at his watch. Four minutes to eight. The competition was set to start in less than five minutes. "Now?"

"Yes. Now." She took a deep breath. "No more competing. Starting right now. Whoever wins, we split the prize fifty-fifty. We make this competition about us. Not yours, not mine. Ours."

Then Leo watched, spellbound, as she extended a hand toward him. She let it hang there between them, ready for him to take hold and shake it. To agree to her terms.

If only he could.

She offered him a smile as well as her hand, and a pang hit Leo dead in the center of his chest. Correction. Those weren't *her* terms. Not really. They were *their* terms. Everything he wanted for the two of them.

His fingers itched to shake on it. To agree to the deal, even though it would have been wholly unfair. He was heading into the taste test challenge at a distinct disadvantage. In truth, he didn't have a prayer. Barring some unforeseen miracle, he was about to fall on his face. Quite spectacularly so. Now wasn't the time to join forces. Not unless he wanted to be another in a long line of Mezzanottes who had no qualms at the thought of taking advantage of an Arabella.

He had qualms. He had plenty of them. Enough for all the wrongs that had been committed in the name of the feud. On all sides.

"Leo?" Confusion—and a dash of pain—shone in Juliet's eyes. She glanced down at her hand as if she couldn't remember why she'd offered it to him in the first place.

He exhaled a strained breath. "I want to. God, I want to. More than you know."

No sooner were the words out of his mouth than the life left Juliet's beautiful green eyes. Her bottom lip trembled. And that tremble just about did Leo in.

How were things going so wrong, so quickly?

He reached for her hand. Not to shake it, but to hold it in his.

She jerked out of reach. "But you won't. Will you?"

"Not won't. Can't." There was a difference. A big one.

The expression on Juliet's face said otherwise. She flinched as though she'd been slapped. Witnessing that look, and knowing without a doubt that he'd been the cause of it, wounded Leo to his core.

"You can't," she said, her voice hollow and distant.

He held up a hand. "It's not what you think."

"Isn't it?" She rolled her eyes. Naturally.

Because wasn't that exactly what people always said when the truth was every bit as awful as it seemed? *It's not what you think.*

Damn it, why couldn't he seem to say the right thing? "Look, I'm serious."

"I'm sure you are. Quite serious about beating me." Her voice grew wobbly, and a hysterical laugh escaped her lips. "How could I have been so stupid? I thought you actually thought you wanted to put an end to the feud. To build a life together."

That's exactly what he wanted. "Juliet…"

"Make up your mind, Leo," she said a little too loudly.

Their families had to know something was going on. Not that Leo cared at the moment. And for once, Juliet didn't appear to care, either. There was fire in her eyes. Fire he'd seen each and every time she was passionate about something. It made him want to grab her and kiss her, draw her bottom lip between his teeth, whisper to her exactly how he felt about her so there would be no more misunderstanding.

She aimed that fire directly at him. "You just said you didn't want to compete with me anymore. So which is it? You do or you don't?"

He didn't. Period.

He was going to have to tell her about his chocolate allergy. He didn't want to. Not now. Not like this. If he did, one of two things would happen. Either she wouldn't believe him, or she'd take pity on him and help him with the challenge. Leo wasn't sure which of those options would be worse. He liked to think she trusted him enough to know he wouldn't lie to her. But he didn't want her pity either, no matter how badly he needed this win.

He ground his teeth together and took a deep breath. "Look, there's something I need to tell you."

"That you gave me the *chocolat chaud* recipe? I already know. I found it. This morning, actually. Clearly, it didn't mean what I thought it meant." Her fire dimmed a bit, replaced by a smoldering vulnerability.

Her words caught Leo off guard. With all that had transpired in recent days, he'd stopped wondering if she'd found what he'd written in her grandmother's recipe book. At first her silence on the subject tormented him. Giving her that recipe had seemed like such a great idea at the time. He'd meant it as a gift. A secret he'd bestowed upon her with which he'd intended to fix everything that was broken between them and their families.

The answer. A few generations too late.

"And what did you think it meant?" Leo crossed his arms.

He knew what he'd been feeling that night when he'd lain beside Juliet, overwhelmed by the storm that had swirled to life inside him when he'd taken her to bed. He still felt it. From the very center of his being.

I love you.

The words pulsed between them. As deafening and colorful as if they'd been spoken aloud or written in the sky in shimmering letters made of stardust.

"It doesn't matter what I thought." Her voice grew hoarse, and her eyes were suddenly glittering behind a veil of tears. "Not anymore."

Enough. "You want me to make up my mind? Done. I don't want to be on opposite sides. I want us to be a team. Forever. But I can't agree to share the prize because…"

He was cut short by the sound of clapping hands echoing off the timeworn walls of the monastery-turned-cooking school.

The contest proctor stood in the center of the room, a barrier between the audience and Leo and Juliet. "Contestants, the time has come!"

Of course it had.

Just when he'd been about to set things straight, fate had to step in and remind Leo who was boss. If fate was indeed real, and if Leo could somehow get his hands on it, he would have happily pummeled fate into the ground at that moment.

"In accordance with the rules of this, the final round of competition, the contestants will be presented with a challenge item which they will be required to duplicate as closely as possible." The proctor launched into a long-winded explanation of the rules.

It was the same old, same old. They would have five minutes to taste the challenge item and come up with a plan. Or rather, everyone but Leo would taste the challenge item. He planned on looking at it, taking it apart, dissecting it, smelling it. But tasting it? No. Even if taking a few bites wouldn't kill him, it was sure to cripple him with a headache. And he'd be counting the seconds until he felt his throat begin to close up. Either way, he was screwed.

Behind the proctor's back, Leo sought Juliet's gaze. Somehow, some way they needed to finish their conversation. It was going to be difficult doing so when she refused to even look at him. She stared straight ahead without so much as a glance in his direction.

Leo looked back at the proctor and found the man staring at him in expectation, as though he'd just asked him a question. And Leo hadn't the vaguest idea what that question might have been.

"Mr. Mezzanotte?" he prompted.

Leo needed to get his head in the game. Didn't he have enough working against him as it was? "I'm sorry. Yes?"

"It's your turn to sample the challenge item." The proctor waved a hand at a silver tray piled high with truffles. Truffles of no special distinction whatsoever. From this distance, they looked like every other basic truffle Leo had ever laid eyes on. "Please, step forward."

He ventured one last, unreturned glance at Juliet. Then he squared his jaw and approached the silver tray.

This is it. The beginning of the end.

He just hoped that on a day as black as this, only one ending awaited him.

Juliet watched Leo push his thumb into the center of the challenge truffle and inspect its contents. She watched him rub the ganache between his index finger and his thumb. She watched him bring the truffle toward his mouth and let it linger a hair's breadth away from his lips before lifting it instead to his nose for a sniff. She watched him inspect it, smell it, feel every miniscule bit of it. He might have even talked to it. But the one thing he didn't do was taste it.

At first she thought he'd simply lost track of time. But when the proctor announced that his five minutes was up, Leo's face showed no hint of regret. He'd purposely not tasted the truffle. Not a single, miniscule bite.

Naturally, she wondered what in the world he was up to. There was a time when she would have thought he was possibly showing off. But that time had passed. He might have been a Mezzanotte, but Leo had never shown an ounce of arrogance when he competed against her. Not even when she'd shown up at the balloon festival with those awful strawberries. Granted, he was French trained. In all likelihood, he was probably capable of defeating her without even tasting the challenge item. She knew it. He knew it. But he wouldn't want everyone else to know it, too.

"Miss Arabella?" The proctor directed his attention toward her. "Step forward to taste the challenge item."

She took a deep breath and willed herself to stop worrying about Leo. He was a smart man. He had to know what he was doing, even if his actions appeared to be monumentally stupid. He was serious about this competition.

Serious enough to turn down her offer to join forces and share the prize.

She realized she'd already bitten into one of the truffles, chewed and swallowed without even being conscious of what she was doing. Now, who was the one acting monumentally stupid?

Forget Leo. Forget him and his chocolat chaud. Don't think about his perfect forearms or his perfect handwriting.

She selected another truffle and took a bite. The sweet,

light flavor of culinary lavender burst on her tongue. That's as far as she got before her thoughts drifted back to Leo again. And the way she'd just stood there, holding out her hand, fully expecting him to shake it.

God, it was mortifying.

No, not mortifying so much as completely devastating. She'd been ready to give him her heart.

Who was she kidding? He already held her heart and soul in his hands. She'd surrendered it to him, knowing full well what she was doing.

Yours.

The trouble was…now she didn't know how to take it back.

Tears pricked behind her eyes, ready to spill over. She blinked furiously and stared at the remaining half of the truffle in her hand. The temptation to seek out Leo's gaze was overwhelming to the point of pain. But she refused to succumb to it. And she certainly didn't want to look at her family. Who knew what they were thinking after witnessing the intense exchange between her and Leo?

Concentrate.

She popped the remaining truffle in her mouth, closed her eyes and tried her best to let go of all her senses, save for taste. As with her first bite, lavender was the overwhelming flavor. Along with chocolate, that is. But she knew she was missing something. There had to be more to it than the obvious.

She let the creamy ganache sit in her mouth for a bit. It was sweet. Sweeter than most chocolate ganache. She'd assumed the sweetness came from the lavender. Unlike lavender that was grown for bath soaps and oils, which tended to be bitter and strong, culinary lavender was known for its delicate sweetness. It was perfect for cookies, tea cakes and flavored crème brûlées.

Not until she swallowed did she detect the barest hint of caramel. But when she did, she knew she'd hit the nail on the head.

Her eyes flew open. Caramel. Of course. Just a dash. Not so much to overpower the lavender or make the truffle sticky, but enough to add another layer of sweetness.

Chocolate. Lavender. Caramel. And probably a dash of sea salt. Because where there was caramel, there was usually sea salt. Not Leo's fancy *fleur de sel* maybe, but garden variety sea salt.

She turned to face the proctor. "I'm ready."

He checked his watch. "Are you quite sure, Miss Arabella? You still have approximately one minute left of your allotted time."

"No, thank you. I'm ready." She didn't want to overthink things. She was pretty sure she was right. If she kept tasting it, she might invent new flavors to add into the mix. Flavors that would overcomplicate the recipe and send her veering off course.

"All right, then." He nodded and called the name of the next contestant.

The name Agostoni was embroidered above the pocket of her chef's coat. Juliet wondered if she was one of *the* Agostonis—an Italian family who'd created an empire out of their bean-to-bar chocolates and then subsequently sold it to a huge food company. Probably.

The Agostoni girl could win. So could any of the other handful of competitors. The odds were that neither she nor Leo would end up victorious. So, in essence, her proposed pact would have been a long shot even if he'd taken her up on it.

Somehow that still didn't take the sting out of his rejection. She struggled to swallow. Her throat was bone dry. She felt sick to her stomach. She could feel Leo's gaze on her, unwavering and as hot as his legendary *chocolat chaud*. She wished he would stop looking at her like that. She wished she could somehow forget he was there. She wished so many things.

How on earth was she going to get through the rest of this day?

The five-minute rounds for each contestant to taste the challenge item seemed to take an eternity. She watched the other chefs taste the truffles, smell them, roll them around between flattened palms and take them painstakingly apart. The head chocolatier from Jacques Torres even held one of the truffles aloft and let it fall to the ground with a splat. What exactly that was supposed to accomplish, Juliet hadn't a clue. The crowd seemed to like it, though. Even Leo's uncle Joe had a good laugh. Juliet was one hundred percent certain it was the first time she'd ever seen the man crack a smile. But then he caught her watching him, and his trademark scowl made a swift and immediate return.

When the theatrics were finally over, the contestants retreated to the kitchen. Happy to be away from prying eyes, Juliet gathered the supplies for her basic ganache and got to work. She'd go back and gather the special ingredients together when the crowd had thinned. The caramel especially. So far, not a single square of caramel had been brought back to anyone's work station. Juliet tried not to get too excited about this fact. The others could be holding back just as she was.

She concentrated on breathing in and out and keeping her

hands steady as she stirred her ganache. Not an easy task considering Leo was working at the gas burner right beside her.

"Juliet." His voice hummed through her veins when he spoke.

How she hated that. Rather, she hated the way she so loved the sound of her name rolling off his tongue. "Not now, Leo. Please."

He gave her a pained look.

She squared her shoulders and removed her saucepan from the stove. "I can't do this. I just can't. Not now."

"Fine," he said, in a way that made it clear that it wasn't fine at all. Nothing was fine. Things couldn't be further from fine. "But know this. We're not finished."

She wasn't sure what that meant, and he didn't elaborate. He could have been talking about their conversation or the tangled mess that was the two of them. Juliet wasn't altogether sure which she preferred. But she couldn't think about it now. She would figure that out later, once this godforsaken contest was over.

She dipped a tasting spoon in the ganache and brought it to her mouth. Mmm. Perfect. It was glossy, creamy and rich. Just as a ganache should be. Time to add the caramel while the mixture was still hot enough for everything to melt together in perfect harmony.

She gathered the caramel she needed from the ingredients table and dropped the tasting spoon in the large ceramic sink on the way back to her workstation. The sink was already littered with dozens of such spoons. All around her, the other chefs were sampling their work. A bite here. A nibble there. A lick of a spoon.

She allowed herself an exploratory glance in Leo's direction. Like everyone else, he was busy. The whisk in his hand was going ninety miles an hour, the muscles in his glorious forearm straining with exertion. His workstation was littered with culinary debris—discarded blocks of bittersweet baking chocolate, upturned cartons of heavy cream, cold squares of butter. His pristine white chef coat had a drizzle of milk chocolate down the front. He was bent over his bowl with a look of fierce concentration on his beautiful face.

She forced herself to look away.

But then her footsteps slowed. Something was missing.

She glanced back at Leo. At his bowl, his whisk, his line of baking utensils—wooden spoon, pastry bag, measuring spoons, pastry brush, cutting wheel, knife spatulas in every size and variety imaginable. There were even a few items over there that were unfamiliar to Juliet. He was surrounded by all the trappings of a chef fully immersed in a taste test challenge, save for one very important item—a tasting spoon.

There wasn't one within three feet of him.

It wasn't just odd. It was patently unheard of. Surely she was mistaken. He had to have a pile of tiny spoons over there somewhere. She'd already used three or four in the course of the past half hour and had ten more ready and waiting in the wings.

She returned to her area with the caramel and went to work slicing it into paper-thin pieces to add to her ganache. And while it melted into her mixture, she sneaked furtive glances at the counter where Leo worked.

Her eyes hadn't deceived her. He wasn't in possession of a single tasting spoon. Not only that, he was already sealing his bowl with a layer of plastic wrap and heading toward the freezer.

He was letting his ganache chill without even tasting it?

Impossible.

She thought back to all the other times she'd seen Leo in action, starting with the time he'd lured her inside the lion's den. She'd sat atop the kitchen counter of Mezzanotte Chocolates, feeling more wicked than she'd ever felt in her life just by virtue of being there, and watched him create. She'd memorized every moment. Every turn of his wrist, every lick of his finger. He'd sampled the *chocolat chaud*. Plenty of times. He'd done the same at her apartment the night he'd shown up with that big bag of groceries. He'd tasted every one of the batches she'd made throughout the day. Numerous times. And he'd sampled cup after cup of the concoctions they'd made together.

So if he normally tasted as he baked, why wasn't he doing so now, when so much was at stake?

He'd eaten twice as many truffles as she had at the Napa Valley Chocolate Fair. Of course, that day had ended in disaster. He'd been carried away in an ambulance. And even though their tryst had been laid bare and they'd been outed to both their families, the thing she remembered most about that day was how awful Leo had looked. Pale, weak. A shadow of his normal self. Much like Cocoa had seemed when she'd consumed so much chocolate that she'd been poisoned.

Juliet's hand stilled. She dropped her whisk, and it sank into her ganache. Or maybe it didn't. She was barely cognizant of what was happening around her. The busy kitchen became a blur before her eyes, and the pounding of her heartbeat came so fast, so hard that she was forced to grip the edge of the counter to steady herself.

Leo had been poisoned. Just like Cocoa.

He must be allergic or something. It was the only explanation for why he wasn't eating chocolate. Since the Napa Valley event, she hadn't seen him eat a single bite.

All of a sudden, everything made perfect sense. No wonder he'd chosen to carve a sculpture for the artistic round of competition yesterday. It was gorgeous. And difficult. But most importantly, it required zero tasting on his part. No recipe to test, no delicate balance of flavors to worry about.

And now he was competing in the taste test without actually tasting anything. He didn't have a chance.

But he could have. If he'd agreed to the deal.

Juliet gripped the edge of the counter so hard that her knuckles turned white. She'd interpreted his refusal as rejection when, in fact, it was anything but. He hadn't been reluctant to share his victory with her. On the contrary, he was protecting her. He knew he wouldn't win today.

How could she have been so wrong? She'd thought his refusal meant that she'd misunderstood what he'd written in her grandmother's recipe book. Those words that had taken her by storm when she'd first read them could only mean one thing.

On this date, a Mezzanotte fell for an Arabella and tried to make things right.

Joy welled up in her soul. How many ways were there to interpret such words? Only one.

Leo Mezzanotte loved her.

And she loved him right back.

24

Leo clicked the door shut to the walk-in freezer only to turn and find Juliet standing behind him.

She gave him a most unexpected saucy smile and reopened the door. "You forgot something."

A blast of frigid air enveloped him as she marched past him. She went straight for his bowl of ganache, plucked it off the shelf and tucked it under her arm. Then she headed for the door with it, as if it was hers to abscond with.

He stepped inside the freezer to block her exit. "What do you think you're doing?"

"Helping you." She shrugged. The nonchalance of her gesture was betrayed by the fierce glittering in her eyes. She looked as if she either wanted to murder him or kiss him silly.

She was so damn beautiful, Leo was game for either.

"Helping me?" he repeated.

She lifted her chin. "Yes. You need caramel."

Caramel. He'd had no idea.

He also had no idea why she wanted to help him all of a sudden. He couldn't help but be intrigued. "And how do you know there's no caramel in that bowl?"

She cleared her throat and shifted the bowl from one arm to the other. "There's not. I know there's not."

He crossed his arms and did his best to stop the satisfied grin that threatened to spring to his lips. "You're so sure of yourself. How interesting. One might even think you'd been watching me."

Her cheeks glowed bright pink. Sure, the change in her complexion could have been a result of the frosty temperature of the freezer, but Leo preferred to think otherwise.

"There's no need to make me sound like a stalker." She rolled her eyes.

He shrugged. He enjoyed teasing her. It brought a modicum of pleasure to this otherwise dreadful experience. "If the shoe fits."

"Says the man who climbed a trellis to get to my room two nights ago." She gave back as good as she got. He had to give her that.

He aimed a smoldering grin at her. "I must remember it wrong. As I recall, we didn't quite make it to your room."

The air in the freezer heated up a notch.

She cleared her throat. "We're wasting time in here."

"Time with you is never wasted." He wanted to kiss her. Right there in the freezer. But he still hadn't figured out what she was up to. "Why are you suddenly so anxious to help me? I turned down your offer, remember?"

"Oh, I remember. What I can't figure out is why you just didn't tell me that you're allergic to chocolate."

Leo stiffened. He still wasn't accustomed to thinking of himself as allergic to chocolate. Hearing it stated so matter-of-factly caught him off guard. He hadn't told a soul about his diagnosis, and no one else had noticed anything amiss.

Not his uncle, not his sister, not his brother–in–law. His family. People he saw day in and day out.

But somehow Juliet had.

He swallowed. "How did you figure it out?"

She glanced at the bowl in her arms, filled with chocolate he hadn't tasted. "You reminded me of my chocolate-guzzling dog. The pieces just sort of fell into place after that."

He narrowed his gaze at her. "I'm going to choose to not take being compared to a dog as a blow to my ego. Is this some kind of trick? Is there actually caramel in that truffle, or is this an attempt at sabotage?"

"Sabotage? Please. I think you know me better than that. Don't you?" Her gaze softened. And the pendulum swung from the murderous end of the spectrum all the way to the side in favor of kissing him silly.

Leo had never been one to deny a woman who so clearly wanted to be kissed.

He kicked the freezer door closed, grabbed the bowl from her hands and tossed it on the closest shelf, then wrapped his arms around her waist. A gasp of surprise escaped her lips as he pulled her flush against him, but soon he was swallowing that gasp as his mouth found hers. His lips were hungry, wanting, demanding. The immediacy of his need took him by surprise. They were in the freezer, for God's sake. But he didn't really care. Not right now. Not when the gulf between them had mysteriously closed and she'd ended up in his arms. Right where she belonged.

Her lips were cold, icy from the freezer, but her tongue was hot. Molten. The combination of fire and ice was almost too much to take. He turned her slightly and pushed her backward until she was against the freezer door. A shiver of desire coursed through him at the familiarity of the posture. Memories of the hotel balcony, never far away, rose to the surface.

He removed his lips from hers before they ended up making a far greater mistake than forgetting the caramel. With his forehead resting against hers, he struggled for air. Their frigid breath danced together in a cloud of vapor and hovered between them.

"Juliet," he breathed, brushing his fingertips against her face.

"Leo." She smiled up at him. "You could have told me."

He'd wanted to, but he'd been trying to avoid this exact scenario. "No one knows."

"No one? Not even your family?"

"Especially not my family." He cupped her face in his hands. "You don't have to do this. I've got nothing to bring to the table. Why should you help me?"

Her lips curved into a bashful smile. "Because in spite of your last name, I'm madly in love with you."

He hadn't realized that he'd been waiting and hoping to hear those exact words until they fell off her tongue. And he most certainly hadn't realized he had his own words, ready and waiting to spill forth. "Mad enough to marry me and make that last name yours?"

It was a preposterous idea.

Or was it?

He tipped her chin upward a fraction, pressed the gentlest of kisses to her petal-soft mouth and whispered, "My love for you is bigger than the moon and stars combined. We can make this work. I swear."

Juliet's lips parted, but before she could speak, Leo pressed the pad of his index finger against her mouth. He wasn't about to give her the chance to say no. Not until she'd had a while to grow accustomed to the idea. He knew he'd caught her off guard. Hell, he'd caught himself unawares. But everything within him hinged on her answer. He no longer cared about the competition or what happened to Mezzanotte Chocolates. Everything he wanted was standing right in front of him. "Don't answer yet. Think about it. Keep your name if you like. I don't care what you call yourself, so long as you're mine."

She grinned against his fingertip and nodded.

Satisfied, for now, he removed his finger from her lips. "Shall we go make some chocolate, my love?"

Her smile was brighter than a golden Italian morning. "Yes."

It wasn't quite the yes he was after. Not yet. But it would do.

For now.

Chaos had come to rule the kitchen while they'd been tucked away inside the freezer. Or maybe it had been that way all along, and the change had been inside Juliet rather than the room. It was a definite possibility.

All around her, chefs were stirring, chopping and swearing. One of them—the biggest, burliest guy in the kitchen—was even crying. He was just sitting on a bar stool weeping quietly into his ganache. Juliet was barely cognizant of any of it. She floated through the rest of the afternoon. Her hands scooped ganache into balls, rolled those balls into perfect truffles, dusted those truffles with cocoa and confectioner's sugar. But for all she cared, they could have been someone else's hands. It was as if she'd gone to Rome as one person and was ending her time there a completely different one.

Juliet Mezzanotte.

There was a time when the very idea of marrying a Mezzanotte would have made her head spin. Now it was all she could think about. She wanted Leo. All of him. Last name included.

And suddenly, the contest was the least important thing in the world. She just wanted it to end so they could get on with more important things. When at last she and Leo stood with the other three contestants, back in front of the crowd in the courtyard, they did so hand in hand.

The contest proctor stood before them and praised the efforts of all the chefs. He thanked them for coming from all over the world to participate. At least Juliet thought that's what he said. Her thoughts were elsewhere, dancing between worlds, through time.

Juliet Mezzanotte.

Leo squeezed her hand. "Ready?"

And she realized her answer was yes. Yes, she was ready.

The contest proctor cleared his throat one last time. "The winner of this year's *Roma Festa del Cioccolato* is Leonardo Mezzanotte of Mezzanotte Chocolates."

Juliet felt Leo's hand clench around hers. She turned to look at him and couldn't help but notice he didn't appear at all happy to have been named the winner. She, on the other hand, was thrilled for him. He'd said himself he would never compete again. Even if he'd wanted to, he probably couldn't. Not with a chocolate allergy. This was exactly the way his final competition should end—victoriously.

With tears brimming in her eyes, she clapped for him as he stepped forward to receive his prize. Then he was surrounded by a crowd of well-wishers, most notably the Mezzanottes, and she lost sight of him.

Her mother was at her side in an instant, with her father, Nico and Alegra following closely on her heels.

Her mom wrapped an arm around her shoulders, and, for a moment, Juliet felt wrapped in the sweetness of a maternal embrace.

Then her mother started talking. "Juliet, dear. Now don't feel badly about the outcome. Leo shouldn't have even been in this competition. I'm going to file a formal complaint. With any luck, we can get this decision overturned."

Nico chimed in, staring daggers in Leo's direction. "That's right. He had no right to be here. You were the winner of the Napa Valley Chocolate Fair. He didn't even qualify."

Why did her brother even care? She doubted if he did, really. If it had been someone with a different name, *any* name, he wouldn't have given it a second thought.

"Stop," Juliet said quietly. "Please."

Her dad moved in for a hug. "You'll get him next time, sweetheart."

"There won't be a next time."

At the sound of Leo's voice, her father released her.

"Leo," he said. "We're having a family moment here. I think it's best if you leave Juliet alone."

"Dad, stop," she said. But no one seemed to have heard her. As usual. They just kept aiming insults at Leo. And he was just standing there with a grim smile on his face, taking it all in. For her.

The other Mezzanottes joined the fray, and soon the lovely clay-colored kitchen was filled with a cacophony of angry voices. Leo's uncle Joe talked over her father. Juliet's mother and Gina Mezzanotte each stabbed angry index fingers at the air. One voice overlapped with another and another until

she could no longer tell the ones that belonged to Mezzanottes from the ones that came from angry Arabella mouths.

She couldn't take it anymore. She just couldn't. How could
they fail to see how absurd they were acting? They were an
ocean away from Napa Valley, generations apart from whatever strife had started this whole mess, and they still couldn't
be in the same room without trying to tear each other apart
limb from limb. Centuries of monks were probably rolling
in their graves right now over the ridiculous behavior on
display at their former place of worship.

"Everyone, would you just *please stop?*" she screamed, her
voice echoing off the stuccoed walls.

A momentary hush fell over the crowd. Juliet found the
sudden silence almost as jarring as all the yelling. She blinked,
looked around and noticed that the judges, the other competitors and the rest of the spectators were beating a hasty
path out of the kitchen, toward the garden and the gentle
shade of the umbrella pines.

She couldn't help but envy them.

"Juliet, really. There's no need to raise your voice," her
mother said, somehow maintaining a straight face.

Could she genuinely not see the irony of that statement?

"Mrs. Arabella." The deadly warning tone in Leo's voice
made Juliet want to grab him and kiss him on the lips right
there in front of everyone.

But as tempting as that might be, she wanted her family to
listen to her for once. Isn't that what this trip to Rome was all
about? Finally standing up for herself and what she wanted?

"Leo, I can handle this," she said.

He nodded, but the angry knot in his jaw was working
overtime.

"Leo just won the *Roma Festa del Cioccolato,* everyone. I

think the decent thing to do would be to congratulate him."
She crossed her arms and aimed a glare at each of her family
members, one by one.

She started with her mother, who just sighed and dropped
her gaze to the floor. Her father glanced nervously back and
forth between the two of them but remained mum. Nico
rolled his eyes so hard that Juliet was surprised they didn't
fall right out of his head.

But finally, when her eyes met Alegra's, something wholly
unexpected and wonderful happened.

"Congratulations, Sparkle." Her cousin's voice was flat,
but she winked at Leo. And the beginnings of what looked
like a smile hovered on her lips.

Two words. Two simple words, spoken with nary a drop
of emotion. And still, it was the most polite thing an Arabella had said to a Mezzanotte in over fifty years. With the
exception of Leo and Juliet, of course.

Leo smiled. "Thank you, Alegra. But the victory isn't
mine to claim, no matter what the judges said. It belongs
to Juliet."

"Leo." Joe Mezzanotte's voice shook. That tiny hint of
vulnerability made him seem less like an ogre to Juliet and
more like a lonely old man. "Don't do what I think you're
about to do."

"I'm sorry, Uncle Joe. I know this means the store will
close, but I can't keep this money. It belongs to Juliet. She
told me what to put in the truffles. I couldn't even taste them.
I'm allergic to chocolate."

Like a well-rehearsed chorus, everyone gasped in unison.
Juliet's mother crossed herself, as though her ears had just
been assaulted by unfathomable evil.

"Allergic to chocolate? Nonsense." Joe Mezzanotte's face was whiter than Juliet's grandmother's white chocolate frosting.

"It's not nonsense, Uncle Joe. It's true. And it's why this belongs to Juliet." Leo handed her an envelope. Not just any envelope, but the one the judge had handed him when he'd been declared the winner of the contest.

Inside that envelope was a check in the amount of twenty thousand dollars.

Juliet stared at it, unable to make a move to accept it.

"Leo, don't be stupid," Gina Mezzanotte said. "What are we supposed to do without the chocolate shop?"

Leo ignored her. "Take it, Juliet. It's yours."

"Not mine." She shook her head. "Ours. And I'm only taking it under one condition."

"A condition? He's handing you twenty thousand dollars on a silver platter, and you want to add a condition?" Leo's uncle shook his head in wonder.

"He's right, Juliet. Just take the check," her mother said.

Then her mother's gaze met Joe Mezzanotte's, and they both froze in place. The fact that they'd agreed on something seemed to have the effect of rendering them both motionless. Everyone exchanged shocked glances. Even Juliet fully expected the earth to fall right off its axis.

"A condition?" The corner of Leo's mouth quirked upward. "Might this condition have something to do with the question I proposed earlier?"

Juliet inhaled a deep breath. Could she do this? Accept Leo's proposal right here in front of everyone?

Of course she could. They were all going to have to grow accustomed to the idea eventually. They may as well start now.

She looked into his eyes, remembering the promises they'd made to one another on the balcony.

Mine.

Yours.

Promises they'd made not only with words, but with their bodies and souls. Promises they'd exchanged under the glow of a full moon and a star-swept Roman sky.

Was their fate written in those stars? Was fate even real?

She had no idea. She just knew that, against all odds, she and Leo had found one another. He'd been a world away— right across the street—but somehow she'd ended up in his arms.

She nodded and slipped her fingers through his. "It has everything to do with your question."

He lifted her hand to his lips for a kiss. "I take it your answer is yes?"

"Oh, no, I think I'm going to be sick," Gina Mezzanotte muttered under her breath.

"Shhh." Alegra cut her off at once. "Pipe down, would you? Can't you see that this is a special moment?"

Gina and Alegra looked at each other, and Juliet was struck with the peculiar sensation that it was like watching two mirror images see one another for the very first time.

"Juliet, in case you've forgotten the question..." Leo dropped to one knee. And right there, on a Roman tile floor that had been trod upon for centuries, in front of every member of their respective warring families, he asked Juliet to be his wife. "Will you marry me?"

She pulled him back to his feet. "Yes. I will."

He drew her toward him, and in the shelter of his arms, she couldn't even hear the protests she was sure were being uttered from anyone and everyone. But when he released her, nothing but stunned silence reached her ears.

"Well." For the first time in Juliet's twenty-eight years,

her mother was at a loss for words. "Well," she repeated, her forehead furrowing in the way she'd always warned Juliet would cause premature wrinkles.

"Congratulations, Juliet. Sparkle." Alegra gave Leo a slap on the back.

"Now that we're going to be related, do you suppose we could rethink the nickname?" he said.

Alegra's expression was one of faux horror. "Sparkle? Absolutely not. I mean, let's not go crazy. It's one thing to completely upend generations' worth of family history, but it's another thing entirely to abandon a nickname. I can only take so much change at one time."

She winked at him. "Baby steps, Sparkle, baby steps."

Epilogue

Three months later

Juliet held the ladder still as Leo climbed to the top and hung the newly painted sign on the outside of the chocolate boutique. The grand reopening of the store was scheduled for the next morning. Everything was ready. Juliet had made countless truffles, specialty filled bonbons and chocolate-dipped fruits of every variety, even her nemesis—chocolate strawberries. Juliet's mother had handled the decorating, tackling every decision from what color paint to use on the walls to the thread count of the window dressings, with her trademark intensity.

Gina and Alegra had become close friends, to the surprise of everyone, save Juliet. She could see the similarities in their personalities right from the start, but it had taken an epic battle of wills at a bridal salon for the two of them to realize they were on the same side. It was a miracle how two sworn enemies could bond over their mutual hatred for one ugly bridesmaid dress.

Juliet would go to her grave defending that dress, not that

she would have ever actually made either of them wear it. They didn't need to know that she'd purposely chosen the only bridesmaid dress hideous enough to make them finally join forces. As far as family secrets went, it was harmless. Now Gina and Alegra would be jointly in charge of the day-to-day financial operations of the chocolate shop. Either one of them was intimidating enough to keep everyone in line, even Uncle Joe, but together they were sure to run a tight ship.

Joining the two businesses had been a delicate process, one that Juliet and Leo hadn't even attempted until after the wedding. They'd married almost as soon as they'd returned from Rome, on a moonlit night at the same vineyard where they'd first met. Under a starry sky, with their families, the grapevines, the sunflowers, and even Cocoa and Sugar as witnesses, they'd pledged their love to one another. And in the time it took to slip rings on one another's fingers, a feud that felt as if it had gone on longer than time finally came to an end. The conclusion was as gentle as a whisper, as delicate as the rose petals the wedding guests had tossed at Juliet and Leo when they departed for their Tuscan honeymoon.

"How does it look?" Leo asked, straightening the sign on its white metal hooks.

She grinned up at him. "Why don't you come down and see for yourself?"

"Okay." He climbed down, until he was beside Juliet on the ground with his arm wrapped around her shoulders.

Together they looked up at the quaint sign with its swirling white letters. A breeze blew in from the bay, grape-scented and gusty, rattling the sign on its hinges and bringing goose bumps to Juliet's skin. She knew it was silly, but she had the feeling it was more than just a simple breeze. She burrowed into her husband's side and couldn't help but wonder if perhaps the whispers of the wind were actually voices from the past. Voices murmuring their long-awaited approval.

"We didn't have to do this, you know." Leo pulled her closer and pressed a gentle kiss to her hair. "I would have been fine leaving it as Arabella Chocolate Boutique. The store could have kept your family name, and the commercial end could have remained Mezzanotte Chocolates. We didn't have to do it this way."

"Yes." Juliet nodded. "Yes, I believe we did."

The wind swirled one last time, kicking up leaves and tiny white flowers from the surrounding olive trees. They danced around Juliet and Leo's feet, as if the two of them were at the center of the storm. The center of everything.

Above their heads, the new sign swayed but remained firmly fixed in place, its letters gleaming in the Napa Valley sunshine.

Welcome to Bellanotte Chocolates.

Acknowledgments

With special thanks to Elizabeth Winick Rubinstein, Rachel Burkot, Susan Swinwood and all the wonderful people at Harlequin HQN. It takes a village to birth a book, and I've been blessed with the best village I could possibly hope for.